The Fire Within

An Antipodean Escape

Sara Beaumont-Connop

Acknowledgement to Country

I acknowledge and respect the traditional lands of all Aboriginal peoples and Torres Strait Islander people, the Maori peoples of New Zealand, the indigenous peoples of the Pacific Islands and respect all Elders past, present and future.

Apology to Country

When I first wanted to know what a white woman like me was doing, living in the wrong country, and impinging on First Nation realms, I had to look to my past. The journey took me back over five generations and has been one of profound sorrow and regret over what I have discovered about the footfalls of my British ancestors, and their impact on these lands.

In this story, which is fictional, but loosely based on fact, I have endeavoured to place First Nations characters, where they were in fact, in charge of their own country and destinies, because anything else is not true.

I want to apologise to the original owners of Australia and New Zealand for the invasive ways my relatives went about colonising their homelands. There has been ignorance and misunderstanding sown by Britain about ownership of country and peoples, that has been ongoing, even into this century, bearing devastating consequences of loss and heartbreak as it's harvest.

It was the expansionistic empire of Britain that profited from human miseries and became callous toward them, evidenced by their historical dealings with the First Nations people. Venally unprincipled men with an insatiable avarice, relentless in their cruelty of greed, men who put their flag up in the backyard of someone else's livelihood and home, told them to live in the swamp and took their wives and children and then introduced addictive substances and epidemics that wiped a great many out.

The story for my family, has been one of successful survival, but I am now well aware of the cost that this has meant to the first peoples.

My wish is that this story brings some of the injustices of colonisation to public consciousness and acknowledges First Nation peoples as the original owners of these lands.

Again, I apologise to the First Nation Peoples of Australia, the Torres Strait Islands, the Pacific Islands and New Zealand.

DEDICATION

To Michael Beaumont-Connop, editor and chief extraordinaire, soul mate from every age, and to the OMDC for supporting me when ever I write myself into dark corners.

Dr Jean-Yves Kanyamibwa, the best emergency medical consultant and friend anywhere, who suggested "putting speech into my writing", and his mother, Marie, for being the first reader of my book.

Chapter 1

In the harshest winters of the 1860s, gold fever glittered, and grew in poor men's minds.

On a remote island of the Shetlands, Gilbert and William, the middle children of thirteen, blood brothers and brethren, shared golden visions; they had bejewelled dreams and Midas schemes.

These came about in no small part, thanks to the frequenting of the makeshift tavern several hours hike south, where the brothers had stood check to jowl with the scurvy Dutch and mainland seamen.

They were too late for the great Californian bonanza of 1849, but the world was wide, and so were their eyes, particularly when they pictured themselves as argonauts, adventurers, explorers, and treasure hunters.

The sailors boasted of duck egg sized nuggets, buried just under the surface, in the land 'down under'.

"Arh, baint nuttin to digging em up, if you've a mind to!" grunted out a wizened old codger, cracking a toothless grin. He smacked his tankard of ale down on the oaken bar of the Voe tavern.

"There those who will give passage on my ship, the Georgiana. I ben seen promissory notes, given to emigrants for fourteen pounds, to help em on their way. Two braw laddies like your good selves could weather the storms of the sea, for the hundred- and three-day journey, tis a doddle for youngsters strong and willin".

Gilbert's face glowed golden in the candlelight, and his eyes focused faraway on fortune. William saluted his brother and downed his draught, then he laughed heartily in agreement with the grizzled jack tar, the richness of the evening drained down to his very veins.

"Maybe we can take Uileen with us?" he eagerly enquired of Gilbert,

"Ock, have you gone soft in the head Will? Ye canna take Uileen, she would never make the voyage, alive" replied Gilbert, as he shook himself out of his rich revelry.

A fire drake of fury flashed into the space between the brothers, Uileen was their only bone of contention; William, romantic, and ready for 'true love' at twenty-three, wanted his sweetheart to be his future bride; his heart swam in his eyes, glistening red ochre with emotion. Gilbert stared hard at the younger man and then he sighed.

"Ah well, we best be gong dee (on our way), the Shelties are awaiting us, they are not fond of the war with the wind in their muzzles."

The seaman nodded agreement.

"Mind what I've ben tellin ye lads, we be sailing in a fortnit on Sunday, come with us and ye'll be glory bound by the end of the month! There's wealth to be found, just a lying in the ground."

Outside the stone ale house, William glanced up, at the star-studded counter pane of sky that encompassed their existence; this was the only stretch of heaven he had ever known, and he wondered, if a sky so bedecked with such gems, could ever exist anywhere else.

Gilbert silently waited for William to move on and when he seemed to be fixated to that very spot, betwixt here and there, he reached out and pushed him to make a start home. William let the ale wash over his fevered mind, as he staggered a bit, caught himself, and started for their ponies; in his mind's eye he drifted back, to when he first saw Uileen, pale as a moonbeam, stretched out on the silver sand she lay washed up on.

At first, he thought she was a Norn, a mythical creature, and so she was, until she stirred, opening her aqua eyes and stole his very soul. Then he went down upon his knees and lifted her into his arms, she threaded her arms around his neck, and they moved with one accord, William sucked in a breath that had been taken by this vision come to life.

That had been a year since and he needed gold, the colour of Uileen's hair, to press his suit for marriage.

Gilbert, meanwhile, grimaced at his brother's loss of focus, for him, there was only one way off the rocky edifice, of too many mouths to feed and no future - that was billowing sails on a stout, seaworthy ship, heading to Antipodean treasures.

Against the midnight ink, Gilbert's mind threw a cloak of glittering, golden dust, and his eyes shone like diamonds at the thought.

Suddenly, as if by some mercurial madness, out of the torpid darkness, came English soldiers on horseback; before they could even react, the loud impact of a club hitting bone could be heard in the silence of the stiff, chill night air.

The brothers knew no more, as unconsciousness overcame any struggle. They were unceremoniously laid out on the sodden ground, then hauled away, by rough rogues who stepped out of the shadows after the deed was done...

It was the middle of a blustery, clouded day; the men looked down at Gilbert and William as cold buckets of seawater were thrown on their faces and they had finally come to the painful realisation of their predicament, choking and spluttering, they rubbed their faces. Staring back at them were weasel faced, weathered beaten, scarred and scabbed sailors.

"Ahah! finally me hearties- Ye be back with the livin, be up with Ye, there's work to be done" the first mate roared into their confused expressions.

For all intents and purposes, it appeared they were on a vessel, headed for open ocean; kidnapped and press-ganged into His Majesty's Navy, ready to serve or feel the lash, strike fear in the heart and flesh from sinews.

The crew were a deviant lot, with miles of missing teeth, and crooked criminal smiles, all shifty and one eyed when they were watching their quarry.

For several months of the voyage, William's anger had not abated at this betrayal, by the Dutch sailors, of their tavern acquaintance.

His back bore the latest whip marks, after he had heaved the swabbing bucket and mop over the side when presented with the curse, of cleaning the vomit off the decks. His heart yearned for his beloved Uileen, even as his mind was torn between thirst for fortune, and future happiness. He did not think this godforsaken hulk would be the route, to anything but perdition.

Gilbert was more sanguine about their situation, even as he climbed the perilously dangerous rigging, to straighten out the lines and make spliced repairs in the ropes. Often, he surreptitiously took out his sunstone, a yellow crystal that turned dark blue in the light, even on cloudy days; it was directional to

within one degree! His grandfather had bequeathed him this treasure, sure that Gilbert would have water under his feet, and wind at his back.

The captain of the Golden Spring was a man with a hard reputation, Jeremiah 'Bully' Brunson, and he always took the 'circle route', to the Cape of Good Hope, fast, furious, and full of misadventures and wild stormy seas.

Often called 'Cape Tormentoto' because of the fiendish weather, that flattened many a ship into the rocks and sure death.

Bully was hoping to catch the roaring forties winds that blew west to east, if drifting icebergs did not find them first, as many a journey ended at the bottom of a hopeless voyage through Drake's Passage.

But Gilly knew they were heading to the great Southern Ocean of Australasia, the land of his dreams and his concerns were only survival. They had already seen the bloody spit of crew, suffering from the dreaded scurvy; weakness and salt water made a toxic mix for many a man at sea. Smallpox, another sailor's scourge, struck a fearful dagger into the strongest mate. Gilbert was all too aware of what his enemies were, and who he was at loggerheads with. He had already fought bare knuckled, and bare chested on deck, going six rounds with Fred West, a large, cockney brawler. They were both broken lipped, black eyed, and bloodied at the end of the final bout; surrounded by screaming tars braying for blood, and Davy Jones locker. The piece of grimy lime rind Gilbert acquired, after his adversary was deigned unconscious by the captain, did nothing to assuage his aching bruised body or battered head.

William and Gilbert had reckoned that apart from the crew, they were carrying cargo of railroad tracks for the expanding colony.

"Will we ever see land again?" William brooded, as the brothers stood watch on deck at three bells.

"Ye must stop yur mourning for the mountains, the heather and yon Bonny lassie, Will, it is on a rich adventure we be". Gilbert replied. "It's a good eighty days, we be at sea, by my reckoning and the sunstone; we baint more than three weeks out from the Australian coastline.

"Huh! What then Gilly?" William questioned. "How do we escape this rotting piece of flotsam?"

"There be whispering down below, that we get ashore before Melbourne, and get to the gold fields first, this Captain keeps hazing the crew, working us day and night; it's mutiny they be plotting."

"Careful laddie, it will be the devil to pay, if the captain hears that talk, the smart money be on watching Jacob Dooley and his henchmen, then waiting for our chance to get away" replied Gilbert.

So, the endless days went on, beginning with tarring, oiling, greasing, painting, varnishing, and scrubbing with vinegar and chloride of lime.

As a land man, Gilbert had once wondered what sailors had to do at sea, now he had no time for such pondering, for as time marched on he learned to watch at night, steering, reefing, furling, bracing, making, and setting sails, then pulling, hauling, and climbing in every direction. William and Gilbert worked round the clock, with just five hours sleep between the watches.

Both the brothers suffered bouts of dysentery, as the rats and mice had burrowed into the provisions, leaving plenty of disease behind them. Algae in the water supply brought on vomiting; some of the sailors fell off the rigging with dehydration, poor broken Ned Grimes and Angus Clayborn were wrapped in canvas cover, mounted on a plank, and commended to the cantankerous depths, to see no more!

It was an orange sky on the morning that the bells rang, to batten down the hatches, as a sudden, full gale squall blew up from the south, 'it be the Williwaw wind" cried the second mate Ben Haddock, "all crew on deck, look out for rogue waves, thirty footers over the bow."

"Rope yourself on Will, it's going to 'be hell to pay', before we've ridden this devil out!" Gilbert shouted above the roar of wind and surf thrashing the ship about, like an unstable compass needle. As the oceans fury drenched over them, William and Gilbert held the wheel together, first and second mate sent the rest of the men scurrying to furl the sails. James Whitlock, the first mate, a raw-boned naval officer with piggy eyes and a turgid temperament shouted out: "Turn the ships prow into the storm, for god's sake, keep it close to the oncoming waves, don't let her broach!" As the siblings fought to keep the rudder in the water, they watched in horror as two ship mates were washed from the jib, trying to secure the mast. The worst nightmare of seafarers everywhere: 'man overboard ', Will looked at Gilly and gulped 'hang on for God's sake brother, tis time to send up a pray, and no mistake',

"Aye!" yelled Gilbert, as he renewed his efforts to stay the course through the watery walls of this hellish marine tempest. Barrels, pots, and anything loose bounced out and over the side, lost at the bottom of that salty savage sea.

For three long days, the storm swallowed the Golden Spring in its raging gullet, until finally, as the relatives thought their limbs dislocated, the ship was spat out into the relative calm of the balmy, Indian Ocean currents.

Much battered and bruised, all the mariners went about their duties, gingerly nursing their many injuries. What was left of the sails were set as all hands started making new sheets and the riggings were replaced; sleep was rare for every able seaman.

Finally, they were just a few nautical miles off the coast of southern Victoria, when the rumble went round the crew, land ahoy! An excited air entered the mealie of men looking towards the shoreline, and they saw Cape Bridgewater.

Most of the seamen had been shangied from poor, destitute neighbourhoods, or harbour towns. They had lived lives shaped by stale bread and poverty. The thought of rivers of riches ran through their very beings, a gambling glint sparked the dullness from their imaginings, what could they lose they had not lost already?

Slowly and steadily, an accumulation of contraband formed, the gains growing in proportion to proximity of opportunities. Barrels of grog were surreptitiously moved from stem to stern, a quantity of laudanum had been acquired from the saw-bone surgeon, one Thomas Mooring, a spy, sent onboard by the British

Navy to pick up on sedition at sea; but the navies knew a snitch when they espied one!

It was a rum lot that their things were searched, and they were spied on, reported and squealed on, they did for 'that traitor' first,

with a large dose of medication and a following small "plop" at the anchor chain, heard by the coverlet of sea, but not a soul aboard saw or heard anything else.

Four bells rang, 2am, the Southern Cross hung from a pitch, black mantle and the wind blew an eerie rustle, through mounted sails. A hushed wave ran before the boat, and bare feet flew lightly, stepping over the foredeck; shadows moved in stealth, as silence seemed to wash over the vessel.

Gilbert sat up in his hammock, listening intently to the sounds of the night, he kicked William awake beside him, "get up quickly and get yur coat on, it's time!"

The brothers crept along the berthing compartment and made their way up the ladder topside. They could just make out the wraithlike figures of Jacob, with several others of a mutinous nature.

Suddenly, the ship's bell tolled, and Jacob Dooley's Irish brogue rang out:

"Listen up, ye lubbers, the captin, stewart, cook and first mate are all 'deora codlata m', or as you would put it - a mite under the weather, me, and the lads here, we're taking command, the second mate is with us, who else is? We're heading for land and anchoring off the briny coast of Victoria, for a chance to strike for gold. Man the topsails and steer her into the leeward wind, look lively ye sea dogs we be landed by daybreak."

The captain and other officers were fit to be tied and that is what they were, in sailors' knots so tight, they squeezed the sweat from each man's face, as they sat lashed together around the mainmast, stripped to the waists and gagged.

The dissenters were winching down the jollyboats as fast as humanly possible.

There were roughly twenty eight men by Gilbert's reckoning, and two small craft, it was going to be a fight for freedom, and no mistake. Gilbert forced his way to the front of the milling 'squid'.

"Not so fast Ye cocky jock", Gilbert felt a hand on his shoulder, and turned to meet his protagonist.

Fred West's leering visage breathed foul fumes into his face, "there baint be room for Ye and that milksop brother of yurn, it's likely we won't be needing the likes of Ye two!"

Gilbert drew himself up to his full six foot two inches in height and shook his head, "Och what we won't be aneeding is a blabberskype like Ye, West" he replied, then he ducked just in time, as William helped out a warning cry "watch out".

Fred West's vacant eyes took on a vicious glimmer, as he stupidly comprehended, he had swung his fist into thin air. But Gilbert was ready for the hurtling, ramming brute and as he bore down on him, he neatly sidestepped the brawler, and with a bull's roar, Fred West hit the starboard side and was lifted over into the foaming waves by his opponent. William ran to the edge where Fred had made his disappearance, naught could be seen except a turquoise turn of water. Jacob Dooley stood watching these proceedings with Ben Haddock and some of the other tars under his influence, "listen ere Ye scab, you'll not be taking up room we don't have".

William stood looking with askance at the mutineers, but he knew better than to take on the villains, especially as Ben had pulled a pistol on Gilbert. "Alright, alright", the brothers raised their hands, and moved away from the group, watching warily as the protagonists had the small boat loaded oars ready to row away.

Meanwhile, the ship was listing heavily, and the captive officers were kicking up a right rumpus, but to no avail. William and Gilbert tried to take the wheel, but without the bracing of rigging and sails, the ship was careering way out of control.

William was searching the coast through the eyeglass, "look out Gilly" he screamed "rocks ahoy!" Just as the words were out of his mouth and caught on the wind to be blown away in an anguished mist, the ship crunched and shook as a piecing sound reverberated through the hull, the fluid, freezing ocean flew through the bowels of the vessel.

William ran to the captives, took out a penknife and cut them free, "it's every man for himself now," James Whitlock cried over the creaking, moaning, groaning of this harpooned marine monster.

"Quick, William", cried Gilbert, "grab this spar and hold on for dear life, we are going down", as the tempestuous sea overtook them.

Wave upon wave came crashing onto the men, tossing standing figures up into the air like rag dolls, the wrath of the reef was awesome in its ferocity.

Now the two adventurers were spun about and agitated in every direction, as they clung to their makeshift float, with one at either end the beam was balanced, but at Poseidon's mercy. Will could feel the cutting, cold water seeping down under his jacket, through his skin and into his very bones and then he felt no more, as a numbing strangeness overtook him. Gilbert clung to thoughts of home and this new country, he thought of his Shetland pony Robbie, how he loved his oats and hay.

"Whist, it was a long ways from the Bonnie isles now", he lamented "hold on for the future, laddie, we'll see you through!" he heard his grandfather whisper in his ear.

The foam and foment, of flotsam and jetsam, finally found its peace on the silver sands of the shore, where the tide's teeth had left its mark and writhed back, seawards to forage for more. Such was the case for our travailing travellers, blethered on the beach of an unknown land, almost sunk in despair but caught up in a netting of hope, that was their salvation...

Chapter 2

It took some time for William to cut them both out of the fishing net that held them fast to the spar timber, and by the time he had freed them, they were both thirsty and exhausted. Finally, they heaved themselves up to scout their surroundings, but as soon as William and Gilbert climbed up a sandbank on to dry land, they knew the confusion of being marooned on desolate beach dunes, with only scrubby bushes, and a few trees to greet their gaze. "Methinks, tis now a long walk to where we are aheading William", Gilbert gravely announced. "Best be on our way, before the sun sees too much of our plight, and shows others the same".

They stumbled forward; William still felt shivering cold from his underwater immersion. Seagulls wheeled away from the pair as they drudged over the sanded steeps, slipping, and sliding forward; mosquitoes appeared and whined around their ears then landed, and started a concentrated attack of their human hosts.

Both brothers were soon victims of these vicious, bloodthirsty insects; their thirst was raging as the insects were slaking theirs.

Dusk was descending like a coral cape, collecting the hum of the evening, as it cloaked them in the grey shadows of cloudscape. Gilbert had noticed William's valiant attempts to still the insidious trembling that his body was being racked by. Fear clutched at his heart, for he had seen this chill before, in winters dark claws. It was the kind of cold that climbed inside a body and became its master, racking the chest with accursed coughing, fevering the mind, and enflaming the senses; it was the demon that made angels.

He felt inside his jacket lining, to see if by the Lord's grace, his small tinder box was still with him, his fingers searched the battered coat, finally finding the small hard stones. Sighing in relief, he called "Will, ye stay here, I'll gather wood and tinder, we have our flint, it will warm up the 'cockles of our hearts', so it will".

"Gilly, I'm as parched as a beached haddock and no mistake, all the water I've swallowed and not a drop to drink!"

"I know, I hear ye lad, first light we search for fresh water," Gilbert answered, his eyes narrowing in determination.

Gilbert walked toward the largest tree he could see, it was of a strange configuration he could not recognise, its skin was a glaucous silver, with slabs of unshed bark that were arranged around its lower trunk.

The lance shaped leaves had a blue, green tinge. As he approached it, Gilbert could smell a menthol aroma floating about the tree's neon aura.

By the time Gilly got back with his parcel of branches and brush, William had descended into a supine position on the ground, where he had been left, his pale skin was dry, his eyes glassy and his limbs threshing with cold. Gilbert ran to kneel at his side, "Och! I canna leave you for a moment", he said wryly, but William has entered his own land of lamentations, it was all beyond his ken.

A bright vermillion fire was started between a ring of rocks, and when he was sure it would not go out, Gilbert pulled out a penny pipe and began to play a song, sung by their parents and grandparents, after the first introduction William began to sing.

"Speed Bonnie boat, like a bird on the wing,

Onward the sailor's cry!

Carry the lad that's born to be king

Over the sea to Skye.

Loud the winds howl loud the winds roar,

Thunderclaps rent the air

Baffled our foes stand on the shore

Follow they would not dare."

Williams shaking eased and Gilbert closed his eyes in relief, the crackle of the fire, the aromatic smoke swirled around them in the solitude of the moment.

All at once, a spear pieced the air beside them and stood sticking into the sandy earth, both men opened their eyes in alarm and out of the darkening, adumbrate bush, emerged the figure of a man, the like of which the brothers had never seen before. Black as burnished coal he was, with white stripes across his face and forehead, athletic and tall, proud he stood, wearing naught but a loincloth and a bandage of cloth around his head.

"What you white fellas do here aye?" the

stranger asked in heavily accented pidgin English.

Gilbert held out his arm slowly, "Our shipwrecked on yon reef," he gestured; his visitor looked silently towards the ever-changing tide.

"You come my land?" he questioned.

"We come not to fight," replied Gilbert "we seek only to find gold."

"Bad white men killed many our men, many our women. We happy, then white fella come our land, give us grog and it make us mad. Then we get white fella sick and go die.

"Och, for sure that's pure boggin - we are sorry for your losses and know nothing of yur sufferings. All we know is what far away English men say that poor lads like us can have a living life, digging gold.

I am Gilbert and this is my brother William, we are glad to meet Ye".

Both the siblings felt the dangerous ground they were perched on, they held their breaths and tried not to think of themselves as roasting on a spit, tasting like pork.

The lithe local looked hard and long at the brothers, then he said, "you must be some lucky white fellas, you see my spear, it finds 'Googar', in black fellas speak, maybe you be his catch."

Gilly and Will turned to look behind them, there, skewered on the point of the black man's spear shaft, lay a beastie from their very worst nightmares; russet shaded, four foot long, a very large dragon, with a creamy yellow underbelly and reticulate patterning down its back.

William cried out "da laek o dat Gilly", Gilbert pale, round eyed and gulping agreed, horror had come to stalk them. At the men's obvious distress and panic, the aboriginal man

laughed out loud "Hah Hah" he said, "you white fellas don't know nothing about our bush, I guess me being Bunjil Jonson, best tracker in this here country, he had better learn you some bush-man's ways. You got any tea? Or tabbie weed?"

"No," Gilbert answered slowly, still staring fixity at the immobile lizard to make doubly sure all movements had ceased. Then he shook his head, still in bemused disbelief at myths sprung to life and said, "I have only my chanter pipe, my flint fire box and some silver coins," he omitted to mention the sunstone, a precious token he could not barter.

Bunjil considered these options stroking his chin, "I take coins for water and food, but tracking is more."

Will searched his pockets and found a small stone carving of a seagull, he had made as a token for Uileen, he knew he must give it up. Reluctantly he held it out,

"Is this be enough?" he asked hesitantly. The black man's eyes lit up at the detailed small bird on the wing, "you catch spirit of air" he exclaimed. "Yes, I lead you to my land, my home, we trade, but first we drink, then eat. From his back, Bunjil took a strange, dried skin bag and offered to William, water, clean and cool. Gilbert drank next and returned the bag, "Now" Bunjil said, "time for tucker!"

In short order he had the goanna skinned and hung over a crackling fire. He laughed again at the brush that Gilbert had gathered- "man, you try burn 'blow up' bush, that no good for campfire."

The black man went a short distance and returned with some brush and threw it onto the flames, a large flare, accompanied by explosive popping, made them jump back. The brothers looked sheepishly at their mentor and cringed at their ignorance of this very foreign land; they were but children in its clutches.

Soon, they were feasting on the surprisingly soft, tender white meat of the dreaded dragon. William was nodding off, when Gilly began to play 'auld Lang syne', Will hummed along, Bunjil sat on his haunches, enthralled, his heart swelling with the music, he reached into his woven dillybag, and took out a wooden pipe of his own, a didgeridoo, a metre long. With vibrating lips, he breathed a circular breath, long, mellow notes mingled in unison with the chanter, the musicians were of one accord.

The three men were encompassed in the soft twilight of a new adventure, wrapped about with excitement and interest, with as much trepidation of the new relationship, as any strange company can have.

The following day the trio set off in a north easterly direction, William still had a cough but was feeling stronger, Gilbert walked in tandem with his native mentor, and tried to learn about his anomalous surroundings.

The Australian hinterland glowed in the mornings dawn, wreathed in a crimson aura, emblazoned with glinting golden highlights.

William thought that the bullion they were seeking might be found within this bountiful bush expanse, for it seemed to go forever. Some of the strange, towering trees overawed them, for they were old; nearly as old as the metamorphic rock they sat upon, these great, grey, green giants were garlanded with blossoms, inhabited by birds of multiple sizes and species. When the siblings started, at a raucous commotion from above them, Bunjil pointed out the large, bright, white birds, as an early morning cockatoo circus, rounding each other up for a feast of blossoms and nuts, crowing at the pecking order of each with the other.

During the unfolding days kaleidoscope rainbows spun out of the trees around them,

ringing like a fleet of bells; rainbow lorikeets joyous in the freedom of their flight.

At dusk, a crazed laughter reverberated and was caught up in the gum trees, William and Gilbert fairly jumped out of their skins.

"Gilly, tiss the mad ghosts of lost travellers come to haunt us", hissed William. Gilbert looked at Bunjil, who once again joined in with nature's joviality, through his laughter he said, "That's old man Kookaburra, in the beginning of time, god Bayame told kookaburra to wake up blackfellos, so we would not miss the wonderful sunrise."

William leapt out of his skin when the tall grass in front of them suddenly burst into bright red bouncing abundance, those queer creatures had him hopping back in fright. Bunjil hooted with glee, and pointed at a two-metre tall, leading king kangaroo,

"That fella box your ears for you good, he a mean beggar, if you cross him, but they is plenty good to eat", at that pronouncement he reached behind his back, pulled out and threw a large bladed, flat wooden instrument.

It was about two and a half feet long, made of mulga wood, painted with ochre and banded with incised designs. As quick as lightening it streamed out into the hazy light, through the dazed air, and like a flash of brownish quick silver, the scimitar like blade, hit its mark.

In transfixed awe the siblings saw that a kangaroo had been downed, as if it had run into an invisible adversary and it jumped no more. A spear followed the arc of the boomerang and finished off the kill.

Bunjil showed Gilbert and William how to skin and prepare the marsupial. They started a fire and used the coals and hot ashes to cover the animal, to ensure it roasted right through, and afterwards he took them to a creek that had a brackish gleam on the top, and showed them how to take coarse grass, growing beside the water, and by placing it on the surface it would remove the scum, whereupon underneath they found clean water to drink.

Portland had been the first colonial settlement in Victoria, but the Aboriginal people had lived in the area in its sublime solitude for thousands of years until the 1830s when sod had been turned and sheep run by the first English grazier lately from Tasmania.

This area would see the harbingers of mighty change in fifty short years. When our young protagonists arrived on a heated January afternoon, on its dirt dusty, colonial main street, they felt like they were walking through a furnace. Still, to Gilbert and William, it seemed to be an English oasis; something they finally recognised after time and tide had taken everything, they were a part of.

They were approaching Gordon's tavern just as two diggers were being thrown out of the door. One of the men went sailing by Gilbert, wearing naught but long pants and a silly smile, the other was cutting a 'blue streak', with language from the Dublin dock gutters to be sure. The large and robust hotelier dusted his hands as he growled out: "you're barred, take your miserable carcass's off with ye and don't come back!"

Both men staggered about in the glaring sunlight, as if blighted by its burning rays.

"Gods mercy Shemus! Why'd ye have to pick a fight with the owner's son?" the first wretch pleaded.

"Ahaha, Flann O'Flynn, my cats curse upon Ye, may ye fall on yur head and may that blatherskype barkeep Henty, may that idiot have red diarrhoea!"

The two Irishmen continued to prognosticate for some time, pushing each other over into the dirt, dragging themselves up to fall again, each as his opponent pulled or tripped the other.

Bunjil was mightily amused by the whole affair, Gilbert was cautiously watching, he had already had one lesson in drunken stupidity. William was quietly resolute, trying to take in the town, his eyes were swimming with sights old and new.

They left the two brawlers holding each other up in the street, smeared in muddy sweat and beer; one of the pair tried to catch Gilly's arm as they went,

"Gif us a shilling lad; begorrah, I'm skint as a March hare".

Gilbert with a shake of his head declined, wryly

he added "don't marry for money mate, you can borrow it cheaper, but no from us, we're skint as well! "

Shemus was then promptly tackled by Flynn and the two drunkards descended into anarchy once more, shouting and punching.

From out of the side street, a melee of dust was sent up, and out of the affray a mounted trouper arrived

"Here, what's this ruckus all about?" he cried, as he held an Enfield musket across his saddle.

"Just what we needed", said William.

"Quick", called Bunjil, "in here!" He pushed Gilly and Will in a side door, just as the policeman was dismounting.

The brothers found themselves crouched in what appeared to have the stench of an outhouse.

"Gilly, this stink is 'geen me the boak' (making me feel sick) Will whispered.

"Hush now, where there's troupers there's trouble," Bunjil quietly said.

They watched and listened through a crack in the door as other mounted police arrived.

An officer spoke to men who had gathered in

the street, while the two Irish miscreants were tied together, sitting dolefully under the watchful gaze of the first trooper.

The officer said to the crowd gathering in the street, "there's been an axe attack on a digger, name of Brown, up near Castlemaine, and we are searching for the culprit now."

As the police dispersed around the town to begin searching, in rode Henry Seekamp, journalist and editor of the Ballerat Times.

He started, from his mounted position, to regale the town's people with the whole scoop on the awful incident.

"Two diggers were gambling, but it was discovered the dice were false. The loser then found out his opponent was a regular flimflammer. He sought out the charlatan and a right royal fistfight ensued with the cheating blackguard appearing to be on the receiving end of a good thrashing from his opponent. Whereupon the villain in question, grabbed a heavy American axe and swung it full force, he smote his adversary upon his left breast, and the razor-sharp blade sliced open a large wound, and although heavily choked with blood, palpitations of the heart could plainly be seen!

The mortally injured man fell to his knees, then the barbarous murderer uplifted his weapon and struck his victim on the frontal bone of his

head, laying it agape for several inches and chopping off a piece of ear. The local Doctor Owens claimed, "that upon examination the casualty was beyond human skill, in the last stage of existence!"

They are bringing him into town in a day or so, after his total demise, for it could clearly be seen by all present, that the working blood vessels of his brain had been exposed!" the newspaperman added.

The crowd crowed in disbelief, angry words like "let's lynch the murdering miscreant," were bandied about, and "we need justice for settlers!"

Unfortunately, at this point in the proceedings, one of the police troopers had a hankering to use the privy, and not just any privy would do, it just happened he chose the one Bunjil, William and Gilbert were hiding in.

As they stared in horror at the approaching

policeman, Gilly felt a tingling feeling, crawling along his neck, he reached up to touch the sensation and when he brought his hand away, he screamed out in mortal terror, for there, holding on to the pale, pink skin sat a spectacular spider from Satan's horde!

It had a shiny, ebon carapace, dark brown, hairy long legs, and a large, maroon abdomen. William saw it just as Gilbert shook his limb violently, and it went flying towards him.

Both brothers took flight, yelling for dear life; as William rushed to the door from his corner, a pail of excrement was caught up in his leap for escape.

The policeman flung himself at Gilbert, grabbing him by his collar while he was thrashing at himself, screaming about spiders from hell, when William and his airborne slop bucket careered into the 'long leg of the law'.

The copper looked down at his stinking, sodden, soiled trousers!

"Right, you had better come along with me, you two, and I wonder what you are doing hiding in there?"

They were summarily frog marched into the glaring spotlight of police and public suspicion.

The brothers were pale and dazed by their experience and as they were thrown roughly into the cell and they wondered, what of their guide Bunjil?

Chapter 3

The blow cracked against the head of Mangus Manson and he dropped as a dead weight, his face hitting into the hard Shetland stones as he toppled forward past his prey; the far-off distant thunder clouds boomed, and rain began to run down in rivers.

Grace stood with her skirts tucked into her waist, she was standing stock still in the chilled creek, the family washing streamed out around her. Uileen stood above her with a heavy iron shod walking stick raised, clasped in both hands, breathing heavily she asked, "Grace are you all right, he no touched, e did he?"

"Och no, he nay had time to get his breeches down, but if ye hadna come when ye did, it would have been a different story," she shuddered in horror at the very thought.

Grace knew that if she did not find a means to escape her exile in this isolated part of the North Sea there would be naught in her present or future except for pigs, both the four legged and the two-legged variety like Mangus Manson.

Uileen stared down at the bestial visage of Mangus and revulsion overcame her, she shook her head to clear it, then she felt the familiar pain of loss. It seemed as though the treasure of her life had been poured out into the sea and sweep away on the fickle currents of fate. They had got word of William and Gilbert's captivity a week after the event and life on the farm had hardened over them, Uileen was desolate for her love's encapsulating embrace, it had seemed almost chimerical in its perfection.

The family had gathered around the old wooden kitchen table, Ma cuddled four-year-old Fanny as her tired lined face looked worriedly up at her grizzled great bear of a husband who held court at the head of the table.

Gilbert the elder was pronouncing his assessment of his daughter's situation, "Och, you girls, it's a power of trouble you've found and no mistake, Mangus Manson is a brute, his four brothers the same".

"Ahh, Da they had no choice," cried Thomas, sky blue eyes blazing, at twenty-six years the eldest and a stalwart protector of his family,

"There's no decency in the man, he canna keep it in his breeches" he added.

"Aye yur right there son", replied Da. "When my father's father, yer great grandsire fled the English, amid the blood-soaked Culloden field, those backstabbing Mansons were there fighting with the English! They are part of the Gunn clan of gobbershites who fought agin us and the young bonnie Prince Charlie. Brave Jacobites cut down by their own treacherous countrymen, for the sake of the sassenachs!" Da spat into his hand then made a fist.

"Their motto is 'either peace or war' and they're always spoiling for a fight! "shot out eleven year old elven lookalike John. Whilst "No in front of the bairn", Ma remonstrated.

"Well, those Mansun boys have been the ruination of lassies up and down the coast" chipped in Fiona, nineteen years old, with silver eyes shimmering like a loch in winter, cinnamon hair waving about her tense face. Agnes piped in with, "they stink those Mansons."

"Hush child", Ma reprimanded, "don't talk so, yer tongue will fall off",

"They are worse than our pigs, Ma, Ye can smell them from thirty paces!" Catherine, 'Miss Eight' year old informed knowledgeably with her gaze brightly focused on the family.

"None of that helps us", retorted Grace, her stare fixed on her parents anxiously. At twenty-one, the beauty of the clan, titian curls fell around her heart shaped face, ruby full lips and dark red brown eyebrows formed a perfect framework for slightly slanted sapphire eyes.

It was not difficult to see the young men's attraction, Ma thought proudly, nevertheless the last thing the family wanted was another swine at the farm! Everyone was adamant about that!

"William and Gilbert would know what to do", said Uileen hesitantly her flaxen hair glowed, a halo in the fire lit space.

"Hah, if it weren't for the traitorous Dutch sailors hogtying them and dragging them away, we would have more manpower" Da bitterly commented.

"We have a plan", piped up George and Angus the ginger-haired, grey green eyes twinkling with merriment, the twins at seventeen summers keep the family highly amused. They had already been in many scrapes and misadventures, Da and Thomas both sighed, "Here we go, not one of yur hair brained lunacies", Thomas said wryly.

"Not a bit of it!" said Angus, "the thing is we have a mate, he's a Norwegian sailor, on a ship in Lerwick harbour now. They're off to Glasgow in a couple of days, then Dublin to pick up Irish girls. Them British are sending unmarried girls to the colonies with new clothes and money for jobs and as settlers. The no potatoes hit Ireland right bad, they're starving in the country fields and the city streets, millions of the pur beggars! "

"That might be the answer", said Grace thoughtfully "I for one canna stay here, with a boar like Mangus roaming about, I know he' no like losing face to two women".

"Ahh so far away", cried Ma "all my babes so far away".

Fanny seeing her mother so distressed began to cry and the whole family descended into a chaotic torrent of crying.

Young Jem at six, demanded to know why he couldn't board a ship sailing to faraway lands too! Finally, Da banged his fist upon the tabletop and quiet descended, "it's been agreed, tis a difficult and dangerous choice, but no other will succeed."

Everyone began to weep again, and the volume of their voices transcended the evening air like smoke shouting out of a pyre of grief as the kin communed their deep love.

Grace and Uileen felt completely rearranged

by events as the sea spray curved up the bow of the clipper they sailed upon. The two women were being showered with chill horizontal rain as cold tears ran down their faces. On that dark winter's morning in the cross winds of the Atlantic and the North Sea, it seemed that the sea gods, Da Midder and Tehran were battling under the waves for dominance; the ocean roiled and so too did the emigres minds. It had been a torn ragged wrenching, the departure from all they had known and felt safe within, the bosom of their kin. At the last, even the jovial Angus and George looked dour as they hugged them goodbye, standing on the jetty under a haloed moon, crystalline in breath-taking clarity, in those final moments they could only see the drama of a deciduous life apart.

Lars Jensen, the helmsman arrived.

"Come" he bid "you cannot stay here, you will be in the way, better you follow me to the steerage deck".

Grace looked up at their benefactor, Lars the Norse sailor, with a cobalt blue stare that pieced her peace of mind. Under thickly fringed lashes, her eyes narrowing in a detailed assessment. Grace thought, he's certainly tall, I'd guess over six feet four, taller than Gilbert, well put together, broad shoulders, wide chested, narrow waist. Just as she was ruminating on all this, Lars looked quickly round at her and it seemed as if he could see into her mind and read her every thought! A bright scarlet flush flew over her face, she averted her gaze, but not before he threw back his shaggy blonde head and roared with laughter.

"Right" Grace huffed, "we'll see about ye, yer chancer!"

Between the decks was only a cargo hold, both Uileen and Grace could see hastily thrown temporary partitions had been put up. They climbed down the narrow ladder through the hatchway.

"This is about the same as the pig pens back in Shetland," Uileen said to Grace who nodded in disgusted agreement. The ceiling height was between six to eight feet with bunks of rough boards placed traversely from stem to stern, small corridors ran between each bunk, to Grace and Uileen's shocked surprise two women already occupied each wooden bed. "Aye they are built for up to five people sharing, like a family" Lars informed the gobsmacked females.

"Well, I don't like the look of this for three whole months," said Grace.

"No, indeed," replied Uileen.

"Well look who the cat dragged in here, misses La de da," called out a strident voice from the coffin like structure stretched out in the gloomy interior.

Grace peered into the dim sepulchral space and froze as she saw one of the last people on earth, she wished to ever lay eyes on, Anne Manson!

Uileen in confusion followed Grace's fixed stare but was unable to discern her distress. "It's Annie Manson!" Grace hissed out of the side of her mouth at Uileen.

"Oh" said Uileen, not really knowing the whole Manson clan, but she understood the danger sure enough.

The two women were deposited at their designated sleeping station, another three female faces peered down at them from the top bunk.

"Yur under us to be sure" said one of the pair, "Yur trunks are in storage, but they gave us all a pillow and a blanket, praise the good lord!" Bridgette O'Connor was a big boned, bright eyed Irish lassie from County Clare.

During the 'Gorta Mor', the great hunger from the potato famine, she was burnt out of the croft that she shared with her brother Sean by the English landowners' henchmen. The very next day Sean was arrested for stealing a sheep and thrown into Dublin gaol. Just under a week later when she went to visit him, he was found hanging from a rope in his cell. Bridgette was detained by the authorities and the sisters of mercy and told that the government was sending her to the colonies along with all the other fourteen- to nineteen-year-old female orphans. They were collectively given a wooden chest filled with calico dresses every hue of purple known, a cloak, mitts, new shoes, soap, towels, a comb, hairbrush, bible, and prayer book.

Alongside Bridgette sat Roisin O'Flynn who was off to parts beyond the seas to find her big brother, Flann, her other family had all expired from diphtheria during the harsh winter.

Then Maeve O'Halloran and Brianna O'Brian, two more young Irish belles who looked pale and wide eyed at their circumstances.

Everything had happened so fast, they had been gathered up like autumnal petals, fallen flowers in the great storm of the starvation. Now their path floated them out and onto a vast oceanic and unknowable future, a first voyage for them all.

Before Uileen or Grace could answer Bridgette began shrieking in horror

"Ug, ug, Saints preserve us, tis lice I'm feeling biting me legs".

"Oh fleas, as well, here is one of the little buggers, they're in the bedding!" cried Maeve. Grace looked down dubiously at the bottom bunk, then she glanced at Uileen, both women squirmed simultaneously, it was going to be a long uncomfortable journey.

The women introduced themselves shyly, trying to adapt to the cramped quarters lack of any privacy and the strange movement of the ship.

The matron came through and began to organise them into teams of eight to ten, every team had to do their own cooking and they ate their meals on a long trestle table that stretched the length of the deck.

The deck was cleaned thoroughly twice a week, mornings were for washing, lessons, prayers, sweeping and scrubbing and in the afternoons, they were allowed topside only in a roped off area. Here they could tell stories, sing, dance and entertain each other.

In the first week, most of the teenagers were wretchedly seasick, Uileen nursed Grace and their Irish companions. No one cared very much anymore about the dark fetid interior or eating ever again.

Lars came up and down with fresh water, finally dragging Grace up wrapped in her blanket, making her set her eyes to the horizon. The wind blew a fresh gale as the clipper sliced the waves before it. Grace felt like she had been swallowed up by the sea, for she must have already imbibed a good amount of the salty brackish stuff. Her innards were knotted in nausea. But Lars was unrelenting, he held her fast, humming a childhood lullaby in her ear, Uileen would join them after tending to her four other patients. Finally, the clouds of illness broke, the roll of wave did not result in a somersaulting stomach, it was time to join the ship of the living.

Grace had not had a chance to see her fellow passengers since she had succumbed to the seasickness as the steerage deck only had light coming down through the canvas hatchway, some filtered in through several tiny skylights, but it was generally always cloaked in twilight.

So it was with a shock that she heard a voice steeped in bile call out to her as she walked onto the main deck.

"Well! Will you look wot the cats dragged in! I canna think why a scrawny wench like ye would be wanted in the colonies!"

Grace stood stock still, searching the groups of girls, for the unbearable visage she knew the bile belonged to. There she was, large as life and twice as ugly, Anne Manson, hair as black as coal, eyes hard like a flint flaying knife and a mouth that was so caustic it would lift any stain from most surfaces. She stood with her hands on her ample hips surveying her quarry, sneering as she gestured at

Grace. "Thought you could run away from the Manson's did e, think again ye slattern. Now I

knows you're ere, we will hav some better entertainment!"

She decreed to her small cabal of cronies who hooted in agreement.

Grace held her ground, she knew Anne was just as poisonous as her bogart brothers, but she called out "Och away and boil your head Anne Manson, I dinna ken what you are on about, but I am no running from anyone or anything." At that she turned her back, and with Uileen walked away to the other side of the rail.

"You'll see, you'll see, shouted Anne.

After this disastrous meeting, Grace and Uileen found dead rats in their bedding, cockroaches in flour and someone had emptied a slop pail on their pillows. One night after they had discovered more foodstuffs had been spoiled Uileen proclaimed "We must do something! "

"Agreed" said Grace, "but the question is what?"

"I have an idea" piped in Bridgette "it would serve them right, sure it would, when their team has a wash, we will put lye in the water."

"Twill burn them sure enough," answered Roisin "But it's too much, how about we swap their dresses for small ones so they can't get clothed!"

With conspiratorial smiles they all agreed.

In the gloaming light of the next morning the sea chopped up, its waters took on a dark polish crested in yellow frothy waves and while the women were all still in their bunks the sudden blaring peal of an alarm bell reverberated through their heads.

On the main deck the Captain and First Mate Dolby stood scanning the horizon while Lars manned the helm. Looking out to port with a telescope Dolby exclaimed "It's definitely a pod of whales Captain!" Given the terrible danger of such an encounter the captain nervously shouted to Lars, "Swing her around! Hard to starboard!"

But before the plan could be put into action a great whale turned and bore down on them with a seemingly intense celerity. The wooden ship was hit with a tremendous force, jarring it

sideways as the leviathan passed beneath it to the other side and with a wild thrashing in the water, Lars could see him smite his jaws together, as if demented with rage and fury. "He's hit us hard Sir", called out Lars as sailors ran up and down trying to sure up ropes, rigging and sails.

"Look lively you men, watch out for that topgallant sail Perkins!" Yelled the Captain, quickly trying to wrest control of the vessel. Out of the watery depths emerged the great grey cetacean breaching the seas surface in sheer abandonment of gravity,

"There he blows", yelled a deckhand

"Keep hold of the wheel Jensen, I'm going to see to the passengers, you are with me, Dolby".

"Aye aye Captain" shouted Jensen and braced himself against the surges hitting the clipper. Just then, the great creature gave another almighty crash into the front sides of the bow and with a wrenching tormented shriek timbers split, and water gushed into the splits below decks.

"We've been shoved in cried the captain, "Get the carpenter up there, double time!"

At the same moment the terrified passengers who had been awakened by the alarm were falling about trying to manage the gymnastics of dressing. They were a jumbled and chaotic herd, some screaming, others panicking, wildly, half awake, as to their horror, the ocean seemed to be pouring in upon them.

"Quick everyone up the ladder" called out Grace, but it was a disordered mission getting the terrified drenched voyagers to focus on escape. The captain called to his men, "get those women up here now"

The sailors pulled the bedraggled wretches from the dungeon like hold, slowly the rescue was expedited.

"Start the pumps and get going bailing out the water, Dolby, take Jensen, and some of the deckhands to help" directed the captain as he took over the helm.

The ships carpenter Roberts arrived with a group of compatriots, "Get those bracing beams and wooden chocks in place quick smart! We'll stuff them full with tar then" he ordered the men.

"All hands to the undertaking, get that water bailed, start clearing the mess", Roberts directed.

As the ship heaved to and control was wrested back from the seas the girls were being accounted for, as they shivered, sodden, standing in the fierce chill gale that permeated the upper deck.

Three saturated stragglers were being herded by the matron, "Hurry up, just get to your station, at the double."

"What a sight" called out Bridgette drawing every man left topside's glances; Cara Grogan emerged first wearing a drenched gown that was obviously far too tight and short, the garment was stretched and plastered against her form, leaving her heaving breast's skin colour clearly visible to the onlookers, her legs, from her ankles to her upper thighs were showing and her face turned red with the effort of breathing and embarrassment. Niamh Jones was next with most of her bust exposed, the cold had hardened her nipples and

doused, despairing, she desperately tried to hold together the front of the frock from the male eyes devouring the sight.

At last, driven by the matron Anne Manson stumbled upwards onto the deck, by this time every sailor on board had their eyes glued to the entertainment. Anne's attire would not cover a hat rack in the agitated conditions, she had been unable to dress in any outfit supplied and was forced to make the most of a small blanket clutched to her front so not only her thighs, but her entire rear was exposed to everyone.

There were gasps and smirks all around the ship as every man leered and many called out and wolf whistled.

"We'll have none of that!" shouted the captain, "What are you up to Miss Manson, coming aboard half naked!"

A canvas sail bag was unceremoniously pulled around the women covering their nakedness while a spluttering furious Anne glared with unmasked venom at the victorious look on the face of her nemesis.

There was no reply but a sudden guttural snarl that emerged from deep inside Anne as she launched herself at Grace and Bridgette raking the air with her nails. The blanket and sailcloth were lost as she careened towards them, Cara and Niamh screamed and joined the fray and the ship's topside actions came to a frozen halt as every man stopped what he was doing and held their breaths should movement cease the scene sprawling out before them.

The captain, as unbelieving as every other man present yelled for the sailors to throw the sailcloth once again over the women and they were separated and corralled. The ships surgeon, Rogers, after some debate with the captain decided upon the punishments with the ringleader Anne and her followers, Cara, and Niamh to have their heads shaved, with solitary confinement for a week and bread and water their only sustenance.

The voyage progressed with a substantial contingent of the younger women coming down with measles; then all hands were needed for their nursing.

Brianna contracted pneumonia and her fellows watched her laboured breathing with anxious trepidation. For two straight days and nights they took turns fighting the fever that brought drenching storms of sweat racking through Brianna's frame.

Just as the ship wove its way into Sydney harbour, Brianna breathed her last. Every one of the friends that had been forged through the ordeal knew that the carefree days of girlhood were now well hidden in the long distant hills and fields of Ballybalgowan.

Chapter 4

Gilbert glared through the steel bars which were as thick as broomsticks, he had squeezed and pulled with all the young muscle and brawn he possessed but to no avail.

"Ah, it is nay good, nay good at all, we're no going anywhere Will." Will looked up morosely at his brother as he sat on a hessian sack stuffed with straw propped against the hard rocks of their prison walls.

"Och I told ye it would nae budge, ah dinna ken why ye continue to try!" he said.

"We'll we have to do something to get out of this jail, I dinna want to be strung up or shot for a murderer Will!" Gilbert exclaimed. Unexpectedly from the next cell, a pure clear singing voice pieced the air.

"The minstrel boy to war is gone

In the ranks of death ye may find him.

His father's sword he hath girded on,

With his wild harp slung behind him.

Land of song, that lays of the warrior bard May someday sound for thee,

But his harp belongs to the brave and free and shall never sound in slavery."

The siblings looked into the dimly lit chamber, there was Flann O'Flynn and his compatriot Shemus Sullivan lying as they were left,

bruised and bloodied by the constabulary. Flann was humming and Shemus sang angels to their rest, the solo in a heavenly choir.

"Och tis a marvel of a voice ye have Irish", William noted.

"To be sure, we have to teach ye Scottie's how it's done", replied Shemus. The men stared hard at each other for several moments, then burst into hearty laughter.

"Och if we're going to fight each other, we should have stayed at home," said Gilbert. "Aye, agreed Flann, "we are all we have in a land that God has all but forsaken!"

Suddenly, two black figures appeared at the barred door, William cried "look out!" and the quartet of prisoners jumped at these shadowed images come to life.

"Shush, now hush! whispered Bunjil, "I bring my friend Black Billy he knows a way out of lockup."

"How?" asked the quartet of desperate men in unison. Black Billy held up a ring of heavy keys, "I in charge now, everyone else gone, I native police! he announced proudly.

"How?" the prisoners parroted once again. Black Billy had curly hair of an iron hue, his teeth were still a brilliant white, his smile winning and pleasant. He had a well knit together form not robust but a physicality that hinted at powers of great endurance.

"We give white fella jailor, gold nugget, I show him where to find more, he come with other white fella police, they go to find more."

Flann and Shemus were up in a shot, "ready whenever ye are Black Billy".

"No one said ye two were going", said William, "Och if we just go, we will be wanted men William," said Gilbert.

"Can't we just make a run for it Gilly?"

"Nae William they know who we are"

"Not really, they havna got pictures", reasoned Will".

"You go with Bunjil he good tracker,

good black fella he see you right", said Black Billy, "I say police already let you out, you long time gone."

Gilbert was dubious about this plan as he knew British officialdom, they were tenacious at times when it came to losing and winning. In the end it was five positives against one's feeble protests.

"Alright, alright, we go, but burn any paper with our names on it." said Gilly.

"Agreed! The chorus replied.

The men were well away from the town when the blaze began. The hungry flames licked its lips and then wrapped them round the wooden structure, gulping down the architecture like a thirsty digger with grog. The smoke was pouring into the night sky reaching its plumes out in an inferno attempt at embrace.

Alarms bells were ringing, townspeople ran into the street. Fire put the fear of Hades in the hearts of all. A bucket line was formed with fifty men and women working tirelessly tolling the heavy pails up and down.

Behind the smoke laden fog of fire, a shadowed form watched the pyroclastic scene then slipped into the stygian darkness beyond.

For the intrepid trail blazers, it was a weary night walk, with creek and a river to cross. They rested seated on logs or lying propped

up against the gums trying with discomfort to let the days exhaustion leave their bodies until Flynn felt something quietly encircling his leg.

It felt like a large cat rubbing against him, he glanced fearfully down, frozen with indecision and saw a large black snake scenting along

his upper leg. "Don't move cautioned Bunjil "just let snake move up to your neck and sniff, if you turn your head, bad luck!"

Flann felt sweat trickle down his face onto his neck his torso, as the creature slithered its way upwards. His muscles began to spasm and contorted with the effort, and he gripped the log for dear life, praying to all the saints to preserve him, but in the last instant his body betrayed him, and he shook violently. The serpent struck and two small fang marks could be seen half an inch apart, Flann looked in horror at his companions as the venom quickly invaded his blood vessels. Shemus looked on in horror, distraught at his friend's predicament while Bunjil whispered to William and Gilbert, "No good now, he go bung any time soon, snake wins the fight".

Steadily, Flann's breathing became laboured and his head began a fierce-some ache. "Shemus" he gasped, "I see the rolling green hills of home, my Ma and Da, sisters and brother, they're running towards me, it's where I played as a boy, my heart was light as a feather, it was so full of joy. Can you see them Aingeals of God streaming light they're singing, Shemus me lad, I think this is goodbye?" The light slipped from Flann's eyes, he saw no more the Australian summer sky, but dwelt forever in the heart of his beloved Ireland.

Shemus slumped with grief against his bosom companion, tears rolling down his ruddy braw face, his pained loss visible to all who looked upon the pair.

A burial off the beaten track was all they were able to achieve. After the last ochre rock was placed on the mound and a wooden cross added. Shemus spoke "Eternal rest grant unto him O Lord and let perpetual light shine upon him O God, may he Rest in Peace!

Once more the journey was cut short for another young life and yet the fevered determination to persevere fanned their endeavour; the yearning for their future trod the past into the ground behind them.

They finally arrived at the Settlers Arms Inn. It had been gnawing away at Gilbert how they were to prospect with no money for supplies and even more important no money for a license to prospect.

The four white men were able to venture in, but Bunjil and Black Billy remained outside as aboriginals were not permitted in white drinking houses.

Gilbert was very angry about this rule. He wanted his mentoring guides with them but relented when he heard that grog drives black fellas mad from Black Billy who said, "it takes us to the Debble, the Debble, many die off, a long time gone now". Sorrowfully Bunjil and Billy turned retreating into their beloved bush for the nights camp.

In the taproom, William and Gilbert checked their dwindling financial situation and apart from paying for a drink and a meal they were almost bankrupt.

Meanwhile Shemus was having an animated discussion with a pair of likely villains at a table in the dimly lit corner. After what seemed the culmination of a heated discourse, he returned to the brothers now propping up the bar.

"They're looking for challengers for the

bare fisted fights this Sunday at Fiery creek, the prize moneys 100 pounds!" announced Shemus. William looked at Gilbert; Gilly for his part avoided his eyes and stared into the candlelight caught up in conflagrations of his past. He was not a born brawler but had always stood his ground well. What wouldn't he do with 100 pounds, it was a fortune on its own, but it would cost dear and no mistake. The fights were for high stakes, and none left unscathed.

Still, it was their only chance at salvation in the hard stare of penury, with the real riches still to be dug up. He finally decided.

"Where do I sign up?" he asked resolutely.

"No need! I've already put your name down, I figured a brau lad like ye 'could take on the world and anyway William there was bragging about ye prowess something shameful!" remarked Shemus laughing mischievously. Sunday morning arrived with the ludicrous laughter of kookaburras renting the dawning day. The four mates and their guides made their way through bog gutted mud tracks to the fight site. Bunjil was shaking his head and canting "Bert Bendigo Caut fella, he no good, full of tricks, bad doings and Black Billy say he deadly and as poisonous as taipan

and not honest!"

Gilbert was trying to focus on the prize money while William was starting to worry about what he had put Gilly in for. Shemus, rambunctious as ever shadowboxed the trees until gravity got the better of him and he went rolling over a small embankment with his unbalanced antics.

It rained heavily overnight, but the air was hot, heavy, and sticky with summers wet humidity. This did not deter the spectators who were laying bets and spoiling for the fight. At 9am Bert 'Bendigo' Caut arrived with his seconds. Gilbert, as challenger and his team took their places. Caut won the coin toss and elected to fight with his back to the sun. He was ten years older, heavier, and taller than Gilly, bred for brawling on the backstreets of Nottingham town. Bare chested, clad only in breeches the two men approached each other and began feinting.

Gilbert struck first and landed a glancing left on Caut's neck; Bert immediately replied with a left to Gilly's mouth saying, "I only want to see your claret blood then I'll make you fight!" Gilbert knew that he had to stay out of Caut's reach as much as possible for if Caut landed a direct blow he would be done for, the man was immense; so, darted endlessly back and forward out of Caut's reach and connected with a stinging set of strikes to an infuriated Caut.

The older man responded with a flurry of punches which Gilbert somehow managed to avoid the majority of, somersaulting around

Caut who became even more enraged. Foaming and spitting Caut grabbed Gilly around the throat and tried to strangle him with a convenient rope he had tied around his waist. A foul was claimed by Gilly's team and the atmosphere changed as Gilly slid down, writhing away from death. Coming to his feet again quickly both men exchanged a barrage of punches before round eleven was called. Gilly fought back with body shots,

"Och mon, ye fight like a wee babe "he taunted. The crowd roared!

"Get him Gilly" cried Will from his corner.

Blood ran down both men's faces obscuring vision except for the red rage of the fierce fighting that was on both their minds, kill or be killed.

Bert was desperate for revenge, and he head butted Gilbert twice with such force that the blows were felt as much as heard much to the shock and pleasure of the crowd who had come for the promise of a bloody fight.

Gilly dazed, shook his head while blood streamed from both nostrils, but the referee would not call a fowl and the fight continued. Coming to his senses he screamed at Caut

"Ye no that good, I thought ye were the champion!"

Incensed, Bert rushed at him; he'd pulled up a pole from his corner eager to skewer this upstart Scotsman for good. Gilly saw the danger just in time to jump wide of Bert's mark. Caut, now a bull at a red rag snorted with frenzied fury as he came round again with his weapon. The referee called foul but Caut, a juggernaut at full speed, just kept coming and then a pandemonium broke out.

Gilly's supporters, and by now there were many, had had enough. The diggers felt in close accord with one of their own. They picked up whatever weapons were to hand.

Caut's seconds realised the danger of being way outnumbered. "Come on Bert!" they cried as they dragged him crazed and screaming blue murder to his coach and pushing him in headfirst. They then attempted to flee the scene lashing the horses, but the mob was too quick. The leading digger's, sensing victory secured the coach's arrest.

"Hold up, stand too, Ye coward", Shemus, who was one of them shouted.

They dragged Caut from the coach, but he roared and squirmed and flayed his fists out into the crowd. His team took a hammering of king hits as they tried to defend their boss.

"Where is he I can't see him" cried William, "There he is!" shouted Shemus; the men turned to see that in the ensuing melee Caut was atop a horse he'd just stolen, riding bareback, lickity split away into the Australian bush.

Gilbert was ceremonially awarded the prize money on points as well as by default and was triumphantly carried away by a hundred singing and drinking diggers. He wasted no time in stopping by a roadside shanty and buying some supplies of tea, flour, salt, potatoes, and mutton for the journey.

He also chose tobacco and a pipe each for Bunjil and Black Billy as a fitting tribute to their unswerving devotion and loyalty; undoubtedly saving their lives up to this point. Both black men were delighted,

"Very good this all the same as me want em long time", crowed Bunjil with Billy nodding vigorously in full agreement.

The mining tools would have to wait till Ballarat district was within closer proximity, Gilbert felt they could not be weighed down with too much luggage for safety's sake, he did however purchase a brace of pistols, some possum skin rugs from the Wadawurrung women and a small pony to carry supplies.

The miners in the bar were pouring back the brandy, loudly discussing the blight of bushrangers on their lives.

William caught a glimpse of a sneering scornful expression on the by no means handsome visage of the shanty keeper.

Will thought that he may have caught an intuitive transient glimpse of a look so profound, with its devilish cruelty and cunning that the man was actively sympathetic to the rangers.

Hearing this, Bunjil and Black Billy were keen to move on, especially as they still had the Black Forest to traverse, it was reported to be full of the wicked malfeasance of the bushrangers and ex-convicts.

The Fiery Creek plains stretched out before them and the stars were not all out of the heavens, it was a bright early morn. The magpie had started the first hymns breaking the mornings fast, joined by the butcherbirds mellifluous feast of warbling.

As they hiked along, the sun seemed to jump up over the horizon, a blaze of light flooded the landscape.

Yellow blossomed wattle clothed the creek sides, here and there, stringy bark

and iron bark tree grew in clumps. This world seemed wide to the brothers; a breath-taking beauty stretched into the infinity of their imaginings.

As they approached from the flatlands the forest fanned out in front of them, prostrate trunks of trees rendered progression laborious. They laboured to find passages through the dense thicket and while trying heard an ear splitting 'coo-ee' echo through the woods around them.

Shemus shouted back "coo-ee, coo-ee, coo- ee ricocheted around the tall timbers echoing throughout the treetops.

"What is it?" Demanded Will, full of dread. Bunjil cocked his head to one side, "that white fella, he in trouble, 'coo-ee' bush sound for 'anyone there'?" he stated.

Black Billy called out "stay here, I see by and by".

William looked around them; this place was full of secluded hollows, honeycombed with untold numbers of ready-made graves, the hairs on his neck stood up at the thought.

When Black Billy returned, he said "two white fellas tied to a gum, they yell, robbers!"

"We had better rescue them", said Gilbert. The party descended into the clearing that contained the captives. The pair were thrashing about trying to unbind their ties. "Help us!" they cried "we've been bushwhacked by the damnable Captain Melville's gang!"

Gilbert and Shemus ran to untie the

strangers. William glanced around to see Bunjil beckoning wildly.

He hung back in the brush, seconds later, the so-called prisoners leap up from their ruse holding pistols at the stunned rescuers. Three dark horses raced out of the undergrowth, bush rangers; side wangled, William's heart sank. Gilbert, Shemus and Black Billy were well trapped by the marauders, they were outnumbered and out gunned.

"A pox on it", muttered Gilbert, as he realised their plight. He couldn't fight his way out of this one!

"Don't resist or yur dead" the masked leader, none other than Captain Melville stated.

"Now Black Douglas, find out if our visitors, hav any loot!"

At gunpoint, the three men were easily tied up to the gum tree and frisked with only a few coins coming to light.

"Hand it out quick and no shenanigans!"

Gilbert hesitated as he thought of all his

pounds stored in his shoe. He looked hard at

the man called Black Douglas and recognition dawned: It was Fred West himself, his adversary on the Golden Spring.

"Thought you were dead", Gilly mumbled.

"A man's got more lives that a Cat o nine tails!" Melville laughed.

Shemus struggled in his bonds, "If you attempt to get away or call out, I'll send a couple of bullets through you! Velvet Ned spat out in Shemus ear.

Douglas came right to the point, "if you don't hand over that bit of dirty rag with notes in it, you're a dead man ", he threatened malevolently.

"We know what's in yur shoe with inside information!" he laughed.

"I fought a man for that money," Gilbert stoically defended.

"Is that so?" Replied Melville. "tell you what mate, I'm a sporting fellow, it's a fair day, I'll

leave you lubbers ten pound to stake yer claims, you can't say fairer than that!" Melville declared.

"Shoot im, I say, dead men tell no lies", Black Douglas growled.

Aye, Captn, make the jolterheads swing fur it" yelled Velvet Ned.

Long Bill agreed, "Now don't be mean spirited about it me hearties, plenty more to come! "

"Damn it! Captain I'll do the deed myself," Black Douglas shouted enraged as he

cocked his pistols to aim and fire. An ear-splitting shot rang out through the forest, closely followed by a second shot which ricocheted around the glen.

Two men slumped over, and the horses were set off in a confused panic. The woods were suddenly alive as from all directions with diggers and native police came scrambling. Birds scattered up to the highest boughs, twittering but quickly falling silent at the clamorous sounds.

Black Billy looked up from his bonded position,

to see Jacky, his kinsman and several others besides coming towards him, "long time till you here, I think we be gone".

Gilly smiled in relief, as he saw William leading some diggers who had managed to apprehend Ned, he turned to stare at an unconscious Shemus.

William ran over to them, bright crimson blood was staining through Shemus' shirt, "he's taken a bullet in his shoulder", William declared as he hurriedly untied his brother and their friends.

"Captain Melville and Black Douglas have scarpered, Long Bill is lying shot dead, ten yards into the bush", William explained.

We had to get back to the Shanty keeper, to round up enough men and return, it turns out that toad eater who runs that hangout, is in cahoots with Melville and his gang, he's been setting up the robberies of customers for months."

"What's to be done there"? Inquired Gilbert as he was binding up the wound on Shemus' shoulder to staunch the loss of blood.

"Don't worry about him, the miners have torched the place and captured the black guard, he's been taken into custody by the native police force."

At last, the cloud cleared over the party and some progress could be made.

Chapter 5

(Balla) camping (arrat) place: Ballarat Victoria.

Ballarat, when the travellers finally found its portals was a canvas city floating on an eviscerated blood red earth in the sweltering Australian summer sunshine, in the ghastly process of disembowelment. To this hot Hades many hundreds had hastened, with anxious reckless speed, through all their journeys dangers, rendered blind by their miser's greed. In this vast array of humanity one half were utter strangers to the other and even to themselves for this was a place anyone could dispose of their old life, create a new one, be poor, then rich in the same day.

After a long look clad in silence, Bunjil spoke, "this place dead to my people now, we live here no longer! Black Billy hung his head in the sorrow of loss so great, that Gilbert and William were pieced by the guilt of their presence in a land not their 'own.'

Shemus grimaced, unable to feel the moment, sweat pouring off his brow, down his face, soaking his shirt, his shoulder burned in its socket with the heat of blazing coals.

"I hate to be a burden boys, but me arm is hurting something chronic".

"Right! Gilbert said decisively, "first port of call, the quack!"

The small band moved amongst the tents making enquiries about a physician and supplies. William and Bunjil went with

Shemus in search of medical succour whist Black Billy and Gilbert went about the monumental task of setting up base camp.

The first doctor who saw Shemus and his wound wanted to bleed him, William had seen enough of this kind of quackery at home. He declined the 'help' on behalf of his friend and hurried him out of the shambles that

appeared to be more a mortuary than a medical care facility.

Some half an hour later they came to a tent that smelled of perfumes so exotic, they had never beheld them in their senses before. Bunjil felt overwhelmed by the strangeness of the air and returned to the outside world of essences he recognised. As he left a small young women of oriental features came quickly forward to greet them at the entry with a bow, her long black hair plaited into two pigtails.

Fascinated by the sight of features of a new human so differing from his own, William starred for some moments, before remembering his errand.

By this stage Shemus was barely conscious, his speech was thick and slurred, they half dragged half carried him into a larger treatment room with a couch and many chests of potions, mortars, pestles, and various jars of dried concoctions.

The young women pointed to a figure in the corner of the room and said "Master Pho!" Master Pho, turned to face his visitors, immediately saying "Please lie him here, on the divan.

"Ah, you seek to solve the riddle of this infection" he said after a careful search of his patients wound.

"Yes Sir, I think the bullet is still in there" William answered.

"Hmm" said Master Pho, after a longer examination of Shemus.

"Much pain to remove, will he take the needles?"

William thought for a moment "Can I see them? he asked, Master Pho nodded.

Ming Toi bowed and brought forward a small cache of fine bone handled needles. Will felt the burden of care for Shemus lay heavily on his heart, these people seemed studiously careful and peaceful. He knew Shemus had few options in this fetid land with so many chances of disease, he agreed for help to be given, praying his instincts were right.

Meanwhile, in this battered town, devoured by the sun, inundated by rain, and swept away by the wind, Gilbert was finding out the frightening cost of being out of the pale of civilisation. The exorbitant price of life's staples made him feel he was being fleeced and then skinned alive. It appeared that salted beef or pork, flour, baking powder and tea, were the only food stuffs on offer. A fellow digger also cringing at the prices shrugged his shoulders and wryly commented "mate, looks like we will have to content ourselves with mutton and damper three days a week and damper and mutton on the other four days". This bought bellows of laughter all-round the shanty, hardship, melded the metal of these men into wills of iron, they determined to scrape victory from the jaws of defeat, wrench their life's blood from these stones and throw the dice until breath was done!

Black Billy and Bunjil looked dubiously at the roll of canvas Gilbert carried.

"That no good 'Gunyah' (house) for you fellas, give us three shillings, we make strong bark wurlie!" said Black Billy.

Gilbert blinked, "you think you can do it, for that" he asked, they nodded empathetically "That's pure dead brilliant!"

They found some relatively flat open ground chopped down some smaller trees with the axe Gilbert had purchased and set about stripping iron bark and pressing it flat under logs, leaving it to dry in the sun, then they erected a timber framework finishing by nailing the dried bark to the frame.

At length William had joined them leaving Shemus to the tender mercies of Master Pho and Ming Toi, reports from Master Pho's gardeners were that Shemus was needing rest but in recovery.

Ninety pounds was not the fortune Gilbert, William and Shemus had thought it was, not at the gold fields at any rate.

"The only ones getting rich are the merchants" said William as he handed over half a crown for a bucket of water, wretched stuff it was. "Just look at it", exclaimed Gilbert as William handed it over, "black as gum leaves could make it, foaming and seething in its putridity! But they drank it when they were thirsty to the last dregs, in the inferno of midday, there never seemed to be enough of it.

Other items such as a pick, shovel, cradle, candles, scales, axe, panning dish, boots, oilskin coats and trousers and a hat for shade were absolutely survival items.

According to the shopkeeper a jovial German, "a miner had to be a jack of all trades, strip bark, fell trees, saw it, dig sods, mend clothes, draw firewood, cook and eat anything to hand, use a spade, shovel, delve, pick and quarry, load, unload, puddle in mud, splash ankle deep in water, bear occasional slushing head to foot, bear sleet and rain, sleep in damp blankets, all with a good spirit and the endurance to withstand it, for three months.

"Then indeed if he continued there would be gold and rheumatism in it for those hardy souls left standing!"

Gilbert and William handed over forty-pound notes of their dwindling stash.

A mining license was procured next for the exorbitant sum of thirty shillings, a month, "Outrageous", Gilbert cried, both brothers felt it was daylight robbery, but these papers were checked regularly by the native police and fines given for working without them. They were also warned the claim had to be worked on six days a week or it could be 'jumped' by another digger.

At the crack of dawn, the next day, Gilbert, and William began to strip large areas of shallow ground down to the bedrock, the 'sinking' was from three foot to six foot in depth with plenty of water. When they first saw the small golden particles from halfway down the hole sitting in their pans, they were ecstatic with excitement, holding each other in sheer elation.

A week later Shemus arrived at the bark house, his shoulder in a sling, thinner, if possible, but of cheerful disposition.

"What ho mates? I guess it's time I lent a hand"!

William and Gilbert looked dubiously at Shemus' disarmament,

"You can make the tea and shoo the flies", said Gilbert "we need some rest from the biting varmints!"

"What about the fleas and mosquitos?" quipped William.

"It looks like we shun the delights and live laborious days", groaned Shemus.

"Welcome home Shemus," laughed the siblings.

The dew was falling heavily, the men were quietly listening to the incessant chirp of insects, the melancholic wail of the bitten, the deep tones of the mopoke, with the occasional yelp of a dingo and a whirr as a flying fox squirrel sailed in on a downward angle from one tree to another. They were in vast an animal kingdom, alive with diversity the likes they could only conjure in their wildest dreams.

Percy Tapp, and Horace Winpole had set up camp nearby. Yorkshire born and bred, or so they said, they arrived about eight at night looking eagerly around the campsite.

"We have been sinking a hole by Tucker's Gully and we had not even the hint of the colour gold from the bottom of our workings," said Horace. "That's why we moved here, my mate dropped the bucket and I the pick by mutual consent, not the ghost of a speck", agreed Percy.

"But further over by Golden Point", said Horace "there were hundreds of tubs, cradles, windlasses and weegees all in motion, injudicious action and mire, a flummoxing phantasmagoria."

"We're thinking of relocating, lock stock and barrel over there in the morning." Percy breezily announced.

If ever a pair were opposites, it was these two, Percy could double as a coatrack, his rail thin spare frame lanky and dishevelled in trousers hanging two times too big, tied at the waist with string. Horace on the other hand, looked as if he carried most of the larder internally, his red striped undershirt was barely covered by a blue over shirt popping at the buttons. His double chin disappeared into a couple of others, lost in the folds at his neck border, how he kept his girth in such proportions the brothers and their friend could only marvel.

"We've brought the beer! The pair went on to declare. This seemed a great fortune indeed to the luxury starved expatriates, however at first gulp, Gilbert and Shemus encountered a curious sickly taste. William examined the bottle a bit closer and saw that it was of a colour such as would be seen by emptying a bottle of ink into a basin of soap suds.

The trio knew they had no fear of addiction from this benediction, it was obviously an acquired taste, and not much to their liking. "When we strike it rich, we'll bring brandy" promised Horace, as the visitors ended their vivacious visit.

It was about an hour later, that Gilbert realised his flint box was missing, he made a thorough search of the cabin, but it had vanished from view into the ethos. Strange he pondered, for neither Shemus nor William took it without asking and it was always in his jackets inside pocket. He made a note to retrace their steps to the claim in the morning, to do another hunt for his lost property.

At the next day's dawn, William asked "have either of you taken the three shillings I had in my jacket?" Both Gilbert and Shemus denied knowledge of the coins. The three newcomers' thoughts turned to their ebullient callers, they pondered on the visitation.

In the very early hours of the morning several days later, Bunjil and Black Billy arrived with three frightened women from Billy's clan the Wadawurrung. All five came silently inside, as quietly as the dew drop of the dawning day. Gilbert, William and Shemus were rubbing sleep from their eyes trying to take in the terrible tale that Black Billy was telling them. "Those white fella squatters with their sheep, they say we steal sheep, we say 'What for you say we steal? We say 'What for you steal my country? You all one big thief. What for you quamby along o here? Geego along o your country and let black fellow alone. Then we go hunting, the women gather roots, those white squatter fellas band together, take guns, they could not find any black fellas they could drop, but they found black women hiding in the bushes, they kill them!"

The three women stood stooped in tragedy's pose, supporting each other in their anguish and sorrow.

"What can we do?" asked William appalled, "Can we get these men, bring them to justice? "No!" said Bunjil bitterly, "the magistrate Gunn will not hang a white man for a black one, neva see a white man suffer for shooting black fellas."

"Aye", agreed Gilbert "self-interest is at the root of these murders, they don't want to share the ground anywhere these sons of the sod."

"These wives not safe, can stay with you? Bunjil asked.

Shemus, and the brothers looked helplessly at the bewailing misery and agreed that the women could shelter in the Gunyah, but sleep in a lean-to.

The Aboriginal women were extremely biddable and useful in helping keep the house clean, the clothes drier and the food a lot better, Shemus could only cook damper one way - burnt!

With their feminine wisdom the trio started to catch and cook fish, birds, and roasted wallaby, accompanied by wemba wemba roots, taro, and berries.

Each one had their own possum skin cloak. The head woman, Alice explained by drawing with a stick in the dust, that the possum cloaks were made at each person's birth and as the baby grew the cloak grew with them. She showed them the skin sides designs, an iconography of country, of totem of place, the owner's identity and when the time came, they were buried in it.

The three men for their part kept their guest's presence a respected quiet knowledge.

Chapter 6

As they docked the women saw a city that was moulded by the history of an ancient indigenous habitat and convict hardship. Sitting sequestered in a beautiful harbour all around the semi-circular quayside were sandstone blocks, hand hewn from the landscape, stacked one up on top of another.

The building labour was of Herculean proportions dragged from in-prisoned strangers, chained to beginning a new civilisation.

But with the gold rushes it was fast becoming an unshackled society, echelons of fine buildings rose one above the other, like seats in a grandstand and glimmering above it all, the new immigrants could glimpse the towering spire of St James church.

Lars tried to shepherd Grace and Uileen off from the herd of other passengers, but he was still a working sailor and was ordered back to the wheelhouse of the ship.

Everyone travelling assisted was rounded up and marched behind an escort of male and female guides all uniformed and correct.

Their destination was Hyde Park barracks, an imposing brick monotheistic building, Georgian gothic, built solid, strong, unimpeachable for the male convicts, but it still had a penitentiary like presence which it imposed on the new arrivals.

On the upper levels the barred windows peered suspiciously at these foreigners. Grace looked around as she felt eyes boring deep into her back. Ann Manson stood hands on hips staring, her black hair just wisping back from its shave, her eyes shot with spiteful promises, Grace felt alarm twist in her stomach. She quickly looked away beginning to make fevered plans for their liberation. Uileen held her hand and together they walked through the doors of this unholy fortress to find themselves new positions in this new country.

The beds were solid iron, with wire wove to hold the mattresses. Everything was built to

regulation excepting that the sheets and pillows were the women's own.

Essentially the prison like accommodation was a respite centre until the sojourners were collected by relatives, employers or hired by one of dozens of married matrons for household help.

There was some female 'inmates' who had been housed for many months, destitute, infirm and from the sound of some of the wild rankings and ravings insane.

"The top floor was going to be transformed into an asylum", the matron said, "in the meantime, the new girls were to leave the residents be, and no mistake!"

That night Uileen and Grace were awoken by the pitiful mewling of a thin, ragged wretch of a woman, clawing at their bedclothes.

"Where have ye hidden me babe? She moaned "I saw ye take it away!"

Uileen tried to soothe the poor unfortunate, but she was too far gone in her obsession.

"I want my littlun or it will be the worse for you me gels!" the crone screeched as she whipped out a pair of dagger like scissors.

"Look out!" yelled Uileen as the attacker plunged them into the pillow narrowly missing Grace's face as she twisted away just in time. Uileen leapt up to restrain the woman who fought with the strength of ten, Bridgette and Maeve came running to the rescue and between the five of them they managed to restrain what was a nightmare of a situation.

The staff arrived finally; Matron was perplexed "Usually mad Meg does not go off like this unless someone had roused her to it" she commented. Uileen looked around the dormitory room to see Ann Manson looking smugly back and then whispering to her companions at her side, the three laughed knowingly.

"The sooner we are on our way the better," whispered Grace when she heard this news.

It was a hiring day, and the hiring room was set up for appointments, all the 'respectable' married women were vetted by the matron Mrs Ferris, to become employers for the likely candidates. Ninety-two applicants had turned up, twenty-four jobs for maidservants were available.

The line of respectability seemed to deteriorate somewhat when the news of the scarcity of resources radiated down it.

Some 'pious souls' were even seen replacing the odd hat pin in their hair shortly after their fellow parishioner was suddenly overcome with sharp stabbing pains in the posterior and pulled out of the running.

One of the prospective employers loudly voiced displeasure when she found out that the maids were Irish.

"We don't want these 'Bad Bridget's', immoral, unskilled workhouse sweepings," she remonstrated, continuing ...

"Catholic castoffs, I will go elsewhere for household help, she exclaimed.

"Aye go", answered Mrs Ferris "there's nothing for you here!"

Grace, Uileen, Bridgette and Maeve sat at breakfast knowing that they would eventually be hired out in the coming weeks.

Grace explained the plan that they would be trying to get to the State of Victoria where the Ballarat goldfields were.

The other young women listened to her plans, "On Sunday, Lars was going to come to the wall surrounding the barracks, Uileen and she were going to church. They would then meet him at the lamppost and receive a note telling them when they could travel south with him. Bridgette was very keen to hear more of the goldfields while Maeve was hoping to become a cook, but at only seventeen, it was likely she would start a kitchen hand.

They all agreed to accompanying each other to church, but when they rendezvoused at nine o'clock Brianna did not appear, so the four remaining churchgoers set off.

Lars was loitering around the south end of the wall, he sighed with relief seeing Grace and Uileen.

"Here is some money and an address to get a cab to. In one week, you must come to this place by lunchtime, I will be waiting with horses but bring only a carpetbag." Las exhorted them.

"Can Bridgette, and Maeve come to?" begged Uileen, "they have nothing here, they don't even want them here, they don't like the Irish girls".

Maeve added "it is all so unreal; it feels like Ireland might not exist anymore. But I am pushed from pillar to post the same. I see mistrust in their eyes and the attitudes towards us are the same, dirty Catholics!"

Lars looked perplexed.

"Please", pleaded Grace "they will be beaten!"

Finally after an agonising deliberation Lars replied.

"Ja ja, very well, but you attend to me young ladies", he admonished.

Later that night after after returning to the barracks Maeve mysteriously disappeared no one had seen nor heard from her. The following day Bridgette was worried, and she took her concerns to her friends.

They decided to split up and quiz the rest of the women and staff about Maeve's whereabouts. Someone saw her leaving the barracks heading to the south side gate, late the day before so Grace asked permission of the Matron to search for her and reluctantly, she was granted it.

Uileen went one way, Bridgette, and Grace, the other, they interviewed and questioned the local shopkeepers. Finally, a cafe owner recalled seeing a young woman he hadn't seen before joining a group of known harlots, he wondered what was going on, but was serving his customers at the time.

'Questa Casa' was located on Pitt Street and Bridgette knew when she saw it what she was looking at, the oldest house in the world, a brothel. This pink Georgian fortress housed those unfortunate women that had come to a new country only to find only the same prejudices, the same poverty and the same

perversions.

Bridgette knew with a keen intuition that within those pastel portals, her friend was captive, being used as bait to hook money from the city's many sharks.

After much discussion and planning Grace and Bridgette 'volunteered' to apply for positions as workers to gain entry to the garish property while Uileen anxiously awaited the outcome in the laneway.

Madam Cyn, the lady of the establishment looked Grace and Bridgette up and down, "Wots your game, then loves? Why're you looking to do business ere? You don't strike me as the sorts who'd want for fancy men!"

Grace was quick to reply

"We don't want to work for tuppence, doing needlework or being somebody's servants for little payment and long hours".

"Well, ducks, it's good money, but you works for it and no mistake", returned Madam Cyn. She was a middle aged and striking individual, dark hair streaked with grey, artfully arranged atop her head, makeup carefully applied around her eyes with crow's feet just crinkling the edges. She had been a beauty in her day, now she was calling the shots, educating her sons, paying her way in the community, she paid fair, played fair and was her own boss, independent of a husband, with the occasional lover just to keep her warm.

"I can take you on trial basis, then we'll see the lay of the land, so to speak! Matilda take Bridgette and Grace to the green suite."

The newcomers followed where they were bid, as they went down a long hallway the door to a room opened and there was Maeve, in the passionate embrace of a young seaman.

"Let go of her," shouted Bridgette, rushing to Maeve's defence, as she saw her friend's entanglement.

Grace following closely behind pulled up hard against Bridgette, ready for the affray.

"No! cried Maeve "don't harm him, he's to become my husband!"

"What?" cried Bridgette and Grace together.

"She is to become my wife!" the young man chimed in.

"Saints preserve us", exclaimed Bridgette, "we came to rescue you."

"I couldn't tell you, it happened so suddenly,

Sven has jumped ship to go to the goldfields and he wanted me to go with him" exclaimed Maeve.

"I take it you found each other on the voyage," retorted Grace wryly.

"Ja, we were friends on the way out here," Sven replied. "What can I say, we fell in love, but knew we could not be together if I am a sailor and she a seamstress. We want a life for each other, we need to be together!"

Bridgette and Grace were at first a little disappointed not being included in their comrades escape plan, but with every working woman in the place gathered in the hallway and Madam

Cyn muttering about their false pretences they decided to accept the inevitable consequences of Maeve's decision. "But why did you end up coming here?" asked Bridgette.

"Sven knew Madam Cyn, and she said we could stay for a few days, to get a start", answered Maeve quickly.

"Tomorrow, we go to the Mt Alexander goldfields, asserted Sven.

"We are supposed to be going tomorrow", said Grace, "Lars is waiting for us, the bullock cart is leaving for Ballarat, and we must leave with it!"

The three women parted friends, with best wishes for the future all round. Madam Cyn however, felt somewhat deceived and put out, until Sven added another twenty shillings to pay for their bill.

Uileen had almost given up hope and was pacing up and down outside the cafe waiting, Grace and Bridget breathlessly explained the situation which beggared belief for them all, however acceptance was fast becoming their biggest asset in making their way in this wilderness, foreign and new.

The bullock cart had left, Lars had disappeared and with him the transportation and guardian evaporated. Grace sat with Uileen and Bridgette, in shocked silence.

There were not enough pence to buy more than a cup of tea each, between them, the plans to reconnect with Gilly and Will had slipped through their fingers.

Now they were at the mercy of the Matron and the married elite of Sydney and money was their greatest challenge.

Chapter 7

Gruelling hours of filling the cradle in surface soil and gravel, searching the obsessive lure of elusive alluvial gold, filled their days.

As William looked out in a rare resting moment from Preston hill, he solemnly thought the camp had the appearance of one vast cemetery with freshly made graves. He thought of his reason for being, Uileen, the very essence of her image contoured the reason for his life, when he panned it was the golden flecks in her smiles he looked for. When he endured the sweltering heat, the rain that brought muddy clag clinging to his every step weighing him down, Wills spirit was enlightened by his love, the load star that kept his bearings.

He saw scattered like seeds around him the ethnic diversity of his fellow toilers, many were sojourners whose imaginations like his had been captured by the promise that all men might acquire the wealth with which to become property owners. Men from every corner of the globe, Germans, New Zealand Maori,

Frenchmen, Portuguese, Americans, and Chinese converged in droves to discover their worth. Money absorbed their every thought, every heart was full of the wanting of it, this dream so raw it was on the tip of everyone's tongue, an appetite, hungering for a way to devour life, it was there in all their waking hours and in the dead of night. Gilbert was amongst his peers, his thoughts were never far from brooding upon the quartz staircase out of penury, the hardships he endured he saw as his apprenticeship to working his own land building a livelihood for kith and kin, although the likelihood of finding a wife in this barren terrain was minimal at best.

This masculine society: six hundred men to ten women, swung from hardships to happiness in an afternoon, a comradeship grew from shared miseries, ministrations, and mate ship, they were the diggers, and this was their domain. On a shopping expedition Gilbert met Colin Couper, Gilbert had not taken enough money to pay for the last sack of flour, Colin stepped forward and bought it for 'auld Lang syne'.

"It's a pleasure to meet a fellow countryman who knows the value of friendship," said Gilbert.

"We sink or swim together, me father was fond of saying" Colin returned.

"Have ye been ta yon butchers shop mon?" Asked Gilly.

"Not yet", replied Colin.

"The air is black with all sorts of flies and its sounds like thunder, Ye will not hear yourself speak," said Gilly.

"Och, I've already had the devils all over ma meat and tattles like an ebon plague", complained Colin.

"Aye, it's crawling with creatures this new land, but none worse than the two-legged ones, I'll be bound." Said Gilly.

He was canny Scottish troubadour who had made the same pilgrimage as his brethren, but he had thrown his lot in with a German named Franz, for they had both been to the great gilded Californian goldfields. Still Colin hankered to spend time and converse with his fellow countrymen, he became a regular at the brother's bark home, the United diggerdom of friendship brought with it laughter, stories, and songs all sung round the glow of firelight and shared adversity.

Well, I'll tell ye true, lads, ye'll never guess what now! Colin declared "I returned to my hut this evetime, it was surrounded by the native police, on the hunt for our licenses. The sod chimney was smoking and the hut door, an old flour sack stretched on a frame of wattle sapling was gaping wide open. My first thought was Franz was out and no escaping the two police marching straight for the doorway, I had to approach to a few yards of the scene, license in hand. Franz had left and I can find no trace of him, the lead troopers checked the paperwork and they left disappointed, no fine money for them, this time. The mysterious disappearance of Franz puzzled them all, Black Billy and Bunjil dropped by with a kangaroo for supper, as they sat down to eat the roasted marsupial. The two wadawurrung women left with Black Billy to return to their clan, but Alice elected to stay with her newfound benefactors and Shemus for one was glad of it.

A week later a shout went up around the digs, "They have caught a thief!"

Gilbert, Shemus, and William ran down the track to shared open ground where a mob of other diggers were milling round. Three miners were tying held down a fourth to keep him captive.

"It's Ben Haddock the second mate from the Golden Spring", cried Will.

"So, it tis, och, he's in for it now, said Gilbert.

The spokesmen for the diggers were proclaiming what the prisoner had been up to.

"Enzo caught him red handed in his tent, had his gold, money pouch and his silver photo frame", the leader declared.

"Shoot him", cried someone, "Lynch him!" called another, there were many calls for rough justice. In the end cooler heads prevailed, Ben was stripped to his underwear, then passed around the circle of vigilantes and doused in sludge.

A fire was started and one of the firemen retrieved a chisel from his tent.

"Now!", he said as he heated the instrument to red hot, "what do we want this sneaksman to learn?"

"Caught stealing from his mates", came the answering calls, from the crowd.

"Right! hold him down lads", said the tattooist, as he carefully chiselled in the letters, that made the words that completed the damming statement.

The screams ricocheted around the encampment, but he was held still in an iron grip of anger. By the time the punishment was done, Ben Haddock could not show his face anywhere, as it would be a permanent reminder of his grave crime against his fellows. "Banish him" went up the unanimous cry. A digger on horseback with a stock whip, obliged the crowd by cracking Ben Haddocks way out of town.

After this furore, when they returned to their hut, William and Gilbert were surprised when they were confronted on the threshold of their lodgings by a smart genteel-looking female, politely asking after Colin.

"I'm Frances", the woman cooed, introducing herself as Colin's sister.

She then proceeded to throw up her heels and cut the most unladylike capers around the dining table. Shemus hurried off to find Colin, who was as gobsmacked as his mates to find out there was a lady asking after him, he could not imagine who it could be, being one of three brothers.

The meeting was indeed one of fascination and intrigue as Colin beheld the damsel who seemed to know him. He could not, for the life of him, place her as a sister, especially with that accent. Finally, the penny dropped, Frances dropped her veil and became Franz, who resolved to never buy a license, that he would continue to wear his new style and mine for gold as Frances and would, from that minute on answer to no other name!

Gilbert, Shemus and William were somewhat stunned by the turn of events, but Colin informed them that by law, women did not need a license to dig for gold.

"I've only got one question", said Will.

"Oh," said Francis, "what's that?"

"How come a Scotsman got a German sister?"

The company roared in shared mirth.

The heavens let loose for a week, everything was wet, the damp drizzled into every shred of fabric the miner's possessed.

"My bones are wet, I think my very heart has turned to water", moaned Shemus, as he rung out his coat and hat.

"Plenty rain," agreed Alice as she put more wood on the fire.

William rushed in bringing the storm blowing after him, "Quickly, quickly, the troopers have Gilbert, "we must come up with five pounds", he shouted.

"What happened," exhorted Shemus.

"The license got so wet in his pocket, it was a mushy crumpled mess, they would not accept it and when he protested, Deputy Commissioner, Nickleby Armstrong; you know, he's an ex-convict, he had Gilly handcuffed to the ring bolt of his saddle and when Gilbert would not trot along with the horse he broke into a cantor! Gilly tried to drag the swine off the mount, then one of the troopers came along, took out his sabre and

hit Gilbert with the blade whichever way it came down. He was still standing, but as soon as he answered back, Armstrong hit him hard, head on, with the brass knob of his riding stick. Gilly fell to the ground, bleeding and unconscious. They held me back and took him to the lockup by the government camp." Will bit out dully.

They found the last few notes they possessed, hidden under the floorboards.

Shemus put back on his soaked oilskin and boots and they made for Gilbert's imprisonment.

Edward Armstrong was handling court when Shemus and Will arrived, the troopers had

guns trained on the diggers, the logs were crammed full, some of the prisoners were 'Vandemonians', Tasmanian ex-convicts, the very demons who sought and gained the lowest abyss of crime, men of the most depraved and abandoned character.

William and Shemus stood their ground "we've come to pay the fine," William declared. "Wait yur turn, you gobbershites", our bisness ain't concluded yet", snarled Armstrong, "Ye lousy diggers, I should lock ye all up, see if I don't."

Two hours later, the tableau remained the same, Armstrong cast his jaundiced eye over the trio, before acidly pronouncing that their fine would be ten pounds!

"But the law is five!" protested William.

"Is he a relative?" asked Armstrong, pointing to Shemus.

"No, but he's mining the same patch," said William

"It's no matter" roared Armstrong, "he needs a separate license. There will be no more digging on that claim, until the fines are paid in full, new forms are filled in and paid for!"

"We only have five pounds", cried William.

"Well, it's not enough and in a moment you will both be joining your brother!"

Shemus had been fiddling with something, in his coat pocket, as reluctant as he was to part with it, he slowly pulled out a golden nugget. It was surely worth more than ten pounds. It was the very first one they had found, the thought of just giving it over, weighed heavily on his heart, like lead. He sighed, handing to the Commissioner. Armstrong's face lit with avarice, as he gleefully accepted the bullion, noting with satisfaction its size and weight.

"Huh, fortunate indeed you have a backup plan, I will accept this as payment for the fines, however you will need to line up for new licenses and pay, before any more mining is done on any claims, my men will be watching you!"

By this stage of the proceedings Shemus and William knew the measure of this man

Armstrong; at least enough to know nothing would be gained in resisting his version of the law.

When the troopers dragged Gilbert out half-conscious, from the cage he was penned in, Shemus and William positioned themselves on either side of his prostrate form and half carried him back to their home.

A shock awaited them there too, Colin was in the doorway, talking to Alice animatedly, Alice was shaking her head, plaintively.

She ran to assist them when she saw them coming and the state Gilbert was in, situating him by the fire, to warm the blueness from his hands and face.

"What's wrong?" Asked Shemus.

"Horace and Percy have jumped your claim" reported Colin, "They heard the troopers had taken Gilly and the weasels leapt upon it like rats on a rotting corpse. I arrived too late to stop them, they both have pistols, the shysters, I suspect they are a lot more rubbish than they seem".

Gilly came to a fuller awareness upon hearing Colin's tale.

"Those thieving heathens, how dare they come here pretending friendship."

The effort to rouse to such anger, exhausted Gilbert's facilities, he fell back to his makeshift bed upon the hearth side. William had stood in brooding silence at the dire news, knowing they were stretched to their limits financially. They had collected in four months only eleven ounces of gold dust between them.

The inhabitants of the hut were inculcated in a sober mood of lost opportunities and negative experiences, Gilbert drifted in and out of a fevered sleep, talking to the turmoil that beset him.

Alice and Shemus sat close at hand wiping Gilbert's brow, murmuring together in a comforting discomfort. William kept watch on the fire, going out to get logs to keep the cabin warm, on a night where the cold was not only weather dependent but came from within, a bleakness of spirit, freezing warm thoughts.

Into the firelight, he projected Uileen's lightness of being, he ran his frigid feelings through the blaze of her smile, he dissolved his chilled fears in the flames of her desire. The passion of their love burned in his veins, igniting his dreams of hope, once more, knowing she was out there waiting for him, he was alive.

Gilbert's condition was not better by the next morning. William knew the gum leaf teas Alice was trying did not seem to break the shaking cold that had Gilly in its grip.

Shemus spoke his mind "Gilbert needs a doctor Will, we need to get Master Pho and Ming Toi, they can treat the pneumonia".

"What do I pay them with?" asked Will.

"Master Pho is a patient man; he will accept a deferred payment" said Shemus.

"You see if he will come Shemus, I will ask Alice to find Bunjil, someone has to stay with Gilly, we need all the help and providence we can get", said William.

Bunjil arrived at much the same time as Master Pho and Ming Toi. Will explained the conundrum that had led them almost to bankruptcy. Both guests listened to the brothers' misfortunes, nodding sagaciously, although Alice and Bunjil found the celestials (people of the sun) difficult to cope with.

Bunjil whispered to William, "Black fellow die, by and by jump up white fellow, but long tails have no place in our stories."

William tried to explain the newcomers' differences, but the divergence was not in Bunjil's ken.

Gilbert was too sick to know who had come and who had gone; a febrile force reduced his strength to that of a babe. The willow bark and other herbs, that he drank, were just a liquid sea he floated in.

As the time slowly ticked by, the blankets and fire began to penetrate the bone chill. Upon finally waking from a long slumber, Gilly looked up at an exotic angel, with almond eyes of amber brown, winged with delicate black brows in an oval face, framed with a long curtain of ebony hair falling around her shoulders. The apparition smiled; Gilbert felt the warmth of the eternal eastern sunrise blaze on his face. He was overcome with elation he had never experienced in his whole life.

Then, Master Pho came forward across Gilbert's vision and with methodical thoroughness looked deeply into Gilbert's eyes. He felt his pulse, then lymph nodes, and noticed the absence of high temperature.

He nodded in satisfaction, "You will continue your journey in this lifetime", he noted.

"I will leave now, however Ming Toi will remain until your strength is greater," he asserted.

Gilly looked at Ming Toi in wonder at the fairy tale that seemed to beckon him to follow, he sank back against the pillows and was enchanted, as she swept a cool cloth across his brow.

Alice and Bunjil took Shemus and William out to look for prospective gold sites. They went down into Golden Gully and Alice looked intently over the heaps of tailings left over from the locusts that had dug there before. After an hour's peering search with a glad cry, she stooped down, plunged her hands into the slurry of dirt and pulled up a small nugget.

Shemus rushed to see this miracle find and Bunjil laughed and held out his hand to William; curled inside his fingers were two more larger nuggets.

Will was ecstatic with the thrill of the finds.

"We no more poor fellows, we plenty rich fellows now", chortled Bunjil.

William shook Bunjil's hand wildly whilst Shemus hugged and kissed Alice most thoroughly, much to his compatriot's bemusement.

With the fortune of finding friends like Bunjil and Alice, the hunt for a fortunate future was still before them.

Chapter 8

Roaring Jack Tucker was one of the gold generations, straight from the El Dorado of the Californian goldfields. In America he had ridden the roads to riches, but gambling had given most of his fortune to fate. Now he threw his dice again, taking a gamble on sinking a deep line on Bakery Hill.

He spun an enchanting tale of digging shafts down to the mother loads, the seams of gold running through the very quartz rocks they were standing on.

"Why yes siree, there's bullion begging to be uncovered, in them thar hills. We are going to extract nuggets and bullion from gravels straight off ancient stream beds, we can achieve more gold in a week here than most people do in a year! All we need is backbone and muscle, we will set up a windlass and winch down buckets, one down, one up, we'll be down to bedrock in no time!"

Round a blazing campfire, Shemus, William and Gilbert listened intently, it had been some months since finding any nuggets and the gold dust was only sporadically being caught in their panning.

Poverty was stretching its gaunt and withered hand on the diggings and elsewhere as the alluvial sites were drying up.

"How do we keep your shaft from caving in?" inquired Gilly.

"We will put a drive in to hold the sides and the ceiling", replied Jack. "It will take six men, but we could raise an estimated twenty-five tons of valuable quartz per week, that's where the bonanza is boys!" Jack continued to expound.

"Well! What are we waiting for?" said William," let's get at it".

Shemus and Gilly agreed it was time to move to a more industrial kind of mining to find the rewards that they craved.

"Whoowee", cried Roaring Jack, "let the good times roll!"

They all paid in for a joint claim on Bakery Hill. They set up their gear, Fig Newton and Luigi Vinci threw in their lots with the Lucky Lottery consortium as well.

The first level they dug down to ninety feet, put in a drive northward for seven feet and struck a reef ten feet thick. The dirt was then winched to the surface and put through the cradle with water sluicing it through. The water was extremely heavy and difficult to lift.

Jack had the men using two buckets, one up and one down, it was a constant weight that took all their strength to exercise.

After a particularly backbreaking session, Luigi was on watch, he had been on the first shift, early dawn, and his shoulders had sunk, and he slumped forward on a walking stick. Will had just surfaced for supper as Luigi took a seat on the bucket that will had just exited.

"Luigi, watch out you don't get too close to the shaft on that bucket," warned William.

"I good, Will, I see you soon, I will come", Luigi sighed, but his eyelids closed as if by their own accord and he sank down into a nodding stupor.

Jack called out "Ain't you for any supper Luigi?"

"I'll come direct, Luigi replied, but fatigue folded his physicality into a head foremost ball and he pitched forward straight into the abyss of the hole before him. Everyone heard the commotion and clatter as they rushed to the windlass...there was a breath-taking silence; the air split with tension as the mining companions looked down, appalled at the sudden accident.

Astonishingly a faint cry out caught their attention: "Heave up" Luigi cried.

"Hells bells" said Jack, "who would believe it, he's got the darn luck of the devil!" as they pulled Luigi, bruised but unbowed from the chasm.

Even after performing a few somersaults down the shaft, striking his head and back he had somehow survived, essentially unscathed!

"Some people, ye just canna knock any sense into," laughed Gilbert, as he ruffled Luigi's hair, when they had checked him over.

Luigi gave a small comical shrug and promptly fell back into a deep slumber, as his company carried him back to his tent.

They were beginning to make their money by crushing the quartz in a stamper, but one chill evening, starting the night shift, Fig Newton looked like a large mole, coated with black and grey mud.

He was in a low, long, narrow tunnel hacking and chipping away with his pick at the hardened rock walls, one hundred and seventy feet below the surface, with only a lantern to hold the small space lit. He struck a large irregular lump of water worn, honey combed, aureate and as he held his lamp to his discovery the purity of its golden glow bedazzled him.

Carefully he removed it from its cavity in the rock bed and pulled himself up in the bucket with the prize.

"Quickly, quickly!" he cried to Will "gather the others I've made a find!"

The whole group assembled around the diggings, exhilarated at the find. They examined it's portend. It was about fourteen kilograms in weight and although not the biggest nugget ever found, its size did proclaim a special place on the gold registry.

The team were jubilant at their good fortune, through it was perseverance that had won the day, and believing in the opportunity for a better life. Most of the town came by to see the "Bonzer" nugget as they named it.

Jack, Shemus, Fig, Will and Gilbert in high spirits accompanied it to the Treasury Office. At the bank, Luigi chose the short straw of guard duty at the dig. The celebration of finding the good-sized nugget meant that the security of the dig had given way to the opportunity to enjoy the fruits of their labour.

Roaring Jack, Gilly, Will, Shemus and Fig attended the theatre, drinking to each other's health and generally living large on the bounty that the blind goddess showered upon them.

"Hurry up Horace", whispered Percy, as he stood over Luigi's inert body, "he's out cold", we had better be quick about jumping this claim!

"What happens if they return?" asked Horace.

"Use your pistol man"! Said Percy disgusted.

"They say gold thirst can be the most horrible demon to deprave the human heart!" Mumbled Horace.

"Ah my friend, we are slaking our thirst, not desiccating from want, our hearts will be overflowing, you saw that nugget! Get on that bucket and get down there this instant!" Percy demanded.

Horace heaved himself onto the wooden pail, his anxious and haggard appearance disappearing down the long mine shaft like a hollow phantom shrinking sadly as he went.

The air smelt damp, reeking of rotting vegetation; suddenly sixty feet from the ground Horace fell out of the bucket, the foul draft smothering his consciousness.

Percy, hearing his friend fall, leapt into the second bucket winching himself down to find Horace quite crushed and broken by the crash he had sustained with the rock floor.

As Percy realised with shock that his mate was no more, he scrambled back into his bucket and started to wind himself madly to the surface in the caliginous darkness.

There was a sudden roar, and an inrush of water caused a collapse of earth and rock and the timbering caved in upon him.

Luigi came to and heard faint cries of help emanating from the mine shaft.

As he peered over the edge illuminating the pit, he saw Percy Thorpol's head waving distractingly around; dirt, dust and rubble completely covered the rest of his body.

"Help me, quickly, I am unable to move", Percy cried.

"Hold on", called Luigi, as he ran to fetch helpers.

For twelve long hours, Percy had stayed conscious, suspended in suffering while the rescue diggers worked religiously to uncover him and release him from his tomb. Towards the end of his torment Percy cried "I no longer feel my arms!"

"We have you now, you are soon free", cried Luigi, as the rescuers finally brought him to the surface. But the physician could do nothing for his patient, except provide laudanum for pain and sleep and some five hours later, Percy and Horace had met their maker, the fickle hand of fate had won its hand.

"Shemus you have a letter", said Gilbert.

"Who would write to me here?" thought Shemus as he opened the small white missive. There before him, inked in every line was his last connection to the 'Emerald Isle', reeling him in to the dilemma of kith and kin.

Ming Toi wrung her hands in distress and despair, her countrymen ate opium with such a concentration, that the lives of many floated away like poppy petals down the endless stream, avoiding the drudgery of this gruelling environment.

Master Pho had not come back from visiting one such den yet, where could he have got to, she thought. Her mind clouded with storms of doubts as she wandered the makeshift surgery that was both work and home.

Outside, the gardeners Lim and Ah Sam, assiduously tended their crops of herbs, vegetables, and spices. With any kind of water and manure they could provide a basket of healthy staples to prevent scurvy and many other ailments dogging the health of the miners.

The peace of propagation was shattered by two of their fellows running and shouting for help. Ming Toi and both gardeners rushed to their sides.

"Master Pho has been set upon, when leaving the opium room", cried the first messenger.

"They have arrested him; he has been taken to the jail on Camp Hill" chimed in the second informant.

"We must go and rescue the master", retorted Lim.

"Yes," replied Ah Sam, "but we will need reinforcements, these people are our enemies!"

"I will go to my friend Gilbert; he may have some plan to aid us in our mission" said Ming Toi after consideration of the difficulties.

The portal of One Thousand Sighs was run by a little man not much over five feet tall.

Ah Sing knew the true secret of mixing opium that made good business and much pleasure.

On the wall a proverb was hung in Cantonese 'If I can attain Heaven for a price, why should you be envious?'

Ah Sing could roll the black opium pill in both hands, he always told people he kept a 'first chop household'. His customers would grasp their big bamboo stem pipe with a copper cup and a jade mouthpiece and then hold the cup over a small oil lamp, vaporising the opium and sucking up the black smoke.

It was very hard to keep count of time in this establishment; one could doze, then sleep into the infinity of a fume.

Master Pho used tincture of opiates for some pain remedies, but he was careful to leave imbibing the opiate to others with needs greater than his own for respite against the loneliness, homesickness, and racial prejudice that they found aplenty in colonial gold towns.

Gaining supply was his only reason for being present in Ah Sings opium den that day. Without warning a band of troopers arrived using their swords to slice their way into the canvas structure. Such was the stupor of the hypnotic, that the denizens of the portal lay prostrate upon their mats unable to lift themselves out of harm's way.

Edward Armstrong followed his men into the den where Master Pho had just completed his transactions and he was accosted and seized by two armed henchmen.

"What have we ere? One of the yellow peril, who is getting airs above his station", Armstrong designated.

"It looks like this one definitely needs to be taught a lesson lads, off with his tail!"

"Sure thing governa!" returned the thugs, who between them held Pho in a vice like grip.

Master Pho tried twisting out of his assailants hold but Armstrong pulled out a wicked long knife, sharpened on a wetted rock while screaming "Let's be having this pigstail off, so ye can't run to market, ye slant eyed scum" sneered Edward Armstrong.

At that moment, Ming Toi, Lim and Ah Sam came hurtling through the tented entrance, "Unhand my honourable Uncle; he has done nothing wrong", cried Ming Toi.

"Huh, that's just where you are wrong girly," said Armstrong, "This ere den is illegal, I am the Police Chief and the law is in my hands, "Ye best stay your distance, or my men will have some sport with you!"

"I will not let you dishonour my uncle with your evil hatred, shouted Ming Toi, as she leapt in front of the razor-sharp blade, just as it was raised to strike Master Pho. The dimly lit edifice, cast candle lit shadows, over the small red, silk flower that lay crumpled on the dirty floor, a crimson stream ran into a pool, the black mantle of Ming Toi's hair covered her pale countenance.

Master Pho looked in horror at the inert form of his niece, his gardeners were transfixed in shock; then they reacted as a single being joined in outrage. A triad of whirling limbs, sweeping around the room, kicking, and chopping, legs and arms akimbo. As they came to a slow halt, the two henchmen were lying on the floor, their heads at strange angles, eyes open, sightless to life's movements.

Master Pho was at Ming Toi's side, she lay holding his hand, feeling her strength ebbing away.

"I could not let you be disgraced, venerable Uncle", she whispered.

"I know my child" answered Pho, "the path of one's life runs where courage takes it!"

"I would like more time to blossom, but eternal summer comes to my door", breathed Ming Toi, and then she closed her beautiful, bright brown eyes to look upon the faces of her ancestors, as they came to claim her.

Master Pho held Ming Toi's slight form close to his chest and felt a burning void where his heart had been beating.

This land had been his challenge, his pathway, and ascendancy to new learnings. This bitter lesson of loss was almost impossible to swallow, what had he gained but sorrow, the white man's greed grasped the neck of all life and strangled the living from it.

Ah Sam and Lim gathered up Ming Toi's lifeless body and sadly with many tears the celestial sons carried their small princess home to be at rest.

As he walked behind his servants, Master Pho remembered his enemy Armstrong, he was not with his confederates in the tent, somehow, he had escaped retribution for his crime, but the memory of Master Pho was long and his patience to endure strong.

A reckoning would be conceived, for a young life would not be given up so cheaply, this man Armstrong would pay!

The news of Ming Toi's death reached Gilbert a week later when Master Pho had occasion to visit. Gilbert felt as if all the colours of his world had turned to ash, the breath went out of his lungs, he was drowning in sensations painful, gut wrenching. Up until that day he had met Ming Toi, his journey had been a simple one to escape poverty and succeed at whatever he put his head and hand to, his dream to have land under his feet, to call his own, seemed all he had needed to pull him through the hardships of this transient life. But the shock of losing the chance of a new constellation in his solar system, a bright hope that his days could be filled with the fragrance of the rare blossom of love was ripped asunder, disappearing like fragile petals in the winter winds.

Chapter 9

Vagrancy was a serious charge and Flag Officer Lars Tordenskjold knew it; according to the police, he had been found consorting with people who had no visible means of support.

"You, Sir, are of a disordering, desperate character, idle and profligate, roaming our streets, in the company of rogues and vagabonds. Furthermore, I have it on good authority that you have deserted your ship, by Jove! We are not the Wild West here Sir, we are a lawful civilised colony."

The magistrate was in full voice, his long, pompous wig bouncing around his round reddened countenance.

"I can only prescribe a sentence of six months at the very least, as a deterrent to others who may be influenced to follow your heinous example, take the prisoner down, officer". After the stunning intelligence that Lars had seemingly abandoned them, Grace and Uileen knew they had both better be employed to find a way to freedom. It was bleak indeed to find out just before being signed up to different households spread out across the city, that Lars had been taken by the police and was almost certainly shackled for the foreseeable future in the arms of the law. Grace felt so impotent to gain a foothold in the mountain of trials that stood before them.

"I canna see a way out," she lamented but Uileen spoke with quiet strength and resolve, "We have the will, we will find the way", as they hugged hard farewell.

Being a seamstress was to be a slave to the needle, Grace thought, as she pricked her thumb trying to hurry finishing the men's

shirts. She had two dozen to finish; the woman she worked for was a cross crabby creature who never thought anything was right.

"Come on girl, get a move on, or you'll be here, all night and no rubbish mind, if you want breakfast"! Mrs Parsons crabbed.

"Yes Mrs Parsons", Grace replied.

Grace worked to eat and ate to work or that's how she felt, she was often sat trapped in the work room at night by candlelit flicker, squinting down at a half-sewn garment. She knew very well that Mrs Parsons and Mr Grimes were taking in out-work, whilst the mistress was confined to her sickbed and the master was working away. The sweatshop labour was bringing in a pretty penny for the pair, if she complained they threatened to say she was the culprit, no one in authority would believe an indentured servant.

Uileen was serving as house parlour maid, her hours were not much better than Graces, up at 5am to bed at 10am, Sunday evenings off, however she only had a whole day off a month. Both maids knew they were dependent on the hierarchy of the households they worked in; everything was regulated around keeping up appearances. Grace had already had to elbow the footman who decided he could take liberties with her, he had a nasty look about him, she suspected he was the go between in the sewing scam.

Meeting on a Sunday evening, with Bridgette in the Hyde Street Cafe, they compared notes, it seemed the sweet notes of freedom, were to be soured by sorrows endless staircase. Both women bereft of their kin's comfort, ached for loves alms to save them from the poorhouses they found no solace in. As the comforted each other, they heard a familiar voice calling their names, they looked up in surprise at the sound.

Cockatoo Island had been laid bare by colonial convicts, it had no fresh water supply of its own and was made into a penal institution by the same brutal labours. Lars arrived at a prison establishment, run by a corrupt superintendent who made most of the prisoners look like choir boys. Charles Wormwood had already been ousted from running Norfolk clink, where he worked his captives' slaves to their last skerrick of energy culling sheep.

At Cockatoo Island Lars found leg shackles and the cat-o-nine tails being used with impunity. The first night was fraught with foul play and fighting as food rations were scarce, he soon found out, most of the prison fare was being fed to the pigs being farmed by the super and his cronies. Anyone who did not finish their work allotment went to sleep hungry, the island was being quarried to build docks, buildings walls, and underground - the superintendent's pride and joy, seventeen wheat silos, all hand hewn out of solid bedrock by brutalised bleeding prisoners.

Lars glanced around in the congested claustrophobic barrack; several men were gasping for fresh air at the iron gratings. The inmates were of all nations, all colours and creeds, all ages, all physiognomies, of recklessness and desperation. A few with features moodily tinctured with desolation, but without the faintest ray of Hope about them.

The surroundings had a brutalising effect upon the convicts, Lars could not help thinking the crimes of the deepest dye committed, terrible in their depravity, were instigated by Charles Wormwood and his guards.

The first week, the leg irons and bullying chafed on Lar's state of mind, mixed with lice, fleas and flies blood ran freely down his legs and ankles. Looking out over the beach, Lars saw the natural prevention system the governor employed around the island shark fins cruised, hungry for the meat carcasses that the guards provided for them, swift sentinels, eerily patrolling the passages of prisoner escape by sea. The second week he was resident, the newer convicts were corralled away from cutting giants blocks of straw-coloured stone to work on building the dry walls for the Superintendents personal garden.

Stumbling in the chain gang, Lars looked up just in time to see the club of the guard coming down on his shoulders and fell to the side of the weapon.

"Hoi, ye prigg napper, hoist up and back in this ere line afore I split yur skull!

Lars spun about as the bully boy lashed out, managing to stretch out his legs as far as possible pulling the chain taut, he then twisted his hips around to catch his attacker off guard, down went the guard, heavily as if a dead weight on the stony ground.

Coming came up bloodied and dazed he spun spitting the dirt from his mouth, roaring demonically at Lars, screaming for his fellow guards to assist, several other guards came hurrying up to check on their comrade. Lars had just righted himself, he was almost in the line and the other prisoners watched warily as the dangerous events evolved. "Right, what's going on ere?" charged the lead guard, as he ascertained the health and situation of his downed man, with a face like thunder, he lost no time in hearing his operative's version of the truth.

Lars was summarily beaten senseless by the remaining guards and dragged back to the solitary confinement cells. After three days, in that tiny dark, dank, caliginous space amongst his worst thoughts he brooded, why had he not declared himself sooner?

Was trust only to be earnt slowly, he knew Uileen had had a tumultuous time since her kidnapping and Grace no longer trusted male attention, but it was in anguish now he sat worrying how it went with them, how would they all be reunited?

As he sat in silent stygian speculation, he heard a faint tapping through the thick sandstone walls, the sound of the small, tapped, repetition continued for syncopation. Gradually it dawned upon Lars emerging out of his fugue state that this was a message, from a fellow sufferer. Having served on many vessels he remembered learning Samuel Morse's sound code for conveying messages across distances.

Was his neighbour using his tapping in this system? He tried to find a stone to tap back with, it took some hours before the two prisoners could understand each other in meaningful ways. As the night wore on, they communicated their stories, both were fairly new to the penitentiary, both were imprisoned for theft, the man who was adjacent to Lars was John Joseph; American born but had also spent a great deal of his life at sea.

A rapport was struck between the two ex-navy men, as they found their plights very similar, John Joseph had been put in solitary for defending his food ration from three thugs who stole other prisoner's fare.

Lars was aware that he had been singled out to be made an example of something regularly done in the prison to reinforce the regime.

The thick planked door opened, and light streamed into the darkness, Lars was blinded as shadowed figures came towards him, he held his hands up to fend of the searing burn of sunlight.

"Come out of there ye dog, the super wants to see you."

"Married to the three sisters" the lead guard announced, sniggering viciously.

Las was dragged from the cell by these lackeys, placed in front of the rest of the prison population and a three beamed wooden triangle and after losing a desperate struggle against his captors he was tied on to this contraption, face first.

John Joseph was soon to follow and be secured to a second such structure, at this juncture the superintendent strolled out of his offices and made his way to the courtyard to regard his newest inmates.

"Now men, you have both been found guilty of insubordination, it is therefore my duty to sentence you both to twenty-five lashes as a lesson to your fellows" he intoned. Having thus made his will known, he nodded to the guards to carry out the punishments.

The guards went about their business with a hearty enthusiasm and the slash of the blows made all the convicts cringe, as they stripped the flesh from Lars and John Joseph's backs. When the stipulated number was attained Lars and John Joseph were cut down and left in a heap at the base of the torture device they had been attached to, a lackey came past them with a pail of salt water, throwing half over each man's back. Both Lars and Leroy clinched their teeth to stop from crying out in agony, as the salt burned deeply into their wounds.

That night, the two suffering men got better acquainted. John Joseph turned out to be a powerful tall African American man from New York City, who had come to the great southern land in search of elusive riches. Both had been imprisonment for vagrancy virtually straight off their boats at Sydney docks, both were suspicious they had been headhunted for free labour.

John Joseph had been incarcerated for about a month he figured; he was working in a boat building workshop as he had experience in this trade. Lars explained his plight, the responsibility of finding his charges and need to escape the island.

John Joseph, cognizant of his own perilous predicament was keen to trade ideas and plans for absconding the island, he had been working on the idea of secreting a file from the workshop somewhere it would not be found for a period.

"If you trust me, could you give me your trousers, for several nights" asked Lars, John was a bit taken aback by this notion, he sat dumbstruck for some moments then slowly nodded affirmatively.

As an apprentice in the navy, Lars had made canvas sails, his sewing skills were quite in demand on the ships he sailed. Their first task was to acquire a bone that Lars could carve into a needle, John Joseph was able to obtain whale bone from a friend working in the kitchen, twine came from the rope ties that held up their pants. At the end of a week the trousers were complete, Lars had fashioned a hidden pocket inside the legs for John Joseph to hide the file.

They set their escape for the follow week when the governor was making a visit to the penitentiary. John Joseph worked as late as he could filing down bolts around the decking of the steamship he was assigned to building. As the guards made their six o'clock rounds and moved on, he carefully secreted the flat metal instrument into the canvas compartment of his pant leg, just as he straightened up, a trusty came around the corner.

"What are you doing there, Joseph?" He asked, John Joseph held his breath, waiting to see if he would be searched.

"Just picking up a tool and finishing off", John Joseph answered quickly.

"Be on yur way man, or no supper tonight", warned the watchman.

The waters of Sydney harbour were cooler in late summer, a deep obsidian blue under cover of a clouded moonless night, Lars and John Joseph had filed off their foot shackles and were entering the water.

Both swimmers had blood oozing ankles from the rasping of metal on skin and as sailors they were only too aware that killer sharks could smell a drop of blood in the water from up to a third of a mile away.

They were hundreds of yards away from shore, heading into the open arms of the sea, when Lars caught sight of a dark lean triangular fin lazily cutting zig zags in the quiet sparkling surface. It slipped in and out of sight seeming not to appear again.

Suddenly its torpedo body, leering chinless face, great mouth with its rows of jagged razor teeth came hurtling up from somewhere beneath them. "Shark!" Cried Lars "shark! shark!" John Joseph saw the monster burst out of the water with hydrodynamic speed in its killer leap, he knew he had to be ready for the next circle it made. With an almost invisible foe in the water, able to use twenty feet of pure propulsion, it was a formidable enemy. Then he saw it begin an inevitable ever decreasing circling round the two defenceless swimmers. As it came twisting through the liquid space, both men could see the beasts blue grey back and white underbelly, they were literally eye to eye with Gomorrah!

John Joseph pulled out the file he still possessed in its deep pocket and slammed it into the creatures rolled back eyeball. The file sank deep into the shark's tissue, even with the protective skin covering the iris the animal rolled away, thrashing wildly to evade the stabbing.

John threw himself upon the monstrous fish holding its girth with his bare legs, retrieved the file from its mark, stabbing frantically at the animals threshed head, whilst Lars tried to pummel the creatures' gills with his fists. Finally, the shark could no longer sustain its attack in the face of the two men's counter force. It took a tailspin away from the protagonists and disappeared into the murky depths, John Joseph breathed deeply as Lars called "are you ok?"

"I think so", he returned, "but I don't want to go through that ever again!"

The Hyde Park Cafe was not difficult to find and a vision of two angels even easier to see, thus Lars and John Joseph were greeted with the latter as he walked through the cafe entry.

"Grace, Uileen," Lars called in excited wonder at finally seeing the living embodiment of his dreams, both his sister and his beloved seated together, on the same plane as he inhabited.

Both young women stared in amazement at his appearance, then rushed to fling themselves into his open arms. John Joseph stood bemused at the show of exuberance, but his face was soon wreathed in warm smiles as the introductions were made.

Grace was still unsure about the obvious caring concern that Lars appropriated towards Uileen, was Lars playing a strange game between the three of them? She could not fathom his close attachment to them both, she needed to know before going any further on this quest what Lars' intentions, were especially as William and Uileen were all but betrothed.

Finally, after the reunion highlights and exhilaration died down, Grace found a few moments alone with Lars, she took the plunge to ask, just what are your further plans sir, and why are you so interested in our future welfare?"

Lars looked at the woman he loved more than life itself and laughed with joy.

"At last, I can feel freedom to tell you my story, I am Lars, my family is well known in Norway, we are Tordenskjold, (thunder shield) a noble family, I am an officer in the Dano-Norwegian navy. Several years ago, our ships were being attacked by pirate vessels emanating from the Shetland islands. I was given a mission to track and infiltrate this enemy, but whilst I was undercover, a clipper bearing my family was attacked and sunk by this pirate gang.

The only member of my family to survive was my sister, she was taken prisoner by the privateer leader but escaped his clutches by trying to swim to shore on the Shetlands one night. She was found unconscious on a sandy beach and rescued by a family of islanders, unfortunately she had hit her head as she was making her get away, her memory was impaired by her ordeal.

I was put in charge of a fleet to roust the marauders and sink as many of their ships as possible, in my endeavours I discovered that the Munson family were in league with some elements in Sweden, dedicated to undermining the Norwegian navy.

Of course, retribution for my family's demise, and rescuing Uileen have been paramount in my covert operation for justice as well.

"It has taken nearly three long years to track her whereabouts without alerting the buccaneers who are still roaming the seas, waiting for vengeance for destroying most of their fleet early last year.

I have been afraid to reveal myself, and put you both in danger, it is my belief that Mangus Munson is responsible for my imprisonment, as he seeks to undermine any who stand against him."

Lars finished his tale with his hand stretched out to his wayward sister, "forgive me for forgoing the truth so long, I saw danger everywhere on our voyage to this new land."

Uileen sat as still as a statue, her countenance pale, searching the corridors of her mind. Slowly, a dark curtain of uncertainty and fear lifted, she gazed at the brother who had valiantly searched the seven seas for her.

"I know you, your name is Peter, Lars is your middle name, our parents... are they truly gone? Uileen asked as tears tracked down softly her cheeks.

Lars hung his head in despair at Uileen grief, he would have done anything to spare her the pain he had endured after losing the progenitors he treasured.

Grace put her arms around the woman who had become her sister in all but name, holding Uileen's slight frame as it shook with sobs at the overwhelming knowledge she had just received.

Long after the cafe closed the quintet of expatriates shared their sorrows, their aspirations and their dreams, Peter and Uileen walked arm in arm with Grace holding Uileen's free hand as they filled in the many blanks that had happened since they were separated.

John Joseph, in the meantime, had made the acquaintance of Bridgette, and the bloom of roses in her cheeks belied a certain fondness for the gentleman's turn of phrase.

When daylight found the reunited clique, they were in the midst of plans to abandon Sydney and find their way to the golden fields that had attracted Grace's brothers and promised the chance of wealth.

Chapter 10

Recklessness often marked the life of the time. At Friars Creek, Murders Flat and Choke- em-Gully, sly grog tents had sprung up like toadstools under the guise of coffee shops. One such tent, had a rather large looking Irish woman, Molly, whose waistline expanded depending on the time of day, for under her clothing, she had fitted a tin container full of grog. A tube out the side of her dress, poured the cups of alcohol for the customers. Unfortunately, Edward Armstrong, had not got his cut from that slatterns' takings that week, that was the second time she had reneged on her payment for his continued patronage and allowing her to continue trading was out of the question, he had to set an example or so he thought.

One dark, dense, dormant night a flame flickered at a canvas edge, smoke wafted in a whisper, woven around the tent poles, then fangs of fire raced up the side of the flimsy calico bivouac.

Men from tents on either side leapt up from sound sleep, shouting and trying to beat out the all-encompassing fiery furore, but in less than an hour, the furnace had done it dastardly deed, the ashes of two lives, were strewn to the wind.

Molly was no more, and her babe wrapped in its mother's arms, was borne away with her, to lie forever in the embrace of angels, out of reach of all earthy evil.

The fragility of this frontier life was always just a hairbreadth away and each occupant of that devil's cauldron knew it.

Anne Manson was pretty-pleased with herself, hadn't she fallen right on her feet and no mistake, meeting Commissioner Gunn's wife in Sydney when she did, had simplified the situation.

Ann had been quite the toadeater to be chosen at the barracks, as her ladyship's personal maid. The journey to Ballarat had been arduous but not without rewards, milady did not keep much of an eye on her silver brush and comb set or her ivory combs, somehow, they were mislaid in the expedition.

"There are so many thieves and ruffians around these days, Manson, I hardly feel safe in my bed", her ladyship had complained bitterly.

"Yes, milady, Och it tis certainly full of marauders", answered Ann, eyes demurely downcast, with a hint of a deviant smile, as she thought of the renumeration she had already accrued, sewn into her corset.

On arrival in Ballarat's Main Street, Lady Gunn pronounced

"Oh, it is a wretched place, destitute of every comfort, is this town!"

Sir Redmond Gunn, looked at his wife, with his usual arrogant, distasteful perusal,

"Pull yourself together Agatha, you are the wife of the High Commissioner, act like one!" "The place looks like a freshly dug graveyard Redmond!" Complained Agatha.

"You will do you duty, as my wife Agatha, or feel the back of my hand, we are not in Scotland now, Madam, you are under my command!"

Agatha had immediately taken to her bed, or at least her bedroom and feigned illnesses that she usually termed her 'megrims'.

Ann was to darken the room and leave her be, which gave Ann an awful lot of time to explore opportunities in this new Eldorado.

It was this elevation in situation had introduced Ann to Edward Armstrong, and kindred spirits were lit with an auriferous excitement, a burning thirst for gold and power.

Ann could not wait to throw her lot in with Edward and fleece the dolts of diggers, the mewling, pathetic dobbers.

Edward had his men stationed around the goldfields, to take bribes from any who aspired to do illegal trade, the grog was a great panacea for many, but the way that Ann made it, it was quaintly called 'Blow my head off'.

For some, it made an early grave. Half was brandy, and the rest her special recipe, she put in some spirits of wine, cocculus indices (poisonous Indian berries), rum, water laced with turkey opium and cayenne pepper, generously supplied by Armstrong.

Sunday 'digger dances', were held at Murders Flat, in a large carnival tent, the men paid their shillings, music played, grog was liberally distributed.

"Madam would you permit me the 'oner' of this dance", a miner asked the blue cotton being, he held at arm's length.

As the strains of a waltz wafted through the ambient convivial air, the men and their Matilda's went waltzing. When Gilbert and Colin first viewed the phenomenon of grown men dancing with their sleeping bags, they were extremely amused at the antics that loneliness could translate into.

It was at such a dance that they encountered the unfortunate fellow who had been in for the chop, when they first arrived in Portland, for a small fee, a nip of grog, he would unwrap his skull bandage and let the voyeur view his pulsing brain as it flexed in its fontanel.

Gilbert inquired as to Smiths' recall of the attack,

"Oh, I remember the swine well enough, it was a cove what called himself 'Captain Melville', I'd know im again I would!"

At first Gilly did not notice the young, dark-haired woman, amongst the crowd of dancers, musicians and drinking onlookers, it took a long minute of perusal to have a lightning strike memory of the Munson clan and their progeny.

Damn and hell fire, what is she doing here, Gilbert thought, not much good he'd be bound. The world was supposed to be a wide one, large enough to lose one's enemies in, not import them with you, hang it all!

He tried to catch Colin's attention, but it was riveted on Ann. Colin had not seen any white women for at least six months, here was a young beauty, complete with drinks, he was captivated.

Gilbert grabbed him and tried to half drag Colin out of the tent, Colin for his part was holding his ground, as the siren swayed towards him, grog in hand.

Ann sidled up to the two friends.

"Och! You're a sight for sore eyes, Gilbert, fancy seeing you here, in this neck of the woods, thought you would be in prison by now. Whose yur friend?

Gilbert went very stiff and still, "Ann", he acknowledged coldly, "it seems you are also far from home."

"Oh, they paid me fare out ere, I'm a lady's maid and a personal assistant to the High Commissioner", Ann smugly replied. She smiled coyly into Colin's face, as she fanned her eyelashes like sable butterflies.

"Och no, are ye a Shetland lassie," stammered Colin finding his breathing impinged and heart hammering, trying to engage this rare bird of paradise.

"Och, of course I am, me Bonnie lad, where else canna real woman be born?"

Colin gulped his throat dry, his brain a turnip mush; Gilbert saved him the trouble of further discourse by abruptly interrupting with "we were just leavin."

"No, we weren't, or at least I wasna", stated a mutinous Colin.

Before Gilbert could object further, Ann had Colin by his free arm, entreating him to "come dance" and was pulling him back into the bowels of the grogshop.

"Colin!", called Gilbert, but Colin was intoxicated with the company he was now keeping, and a large swallow of alcohol he had just been supplied with by his seductress. Gilbert went cold with dread for his companion, he knew it would be impossible to get Colin away without a fight, not only with Colin himself, but Ann and her cronies.

Gilbert arrived back at the bark abode to find William trying to write a letter home, after trying to iron some blankets dry and burning one.

Upon hearing the alarming news of Ann Manson's sudden arrival and residence, with the notorious High Commissioner, Will looked grimly at Gilly,

"What do we do now?" He asked.

"Somehow, we have to extricate Colin from that den of iniquity" answered Gilbert "Before he gets into real trouble if he hasn't already" agreed William. The brothers went to Master Pho's residence and spoke to his gardeners, enquiring after the purchase of firecrackers.

The Chinese community was often vilified by the townspeople, for illegal firework displays, but they continued to pursue this piece of their heritage with vigour, on any of their holiday occasions.

Ah Sam nodded furiously about the crackers, he went into the storehouse, returning with the goods, with much bowing Gilbert and Will took the contraband.

It was dusk, the dance hall and grog shop were in full swing when the two conspirators arrived back.

"Just cause chaos", cautioned Gilbert. William lit the first bangers and threw them into the turgid dirt just beside the canvas walls.

The almighty banging, cracking, explosions, smoke, and confusion were just enough to break through the musical, alcoholic mayhem inside the structure.

Then pandemonium broke out, Gilbert took out a hunting knife and cut through the canvas wall, men were reeling half-drunk, half mad for the exit, blinded in the billowing smoky haze.

Colin was reclined over a chair, deserted by temptation, bedraggled by the strong spirits mixed with malefactions, the pathetic wretchedness of his situation, lost in drugged stupor.

Gilbert called out, "William, help me drag him out the side we opened, we canna risk the front exit, they will be waiting for him".

By the time the siblings had dragged their compatriot halfway to safety, he was moaning softly about his head, stopping to empty some of the gut-rot into the nearest bush or convenient hole.

After the fevered pyrotechnics and for most of the night Colin slept the sleep of the blissful ignorant, awareness slowly dawned with the sounds of kookaburras and some bitter gum leaf tea.

When he finally had his wits about him once more, the damage of the previous evening also rose to the forefront of his foment, his friends sat camped round the fireplace, watching his confusion.

"Och ma heid, ma stomach, am I still alive or did I drink hades last night?"

"Aye, yer fortunate to be here and na about last night ye pudding head", Gilbert said roughly.

Paul Crouch's store was broken into, the looters stole forty-two ounces of gold, pork and other property, worth two hundred and fifty pounds.

"Night fossickers", announced Will, now we have honest men and thieves warring like hostile tribes, it seems not a night goes by without disturbances and robberies" put in Shemus.

"We are going to have to sleep armed, loaded for trouble, from now on my friends" cautioned Gilbert, "the women you tangled with last night Colin, is related to an old country enemy, the Munson's, and she is as devilish as her kin. They have you tagged as a drunkard, and no surprise, that black brew they call brandy rots the guts and the brain. Just last week, Johnson went for a swim in the creek after a skin full, they found him floating by the rocks, at Golden Point, face down, drowned in his own vomit" Gilbert went on to explain.

Colin's face turned a sallow pale pea green as he gagged at the gruesome description. Brandy, the great panacea for many, appeared to be Colin's one weakness, he was equanimity itself when sober, but as dumb as an ox, when drunk.

William who had been concealed behind the half open door, began to squirm with an unusual bulge in his jacket, which began to yip and cry for release.

The occupants of the hut, turned to look in some astonishment.

"With Anne Munson and cronies about, we needed a watchdog,' said Will, as he magically brought out a small brown, blue wriggling bundle from his clothing.

"Another mouth to feed", growled Gilbert as he took the puppy and thoroughly rubbed its small brown head and neck.

"How much did this mongrel set ye back" asked Colin.

"Only one pound", replied Will.

"Cheap at half the price I'd say", laughed Shemus, as he held the writhing canine by the scruff of its young neck.

"What you call him?" queried Alice

"Haggis!" Pronounced Gilly, before anyone could intercede.

Haggis grew apace, fed on chop scraps, abundant head rubs, and bush excursions with Alice. He seemed impervious to fear, above or below ground, taking goannas, wallaby's, spiders, numerous birds, including a run-in with an Emu, leaving a crossed scar across his muzzle. He even took pythons in his stride, much to Alice's amusement.

His ability to snap, and shake airborne sticks, impressed even the hardened Gilly.

"This dog, one good dog", Alice decreed as she brought him home one day complete with a good-sized lizard in his jaws, "he sniffs, he digs, he hunts, not afraid, he dingo blood, he find water in ground."

Haggis always bristled with excitement at the chance to best another beast, he was amiable around his owners, but outsiders he saw as invaders, who needed to be seen off. Other dogs were his sworn enemies, if a fight was in the offing, Haggis would lead the charge, his copper eyes, blazing with the fire of battle and Alice spent quite some time sewing up his wounds.

One autumnal evening when the men were still working night shift, the wind blew an uneasy air into the cabin. Alice was seated before the open fireplace as a low flame crackled on the hearth, dozing in Dreamtime, Haggis resting at her feet. A zephyr stirred the stillness, Haggis lifted his pointed ears into the smoky warm ambiance, his hackles lifted as he scented the presence of another. On the left-hand wall, a plank of wood was split, and Haggis fixed his gaze upon the spot, waiting.... he watched, fixated, as a statue. The black, beaded eyes of Beelzebub stared straight out of the crack in the wall, then a malevolent maw slid through the gap, an obsidian, sinuous serpent slid silently into the room. Haggis growled menacingly, Alice awoke and reached for her knotted walking stick; the basilisk threw itself back on its muscular tail, arching its back, in a viper position, it stood five feet in the air. At that moment, Haggis sprang up to grab the reptile's neck nearest the head and Alice brought her stick down hard, on the creatures' body. Haggis shook his prey, and the sparks fairly flew around the room from the dogs attempts to shake his catch to death. Alice used her club whenever the brute's sidewinding was still in evidence. Finally, the death knell fell, Haggis stood panting above his conquest, his nose bloodied and bruised from grazing along the floor on the battlefield. Alice stood leaning on her stick, knowing they had had a lucky escape, this snake was deadly, it was unusual to see it so far south, she mused on this fact, then she took her stick, picked up the dead sidewinder, and threw it on the dying embers of the fire. She put on more wood, picked Haggis up and they sat together watching their adversary burn in the fire. Sometime later Haggis went to the door scratching and whining. Alice took the lock board off and searched the ebony darkness, as the light of her lantern traversed it, a flash of red cotton flicked past a cord of bush.

Haggis, with the speed of Houdini, ran through Alice's legs as fast as his stocky ones could carry him, out into the darkness, snarling as he ran. The hunt was on again, his terrier nose scented danger, just beyond, in the bottlebrush bushes.

There it was a cloaked figure, lurking, Haggis vaulted up at his quarry, jaws bared, saliva dripping over rows of sharp, yellowed incisors. He met his mark, sinking his teeth deeply into cloth covered flesh. A scream rang out, along with a shot, Haggis yelped, he fell to the ground, the bush became a blur, as William and Shemus came on to the scene.

"Is he alive?" asked Shemus anxiously.

"I think so", said William solemnly, as he looked at the wound in Haggis' hind quarters.

"Och, it looks like the bullet just grazed his hind leg, but it's an ugly wound, we had better get him by the fire and Alice".

At that moment Alice hurried up, she had some broad=leaved paper bark bandages and took charge of her brave protector. Shemus carefully picked up the injured pup, as William examined a piece of red cotton cloth that Haggis had managed to

rip from its owner.

"This looks a lot like the red cotton from the dress Anne Munson wears", he commented. "We will have to check with Gilbert and Colin, then look into this in the morn", he said.

Gilbert looked hard at the claret-coloured cloth, "aye" he agreed, "it looks just right for the skirt Anne was wearing when we rescued Colin.

"Aye", Colin concurred, "it the same colour exactly."

"One of us will have to go and see if she's walking funny", said Shemus.

"Well, she knows us all, except for you and Alice, said Gilbert.

"She sure knows Haggis!" laughed Will.

Haggis was bandaged up and lolling on a possum blanket in front of a warming fire, his ears pricked up at the mention of his name.

"He was worth every penny I paid", William said proudly as he bent down and ruffled the hounds head and ears, "extra chops for ye my lad," Haggis licked his face and sighed, content for now, until he could get up for the next big adventure.

Alice and Shemus ran a reconnoitre on the grog tent at Murders Flat, sure enough Ann Munson was limping lividly about, on a tee tree crutch, berating anyone in earshot, about the vicious curs in town, that should be butchered at the first opportunity.

Once again, the old country scores were being enacted in blood even on new soil, fortune favoured the bold, but when Gilbert heard their suspicions were confirmed, he could hear, the auld Munson battle cry of vengeance and he knew, another affray would be just round the corner.

Chapter 11

For the 'colonial belles' sailing to a land down under, it was at times difficult to keep their girlish hopes and aspirations sailing lightly around the Cape of Good Hope with them, each one painting their own castle in the air, as life on a sailing ship was often more endurance than plain sailing.

Maeve's future glowed golden in front of her shining eyes, until the morning she awoke, and Sven was gone, the house was as silent as the grave.

A note was left on Sven's pillow, "I have met some prospectors who I can work with in Bendigo to help put down mine shafts if I team up with them immediately. As soon as I strike paydirt I will come for you, be patient my love and your trusting investment in me will pay off, our marriage will be our reward. Find housework for now and send a little money, if you can, for our new start. Madam Cyn has a place for you, she has told me."

So, Maeve became the housemaid, for the 'gilded cage'. She waited one month, the two months, and then three months; the pink surroundings blurred blue through her tears, for she knew that if Sven did not return soon, joy would turn to shame, for in the mist of love's young passion, she had forsaken her mother's warnings, her father's forebodings and consummated the union, in anticipation of the holy communion of a ring and the safety of a marriage.

As the dragging of the days became longer, Maeve's weary waiting was weighted with the certain knowledge, that a child would soon be joining the world that worked at night and slept by day.

There was no word, no whisper even on the wind, the mail came and went, money earned and sent, with no reply from Sven. In desperate straits, Maeve remembered her eldest cousin Shemus, who she heard family tell, had packed his bag for Ballarat some time before.

Composing a message to Shemus, was the most difficult task Maeve had to do, for the sake of the future, she had to try. Then she waited with bated breath, going deeper into debt, every long ardour day, and still there was no answer. The wind of ill-fortune blew through her mind, she fumbled with her worries in the pitch darkness of night, turning them over and over, like rosary beads of guilt.

It was unbelievable; Shemus finally arrived, bearing with him money that Maeve had only dreamt of, he was the sandy-haired, smiling knight in shining armour, she remembered as a small girl, who piggybacked her round the hamlet.

"Come with me to Ballarat", begged Shemus, "Alice will care for you and the baby", "What about Sven, he may return, I have to be here for him", Maeve replied sadly.

"You can't have a child here!" protested Shemus.

"I can't leave without knowing what Sven wants", said Maeve.

One fine, azure tinted day, Sven arrived, work roughened, ragged round the edges, but blue eyes blazing with dreams and schemes. Maeve was ecstatic to see her darling man, Sven was apologetic about his absence.

"I have been on a golden crusade, part of a giant stampede to find our Shangri la", Sven expounded.

"Will clean air smell any sweeter? Will sunny days be any brighter? Will starry nights hold any more wonder? Will our love be worth anymore? Or could we lose all that, to a fool's gold? Asked Maeve. "Come, let us make a home working together and discover the riches, a loving family can mine." she pleaded.

It was plain for all to see, that Sven was a dreamer with little substance behind his wild ideas and plans.

So far, his wealth had dematerialised as soon as he found any, Shemus thought, after meeting his cousins intended. But Shemus wanted his cousin's happiness more than anything. So, he took Sven under his wing, and introduced him around his circle of friends, even offering him a part share in a dig.

However, this was declined, as Sven talked of big ambitions in Bendigo, mining. His partners were on the cusp of a gold reef for certain. So, in support of his cousin's future fortunes, Shemus spent his last nugget gambling on Sven's certainties.

Suddenly, Sven seemed to evaporate with the evening breeze, he was nowhere to be found. A night porter reported seeing him with his swag, making tracks towards Castlemaine town. Maeve mourned again her lovers passing, she walked in the shadows of sorrow, only held by the promise of loves reward, her babe close to her heart joining its life with her own.

When it was time for Shemus to return to his work fellows, on Bakery Hill, Maeve was in Madam Cyn's care until the child was born, then she would follow on to Ballarat. Maeve's babes birth brought the light back into the world for its mother, nuzzling its soft fuzzy forehead to her breast; Maeve was not so alone anymore. But slowly the baby failed to thrive, its frail form seemed to melt into itself, Maeve dementedly tried to arrange passage to get to Ballarat.

Finally, a dray was willing to transport the young mother, arriving in the Main Street, Shemus and Alice met Maeve off the bullock cart, the pitiful, high pitch wail of the sickly infant could be heard all down the street.

"What has happened to you?" Cried Alice. Maeve laid her head on her brother's shoulder, her slender body wracked with sobbing, she could not bring herself to speak of her abandonments.

As Shemus and Alice fought to tend to the two waifs, they felt lives slipping away, as day by unending day the small baby retreated into itself a little more, until a lifeless, faded form was all that its mother carried.

As night fell around the shroud that was Maeve, broken in grief and disillusionment, her shaded figure slid softly into the darkness and disappeared.

Morning found the emptiness of Maeve's cot.

"You must go after her" pronounced Alice.

"I'm getting my swag together to track her", returned Shemus.

Beyond the bush borders of Ballarat, lay many gullies and rivers, swift and strong. Shemus could only guess at the route that his sister had taken, although Alice and Bunjil went with him for a spell and found a piece of cloak that closely resembled Maeve's, caught on an overhanging branch of a scribbly bark tree.

The track Shemus traversed, brought him to a river sleek and wide, with gushing rapids running over smooth boulders, down into eddies and ebon pools silted in tee tree detritus.

Shemus searched for Maeve with a fevered determination, borne of fear for her fragility of mind and body, his sisters very existence hovered on the edge of a precipice, he felt the tenuous situation they were in, as the rivers ominous presence bore down upon him.

As he doubled back down the river Shemus saw the figure of a man, plodding alongside the riverbank, seemingly searching through every bough and branch, every root and hollow. Finally, Shemus recognised the desperate seeker as Sven, Maeve's erstwhile fiancé, the man responsible for all the trials and tragedies of two young, delicate lives. As Shemus stood staring at him, Sven called out,

"I'm sorry, so sorry, it was the madness of gold fervour, I am so ashamed by what I did, I need Maeve to forgive me".

Shemus nodded his head at Sven's contrition, and they joined together in their determination to rescue Maeve.

"Oh no, dear god, what is that tangled in the weeds over there? Cried Sven. Shemus leapt into the fast-flowing river, Sven went in after him and the two men dragged the heavy water-laden cloak to the rocks along the bank.

"It's Maeve's cloak!" Shemus decreed, as he grimly recognised the garment.

"You blackguard, you have killed her", he roared as a sudden, frenzied rush of anger struck him. Shemus dragged Sven back towards the murky depths of the river, punching the flailing form of a man, a red mist had sunk over his vision beyond it, he could only see Maeve holding her babe.

Sven struggled, fighting back with any strength he had left, and they wrestled each other until they both tumbled into the roaring rapids further down the swirling stream. In the bright blue light of midday, a body floated, around and around in the rippling surface.

A dragonfly flew a contrary route over the fixed, wet features of Sven, his eyes open and glassy, staring at a distant peak he would see no more. Death clutched to its bosom all the blossoms of youthful obsession.

Down river, Shemus lay buoyed by the water, his arms flailing to keep afloat, his left leg was caught in the rocks and debris was holding him fast in its watery arms. Like a fish snagged on a line, Shemus writhed about trying to secure freedom, but the harder he struggled, the firmer he became ensnared.

Suddenly he heard, "Hey white fella, what you do, fight a bunyip?"

Shemus knew from the pidgin English and accent, it was a young aboriginal man. With all his last might Shemus yelled out

"Help, help me I'm caught!"

"Don't worry boss, Jackie will get you out, from bunyips hold." A splashing was heard then a slightly built wiry youth of about eighteen summers appeared at Shemus' side, "Hold breath", Jackie cautioned, as he dived under the water and lifted the rocks away from Shemus' foot.

Later, as Shemus dried in front of a small fire, Jackie smiled his gleaming smile in the glow of Shemus' thanks and praise.

"Jackie helps, he always helps, even white fellas, Jackie takes care".

Shemus stared into the fiery depths in front of him; he felt a million miles away from Ireland, but this land had taken its heart and wrapped it around his aching own, he smiled back at Jackie, at peace.

Bullock drays were not for the faint hearted as Peter, Grace, Uileen, Bridgette and John Joseph were finding out; the expedition by wagon was so jolting, that they spent a good deal of the journey walking.

Travel sickness seemed to be Bridgette's constant companion, so the tedium of travel was intermingled with stops, and the pungent aroma of grass trees and the peppermint bushes that lined their track.

'Bowyang' Yorke, the bullock driver, wore a permanent frown due to the state of the nation he would say, a twill shirt, moleskin trousers, blucher boots and a cabbage tree hat, most of the time he was reciting his poetry, turning a blue streak at the bullocks, or working out how to navigate the constant mires, and obstacles that were the Australian bush trails.

Bowyang had just gone into full voice with his lastest poem:

Bill The Bullocky...

As I was coming down Conroy's Gap

I heard a maid cry:

"There goes Bill the Bullocky,

He's bound for Gundagai.

A better poor old bastard

Never cracked an honest crust.

A tougher poor old bugger

Never drug a whip through dust.

"His team got bogged at five-mile creek,

Bill lashes and swore and cried,

"If Nobby don't get me out of this

I'll tattoo his bloody hide'.

'But Nobby strained and broke his yoke,

And poked out the leaders eye

And the dog sat in the tucker box

Five miles from Gundagai".

After he had finished his rendition, his offsider Jones, pointed out the sea of slurry about to envelop them. The roads from New South Wales to Victoria, Ballarat were in a 'state of nature', rough, narrow, and steep. But this one had been flooded recently so the going just got a lot tougher, as they rode into the mountainous sludge.

Peter and John Joseph had negotiated long and hard, for passage on the bullock dray, with Bowyang. As they were sitting now, hopelessly bogged over the axles, down to the bed, they wondered why they had bothered.

Uileen, Grace and Bridgette had exited the jinger, a timber four wheeled, flat-topped cart, as the Bullocky driver Bowyang, coloured the air blue-black with expletives. Bowyang's whip knew no effect, Jones looked ready to cry as the animals just stood chewing their cud, refusing to budge.

The eight bullocks were yoked together in the quagmire,

"A sorrier sight could not be seen", said Peter and John Joseph heartily agreed.

When the whole party had been stuck in the accursed bog of that place for some hours; myriads of flies came swooping down, biting the curses from their victims' lips.

Broken wagon wheels, and the skeletal remains of worn-out horses, and bullocks could be seen down the side of the facsimile of a track, Grace shuddered at the sight, it was obvious they were not the only wayfarers who had the misfortune to be caught in this slough trap. The men decided to unload the wagon, everybody put their shoulders to the wheels, whilst Peter tried to dig the bullocks from their gluepot.

Unfortunately, apart from becoming encrusted with sludge, the attempts to unwedge the animals and wagon were largely ineffective. The team of travellers and beasts were becalmed, the solitude of the situation was sobering, as they sat resting at the barked base of a great, grey gum.

A noise sounded somewhere in the distance, rattling, followed by cussing and what sounded like throat singing! A dray, dragging its way along the same pinches, drawing its collective breath to the sound of the teamster's swearing.

"We are redeemed", cried Uileen, the bullock team was led by an old white, bearded, travel-stained battler of the track. He and his younger apprentice, and between all the company the new bullocks hitched in front of the trapped ones, the three bullockies and five pioneers heaving, the cart lifted from its cavernous mud prison, and they finally freed themselves to finish their lengthy journey.

They arrived in Ballarat town, just in time to see a whole flock of sheep stampeding through the dry goods store and into the boot store next door, with a drunken horseman weaving wildly some yards behind.

The pandemonium that followed with shopkeepers up in arms, guns being fired in the air and packs of dogs racing about barking crazily at the melee, combined with the opportunity of mutton on their menu made the newcomers raise their eyebrows in stunned disbelief as they watched the comedic events unfold before them.

A drunken digger, Bert Brown was protesting loudly to the magistrate and two troopers who held him upright to stop him from toppling over.

"It twernt me yur honours, it's me horse, he's the guilty one, he's drunker than a lord on St Pattys day."

Then the major arrived wearing his office robes, after stepping in something brown and unsanitary his face became a vivid vermillion and he began officiously remonstrating loudly.

"I won't allow drunken donkeys to be ridden on the footpath!"

"Oh no, yur worship, he's no donkey, not my Rocket, he's a thro, a thorough, a through bred he is!" Slurred Bert.

"Yes well, that's no excuse" the Major remarked sourly, smelling the culprit's breath from five yards away. "Fine man and beast, ten pounds for the trouble, will you? The Major enquired of the Magistrate

"Certainly sir, it is already decreed."

Bert, seeing a way out of his predicament, dragged his hands through his deep pockets, pulled out the necessary cash, leaned forward in a staggered bow, before dragging Rocket down the road to the raucous laughter of his peers.

The Goldfield's Wild, Wild, West came into sharp relief that Monday morn; Peter, John Joseph, Grace, Uileen and Bridgette could see it was obviously a roistering place. They were to learn that there was a Ballarat east and west, divided by the Yarrowee creek. East Ballarat was more calico than timber, and when not menaced by flood, it was often on fire.

"The rougher, poorer side of town, the east-side, incorporated houses of ill repute and the 'unholy celestials' camped down that way," a shopkeeper warned them, "not a place for real ladies" he said, staring at the three young women, who blushed in confusion.

The west side had the utopian presence of civic buildings such as they were, a small library, the glorious minister of a church, the post office and council rooms opposite the unicorn hotel, not to mention various shops.

The population was located mainly on ground traversed by the streets of the eastern borough and along the lines of mining leads now built over, covered with gardens, yards, crossed by roads or on the edges of the mingling boundaries of borough and bush.

The party decided after some discussions to obtain rooms at the Unicorn Hotel, it appeared life was rough and eventful and when Peter went for some supplies, he carried them back to his room he shared with John Joseph, hidden in his handkerchief.

As Grace looked out of the window of the hotel, she thought she caught a glimpse of a face that was familiar, but this seemed so unlikely, she shook her head to clear the thought. Bridgette was talking excitedly about the tent theatre she had seen on the way into the town.

"I could enquire if they would employ a dancer" she warbled.

"Sure, you could" encouraged Uileen "when you danced on the ship, you could dance on a sixpence." Bridgette's face glowed at the praise,

"Mayhap John Joseph will come see me"

"Och! Aye, maybe he will like what he sees", laughed Grace coming back into the discussion with a teasing tone. Bridgette's porcelain skin glowed crimson at the remark.

Uileen threw herself into William's arms, Grace had already flung herself at her big brother Gilbert. Peter, John Joseph, Alice, Shemus, Colin and Bridgette looked on, bemused at the hugging, laughing and weeping foursome. There was so much talking at once that the babble of voices drowned out even Haggis's warning barks and a kookaburra chorus just above the reunion on the branches an old, knurled gumtree. "Well, you took your time lassies, Och ye look like the cats' whiskers and no mistake" exclaimed Gilbert finally, as the excitement died down a bit.

"Humph, ye didna know we were even coming, ye big lug"! Grace returned laughingly.

"Well, ye had better come in and tell us yer story, from the beginning mind" invited Gilbert.

Uileen and William gazed at each other, as if the world had stopped just for them and they were the only two people there. Each drank in the features of the other with a thirst that could never be quenched, in each other's eyes they saw an eternal procession of stars, they seemed entwined it an ethereal bliss.

Grace looked at the pair and sighed, no hope there for illumination, she introduced Peter, Bridgette, and John Joseph, whilst being introduced to Alice, Shemus, Colin and of course Haggis.

The story of Mangus Munson filled Gilbert and William with a burning rage and it was all Uileen and Grace could do to stop them from taking their firearms to find him. Peter helped calm the situation down with his part in the tale, and long into the wee small hours the party held each other enthralled by the adventure and adversities they each had traversed.

William and Gilbert explained the situation at the diggings, the unfair taxation and the digger hunts, the violence and the confrontation that was shaping up to occur.

John Joseph listened intently because as a free man, he was more than supportive of male suffrage, even female suffrage he said, smiling cheekily, and winking at Bridgette, who again adopted a scarlet complexion.

Chapter 12

The cry went up – "Eureka!"

On the frontier, you are always on the brink of eternity, but this uneasy border became an endless seek and hide. The diggers were becoming fair game, Sir Redmond Gunn, the commissioner, had ordered the police to redouble their exertions in collecting the license fees. Raids were happening almost daily. Colin, Gilbert, William and Bunjil sat morosely looking into a dying fire,

"They've made a sport out of it, you can see they enjoy hunting us down", Colin stated blackly.

"Aye, it's like they are rounding up sheep for fleecing" agreed William.

"Or worse," claimed Gilly, "the foot police in skirmishing order drive the stragglers, advancing in formation with the mounted police coming up the rear."

"Three days ago, a great haul was made, sixty prisoners marched off cuffed together", said Colin.

"White boss, think everyone criminal, use black fellas to police". Bunjil said. "But now most black fellas go away, don't work for bad men anymore", he added.

"That is so," agreed Colin, "

Most of the so-called police are being recruited from Tasmania, they're ex-convicts, who are using brutality to achieve any outcome they please. Twice a week now they can legally hunt us, by government order, with a bounty paid to bent coppers, on every man without a license on his person, even if his name is on the registry as paid up!" Gilly bitterly decreed.

"It's time we pulled together, we are free men, no body's slaves" Will cried.

This raw, dangerous frontier had created a social collectivism, the diggers knew their mates, life and death were hand in hand, the miner's survival brought closed fists to those who would try to reign in their freedom.

The goldfields population was in an inflammatory state, and kindling into an extensive revolt, hostile feelings were expressed in small and large gatherings.

The fees had to be opposed, miners needed to have a say in governance of their own livelihoods, ten to twelve thousand diggers met to agitate in proper manner for a fair solution.

Rafaello Carlotti, an organiser of the meeting, stood before his comrades and pleaded "whatever is done - don't let us take the law into our own hands, let us adopt constitutional means!"

Then, finally, Lawrence Jones, a Welsh journeyman, got up before the crowd and addressed it.

"I see before me thousands of men, which any country in the world might be proud to own as her own sons ... this very cream of Victoria and the sinews of her strength. We have received intelligence that the license fee will remain, and indeed double! Will you tamely submit to the imposition, or assert your rights like men? Ye are Britons, would you accept further oppression and injustice by paying double fees?" "Never!" Roared the crowd.

"Then wear a red ribbon as a sign of rebellion against this tyranny, it shows our just cause and they cannot call us criminals and arrest us further!" He reasoned.

"Well how come the squatters can lease hundreds of acres for much less than what we do", yelled a voice from the crowd.

"Not fair! it ain't bloody fair!" roared the surrounding miners.

"Yeah! and dead lead mining can take months, then you find nothing, we still must pay, wot with? I ask," another man called from the back.

Universal agreement ensued. Along with the miners in the crowd, stood business and trades people, Ann Manson was there with Edward Armstrong, after all they were running a public house now, a respectable business for sure and they paid license fees too.

"This could be to our advantage Annie", murmured Edward, "they'll wanting more grog and guns!"

"We could alert the army and the commissioner for a fee", Anne whispered back, as she smirked at the melee of agitated men.

"Line up then lads and sign this here petition" called out Rafael.

The men assembled in a line that snaked around the room and out into the mud-strewn streets. Eight thousand diggers put pen to paper in the pursuit of male suffrage, the tide was turning, a democratic charter was birthed.

A few months later, around midnight in East Ballarat, Edward Armstrong had just locked up his new establishment, the Court house hotel, and was checking every window, when Colin Couper and Angus McKinnon arrived at the entrance.

"Canna we have a last wee dram for the road mon?" Yelled out Angus.

"Aye, just a wee tipple now, to help with the frost bite, Ye understand", called Colin.

The two men proceeded to bang on the door, setting up a calamitous din.

"Ah, replied Edward "cease yur prattle, or I will part yur hair with my pistol, so I will, Ye drunken sots; we're closed!"

The two Scots men had started a raucous, voluminous set of Auld Lang Syne at the tone of Armstrong's voice.

"What is it, Edward?" called a voice from the stair well,

"Nothing for ye to worry yourself over Annie, just some Scottish scum wanting more grog."

"Well, give them some, Eddy me dearie, I've just the treat for such as they, so I have, it's been brewing in the cellar for a few weeks now"

"Have you indeed my dove? Well, we must be hospitable, mustn't we?" Edward returned.

Anne found the brown bottles she had titrated, she took the cork from one of the mixes, a foul odour filled the air, like rotten eggs and bacon. A sticky, yellow-greenish substance slithered into a flask. Ann added a splash of black rum, that will put fire in their veins, she thought and keep them quiet for a good long while!

Edward handed the flasks through the open window, took their money, then promptly latched it shut!

"Well, another day of pocketing more coin he thought.

Colin and Angus had staggered arm in arm into an alleyway, they collapsed together against a shops wooden wall, some of Colin's concoction splashed out, down his blue flannel shirt,

"Och, will you look at tha now, mon I'm losing it on me bib"! he exclaimed. Angus was too busy guzzling down his draft to take a lot of notice, he hiccupped at the final gulp, then lay against the support, with a drunken stupor drowning his senses to his surroundings.

Colin had but a few drops of liquid left, "arh!" he exclaimed again to the empty alley and his comatose companion. Both men sat in satiated silence, until Colin began to feel the sobering effects of a chill winter breeze, he tried to rouse his mate.

"Come on Angus you'll be colder than a puffin if you stay plastered here!" Colin tried to pull Angus' arm, then he shook his beefy frame, but Angus fell to one side with an eerie stillness overtaking him. Colin could not think through the muddle of 'medicinals' he had imbibed, but he was sure at the back of his addled mind somewhere, that they were in trouble, then he blacked out!

Gilbert, William, and Bunjil made their way hurriedly to where Ah Sam had told them he had last seen Colin and his friend at midnight the previous night. The Chinaman said he could not stop to check the two men, as he was on a mission for Master Po, of much urgency.

It took the three men sometime to trawl through alleys and lanes to locate the two men, lying in prone positions, seemingly unconscious.

"Och! it's not the grog again, is it? queried Will,

"Aye, I fear so," said Gilbert.

"White fellas fire water makes sickness for all", said Bunjil, "sometimes not just sick, maybe bung?"

Gilbert anxiously approached Colin and looked for signs of life, he was relieved to see Colin move his arm across his body. However, when William checked Angus, he could find no breathe or heartbeat, just a cold, clammy, grey face devoid of animation.

"I think Angus has met his maker" said William solemnly.

"Let's get them out of here" said Gilbert, "we'll have to carry or drag them, Colin is going to need some medical help I'm guessing!"

It took the three comrades some time to get help with the two unfortunates.

Some hours following his discovery, after Alice had administered her tea, plus a drugged sleep, Colin came floating up from the groggy depths of hell, or so he thought. His head felt three sizes two big, with forks being pushed into his brain, his stomach heaved and he vomited a puce coloured bile into the wood bucket, then he continued this practice until Master Po arrived some fifty minutes later with his acupuncture, and the torture finally came to a blessed end. Colin lifted his watery, red-rimmed eyes to his saviours and tried to talk, but his throat was as dry as the sands of

Persia, his tongue was swollen, and a thick, white mucus lined the inside of his mouth.

Alice brought water and then Colin said one word "Angus?"

"Och, mon, he didna make it, he was dead when we found you", said William quietly. "But he canna be dead! rasped Colin, "he was only twenty-four years old and as strong as an ox!"

"I'm sorry Col, he's gone, the doctor checked him over, nothing could be done", said Gilbert.

"Och, I canna believe it, we just had a dram, just one dram, it couldna be that strong!" "Master Po has taken some vomit to test what you drank," said William "then we shall see".

Colin lay back on the cot he had been sleeping on, sickened and dazed by his friends demise,

"I canna take it in, he was fine, fine, before we had that last drink!"

Master Po returned late the following day, armed with some bitter truths, the grog was made up of raw spirits, probably from an illicit still, combined with spirits of wine and kerosene, Very definitely hazardous to health and morality.

The hair that Bunjil had saved, from the child of the sheep station massacre, had traces of strychnine poison in it. It was obvious that a farm pesticide had been planted in horse meat given to Bunjil's people to eat,

"The farmer was saving on bullets!" said William caustically.

In the case of the poisonous grog, it was only Colin's fumbling fingers, dropping most of the contents of his drink that saved his life, the Master was sure, after hearing the whole, sorry story.

Gilbert and William went to see the commissioner at the police camp,

"It's the murder of an honest working mon, yer honour", said Gilbert.

"Edward Armstrong sold poisonous liquor" put in William.

"Can you prove any of this, you men?" demanded Sir Redmond Gunn.

"We know the grog had kerosene in it, the doctor examined it", William added.

"Ah, you mean that Chinaman? Yes, well, that is not proof… It's probably nothing, but another careless mining accident! Case Dismissed! You may go on your way, both of you. And don't waste my valuable time anymore!" spat Gunn.

The brothers looked at each other in disgust and departed, it was time to put this to a vote, would the working men accept their lives were worthless and meaningless in the face of blatant, murderous practices by the governmental hierarchy?

It was as if a dam of frustration had burst, diggers overflowed into the streets, marching to the largest rally they had thus far seen. When the case was set before them, rough justice became their retaliation, the men went into the township such as it was, smashing windows, chanting for equal rights and justice for the mining man.

Darkness was falling, down by the Courthouse hotel lights blazed, or did they? Why was the air orange over the hotels peaked roof?

Suddenly, from out of the darkened byways, someone ran shouting "fire!"

An explosion of men expelled onto the streets, somewhere in the distance the church bell rang; water from the creek was being bucketed and thrown in disorganised disarray as the general populous was in an uproar.

A large group of unruly dogs ran helter-skelter around the laneways, no one took much notice of the uncontrolled, mangy curs, for if they did, they would see the whitish frothing foam, dripping at the corners of the bared canines mouths. The maniacal foment glinting in their eyes moved many a man from his standing place, as they snapped their jaws together menacingly.

Blacken in soot and ash, Edward Armstrong was hefting buckets of rancid water at the blood red, burning interior of his hotel, as he swung around to grasp another load, the horde of marauding, mangy curs hurtled around the corner.

The heat, smoke and confusion maddened the situation further, somehow one of the lead dogs had flames, leaping down its back, incensed, it flew at its perceived protagonist, and sank its sharp incisors into Armstrong's upper thigh.

He screamed in pain and rage as the deadly teeth pierced his flesh to bone.

"Get it off, get it off!" he cried. Anne ran over with a pistol, took aim and fired, putting the miserable animal out of its sufferings.

"Come on!" she yelled "we'll have to leave it, it's too far gone!"

Two troopers ran over shooting at the wild, mongrel pack and dragged Armstrong out of the way of the burning building's final total collapse.

Two coolies ran from shadow to shadow, only the outline of their conical hats gave away their race, whether they ran to, or away from, the scene, could be debated, but their charge was well taken care of, their steps disappeared into the vapours of the night.

A physician was summoned to the police camp, the bandage around Edward Armstrong's leg was brown and bloodied, he was sitting up, fuming at the incompetence that surrounded him.

"But sir, I cannot treat a bite. I can take your pulse and check the colour and quality of your urine, but you will need a surgeon for any stitching or surgery that's needed." "Where's he at then?" asked the moribund patient.

"The nearest one is Melbourne town", replied the doctor. "I can give you a physic that will purify the blood!"

"Huh, fat lot of good that will do me", retorted Armstrong, "get along with ye, yur no bloody good to me! Damn ye!"

The erstwhile physician gave his recalcitrant patient a look of dislike and departed as quickly as he could.

Meetings of Diggers were held on Bakery Hill, near the Eureka lead. A spokesperson stood atop a tree stump, the rebellion sought only the 'rights of honest free men'.

Gilbert, Shemus, Colin and William, stood listening to the moral persuasions, they were part of the cosmopolitans, the golden generation who aspired by their blood, sweat and free will, to no longer serve a master who owned the very soil they stood upon.

"Och, our lives are worth nothing to the bloody bosses, Angus Mackinnon is bashed and poisoned by Edward Armstrong, there's no justice for the mon", exclaimed Colin.

A miner in the front called out, "Did you hear about poor Tom Black? He got so afeared he jumped in a hollow log to escape and found a four-foot snake in his spot, that poor bloke, we finally found him crouched ridged with fright, and had to cut him out, the snake had found another abode."

All the company guffawed at this tale, but Vern Dobson was quick to remind the company that "We are being often violently abused by the troopers, called 'sons of whores', when they accost us for the accursed license for the tenth time that day,". "They must not be able to jail us for not carrying a license, if we are legally registered with one", shouted out another man.

"Those are the salient points, fellow miners, we must have the abolition of the license, safety as citizens, the ability to vote, and own land in this, our new country", the lead organiser Vern Dobson stated.

"All this lollygagging is humbug, there's nothing convinces, like a lick in the lug" called out Amos from the back,

"Aye!" shouted a dozen others.

"It's time we stood our ground, give them a taste of their own medicine. Men are made mad by bad treatment, its time the police are taught that they may exasperate to madness, the men they persecute and ill-treat" yelled Ned Kelly.

A standard was raised, and thousands of diggers stood about it encircling their beliefs, the Southern Cross emblazoned on a background of blue, blew free in the cerulean antipodean sky.

Men turned their faces to their flag of redemption flying in the heavens.

Looking across the crowds of people, William could see every body shape, height and size, every style of beard and hat, bohemians all, a whole world of diversity and difference all united in their just cause. In silence, every head was bared, and steadfastly an oath was taken by the five thousand, to defend the rights and liberties of all free miners, no matter his culture, creed or colour.

Someone lit a tinder. A flare of light flashed from a rebel's hands as the despised license went up in a blaze of defiance, others followed, until the bonfire of rebellion was well underway. Timber palings were taken from the Eureka leads and construction, for a fortification was deemed a necessary evil.

Vern Dobson and Rafael Carboni organised the building site. Military drills were set up as the diggers collected guns and pikes for their defences. William and Gilbert gave what help they could, hastily grabbing supplies and setting up a tent within the stockade.

"Come on men" cried Rafael, "we are wasting daylight, we need these defences now!" "Are you sure they will attack, Rafael? asked William.

"They are bound to retaliate, if I know anything about Sir Redmond Gunn, he's been looking for a good way of taking the flashiness out of the miners." replied Rafael.

When the brothers went to their cabin, they arrived to see a sight that made their eyes sore for the wanting of it.

Redmond Gunn looked up at his visitor,

"Well my boy, how's my nephew this fine morning, what do you think of this new land?" "Och its fine! Plenty of opportunities, Uncle Redmond, thank e for the dragoon finery, it sits well upon me don't e think?" crooned Mangus.

"Yes, Mangus ,you have your father's broad, strong shoulders and your mother's canny mind, we'll make a soldier out of you yet!"

"Aye, I'm here to serve those bloody blighters a good hiding!"

"That's my lad you will be sergeant at arms in the 12th mounted Calvary. Report to the command tent and your commanding officer, they will get you a horse. I have sorted out the documentation for your commission." said Gunn.

"Yes Sir, thank you sir" Mangus snapped back.

Sir Redmond Gunn smiled a smug, satisfied smile as he watched his kin march out of his study and into his line of duty, wait till those dissentient diggers cop the sharp end of three hundred military bayonets, half of them mounted, they won't stand a chance.

He had also sent for reinforcements of police and troops to follow up the challenge.

It was a Sabbath dawn, sacred to some, celebratory to others, many of the resistance had chosen to leave the stockade, to be with loved ones, drink to friend's health or find some sleeping solace in the familiar surroundings of their lodgings.

With those who stayed at their posts, John James and Bridgette sat, John James had sentry duty and Bridgette had come to keep him company.

"In Ireland, they had a famine uprising, against the English, in Farranrory, south Tipperary, the Irelanders, they were called, they just wanted an Irish nation, independent and free! They fought, and some died to overthrow British rule, and we need to do that here, in this new country, some of those rebels were sent here as punishment for seeking justice and liberty" stated Bridgette bittersweet .

"My people have been enslaved for one hundred years at least, I don't intend to be enslaved again in a new country!" retuned John James.

They heard the rhythmic thudding of the kettle drum, as the light pierced the gloaming. William, Gilbert, Peter, and Colin were stationed with rifles primed at the peaks of the palisade, only one hundred and fifty people had remained in the enclosure, many were awakened only when the drumming marching had reached the first gully.

Shemus had gathered Grace, Uileen, and Alice together. After many tears, protests and regrets, they had sadly taken Haggis with them into the bush to meet with Bunjil. They were heading for the caves, some miles safely distant from the rebellion encampment.

The two sides stared intently, each at the other, over a small distance of two hundred yards. The air stood on end, electrified by a single gunshot, the drummer boy lay wounded at the feet of his captain.

"Advance" roared Mangus Munson, as he rode his black charger into the front of the fray, pointing his bayoneted rifle at his foe. "Charge for their guns men", Mangus shouted.

William fired as fast as he could, looking as he was into Hades maw, Gilly ,beside him loading and reloading shot and shell, as dozens of soldiers stormed the barricades, shattering asunder the pikestaffs with decisive force.

"Pull back, pull back ", screamed Vern Thomson.

Peter took careful aim at his quarry; he had seen the popinjay parading about killing anyone who tried to escape unmercifully. Unfortunately, two soldiers leapt in front of him, and he was forced to shoot one and fight off the other and by the time he looked out at the fray again, the brute had relocated.

Mangus Manson was enjoying himself, being paid to be mercenary suited his very nature, and damn, he was good at killin! It was when he saw the black man, sheltering the frail form of a woman beneath him, that he became enraged imagining the black man, soiling a white woman's honour. How dare he, and she was just as bad for being there. He took up his pistol and fired straight into the skull of John James.

A dull noise sounded, and Bridgette screamed with frightened outrage as bloodied bone and brains exploded, shrouding her face, neck, and arms. She picked up the sabre lying beside her sweetheart and stabbed it with all her might at the beast that bore down upon her, straight into the curve of its chest, went the razor blade, and the monster went down in a neighing, yelling heap at her feet.

Just as she raised the sword once again, to plunge it into the demon, her body was buffeted by a bullet, then another, and another, still she stood swaying on the blood soaked ground, like an avenging Joan of Arc, until finally, a projectile pierced her heart, she looked down to see the lost expression of life at her feet, she buckled, she bled, and at last she had her freedom, on the island of her dreams, with the man who made her dance for joy on a sixpence in the sunshine of their love.

As the sun shone its spotlights on the mourning, the moans of the wounded were silenced one by one. From his vantage point, Will could see the shot and hewn bodies of the dead, as he half choked on the reeking stench.

Mangus Munson had done more than a day's work, after he had set the soldiers wreaking vengeance on the insurgent diggers. He dragged himself from underneath his slain charger and had set about cutting down as many as he could find.

Through the smoke and confusion, he was sure he had seen faces of an old foe, Gilbert, and William, oh he would dearly love to settle those old scores in torturous agony.

How he longed to be victorious in all his battles, new and ancient, unfortunately, another platoon had been sent from Melbourne and he had a new commander.

His troop were required to leave the fields and seek the leaders of the insurrection as quickly as possible, this was done in part because many of the townspeople were not particularly in favour, of the army's bloodcurdling tactics in dealing with their own countrymen.

Later that same morning, Peter and Will watched warily from Maggie Murphy's farmhouse windows, as Mangus Munson rode away on a requisitioned military mount. It seemed the devil had the luck this day, it was time to reconsider their options. Late into the afternoon they had searched for Gilly and Colin for hours with no results,

"They may be back at the hut" suggested Peter,

"Aye, they may at that", said Will, "we had better go and see".

Gilbert had been covering Vern and Rafael; they had all made a run for it and were hidden down an old mine shaft, Vern was shot in the arm and bleeding profusely. Gilly pulled some planking over them to give some cover from prying eyes.

It was a sodden, muddy puddle in the bottom of a dank pit and the men only had the clothes they stood up in and their guns.

"It's going to be a long day," said Gilly,

"We have to get Vern to a surgeon, I don't like the look of his arm", replied Rafael, grimly.

"Och, neither do I, but for certain he will die if bloody Munson gets his hands upon him!" swore Gilbert.

The moment, minutes, hours ticked by, the three men were chilled to the bone, Vern's teeth were chattering like castanets.

"It's nae good we canna stay hidden in this hellhole any longer," Gilbert finally announced, "I'm going fer help"

As he was ascending the deep tunnel, he looked up to see four sets of eyes peering down had him. Looks like we may have lost this one, he thought, as he heard the thudding of his heart in his ears and the rushing of blood to his head.

All of a sudden a voice came booming out of the blackness, Gilbert recognised it at once.

"Och, will ye stop lollygagging around down there mon and let us pull ye up", Colin called down.

"I've got the whole gang of Maori land here to help!"

The muscular, young Maori men made short work of extricating Rafael and Vern.

"Just like pulling a full fishing net in" said one young rescuer.

Colin explained

"I pulled back early in the fighting, to help two wounded souls escape away from the conflict to safety. I saw the bloodthirsty swine, killing randomly, unarmed men who were hopelessly outnumbered. I tried to return nevertheless, but it was too late to keep fighting. I thought I saw a glimpse of ye Gilly, with Vern and Rafael leaving the stockade."

"So, I hid in a dry well, waiting for the bloodshed to subside, Och, the wounded, they were screaming something terrible, it was hours before the troops finally departed, then I could follow".

"Mon, yer were na easy ta find, I had the devil's own time deciding which shaft ye had chosen to disappear into, it was yer luck that Tane, Rua and Rawiri here, have such sharp eyes and were in the neighbourhood helping the wounded."

After getting Vern to a surgeon and hearing the bad news, that the arm would have to come off, the remaining six sombre companions shared a brew and a comfortable pipeful of tobacco, and traded notes on everything, where they came from, being part of the antipodes, life as a prospector, civil liberties, why and what they fought for.

Return of the Redcoats

The path laid out before him was cinder red, a parched creek bed of pulverulent dirt, the grime of the road desiccated on his neck, and he was in a brittle mood.

Mangus Munson's journey to the outer reaches of Victoria, chasing tales of real and imagined traitors, had been an exhaustive dissipation of troopers and time.

The exploit had brought to grief, some of his men who had deserted when faced with a desert of dust, unforeseen circumstances, and very little recompense.

The Eureka was a debacle, the men demoralised, fighting their own countrymen, the desert held no shade for these unsavoury truths.

The Great Victoria Desert stretched its arenaceous arms in every direction, the sparse marble gums, mulga bushes and spinifex grass dotted the landscape green and gold ornamentations, as dingos howled in the quiescence of the nights.

During the long hours of riding, marsupial moles, mallee fowl, rock wallabys, geckos, dunnarts, skinks, parrots and a multitude of other abstract Australians made their presence known. But the scenery palled as the supplies ran low, the morale was lowered by monotonous, makeshift camping in a no-man's land of ochre sands.

To add insult to injury, the whisky and the water were mixed in a galvanized tin, resulting in a rather nasty, zinc poisoning of half the men, including Mangus.

The only upside of the sordid debacle was the chance to get back to Sir Redmond Gunn with the new intelligence he had picked up whilst reconnoitring in Melbourne. Bumping into Fred West, in a sleazy dockside inn, was a stroke of good fortune, the mutiny on the Golden Spring was even more absorbing.

They had not yet tracked all the mutineers down, and had not found the Shetland brothers, Gilbert and William!

Mangus was riding the troop hard to return to Ballarat, it was time for some reckoning!

Chapter 13

His head ached and he felt more tired than he could ever remember being, on top of that, the site where he was bitten by that bloody wild cur, was alternately burning, prickling and itching, Edward Armstrong thought he would claw his upper thigh raw, if it did not hurt so much when he itched it.

It had been several weeks since the night of the fire, he had been trying to sort out the unholy mess, and avoid the diggers who were blaming him for Angus's murder. Twice the magistrates had been to call, and question him about his movements that night, there was hell to pay in the city, the way the rebels were going on with their meetings and mayhem.

"I don't want any water get that godamn glass away from me" roared Edward.

Ann Munson flinched as if he had hit her,

"What's got yer goat, Eddie? She tentatively asked.

"I don't know…. I feel like I'm burning up, my head hurts. Can ye pull the curtains, the light hurts me eyes."

Ann pulled the drapes, she looked at him with concern in her eyes,

"This is na going to interfere with our plans, is it? She asked anxiously, "I'm really to ship out a lot of stock in the next week or so" she informed him.

"I dinna no, I will be okay in a while, just stop yer prattling at me woman, I need to rest" Edward grumbled. Ann took her leave gladly, not bothering to say anymore, it was coming to the time when she needed to move up, and she was making some interesting advancements of her own.

Raised voices were heard shouting over the campfire tents and covens of campers, "Have ye been at the whiskey agin mon, och, will nether leave it alone? Gilly grumbled.

"A mon must drown his sorrows mate, it's a long way from Loch Ness ye ken, Bonnie Inverness and the highlands in the heather bloom, ma soul is like a broken shell for the keening of my kin." Colin lamented.

"Aye, aye, I know ye are bereft, but we need ye to sober up, and put yer back into the dig, yer no good to us or yerself lying about like sleeping beauty." Said Gilbert.

"Och, I canna go withoot a wee dram, it's me only consolation, in this godless wilderness", Colin's voice raised in angry retort.

"Well, ye know wot happened to poor Angus, you've got to pull yourself together. All yer moneys going down yer gullet", Gilbert shouted "we agreed to work equal", he added "but you've bin smashed for days."

"Ah, go to the devil, with ye, I do my share, like is not, yer no my kith." Yelled Colin as he lurched away to disappear into a fringe of mulga. Gilly shook his head, picked up his pick in disgust and headed to the shaft they had been working on to continue digging the lead.

Dusk had already fallen, it coloured the camp in multiple shades of grey, Colin bumbled his way along, mumbling and cursing the world and its melodrama's. It was rapidly coming to the end of the day, he and Gilly had always shared everything by the end of the day, they had always laid to rest, at peace in their friendship. As he sat down on the damp base of a stringy bark, Colin knew, he was a man who had his father's short fuse, but his mother's sensitivity, it was always the whisky that won the war between them, until his mother and sister intervened.

Gilbert and William were the brothers he never had; he did not want to be his father's folly. It was a reason to come to the fields, to make something of his life, not drink it away like his sire. But how he yearned for home, the family, the friends, the land he was part of, belonging in these foreign fields was only by dint of will, whisky and his Scottish peers ,and now the day was ending without resolve.

At that moment, one of the Maori diggers, Tane, came running down the track

"Col, Col, come quick, there's been a cave-in at Bakery hill! Colin's head cleared, as he came upright from his prone position, where he had been ruminating over his pipe tobacco.

"Hurry, hurry", cried the young man. Colin jammed his hat on, and outpaced his mesenger, running as if the hounds of hades we at his heels.

"Whose down there?" he called as he arrived breathing hard...

"It's Gilly" said Jack Tucker, he took the night shift. Colin looked down the shaft, the sides were closing in, and had not been reinforced with timber, the ground was perilous, it would be insanity to sink without sidings. Then he remembered an old side lead they had dug that was still open, he rushed to the tunnel with a shovel and a pick, and he began digging.

It was a race against time, it was five to seven feet along, the dark was almost upon them, and the air left in the drive would not last much longer. Colin knew that if Gilly was even still alive, he had to reach him soon. Into the soft clay he drove the pick, oozing great glops of sweat, heaving gulps of air in a sob.

At last, he heard a faint tapping from the other side, he worked maniacally, fiercely attacking the earthen barricade between them, the distance narrowed quickly. Finally, he opened a face sized hole, a wheezing strained voice on the other side called out, "Thank god, I nearly suffocated."

Colin put his arm in the aperture, Gilbert grasped it, and the two men pulled the orifice open, Colin climbed into the vent that Gilbert had been entombed in, to help push him through the space, as he began to follow, a loud booming noise was heard from above, he turned just as tons of mud-laden debris, fell, full force on his lower body.

Gilbert heard, and reached to pull his friend free from the disaster, Colin held out his arms to his compatriot,

"Och, I canna feel me legs Gilly, I think I'm dun fer,", he whispered.

"No, I'm going to pull you out Col" cried Gilly.

It's too late mate, it's the end of my days, just hold me hand in friendship brother, so I may hold a part of Scotland once more, before I go"

Gilbert grabbed his comrades hands, and held them to his heart, as the 'married dancers' went out of Colin's eyes and his breath escaped to the highlands.

Rasping breathing was coming from a different part of the camp, as Redmond Gunn, lifted his head from the kiss that Ann Munson was returning.

"You are supposed to be my niece, what enchantment have you cast on me, I can scarce mind my work when you are near."

Ann gave him a sultry, slanted look, full of carnal promises, and again they kissed long and passionately,

"Och, it doesna matter, ma body craves a strong mon's touch, to satisfy it's desires" Ann boldly murmured as the two relatives surrendered to the burning ardour driving them on, like a furnace it consumed them, as they sank to the floor of the private reception room. As she allowed his hands to roam at will over her pliant breasts and body, in the mirror Ann's closed face held a sly secret smile.

Agatha Gunn looked at the reflection she could see through the slightly open door, with distinct distaste, to think that, that guttersnipe would manage to wheedle and manipulate, using her overblown charms was more than her body could bare. How dare she! After all the years of abuse and loss, that Agnes had suffered at the hands of her husband, she would not have him flaunt a younger bitch in his kennel to shame her.

She flew upstairs to her portmanteaus, recovered her ladies pistol and carefully crept back down, taking careful aim at the two lovers entwined in arching ecstasy.

Ann felt a searing pain in her shoulder ,and looked down at Redmond in confusion, he for his part, was still latched on to her crimson, red nipples.

Scarlet blood ran down Ann's alabaster skin, she pulled away from his embrace, and sank back onto the Abyssinian carpet, a gaping hole in her upper chest. Redmond stared at his niece's wounded predicament in horrified shock, his mind reeling at the sight and the consequences.

He did not notice Agatha, glide quickly away from the tragic scene, as she calmly put on her gloves, hat, then took an umbrella to exit out the back door, perambulating her way to the nearest shops.

Redmond Gunn knew he had to find someone to deal with their situation discreetly, a surgeon would be out of the question, no, it would have to be the yellow peril, the Chinese doctor Master Po!

A closed in buggy pulled up to Master Po's humble headquarters and Redmond Gunn climbed down, carrying an unconscious Ann Munson in his arms, he had wrapped a cloth around the wound to staunch the bleeding, more than that, he had no notion of. Ah Sam, came cautiously forward to investigate this new and potentially dangerous situation...

"I am Sir Redmond Gunn, and I demand your Master save this poor, young woman who was wounded by a drunken lout outside my home", Redmond stated.

Ah Sam looked closely at the raven-haired damsel, his blood ran cold as he recognised Ann Munson, the cohort of Edward Armstrong, their sworn enemy, maker of the poisoned brews.

"I have no time to dally so I must leave her here now, get your Master to fix her up; your pigtails should be good for something", Redmond Gunn growled, as he quickly put his burden down on a small sedan, he made his way to the exit, and he did not look back!

Master Po looked at the unconscious nemesis, he could see by her pallor that she had lost a lot of blood, a further inspection showed the bullet was still in the wound, it would have to come out! As he examined his patient, Ming Toi's beauteous visage floated before him like a cherry blossom, on life's river, he felt his body tremble at the rage of injustices that had befallen his people at the hands of the likes of Ann Munson, Edward Armstrong and Sir Redmond Gunn.

Edward lay stark naked on his pallet bed, his eyes staring at the wooden ceiling, he could not make out where he was, it seemed familiar to him, was this the prison he was incarcerated in, at fourteen, for stealing and thuggery in London Town, the clink?

Or was it Port Arthur in Tasmania, where he was sent as an incorrigible, from the hulks on the Thames at twenty-five years. Suddenly his whole body was seized in a spasm that raked him rigid, his groin ached with a painful, uncontrolled erection. Was he just foaming at the mouth, or just going to vomit again? Then, the next minute ,he bolted upright, he could see the dark outlines of his enemies come to claim revenge, all the diggers he had set afire in their tents, all the men he had run through with his sabre on the hunts, the first people he had shot where they stood, men, women and children as he had run roughshod through this backwoods. Hush wait, look, there they are, just waiting to have at me, he could see their laughing countenances at the windows. He dragged himself up, and grabbed a brace of pistols and a rifle he hung over his shoulder, he wrenched open the wooden portal, advancing into the blackened night ,firing into the pits of hell.

He lay in the Main Street convulsing, his face contorted in rage, thrashing and snarling at his onlookers, hands twisting, anyone who got to near, he tried to bite, as bile dripped down his jowls.

Master Po, Lim and Ah Sam stood at the edge of the crowd watching.

"It will not be long now", Master Po said in a low voice.

"A man, who is a vicious cur, deserves to die like one!" Said Lim.

"We will go now, knowing that Ming Toi's memory has no shadow cast upon it", Master Po replied. The herbalist, and his gardeners slipped silently away, to continue their healing pursuit, safe in the knowledge that one predator less preyed on their safety.

A ring of the town's dogs, yapping and barking surrounded Armstrong as his fitting became extreme, the police were called and only after firing their carbines directly into the pack did they disperse, but not without taking a few bites of their quarry.

A doctor was found, one that would attend, he had seen this malady before, and knew it was just a matter of time. Armstrong was tied to a sturdy wooden bunk by his arms and legs until, at last, his raging lapsed into a deathly coma, and he screamed no more, as Cerberus the hound of hades had come to fetch him.

Ann was up and about, her shoulder wrapped in a sling bandage, she knew she had to make herself scarce now, as Redmond Gunn would no longer protect her when she had so many foes.

As she had been attended to at the heathens, herbal tent, it had occurred to her that the 'luck now' nugget had been found, and she knew where some of the gold had gone. It was twilight when she stealthily made her way to the cabin, it seemed quiet, only a small light flickered in the cracks of the walls.

She knew the men had been doing night work, so they would not all be home, it was that mangy sentinel that she had to watch out for!

Grace had gone down to the creek for some water, she and Uileen had returned from the caves to check up on her brothers and Peter, her betrothed, the Eureka altercation had taken its toll on them all.

Alice, Haggis, Shemus and Bunjil had stayed in the bush and were camped at Lake Wendouree with the Wathawrung people.

Uileen felt the hairs at the nape of her neck stand up, as she felt a presence, looking at her through a gap in the woodwork. She hoped that Grace was not far away, as she did not have a lot of weapons at her disposal, the men had their guns with them.

Uileen picked up a walking stick, and lit two candles to illuminate the small room further, Will and Gilbert were still at large after the battle and Peter was supposed to be guarding the dig, from the many claim jumpers who had invaded the area after the big find.

Ann looked twice before she could believe her luck, only a woman at home and a weak one at that, she pulled out her revolver and knocked a hole in the plank she peered through.

"Stay, very still, or ye'll have a bullet in ye right enough, miss high and bloody mighty" she spoke in a firm menacing tone.

Uileen jumped with fright, she had heard that voice before, Ann Munson, how did she get here? Uileen thought desperately seeking to delay the situation.

"So, ye made it Ann", Uileen said trying to stay calm.

"Och yeah, I've done alright for me self, but I'm here to do better by god! Hand over the gold from that big nugget ye menfolk found, or they'll be finding lead next!" Ann threatened.

Uileen tried to bluff.

"They sent the gold to Melbourne in the police strong box".

"Och, ye best not be telling me porkies, or it will be the worse fer ye! Now get that gold and any coin right now!"

Uileen tried again, "I dinna ken where it tis Ann" she cried.

Ann pulled the trigger ,a bullet blazed it's way into the room, an ugly gash appeared on Uileen's upper arm, she stumbled back as pain seared through her, and her side felt numb.

Grace heard the shot, dropped the water bucket and ran for the hut, with the number of marauders, about she did not hesitate to imagine that Uileen was safe.

Ann had made her way into the cabin and was standing over Uileen pointing her weapon directly at Uileen's head.

" It makes no odds with me, if I kill ya, I've already got police admirers, I will kill ye if there's no gold. I owe you and that cow Grace for the boat over here, where is she by the way?

Uileen was dizzy from the shock of her wound, the world was spinning around her head, all she could hear was Ann's demonical demands.

Grace saw the situation from the open door, and sprung into a surprise attack, using a supple branch of springy bark, she swung full force at Ann. The astonishment of being caught off guard jolted Ann from her purpose, and she turned to face her assailant. Uileen made a supreme effort and launched herself against Ann's legs, knocking her off balance. Ann flailed her arm in the air, as she grabbed at Grace. The two women grappled with each other, Ann was however hopelessly encumbered with her shoulder injury, and Grace was able to push her aside and kick the gun away, Ann tried to pull herself up on the table, but she knocked over a candle onto her blouse, and the hungry flames licked at the cambric fabric.

She screamed, as the incendiary caught her long, ebony locks. Ann ran shrieking and screeching from the hut, wrapped in a fiery embrace, looking like an incandescent inferno, as she disappeared into the grey gums.

Grace, meanwhile, was too busy half carrying, half dragging Uileen from the burning habitation, as Uileen was almost unconscious. She then tried to beat out the sea of flames that was searing its way across the tinder dry hut.

Half an hour later, William and Peter ran into a smoking remnant, that had once been their shelter, the cinders were still being blown around in the sharp nightwind, sparks leapt out of the timber, Uileen's face was ashen and Grace looked like she had joined the first people, so sooted was her countenance, that even her own mother would not have known her.

Peter and William, thanking God for sweet mercies, gathered into their strong arms the two women they loved more than life itself, as Uileen and Grace wept their tears of trauma and relief into the flannel of their loved one's shirts.

After the initial shock and anger of Ann Munson's perdifity, Peter tenderly examined his warrior princess's wounds. Uileen's upper arm and shoulder were grazed, but the injury was not too deep, just superficial enough not to need a surgeon, it was Peter that did the stitching.

After assessing the damage, the four homeless aching hearts, made a haven in each other, as they walked back through the tortured tracks of the camp. They were cautiously vigilant about Ann Munson's final resting place, however!

A lot had happened in the short space of time the quartet had been separated, the Eureka stockade had been fought and lost and in the chaos of the furious fighting, Peter and Will had misplaced Gilbert, Colin, and the leaders of the rebellion Vern and Rafael. They were all worried that the civil war had taken more than just the roof over their heads, Gilbert was their mainstay and Colin, his best friend, their family's firm supporter.

"Haggis, Haggis, where are ye, yer mongrel, we haven't got time for yer shenanigans", yelled Shemus.

Alice, Shemus, Bunjil and of course young Haggis, were coming down from Mount Misery, they had been out hunting and gathering for the clan.

Haggis had got the wind up as usual and followed his fertile nose to see what mischief he could get in to, they had already had to dig him out of a wombat hole.

"That mutt could make a man mad, with the mayhem he contrives!" mumbled Shemus, after Haggis had found a rather large nest, of very irritated, marbled scorpions under a hollow log. After both man and beast had been stung a few times, by the mottled menaces, they had both learned their lesson.

Alice smiled discreetly as she saw the arachnids clapping their claws together in triumph over the intruders.

"Bundungu, the stinger is small, but he beats white fella and his dog" she laughed out loud at her joke.

The creek was running wild, bubbling over rocks, pebbles and old tree branches left in its watery depths. Small eels darted in the fluidic gloom. Haggis hung over the side of the stream, splashing at the wriggling shadows, he reckoned that he would have one of the blighters sooner or later, with a bit of splishing and snapping. Unfortunately, Haggis had a rather large head and chest, and it had been raining heavily in that region, so the side of the bayou were just about as slippery as the eels. Haggis tipped headfirst, bottoms up, into the green, glassy expanse of river, and went under.

Now, Haggis was a land canine, not much of a swimming sort; being still young and inexperienced. So, he was no match for the rushing current that the rain-swollen gutter produced. All the unfortunate dog could do, was frantically paddle backwards against the tide.

Alice heard the commotion and Shemus came right on her heels. Haggis was going under in the deeper water. Alice leapt into the freezing water, swimming to reach the distressed mutt as Shemus waded into the shallows, over the sliding stones to take the drenched dog from his saviour.

After a brisk shake all over Shemus, and a towel down with his swag, Haggis sat somewhat shamefaced at his fall from grace, he put his paw over his nose and lay down, as he now was a low-spirited dog, meanwhile Alice was showing Shemus some rocks she had seen in the creek-bed after saving their pet.

Shemus looked hard at the stones, he blinked in the sunlight as he saw the glint of gold off the brilliant facets.

"Lord be praised Alice, ye have struck it rich my girl! These here are nuggets, bigger'n than any I've seen".

Alice looked bemused by Shemus' excitement, but she was all for joining in.

"You like rock, I find more," She promised.

"My darlin, you are the best treasure of all, how did I get so lucky?" Shemus exclaimed, as he swung his ladylove around in dizzy delight in the wooded clearing, as the kookaburra laughed, even Haggis brightened up after watching this turn of fortune.

The reunion took place in Maggie Murphy's farmhouse. Peter had found Gilbert wrecked on the shores of loss, swept out in a sea of grief, drowning in grog, as wave upon wave of pain hit him in his solar plexus. Tears streamed from his eyes, flooding the front of his flannel shirt, unseeing, unmindful Gilbert could only feel deluged in the agony of loss.

He was submerged in thoughts of his homeland and countryman. With Colin there beside him, he had felt buoyed by his strong heritage, kinsmen working together to build better lives on the new land.

Now one of the foundations of his fortunes had been kicked from underneath him, the ocean of all sufferings seemed to unleash itself over his labours, he was engulfed in that hour, this world had lost its meaning. All he could do was keep going over all that he had lost, and the heartache that he now endured.

William, Grace, and Uileen stood anxiously around their brother, helpless to offer succour, for the blow of finding Colin deceased took the rest of the energy out of their sails. No one mentioned the cabin, Ann Munson, the fire or Uileen's injury, they all knew Gilly was too far away to hear anymore hurt, he was on another plane of suffering that they could only begin to imagine.

Colin's funeral was the whole camps concern, a hero should have a send-off, and the miners would have it no other way, many lined up along the coffins path, caps in hand, if liquor hadn't conquered their consciences, but if so, they then sat in a stupor of sad expression watching the grave proceedings.

Ballarat cemetery was a void, of sparse grasses, dusty gravels, and a few gnarly gums. Cinereal clouds hung over a leaden procession, the town had been burying a lot of its sons in the last weeks. Gilly trudged along behind his friend, in a dirge of guilt and recriminations. Will accompanied him, behind them, Grace and Uileen were supported on Peter's stoic arms, as they walked, weeping behind their brothers.

Shemus, Alice and Haggis had heard the tragic news, they waited at the cemetery for their friends, what there was of it. Roaring Jack Tucker, Luigi Vinci, Fig Newton, and many others wended their weary way behind the bereaved, grieving the going of another good man.

Standing straight and silent, at the corner of the clay acre designated burial ground, was Master Po, with him Lim, and Ah Sam, their heads bowed in quiet communion.

Gilbert looked down at the narrow hole in the ground, and thought of life's irony, just a few days before they had been making holes in the ground and here was one, Colin would not be coming out of.

Gold seemed a cold, hard, and bitter poverty next to the treasures of his friendship with Colin, no coin could buy those kinds of riches.

Sod thudded down upon the lid and Gilbert felt like thudding down with the clods. William's arm steadied him as pearl sized tears dropped down his whiskers as he remembered the ring of his family's support.

Colin was laid to rest, his labours were not in vain, for the value of his contribution was priceless, Gilbert was the living proof and when the memorial stone went up, they caved his name with pride.

Grace and Uileen were staying at the hotel, Alice, Shemus and Haggis had relocated to Lake Wendouree, Gilbert, Will and Peter were back under canvas in a tent. A fireside meeting was arranged, time to take stock of the situation.

Money was tight, Gilbert had not been able to find the small cash box he kept their nuggets in.

"We have rocks to spare, don't fret yur selves," Shemus offered, "we can sort out the rest later, ye saved me life more than once as tis".

"Aye," agreed William "but yer not that much of a prize", he joked.

The company laughed as Haggis, seemingly able to pick up the groups mood, dragged in a small lizard and dropped it on the ground in front of the firelight fraternity.

"I have money, from Norway, Grace will be my wife, yes?" Peter asked. Grace put her hands to her face, flushed with happiness. Maybe losing the cabin was not the end of the story, just the start of a new chapter!

Will cleared his throat, "Well, ah, yer see, I was goin to say the same thing to Uileen until Peter stole my thunder", said William sheepishly.

Gilbert looked at the two men, then at the two maidens, then he shook his head,

"Och, are these two larrikins good enough for the most beautiful lassies on God's green earth?"

He pondered his own question quizzically…

"I don't know as I could rightfully say.

"Oh Gilly!" protested Grace "Stop foolin around and give us yer blessing, we could make ye mighty uncomfortable if'n ye don't."

"Aye" chimed in Uileen.

"The women have spoken," said Peter.

"I've already got me present!" said Shemus, and he laid down a gold nugget the size of a Robbins egg.

Gilbert stared hard at the auric metal. How he would give it all to see his friend again, but that alchemy was beyond his ken. He kept expecting Colin to just walk into their diggings, as if he'd been out for a smoke and a 'wee dram', he dragged his thoughts back to the moment, like pulling wild horses into line, and smiled a sad smile.

"Ye'll be spoiling them something rotten Shemus, they will be expecting it all the time", he teasingly warned his Irish friend.

"We have more, lots", said Alice proudly "Haggis find in river, he one good dharug!" Everyone laughed, as Haggis heard his name and raised his battered head from his mutton chop, grinning at the group, before returning with all diligence to his dinner. After supper, the men talked again about what the future held.

"The goldfields seem to be getting harder and harder to mine, said Will.

"It's not the same after Eureka and losing Colin," said Gilly.

"Ya, there is also Munson to contend with", Peter reminded them "He is here at large, and extremely dangerous!"

The other men agreed, especially after Ann's demise and their involvement in that, it was only a matter of time before their luck ran out in avoiding him, and trouble found them wanting.

The proceeds from the 'Luck Now' nugget seemed to have vanished into thin air, it was difficult for William to comprehend what had happened to the tin box they had buried secretly. Only the immediate male company knew of its existence, they had racked their brains over the mystery, but now, knew time was running out for them to keep searching for it.

"I've been talking ta some of the fellows from the 'land of the long white cloud' they call it, Tane and Rua", said Gilbert, "they say they know where gold can be found in Te Waipounamu, the South Island. I'm thinking it might be a new start fer us, maybe?"

"We canna stay here, how far is this southern island", queried William.

"It'll take some seven days sailin to get through the Tasman sea they say", answered Gilly, "it's a oceanic wilderness that far under the earth!"

The skirl of the bagpipes echoed through the gullies, as the two brides, one on Gilly's arm, one on Shemus' arm walked to the tune of the Wedding march.

Uileen and Grace would only consent to a double wedding, they felt it was only right and proper, money was an object that they had to consider. But the women of Ballarat wanted a double wedding, and a dual wedding is what they came to the party for!

A sumptuous wedding feast was prepared, and the contributions poured in, the Sunday arrived in brilliant sunlight.

The minister from Melbourne had travelled to Ballarat to officiate, his round face beamed at the congregation, as he stood sweating in the late morning summer heat. William had composed wedding words, Peter shared Will's bards' gift and both men stood facing their love's guiding lights.

They exchanged their vows, as they were hand tied together with cords, the men spoke their heartfelt poetry to their brides.

"When we came to the waterfall of Life's forces,

You put your hand in mine, I put my hand in yours.

There was no turning back, we jumped handfasted.

Past the rocks of despair and desperation.

We were not broken.

My hand is still in yours your hand is still in mine.

Now we have a lifetime, hand in hand.

Two hands, two hearts, Entwined."

The couples exchanged a single kiss before, a broomstick was found and in ancient Celtic tradition, the couples, handfasted, jumped the broom, to much cheering, shouts of laughter and tears of joy.

Then two brides were snatched away from their new husbands by roaring Jack Tucker, Shemus, whirling from one to the next and kissed on their cheeks soundly, until they came to rest in their grooms arms once more.

The whole wedding dissolved into a crush of merriment; the crowd of well-wishers stood cheek to jowl in the bright sunshine to be part of the joyous occasion.

A tent had been set up; the array of food excited everyone, especially the flies so sheets were draped over the roasted meats.

Bunjil and Black Billy had given kangaroo meat and emu eggs as a delicacy for the occasion, they sat with a small contingent of their clan, listening to the piper, trying to understand the bagpipes, and examining them closely. They were told what they were made from, tulipwood and whale teeth, and marvelled at the magical sounds they made, when the pipe tuned up again.

Two quaich were produced and these Celtic love cups with two handles were filled with a bottle of fine malt whiskey from the auld country and the couples drank together in a toast to long life and happiness.

William made a toast to the piper, Peter toasted Gilly, and everyone toasted the brides, the alcohol flowed and the ceilidh dancing began with the wedded couples in a grand march, Shemus escorted Alice into the procession, and men with no partners escorted each other.

Eyes met each other across the room with warm regard, holding promises each was anxious to collect.

Chapter 14

Manaia had voyaged from New Zealand to the Tahitian shores and then to Californian, he had been part of a heady mix of gold mania, and masculine license, that combination travelled with him to the Victorian Valhalla.

He knew the first signs of yellow fever, and he felt them within himself, a restless sensation, an excited state of his nervous system, a wild expression when he looked in his eyes, his tread was light and elastic.

Manaia had quickly collected his implements for digging and washing gold, he tried to pay gambling debts, obtain a passport, jump the first boat, and pass quietly out of the northern hemisphere, adventure bound.

The stockade had just been fought as he arrived to try his luck, fresh Californian colour in his pockets, with sufficient resources of spirit to cut free, from the cramped society of the old world, in order to begin afresh in the new.

The road into Ballarat town had been converted into a slough sea of mud, in the winter Manaia arrived, the power of bullock flesh could scarcely draw a lightly loaded dray. His coach floundered and plunged as if it were the ship, he'd previously travelled, on caught in a gale, trying severely his bones and temper, weary as he was.

This "pakeha ferro", or white people's gold, was a gift and a curse, he had been hunting it for months in California, and it was becoming like the presents and promises of white settlers in New Zealand, easy to get to begin with, but as time goes on, and more people come, it evaporates into nothingness.

Finally, he had arrived at his destination, Ballarat. As he heaved himself from the dray cart and hefted his swag, in a split second between the quagmire of the road, and the side of the dray, a Cobb & Co coach horse team reared up at him, he held his swag up as a shield from the horses' hoofs.

The next minute, he felt a body tackle him round the waist, and roll with him away from the creatures striking hoof. It took Manaia a few moments to realise, that another man had him pushed into a big puddle on the side of the road, out of harm's way. Covered in dirt and detritus, the two men eyed each other.

"Yer were for it their mate", said Gilbert from his prone position, "are yer alright mon?" Manaia nodded his dazed head, as he viewed his rescuer from sodden, close range.

"I ok, I ok, he replied.

"I'm Gilly", Gilbert introduced, as he pulled Manaia up out of their shared misery, both men were saturated, mud, leaves and sticks stuck to their wet dripping clothing.

"Och, Grace and Uileen will give me a going over, ye had better come with me, back to the Union Hotel, and save me from their sharp tongues", invited Gilly.

Manaia knew better than to look a gift horse in the mouth, especially when his life had just been saved, "let's go" said Manaia.

In front of a blazing fire in the hotel, Gilbert and Manaia stood drying out with a drink. Grace, Peter, Uileen and Will sat round listening to Manaia talk about his homeland, New Zealand, and his adventures in America.

"Ah, Californian goldfields hard, I make half ounce a day, twenty miners make nothing, in the winter the lice eat me, in the summer, fleas wake me up. Then the sickness comes, the cholera, I am sick, can do nothing, for many weeks, I cannot move, I am fever, I am cold, some women helped me bring clean water."

"You will find some golden flakes here, but competition is fierce," said Will. "Tane, Rua and Rangi will be working up by the eureka claim, we had better meet up with them at the diggings to introduce you and show you the claim."

As they continued to discuss their circumstances, Manaia explained the use of his word Pākehā for his white friends.

"For the early Maori, meeting European people for the first time, they saw them as 'pale imaginary beings, resembling men' their word to describe this phenomenon in Maori was Pākehā.

An ice-white, sickle moon, glowed anaemically, as its monthly cycle came to an end, Mangus Munson and several of his men waited like phantoms, in the Cimmerian darkness of the United Hotel's back stairs.

"Remember, men, I want as little struggle with the hellcat as possible, wait for Reynolds to give the signal that the men are out of the way!"

"Yes Sir! Sergeant", replied the troopers.

Stealthily, they crept towards the window of Grace's room, a lit candle gave off a thin smouldering light, to an otherwise umbrous interior; Mangus could see the outline of a woman's body reclined on the iron bed frame.

Reynolds arrived, as the small gang of soldiers loitered in the shadows.

"Report man!" ordered Mangus.

"Sir, the two men you had me tail, have both gone to Bakery Hill diggings.

"Right! Men, it's time to settle old scores and set a few new ones, by God" Archibald ye broke the latch on that casement like I told you too?"

"Yes sir, all taken care of sir!"

"Stand guard Reynolds! Whilst we secure the prize, and make our escape unnoticed" "Aye sir", Private Reynolds replied.

Incrementally, the window casing was eased ajar. Grace did not notice the influx of cool air for several moments, as she was floating on a warm cloud of loving visions of Peter, and his tender, passionate lovemaking.

All at once, a shroud of caliginous black was thrown over her face, her head was struck, as if by an anvil, and she knew no more.

The abductors easily picked up the concealed hostage, climbed out the aperture they had entered by, hauled the unfortunate captive up onto a sturdy, grey stallion, and rode swiftly away into the darkening gloom.

"Hullo my love," Peter Lars Tordenskjold called out in a whisper, as he entered the hotel room some hours later.

"I am sorry, I am so late, the men found some nuggets, we were helping them dig out". Peter stopped speaking as he reached the bedside, and realised that Grace was not present in the room, the hairs on the back of his neck began to prickle, from a small side closet, a frightened shaking maid emerged.

"Oh sir, tis Mangus Munson and his men who hav yer lady," the girl quivered, bursting into anguished tears. Peter thrust his handkerchief at the young woman, but his only thought was Munson!

William, Uileen and Peter met in the hallway adjoining their rooms, Uileen's face was drained of colour, her sea-green eyes flashing in outrage. William, his features grim as his mind seethed at the feeling of inadequacy that he felt, losing his sister to an enemy such as Munson.

"I should never have left her alone, unprotected!" Peter remonstrated.

"None of us should" said Uileen.

"We all know Mangus Munson and his ways, och, we canna waste oxygen on angry words", William decided. We need a tracker. Bunjil is our only hope to find our way to a rescue, we have to know where he would take her!" he added.

Bunjil and Black Billy walked with speed, following horse tracks and boot prints, every change in the bush they noticed, the bent branches, the hastily constructed fires, kicked out. After two days of sleepless, hard travelling in arid terrain, after looking at the tell-tale signs, Bunjil said "Looks like soldier's heading for mount Kooyoora and caves there! Several hours later, as the dawn broke on the escarpment, Peter, Will, Black Billy and Bunjil finally reached the gigantic, rock boulder formations, which were staggered across the mountainside, they were stacked on top of each other to form multiple caverns.

"Jaara Jaara people use these caves for shelter, springs for water nearby" explained Black Billy, as they climbed the steepening slopes ,the ground became uneven, and sudden cliffs materialised on the tracks.

They looked out over the views of box ironbark forests, to flat plains in the south, there they could make out several geldings, grazing in the morning sunlight.

"They are here alright!" said Peter, "I recognise the army issue saddle."

"Have ye any idea how many there are Bunjil?" asked Will.

"The fingers of one hand", replied Bunjil. "what do we do now?

"We trap them!" replied Black Billy, his dark face lighting up in an incandescent beam.

The first two men who came down to water the horses were incapacitated quickly, quietly, and with great skill by Bunjil, and Black Billy's boomerangs, from one hundred and fifty feet away, the troopers did not see the hit coming before they lay unconscious. Mangus Munson began to wonder what was taking Reynolds and Pitman so long with the horses.

"Archibald, take a rifle and check on those layabouts I sent hours ago. Thomas, you go gather up firewood, and take your pistols!", Mangus ordered the remaining two men. Grace sat bound and gagged, glaring at her nemesis.

"Och, ye'll get nowhere with that attitude me gel, I've mind to show ye my highland fling, now we have some privacy!" Mangus jeered at his prisoner.

Grace poured venom into her gaze and stared at him, hating his every breath, Mangus laughed into her expressive eyes. Abruptly Grace turned her back to him, realising he wanted to goad her, he was enjoying making her react to his verbal abuses. Mangus frowned at her sudden departure from his tortuous taunting.

"There will come a time, 'miss high an mighty', you will beg for yer life and that of yer brothers!" Munson sneered.

Grace retreated into herself, disassociating from the awful threats and taunts, and the bruising, violent, groping pinches that had been perpetrated upon her, as she had been summarily dragged from her wedding bed. The ropes cut into her wrists, but she had been assiduously working on loosening their grip, whenever her captors were otherwise engaged.

On the edge of fantasy, in a dreamtime, Grace knew Peter was coming, she could feel the drumming of his heartbeat thudding on the ground that distanced them, all she longed for was his arms around her, his mouth breathing her life back to her, and so she waited.

Meanwhile, Archibald and Thomas had met with better warriors than they were, for all their mechanical weapons, both militias were way out of commission as they hit the hard stony ground.

Mangus walked to the cave opening and looked out into the distance across the southern plains, the silent stillness was strident in its portent, he narrowed his vision to feel the threat of the taciturn bush.

Motioning to Grace, he reached over to wrench his prize up off the dusty, cavern floor and place his arm around her delicate neck, as he dragged her out of the entryway. As he pulled her with him, Mangus began to shout.

"I know yer out there Gilly, Will, Tordenskjold; I hav yer precious woman, ye won't be having her back alive!"

At the sound of Munson's malevolent threat, Peter froze. The comrades crept up the sides of granite outcrop's crags formed by the ice ages; the friends looked at each other in united disgust.

Mangus waved his revolver in the air, taking aim at the rocky outcrops surrounding him and he waited. Grace had at last managed to free her hands from the iron grip of the ties that bound her.

Suddenly, Black Billy's countenance appeared above them, like the avenging dark angel Azrael, Mangus levelled his gun and fired, but Billy was already gone, vanished into the rockface of his ancestors.

Mangus watched for a sign his shot had achieved its target, but was answered in silence once more, except for distant bird chatter. He turned, to force Grace back into the caves interior and Grace took her only chance. With all her remaining might, she released her hands and pushed Mangus, the edge of the precipice was a few yards away, and he stumbled at the unexpected attack, his pistol gave a fiery blast into the bedrock, Grace threw herself sideways from his grasp, feeling herself falling from the rocky promontory. Peter leaped off the ledge he was stationed on, and lunged at Mangus, the two men grappled in a deathly fight on the prominence of boulders.

Bunjil lay across the huge, smooth stones, stretching his arms out to pull his burden up from the precarious perch that she had landed on. William helped Bunjil tug Grace up the last few feet, until at last, she was back on firm earth; meanwhile an epic battle was being fought inside the grotto that had been her prison.

Peter feinted to the right, Mangus rushed at him with a bull's roar of rage, Peter ducked away, but came back with fists flying. Both opponents were bloodied, Peter was taller, and lighter than Mangus, whose muscular girth was somewhat cumbersome in the enclosed space, they circled each other menacingly. Peter backed towards the opening and Mangus flung himself at his adversary. Peter slipped on the gravelled surface of the entrance, he fell, and as he felt the ground rush up to greet him, the sound of Munson's body and breath going over the edge of the cliff assailed his ears.

It was time to say goodbye, Grace stood in her ground floor hotel room, staring into the spare street corner, contemplating her future life with Peter in Norway, although she felt she would leave half her heart behind her, leaving her brothers. She knew she had met the other half of her heart and that, would complete her.

The northern lights beckoned, Grace felt secure, safe, wrapped in the cocoon of care that had eluded her, until she had, at last, found Peter Lars Tordenskjold.

Peter had his mission to complete, before they could secure their future, he arrived bearing a letter from the Norwegian navy, with orders to set course for the Orkney islands.

"Will we see my family?" asked Grace, surprised at the turn of events.

"Of course, we will endeavour to sail by, my love, you are a naval wife now, your wish is my command. I will sweep you over the oceans of the world, wherever you dream of going."

"As long as you are by my side, I am home" said Grace, serene in her requited love, they stood upon the bow of the Aurora Borealis looking forward to the lands of their forefathers.

They had already seen seventeen icebergs, castellated, floating masses, lifting their pinnacles on high, and glinting in the rays of the sun, whilst sailing due south, the ship was headed into the windy, roaring forties, passing under the south west cape of New Zealand's Stewart island, at a latitude of 40 to 50 degrees.

Grace peered into the soup like fog, Peter was patrolling the deck. They were altering course, both day and night to avoid ice. For several nights they had to lay to, until day light, Peter had already seen six mammoth bergs, one hundred to five hundred feet high, two to five miles from the vessel. He knew that fragments of ice were more menacing, more difficult to be spotted or avoided, during the darkness. He knew very well, from arctic navel adventures, how burdensome it was to avoid a collision with these terrors of the deep, and he dreaded this part of their voyage for its duplicitous nature.

Boisterous winds blew the sea rough and rambunctious, making the conditions even more perilous and precarious. Peter rarely changed his clothing, he remained on deck nearly the whole night. Grace appeared, as like an apparition on the forecourt, swathed in a fur blanket, anxiously she greeted the first mate

"How is it looking now, Jamison?"

"Still hanging in the balance mam" he replied.

Peter's wearing countenance told Grace all she needed to know.

"I brought you officers some hot mutton stew" she said, caressing his face with her soft smile.

"Just what the doctor ordered!" said Peter, his tiredness dissipating in the uplifting warmth of her care. Grace stood holding her husband's hand, staring through misty blackness as downy, feather-like snow fell around them.

Very few passengers could sleep through the leaden night dramas, as they repeatedly heard Captain Tordenskjold and officers calling out to the quartermaster at the wheel to alter course "port, ice! Starboard! Ice!"

Eight o'clock, Easter eve, Peter returned up on deck, after checking on Grace and the other passengers, when he heard distinctly, breakers on the starboard side of the clipper, near her head. A smidgeon above the horizon, he saw the outline of an enormous growler.

"Alter course to port, hard to port!", he cried out to the helmsman, even with thick fog smothering it from view, he could clearly hear the waves rolling on it, ten minutes longer in the folksale he thought, and they would all have been sent to another world, with no one left to tell of the disaster!

"As we've sailed, I've counted fifty five icebergs sir, just during the daytime", Mate Jamison reported.

"Aye, we are in ice territory now Mister Jamison, batten down the hatches, it looks like we are set for a blow" said Peter.

The dining room had been set for the twenty-seven passengers and some officers, Grace and Peter were together at one end of the long mahogany table.

Outside, the decks were frozen, ropes and sails too, the sea rose with the wind in orchestrated fury, they were nearing Cape Horn and true to form, a turbulent cyclone blew off the Andes Mountain range.

As they were preparing for the meal, the ship went into a tremendous roll, dinner plates, dishes and glasses precipitated onto the floor in utter confusion. Mrs Andrews was thrown against the wall with a hard thump, Jenny MacLaine's hands were cut to pieces. Just as they tried to get up, the vessel rolled staggeringly, back the other way, bobbing like a cork in a shaken bottle of water. Three times it rolled on the broiling ocean, finally Peter was able to catch hold of Grace and a skylight. Mister Nicks, the second mate caught Mrs Gilmore, Mister Jamison narrowly escaped the heavy table crushing him, as he threw himself sideways to avoid it but, unfortunately, his right leg was pinned beneath it and received a heavy blow, it was severely injured.

Grace watched, as the wrecked dishes and plates, along with the curry, rice, ham, chairs, and tables moved from side to side of the boat.

"Twelve times sailing this route, I've never struck weather like this," said Peter.

Nerves were taut and tempers frayed, nobody was at ease now, anxious moment after anxious moment assailed them, like the waves breaking over the bow, emotions bobbled up and down, round about.

Jamison was contemplating the worst, with his leg so broken, he tried to quantify what being at sea meant to him, as he spoke to the captain and his lady.

"The ocean began just outside my window. When I was a lad growing up in Bergen, I had my heart set on going to sea, my greatest delight was to roam the waterfront and watch and listen to the sailors at work in the ships. Rigging, singing, hoisting, and bending the sails to the yards and spars. Voyages to faraway places, there was romance, there was life!"

Grace listened, trying to understand the gravitas of Jamison's predicament, as she wiped a cool cloth across his forehead. The ships surgeon, Limstrom, was examining his wounded leg and the prognosis was not good.

"The chances of losing it", he said, "were very high!"

Captain Tordenskjold had been considering his first mates' situation, he knew that he would rue the day, when the fever of the sea no longer made Jamison's pulse beat faster, and he was no longer able to fulfil his longing for new experiences, renew his wish for new horizons.

"No", said Peter, defiantly "we will not take Jamison's leg from him! I have seen legs put back together and splinted with wood, let us try!"

Grace assisted Dr Limstrom, as he gave Jamison rum and laudanum, he then found a splinter of shinbone thrust through the skin of Jamison's leg and he set about restoring the bone back to its proper place.

Nature gave Jamison the blessing of unconsciousness, as the pain assailed and overwhelmed him. Limstrom set the bone in the thigh as well, then he and Grace bandaged the whole leg to render it immobile. The best treatment for wounds, the surgeon told Grace, was a light diet, laudanum, antiseptic and watching out for pain, swelling, and itching, as well as changing the bandage to prevent gangrene.

Grace cringed at the repercussions for an able seaman with a missing leg, with gangrene, the outlook was grim, and she resolved to nurse Jamison thoroughly, to avoid the worst!

Mercy Andrews was coming in and out of consciousness, Grace checked her bruised face and side, Dr Limstrom said "it was difficult to do anything, except give her laudanum for the pain and wait."

A final break in Cape Horn's wind tunnel of roaring forties, furious fifties, screaming sixties and miasmic murky fog, brought with it a glorious sight, sailing ship Aurora Borealis meeting with Aurora Australis, southern lights that were stretched out over Antarctic skies, like a hallelujah chorus, singing to angels earthbound, a glittering star bound heavenly choir. It was a breath-taking panorama, elevating the spirits of the battered sailors all, bringing hope out of an ocean, heavy with despair.

At long last, the Aurora Borealis was having plain sailing up the coast of South America, past Rio de Janeiro, through the southern Atlantic and into northern Atlantic climes.

"Ship ahoy", cried the lookout. Peter used the telescope and saw an ancient brigantine, listing off the leeward side. He could just make out some poor devils, alive and clinging to the ship's carapace, of planks and timbers, the mainsails were broken, bent and askew, it appeared a rudderless craft, an all but abandoned hulk.

They heaved to and put down some jolly boats and rowed over to the 'Redemption'.

It was in awful condition, taking in water, slowly sinking, wallowing up to its waist in deep waters. Peter could see it would not last long afloat, he had heard of the coffin ships, emigrants were crammed in and not really expected to survive the journey they had paid for!

They discovered the few crewmen still standing on deck, and when Peter went down the hatch to the steerage deck, a vile stench assailed him, such that he had only come across once before, when he had been at war, fighting on a battle ground. Incongruously, as he made his way through the ship, in the captain's cabin, he redeemed a despondent canary, perched within an oxidising cage, swinging like a pendant from the centre of a skylight.

The smell of death became stronger still in the steerage compartments, pervading into the very timbers surrounding him. About twenty people, men, and women, tottered about in confusion, and a few children crawled up to him, holding out their hands in silent supplication. Peter could see they were skeletal with starvation, one of the supplicants spoke, an emaciated man of indeterminate age with fine brown eyes.

"Please captain, sir, yer honour, help us, we are Irish crofters, cleared from our lands, by merciless English landowners, headed for Ameriky. The captain of this ship missed his reckoning in a blinding snowstorm, and in the blackness of night, one stroke of an angry wave swept the ship clean, Captain and most of the crew, gone to a watery grave.

We were carrying four hundred and ninety-six passengers, most are dead of the fever, there's been no doctor, precious little provisions, and no fresh water for drinking, for days."

Peter had seen ship's fever, typhus and typhoid, on slavers, that had been picked up in the Caribbean, and he was appalled at the passenger conditions. Berth stacked upon berth, with less room than a coffin, three people squeezed into six feet square.

Peter later said to Grace "they were stowed away like bales of cotton, lying in their own excrement, the floor was like a cesspool, those on top bunks evacuated over those below, no wonder they are so ill, no fresh air or clean water."

Dr Limstrom appeared at his shoulder saying "Captain, there is an epidemic on this ship, we must quarantine it, with all souls remaining aboard, our own health is in jeopardy, Sir!"

A woman, gaunt and wretched, approached the sailors, her long hair falling out, naught now, but a few matted black strands, her eyes glassy, red and rheumy.

"Yer honours, she cried, "we thought we couldn't be worse off than we war; but now in our sorrow, we knowt be differ, for sure, supposin we were dyin of starvation, or if the sickness overtuk us. We had the chance of a doctor ,and if he could do no good for our bodies, sure the priest would for our souls; and then we'd be buried wid our own people; in the auld churchyard, with the green sod over us; instead of dying, like rotten sheep, thrown into a pit, and the minit the breath is out of our bodies, flung into the sea to be eaten up by them horrid sharkes!"

Peter looked at Lukus Limstrom.

"We must do something for these people, they cannot stay aboard this carcass for long, it's disintegrating", he said.

"They have to be kept apart from our ship", repeated Lukus.

"What can be done?" reiterated Peter. Lukus sighed thinking hard.

"This typhus is carried by body lice, it has a forty per cent fatality rate, everything must be burnt; clothing, bedding, linen, bring the stronger passengers up on deck, scrub everything down, including the people and cut their hair", he said, "and wash with lye soap."

Some of the afflicted started to scream out for water, delirious in their sweaty overheated hells.

"How much fresh water do we have?" Asked Lukus.

"We will need to give it to the most fevered" and Dr Limstrom began ordering the Aurora crew to set to work removing infected material.

"Right men, get everyone up on deck", announced Peter, "help those lying in bunks, who need it", he directed, "bring fresh water, then scrub yourself down with lye!"

A week out from recovering the 'Redemption' passengers, Grace was the perfect thrall, kept endlessly, busy washing and refashioning clothing for all their new charges, nothing could be saved, so new garments were a necessity. Canvas, cotton and donations of dresses, jackets, pants, bonnets, and hats were collected, men and women patients cordoned off from each other.

Grace oversaw a convalescent being assisted on deck, he seemed revived by the untainted air. He was a miserable being, his face, being jaundiced and withered, was transliterated ghastly by the ebon streaks that encircled his cavernous eyes.

Grace's spirit shook with empathy, 'many and fathomless are the lacerations, that the perceptive heart wreaks upon its possessor, as they traverse midst life's odyssey', she wrote in her diary, as she tried to make sense of life when being beset by a crowd of poor creatures, each having some request to make.

Life became a mission, to somehow supply water for burning thirsts, food for starving bodies, and hope for suffering souls, the captain's cabin had become like an apothecary's emporium.

One of the crew, Jonas Jones came knocking at the cabin door, Grace bade him come in, "Begging yer pardon Missus, but some of the Irish beggars are asking for meat, they've got the dysentery and I seen a shark following us all day, it's a certain portent of death, that's what it is!" Jonas ascertained worriedly.

"Have ye spoken to my husband, Jonas?"

"Aw Mam, I've been on watch for hours, Captains organising the supplies with the Mate, and I hav this ere headache, wot won't leave me temples" complained Jones.

"What about Dr Limstrom", asked Grace.

"He's too busy seeing to the Irish, Mam."

"Alright." agreed Grace, "here's some opium drops, they should help you sleep, Jonas", "Yes Mam, thank ye Mam" said Jonas.

Grace went up on deck, the sky was covered with heavy clouds and a cold northern wind blew without interruption, Grace shivered in its presence. How they were going to get everyone to a home would be a miracle, but if anyone could achieve it, it was Peter Lars Tordenskjold she thought fondly.

She took this small time to relax. Looking over the railings, she observed the curling of dolphins, the Ariel flits of the flying fish, with the gambols of fleets of porpoises prancing in the waters around the prow.

The very next day, Jamison arrived up on deck to see to the rigging. First mate Jamison had made a remarkable recovery from his injuries, and although lame, the mate was extraordinarily active, he was one moment in the hold, helping some severely ill soul, the next, he was stretched across a yardarm, reefing a topsail. One of the male passengers commented to Grace.

"Och, your ladyship, isn't Mr Mate a great bit of a man?"

"How do we fair Mr Mate?" asked Grace.

"As well as can be expected Mam, under the circumstances, we'll be in Cork within two days with a fair wind."

At that moment, Jonas came running towards them, his hands holding his stomach, he fell to the ground, writhing in convulsive agony, Grace looked at the fallen sailor in horror, Jamison called out. "Fetch the surgeon! Get that man below!"

Grace came to her senses and ran to her cabin for medications and clean linens.

Dr Limstrom was examining his latest patient, as they carried Jonas in groaning and retching into a bucket. It was the doctors worst fear, the typhus spreading to the Aurora's compliment. He quickly made his way to Jonas, to investigate his symptoms such as they were.

Peter met Grace halfway between decks, both were sombre at the prospect of the illness spreading to the healthy aboard.

"All we can do is wait and see", pronounced Peter, as he cuddled his precious wife to his chest.

"We will be in Ireland soon; they have fever hospitals there".

"But this sickness is so deadly, Peter, so sudden, can we outrun it before it burns through us all", worried Grace.

Peter held his darling wife close to him and said, "In this winter of despair, Hope is our only spring, and we must hold on to each other to fight the cold fear that is more contagious than this disease."

They went out to the helm, the phosphorescent appearance of the ocean at night was very bewitching. They seemed to be gliding through a sea of liquid embers. Holding each other, they stood silently, drinking in the moments of oneness in a universe of uncertainties, they knew their love enveloped them eternally.

Lukus Limstrom washed his hands in salt water and yawned, he had been awake for thirty-six hours and his very eyeballs ached, his back breaking and his stomach was sticking to his ribs. 'Aye, life was grand alright', he thought wryly, as the last sufferer seemed to be sleeping at ease. He felt like he had lost the battle but won the war, the symptoms seemed to be dissipating in most patients. Using 'Dover's powder' and cleanliness, none had died in several days, although they were weak, and time would tell about real recovery.

Thank God, Jonas Jones only had food poisoning from rotten mutton, that he had been hoarding for several days before the stupid man ate it, because of his belly aching, the ship had been on tender hooks, waiting for the next victim to fall.

On deck that afternoon, the day was diaphanous, with a gentle zephyr which formed a ripple on the surface of the water, giving it a marvellous appearance to the reflection of the diminishing sun, looking like jets of vapours bursting from the deep.

Grace, who had been comforting a mother and her child, came up to stand beside Lukus, and behold the beauty of such a mellow day.

"Peter says we will be in Cork in the morn", she said.

"At last, land, I cannot wait to see soil again and have the responsibility of these emigres in someone else's pocket," he said.

"Aye, we canna do more for them now, but some will travel on to the Orkneys and Shetlands with us, then to Bergen, they still need a new life; Peter will find them situations in Norway." said Grace determinedly.

The stop in County Cork, in the province of Munster Ireland was short indeed, they sailed right up the capacious, natural harbour and Lee riverine estuary to the waterfront at Cobh, Queenstown, named after Queen Victoria's 1849 visit. It was situated on the great island in Cork seaport. This transatlantic port was the ebb and flow of emigration in Ireland. Six million men, women and children would funnel through its water way to seek new pastures abroad.

Of the twenty survivors, three had died shortly after they were found on the Redemption, the rest were recovering, eight went off the Aurora to recuperate in their motherland. For the remainder, too soon they left the quay side, loaded with supplies. Then the ten expatriates left their last footprints on their native land. The boat pushed off, in a few minutes they were on board the clipper that was to waft them over the northern seas to the Orkney and Shetland isles, then on to the fabled Norseland.

Chapter 15

Aotearoa New Zealand

Te Waipounamu - the Middle Island South

A kotuku lifted its gracile, alabaster wings from the surface of a mirrored lake, that saw giant alps draped halfway up their precipitous slopes with evergreen beech trees, whose presence ended suddenly where the ice and snow began.

The sharp delineation of vegetation against an ethereal azure sky was only apparent when a cleared saddle was attained, and Gilbert and Manaia looked down over bush clad, folded hills and valleys, rolling away inland before them.

Only then, could they turn their eyes seawards, to the bold, bouldered East Coast, with its many rivers, whose wide mouths foamed way out to where the great Pacific waves tossed under the brilliant winter sun.

Manaia said "This is the land of mountain, taniwha, and treasures that only the Maori know. They are hidden in the depths and recesses of these mountains. The mountains are a place where my people find peace and are sacred, tapu, each one an ancestor, brought by a canoe to Aotearoa, New Zealand.

But a great storm had overturned it, the crew struggled to shore and came inland, but by the dawn light they had turned to stone. Maori have always known of the ferro, golden metal, but our hearts belong to the green stone, pounamu. Our stories are handed down, carved in this stone."

Gilly was silent as he took this in, and then he replied.

"Och, Mon, we have a similar understanding of how we arrived in our land to, I ken with ye."

Volcanic eruptions, one hundred million years ago, had caused Cretaceous alluvial concentrations to be deposited in the schist, as part of river sediments, endlessly washed into the blue spur conglomerate, cemented with calcium carbonate and a blue green clay mineral, an antipodean lapis lazuli.

The mightiest river, known by the first people, the Maori, as the Mata-au, by the French explorers as the Molyneux, and by the English settlers as the Clutha acted like a huge sluice, leaving fire particles behind where it's currents flowed, the gold specks became a bonanza of bullion in the 1860s for the South Island prospectors.

The first European miner, Tasmanian, Balfour Jones, found substantial amounts of auric metal, he was an expert in mining methodology and had been to California, Ballarat, and Bendigo, all the recent goldfields. His knowledge of prospecting was extensive, he had heard from Black Peter, an Indian miner, and Maori diggers in Victoria that gold was resident in Aotearoa, New Zealand too.

Gilly had received a missive from Balfour Jones, several months after he had set out to conquer this land of new opportunity.

By the time Balfour's letter reached Ballarat, Jones had already sailed on the ship Don Pedro with a load of horses, landed at Port Chalmers, Dunedin New Zealand, and trudged on foot to the Tuapeka river with a forty kilogram swag.

In the letter Balfour wrote to Gilbert, he said

"The rugged terrain, unformed tracks and freezing conditions, are more than a match for any man. It is said 'Victoria only wants fencing in but this island needs hammering out flat!' It's a mountainous tussock land, isolated, barren and devoid of timber on the flats, the fuel has to come from buffalo chips, dung made from sheep and horses! But, nothing is impassable when it comes to reaching gold!"

Gilbert and Manaia lined up on the steamer, Gazelles, gangplank with dozens of other 'Travelers', waiting 'to cross the ditch', from Australia to New Zealand, to rub the Aladdin's lamp of an untamed land, rushing to see what alchemy they could conjure up, either in the form of gold or land.

The vessel was bound for Port Chalmers Dunedin, to the east coast of Te Waipounamu, the South Island. It had a mahogany hull, specially designed steam engines, displacing 580 tons. She was 166 foot long and built on the mahogany diagonal principle, a barque rigged royal, and capable of 12 knots under steam, or so the captain boasted.

The food on board, in steerage, was salted mutton meat that tasted as if it was made from bits scraped off the hide of the old sheep, and grey porridge, occasionally cabbage leaves were supplemented, and everything was followed with a dirty looking tea you could stand a spoon up in.

On this voyage Gilly and Manaia were hungry alright, but after the repugnance that followed eating each meal, it was hard for them to rustle up much enthusiasm for any food served.

The only lucky draw during their passage, was a cargo of fruit 'found' on board, without this treasure they would have faded away or even had a revolt, as three pounds a man for the journey to starvation was no laughing matter.

They were halfway out in the heavy Tasman Sea, when the ship rolled and lumbered, the bow rose high in the water as a colossal wave ran beneath the hull, higher and higher the craft leapt, then topping the breaker, rose and plunged deeply into the wall of swirling ocean, with what seemed to Gilly, mammoth waves surrounding them on all sides. Wind tore at the rigging and the dull thump, thump, thump of the steamer's engines could hardly be heard over the screaming roar of the storm.

Gilly could see the imminent upset of the ship approach.

"Hold on everybody!" he shouted, as he grasped the mast firmly. Seconds later, tons of water flooded the aft of the boat, washing crew and passengers under the forward guns.

Manaia was lifted by the gigantic wave and swept over the side, he clutched on to the gang plank's roping and tenaciously clung on to the frame. Gilly waited with bated breath as his friend held fast, after what seemed like hours the wind died down a bit, and Gilly was able to help Manaia back into the ship.

"Tangaroa, my Maori God of the sea, not taking this man today," Manaia joked.

"Aye, yer staying with me, if I have to tie us together!" said Gilbert and the two mates laughed, Gilly gave Manaia his jacket and shared a contraband orange under a canvas awning.

The adventure had begun again! As they came into the harbour, they saw an anchorage port surrounded by an amphitheatre of hills with immense bush adorning the banks of their destination right down to its rocky baseline.

Dunedin, meaning Edinburgh in Gaelic, was a somewhat staid religious settlement, set up in 1848.

"Not more swaggers," spat the musterer, as he saw the steamer approaching, "that's all this bloody place needs, more heathens!"

The village was one unpaved road of small wooden shops, it already had an old identity of the first immigrants, Presbyterian merchants and farmers from Scotland.

To say the locals were jaded by the influx of outsiders, may have been an understatement, Gilly and Manaia were soon to find out, when they disembarked.

A 'swagger' there, meant a man who might rob or murder you in your sleep, after you had fed and housed him.

There was also the quieter, seemingly more virtuous men, unafraid to jump your claim or hang around to spy on how much colour you found. As the two companions walked this dirt track street of suspicions, it appeared that every seeker distrusted a stranger, there was a powerful shortage of goodwill to be found.

As they were walking along reconnoitring, Gilbert heard his name shouted out, he turned to see Captain 'Edward' Baines, a merchant mariner, who had been on the Gazelle with them.

"Ahoy mates", he cried again, "come and have a drink, I have a proposition for ye!" Manaia and Gilbert looked at each other dubiously, wondering what trouble this would possibly lead to, however, they went into the modest Provincial Hotel accommodation. Captain 'Edward' Baines had been notorious on the Gazelle for gambling, he would bet on anything, having shooting matches on board with anyone who would participate, often bagging mollyhawks and cape pigeons, then raffling them off to passengers to supplement sparse rations.

He was a tall, bluff sort of man with red hair, a large red beard, and blue eyes that twinkled at the thought of mischief.

"I was a captain with a fine ship, the Pearl, after I secured the funding from various investors, for a cargo of copra oil and sandalwood. We set sail for home, alas the reefs around Samoa were treacherous and we ran aground. The Pearl quickly sank, and we only managed to save the crew! I made my way back to Sydney, but the blighters wanted their pound of flesh, I could not pay, so I spent six months in debtor's prison. That's when I had the idea of investing in a theatre company, the 'Allinghams', they're coming to New Zealand on a tour of the gold fields," Captain Baines boasted to his audience.

It was obvious Baines was a scallywag, an enterprising rogue, with stars in his eyes overlaid with pound notes!

Two young roustabouts were sitting at a table with the captain, they had just arrived from the hills with six months wages, fifty pounds had been supplied to the publican and the drinks were just arriving.

"Righto lads, let's see yer drinking muscles", Baines invited Gilly and Manaia to join in the betting, and it was obvious by a few rounds in, that a real gambling spirit had been aroused, the eager eyes, bated breath, the ominous silence, and the young farmhands' tremulous hands.

Gilbert could see the lay of the land, he had not been pursuing the urge to lay down his hard-won golden stake, as he knew they were without any mining supplies, bar a few pieces of equipment, pick, pannikin, swag, and tent.

Manaia had made a few bets, but did not enter the drinking competition, the gamblers were all glassy eyed, but it was clear that the captain was the more hardened drinker of the trio, finally the smallest, younger gambler, fell from his seat insensible.

"Och, let's call it a night mon, we need to find a place to sleep," said Gilbert.

"Ye can't go now!" protested, Baines, "we ain't finished, by a long chalk!"

"We need to go, find bed", agreed Manaia.

"Tis not sporting to leave before the end", insisted Baines, however, Manaia stood up with Gilly and they made their way to the door, whereupon several patrons stood across their path.

"Ye canna leave before the end of play, said a heavy-set Scotsman, folding his bulging biceps across his barrel chest. Gilbert and Manaia decided to find their way out the hard way, fists began to fly, men flew bodily at each other, in varying drunken states of anger. Gilbert used his sobriety, and right hook rather effectively, to punch a young whipper snapper under the nearest table, he was out for the count.

Captain Baines, whose auspices it had been under, to start the brawl, was having a few second thoughts, although he had managed in the melee to extricate the winnings from the game into his breast pocket, as he fought his way to the public bar door.

Manaia had copped a split lip from the Scotsman, who then drunkenly apologised, "Sorry mon, I thought ye were someone else, I'm after that blabberskipe 'Captain Edward Baines', he has nae paid up his gambling debt from his last visit here!" He explained.

"Let's get out of here", called Gilly, and Manaia retreated as fast as he could, putting his head down and pushing through the raging men. They found themselves out on the dirty sidewalk. Manaia, Gilbert, Baines and the Scotsman, Rory Ramsey; the wind blew icy in the unprotected faces of the foursome, a sobering cold lash. Rory was deciding upon some rough justice for the captain's perfidy; however, Baines was deciding that size really did matter in contests of strength, he rapidly found the money to pay Rory, with interest.

At that moment, a lovely young woman arrived on the street,

"Baines, there you are, we have been waiting hours for ye to return, we have had no supper!"

"Bella, you shouldn't be out on the street at this time of night, there's a fight in the bar", Edward exclaimed.

"Huh, you think we can't hear the caterwauling from the rooms, mother is most distressed by the goings on!" Bella complained.

"Now don't you worry yourself, my dear, it's a storm in a teacup, be right as rain soon as the boys have passed out!

"Eddie, ye promised us a performance hall, we've been here a week already", Bella cajoled.

"Yes, but as you are aware Bella, me darlin girl, I have only this moment arrived and have been working out the details and the funding necessary for our needs" Edward hastened to point out.

Meanwhile Gilly, Manaia and Rory had closed their mouths at the sight of female pulchritude such as this, Gilbert came back to earth first, leaving the two dramatists to their animated discussions, dragging Manaia with him down the roughshod road with Rory following them.

In the chill night breeze, Gilbert and Manaia set up camp on the edge of the town, the stars hung in the sky, making the universe seem a sea of lights, so clear was the alpine atmosphere.

As a fire crackled in a stone circle, Rory talked of arriving in Dunedin as a lad from Scotland in 1848.

"My mother died of pneumonia when I was twelve, my father had gone off into the hills, I think he died from sick of living, anyway. My two brothers and I were taken in by the Scottish church society, we lived in a boy's boarding house. Now I work on a sheep station just outside Cromwell as a farmhand and shearer.

"Och," he said, "life was pretty boring, we work six days a week, except for the odd trout fishing and boar hunt. The only fun to be had was coming to town drinking, and gambling. This is a wilderness where man, dog, and sheep are united in an alliance to defy the elements that threaten, snow, ice, fire, flood, avalanche, and landslide. It is the ends of the earth, only the seals and the whales know what else lies south of these towering peaks, it canna be worse than winter here".

Otago New Zealand was full of the lost characters of life's plays, men and women who played out the comedies and tragedies of colonialism, Dunedin, in particular seemed to set the stage for them.

Shadrach Jones was nothing if not entrepreneurial, when captain Baines approached him, he had leant down and scratched his bulldog's ear, Sampson had drooled on the carpet and licked his master's hand.

Shadrach wore a checkerboard waistcoat, smoked a fat cigar, and had a penchant for the bizarre. He was the proud owner of the Rose and Thistle public hotel.

Everything was a gamble to Shadrach Jones, at five-foot five inches stout with a ruddy face, wide side whiskers, and curly, dark hair, he cut quite the dashing figure in the stoic Scottish community.

A theatre room was set up in the hotel, flyers were made, advertising drama, comedy, and song straight from the bright lights of Sydney. Isabella Allingham, the dancing nightingale of

Australia, the odd couple, comedians Charlie Chester, satirical songster, and the Allingham brothers, acting acrobats.

The stage was set for action, the troupe opened to a packed audience, Mother Allingham walked amongst the patrons, giving out programs and animatedly engaging the concert goers.

As master of ceremony, Baines presented his diva, Isabella stepped onto the makeshift stage and sang.

Song of an exile

Oh, the limpid streams of my own green land!

Oh, the limpid streams of my own green land!

Wo, Wo, the exiles and the exiles parched hand

As she calls upon the rivers, of her far off land.

There is a fever in the pulse, and deep and restless eye

A cold and pallid brow, but the cheek is flushed so dry.

Oh! The limpid streams of my own green land.

After the applause died down, Isabella departed the stage and the acrobat and jugglers, who were her four brothers, began a non-stop carnivalesque performance, jumping one atop the other, balancing bottles on their heads, juggling items from the audience as they were thrown from the stalls.

After this sprightly gymnastics display, the lamps were turned down and a hush fell over the company, the musicians muted their music, the curtains were drawn slowly, a spotlight shone on centre stage, as the on lookers fixed their eyes on a gauzy, topaz veiled figure, lying face down glistening in the luminescence.

The mellifluous melody of a flute swelled into the room, as the hourglass shape of Isabella undulated to its enchantment, her quivering breasts, heaving belly, and tossing thighs were thinly shrouded, as a million amethyst suns reflected in the incandescence of the veil dance. Her undulating stomach was translucent in the thin, coiling mists surrounding it, she was the embodiment of undying lust.

The swaggers and shagroons went wild, stamping and cheering; some threw coins, the women hide their eyes behind programs, some had already left. The Presbyterian contingent were most aggrieved, although the minister took his time leaving the room backwards. The crescendo of music had reached a climax, with Isabella dancing on her hands, sheathed in a sensual richness of silken fabrics, finally she sank once more to the ground and the roof came down!

Gilly, Manaia, and Rory sat in the hotel bar listening to the music above them streaming down the stairs, Gilbert thought of home, he felt the loadstone warm, nestled next to his chest and he sighed with the knowledge that the bedrock of his family now hung round his neck, a world away from their beginnings.

Most of the men of the town had gone to the performance, such a diversion it was, it was the centre of most of the inhabitants' attentions.

Manaia was interested in why Mother Allingham appeared to be exiting the hotel by way of the back stairs, he could see her stealthily descending in the shadows, just illuminated by the light from above her. The figure of a man appeared from behind the hotel, Manaia went over to the windows to peer out into the pitch darkness, all seemed draped in a cloak of coal black. Manaia shook his mind's eye uncomfortably and went to sit down.

"What's up mon?", questioned Gilly.

"I dunno, maybe nothing, old lady outside with stranger, why?" asked Manaia.

"Hmm", said Gilly, "unusual for her to leave the concert, maybe she knows someone in town!"

"Maybe", said Manaia. They left it there, Rory had already slumped onto the table, as the alcoholic alchemy overtook his senses.

"Let's go", said Gilly, "trouble seems to follow too many questions".

"Yeah", agreed Manaia. The companions hauled up their drunken mate, and staggered out into the starlit evening, the lamps of the upstairs dramatics were blazing, as the trio made the journey to Morpheus through the mud lined street.

The next morning, pandemonium seemed to have erupted from the town centre, a crowd of angry men, shouting questions and threats were heard, as Manaia and Gilbert stuck their heads out of their canvas retreat.

Rory arrived at the run.

"It's the hotel, all the audience from last night have been fleeced!" he cried.

"What!", exclaimed Gilbert, "ye mean they have been robbed?"

"Yeah, they've had a tooler in there!" said Rory.

"What's going on now?" asked Gilly.

"Och, a mass robbery, they're all up in the boughs about it, it's a circus", said Rory. "Time to leave" stated Manaia.

"Aye" agreed Gilbert, but before they could collect their meagre supplies, the police constable arrived to search everything they had, and question their movements.

"We dinna know anything about it constable", stated Gilbert.

"You had better come with me anyway lads, it's best to be out of harm's way for the time being", senior constable Robert Laing retorted.

The friends soon found themselves in a small wooden box of a jail, twenty-one feet by fifteen surrounded by a tiny dirt yard.

"Ye should be looking fer that shyster, Captain Edward Baines", complained Rory, "not us."

"Yes, well, we have searched the theatre company, but came up empty handed", replied constable Laing.

"I think I remember something about last night", Manaia hesitatingly offered.

"Spit it out lad, we need fresh information," said Laing.

"Mother Allingham met a man on the backstairs around eleven last evening Sir", answered Manaia.

"A 'fence' said the constable,

"Maybe", answered Manaia.

"Alright, but we will have to search your gear and person, the townspeople are in a dour mood today, stay the night and be on your way tomorrow."

The three prisoners knew that they were at the mercy of an inclement incident and tried to make the best of the tight respite, Gilly pulled out his chanter and played. Constable Laing was pleased at the composed nature of his inmates, and deigned to take out his violin, a leading passion, besides the law. It was a strange musical repast that played into the night, and it was not until the following morning that Constable Laing arrived with the resigned air of one who was not winning the war on crime in the community. "The Allingham theatre group has cleared out in the early hours, if you blokes had stolen the loot you would have made a run for it hours ago, not gone to sleep, to be woken by me", Laing sighed.

"Watch out for the townsfolk, they already think you're madmen from Victoria, now they are after thieves, your ongoing safety is in mortal danger."

Gilbert, Manaia, and Rory gathered supplies of food and fuel. In their swags they still carried the possum blankets from Bunjil, knowing that there were thousands of men going to the diggings, ready to start at a moment's notice, having neither luggage nor good luck to detain them.

At this first opportunity of a new field, they shouldered their picks and shovels, threw on their forty five kilograms swags, and walked away with all the speed they could put forth.

'Sensationalism' made a swift, horizontal written passage, along with the finding of gold. Many a creative individual, crafted their own fortunes, from the misfortune or riches of the diggers.

Seymour Silver had departed Victoria, the weekly grind of the daily deadlines, in editorial newspapers that rarely printed the reality, of insanity, the aurous obsessions that diced with men's minds.

In a new land, he felt a new identity, a reinvention, a reinvigoration of his copy was in order, and as a writer he had a voice, words he wanted to be heard.

In the hotel, he met with Abraham Engels. Dunedin was on the cusp of a pandemic of panniers, it seemed to be a good place to literally become literate again.

Besides, this insolvency track, was a shortcut well-trodden by 'out of luck' itinerants skipping town, and the ever-mounting debts that were accruing. Seymour knew his fortunes turned on the luck of a penny newspaper.

The first goldrush edition written by Seymour Silver for the Otago Daily Times read as follows:

"The profusion, heedless of routes, reckless of previsionary requirements, start in their multitudes for the current and unsurpassed Dorado!

The fanned flames of 'Rush Conflagration', the speculative character of good miners endeavours, invariably produces a degree of restiveness and want of fixity of purpose. They will perpetuate the craziest extravagances in the obscure belief of seeing that come to pass. They will endure the marvels of adversities and fatigue, they will hazard starvation and exposure, loss in the bush, in short, every evil, anguish and mishap on the strength of gossip, that falls to pieces as soon as it is sifted. The further off the bonanza is, the more clouded and uncorroborated the accounts conceding it, the more allure it appears to possess. The origin of the rush is often shrouded in obscurity!"

Seymour was only just settling in as a 'new chum', on Dunedin's commercial conundrum, but his journalistic observations and endeavours had been honed to a fine art, based in the fields of California and Victoria. Many a man had lost their way to become deranged in the obsessional abyss of 'Midas madness', hence the appellation 'mad hatter', reduced to mere 'Hatter', by those in the trade.

After much heated discussion, Gilbert had left William and Uileen to hold the fort in Ballarat, the brothers were both worried for Uileen on her own, going to such barren terrain in New Zealand. They knew the fortunes of a gold town, the woman's reality of a lonely, harsh life, hands worn raw, bloody with the constant fight to mend, wash and dry clothes, the stress of uncertainty, and the continual dangers of Wills work.

Finally, it was agreed the young couple would stay, Gilbert and Manaia would run reconnaissance for the group, just to take some of the leg work out of the move.

It was a difficult parting for William and Gilbert, their shared sojourn had been scattered with heartaching, gut wrenching adversities, endless escapades, and a tremendous allowance of jollity. Neither would ever be the same, without the other in his orbit, they had grown up together following their yonder gold star, it had forged the blood ties of their youth, crafting an enduring trust of lifelong friendship.

As they watched the ship sail from Melbourne's Victoria Port dockside, Uileen's canary handkerchief waved limply in the prevailing breeze, everyone had hugged till it hurt, lips trembled, eyes teared up, the rift of parting seemed cavernous.

The raging emptiness of Ballarat, enveloped William and Uileen as they arrived back by coach, just in time for the 'Willy Willy' winds; whirly winds, dust demons that Bunjil explained "as a spirit who sometimes in madness stole souls".

Watching the convective circulations winding from the ground up, gathering gritty dirt, dust, and debris, twirling in spirals about the countryside, relocating the tailings of the diggings over the inhabitants, and their cups of tea, Uileen wondered how bad it would have really been to relocate to a new island.

Redmond Gunn had not been idle in their absence, the stockade had been a decidedly difficult downturn in his fortunes and career, not to mention his marriage, and the loss of a comely, cunning niece, his taste for revenge was hardly wetted.

News from Melbourne had reached his ears concerning the mutiny on the schooner, the Golden Spring, most of the mutineers had been rounded up, but two brothers had escaped the judicial net.

Gunn knew the reputation of Gilbert and William, they had been part of a conglomerate that found the Lucknow nugget, they had been at the stockade. Now they were on the list sent to him by Fred West, aka Black Douglas, bush ranger and police informer.

"Sergeant!", he yelled out his office window at the passing policeman.

"Yes sir", called the Sergeant.

"Track down these two diggers, clap 'em in irons, and take 'em to the police camp, they're mutineers, look smart about it, man"! shouted Sir Redmond Gunn.

"Very good sir" replied the sergeant, as he saluted, turned, and wheeled away.

Now where is that nephew of mine? Gunn asked himself, he's another pawn in this charade.

William was at the Bakery Hill diggings, when Ah Sam ran up to the site.

"Sir, Sir, many dangerous, many dangerous, the troops look for you."

"Why?" asked Will.

"You wanted for mutiny boat, brother too!" answered Ah Sam.

A sick, queasy feeling hit William in his gut, all the air seemed squeezed out of his diaphragm. Uileen, he thought, I must get to her, she must not be in this danger.

He downed his tools, took his leave of his mates, Roaring Jack Tucker, and Luigi, then he ran at full gallop back to town following his guide Ah Sam.

Stealthily, they approached the back of the union hotel, Ah Sam knew every alley way and escape route in the rookery, that was Ballarat town. Ah Sam had already ascertained that William's beloved wife was not in their room.

Dread clutched at Will's heart, as he felt the full trepidation of their predicament. He could not be seen on the streets, he could only abide forbearingly, hoping against hope his sweetheart would somehow be restored to his side, but it was a torment to think of the dark, future consequences.

Fortune finally smiled when Uileen, who had been shopping for supplies, passed the very alleyway that William was waiting in.

"Come my love", he called out quietly, "we must away!" He was so relieved; she was safely within his orbit once more.

"What has happened?" Uileen begged.

"We are not secure anymore, Sir Redmond Gunn has an order out against me and Gilly, thank God he's safely away in New Zealand. It's about the mutiny on the Golden Spring and the stockade, we have nae choice, ma darlin girl, but to flee whilst we can."

But where shall we go? Uileen enquired breathlessly.

"Och! we'll have to take a horse to Melbourne, try our luck to get on a fast ship, maybe a clipper, to wherever we can afford to go immediately, no questions asked" said Will. Ah Sam had managed to pry the window of their room open, without alerting suspicion, he returned with a small satchel of money, handing it to William, he said to the pair "You go now, or jail will be waiting for you."

William accepted his money pouch gratefully, he drew out a sovereign and handed it to Ah Sam, Ah Sam bowed but refused to take the money.

"If in your travels, you find a countryman of mine in bad circumstances, you help him, that is payment enough for me," Ah Sam said.

William and Uileen solemnly promised to help any man of the 'celestial sun' to his betterment whenever they could.

Clippers were notoriously fast, the 'Wooloomooloo' was faster than most, with two decks and a half poopdeck, three masts, forecastles, standing bowsprit and a magnificent, female figurehead representing romance.

'Wooloomooloo' had substantial yet elegant proportions, with green gold and white paintwork. She weighed 937 tons, carrying capacity of 1500 tons, three thousand, three hundred and sixty-three yards of sail, and made from mahogany, teak, iron bark and stringy bark.

The newspaper reported 'the 'Wooloomooloo' well might be expected to walk the waters, like a thing of life', as the chief officer put it to the passengers.

"She will stagger yer faith in steam".

I am up to here!

Erehwon, Aotearoa

Wife's lament

'I'm weary of Otago

I'm weary of snow

Let my man strike it rich

And then we will go!'

Savager than any emplacement they had ever known, the journey to Tuapeka river was made on foot, 'shanks pony'. It was made by way of the Dunstan Trail, with only their swags for comfortable living.

Gilly, Manaia and Rory trekked their way up the east bank of the mighty Mata-au river, then headed south to the Outram settlement, and across to the desolate Lammermoor Range.

They trudged up gullies, overlooking russet red tussock lands, vast chartreuse peat swamps, with alpine grasslands, rocky lands with scrubby natives, bonsaied by the biting, bitter winds, and scant topsoil. Barren and woodless, a brutal mountain realm with revengeful rivers, glacial winters, then midsummers sweltering with little shade respite.

They were living on a diet of flour and muddy tea, looking down into gorges where the sun never reached the floor, dressed in moleskin pants, blue shirts, 'wide awake' hats and dirt boots, the quintessential Aladdin's, searching for their lamps.

The incessant, chill rain had poured through everything, blankets, swags, jackets, coats, and hats. Gilly could feel it drenching down to his very bones, Rory's boots squelched as he walked, his sodden socks rubbing his feet raw, rivulets of raindrops ran like streaming tears down his face, he wiped his eyes to gain a vision of his passage. Manaia stoically put his head down and finding the rhythm of his forefathers in the mists of time, walking the paths of ancestors of bygone eras.

As the track widened down into a gulley, Manaia saw a rundown shanty, as he pointed the dwelling out to his companions, a male shape emerged through the deluge, and hovered about a stack of wood before retreating undercover once more. With further inspection the trio could see a thin stream of smoke issuing from a tin chimney.

"Ho, old timer, have ye a dry corner of ye crib for bedraggled travellers", Gilly called out, after a marked silence, a rusty sort of voice called back.

"What do ye want, there no gold ere."

"We only need shelter for the night sir", Gilly replied.

"Do you hav any tin?", asked the voice voraciously.

"We can pay", called Rory.

Slowly the ramshackle door creaked open on rustic hinges, the three seekers trooped into a dimly lit, wooden shack. Sitting, staring at them, sat a middle-aged man with a salt and pepper beard. As he stood up, it became clear he was a tall man, angular, straight spined, clothed in patched flannels, his green, grey eyes were wreathed in wrinkles, his cheeks creased and burnt red, by the wintery southern winds. In his long gaze, they saw that he had seen a lifetime of suns, raising, and setting over the hills, gullies, and mountaintops; he was indeed a product of this enduring landscape.

"Moonlight George, the only name I'll answer to, you fellas will have to git used to it, come in, if you're coming in!" Moonlight grouched.

A small fireplace in the corner with a few logs hissed and fissiled, as flames tried to burn their way around the wet wood, it smoked distractedly, in disgust of its fodder.

In the other corner a copper kettle stood, with funnels and bottles strewn around it, "Och that looks a lot like a grog still", said Gilly.

"What do you know of it? the hatter asked suspiciously.

"Well, we made a wee bit of o malt whiskey in the Isles ye Ken? replied Gilly.

"Did ye now?" said the stranger, and his rigid stance relaxed a bit, his sharp gaze sharpened.

"Would ye like a drop? he asked.

"If ye have some to share", chipped in Rory, licking his lips with anticipation.

"Och! ye swaggers are all the same, thirsty for anything gold," Moonlight cackled, as he poured out three mugs of corn whisky and saluted the moon.

"Ye know, this place afore the gold had twenty thousand sheep, and less than three hundred people, ye could breathe in a quiescence like that, there waz room to move, no one tripped over yer hut! I heared the words of the winds, the mountains breath, the rhythm of eternity beating beneath the granite ground". Moonlight murmured more to himself than his audience.

Gilly took out coin, handing to his host.

"We could get ye provisions if ye need some", he offered.

"Nae, I need naught but me own company, sides the dog will be back soon, I'll have him wanting his grub", Moonlight replied.

The friends stayed a few hours listening to the 'olden days' when times were tougher, but people easier, life was full of adventures then. They lived every day to the fullest for 'every tick of the clock was another small death'.

Moonlight was sure of that, and when the travellers took their leave, the old man stood enshrined in his doorway, a relic of all the yesterday's left on the mountainsides, looking for dreams.

'The Hatter'

When he dropped in at the shanty,

He was much the worse for wear,

For his clothes were torn and scanty,

And his boots were beyond repair.

ZV Webb

The Tuapeka river diggings, looked like a moonscape of pockmarked earth, with tents hugging the hillsides, like molluscs on the waterside boulders.

Gilly soon saw that on these riverfront claims, rations and fuel became imperative, it was the sustenance of survival, or perish.

Standing calf deep in the waters course, Gilbert felt his feet ache with the cold, glacial water saturating his boots through his socks, penetrating his skin; but the heavy gauge, tin pan he was aggressively agitating, became his only focus.

In his mind's eye it was his dish of fortuity, the way forward to freedom, a farm of his own, a family, a future as a freeman.

All that glitters,

Against the purge of poverty,

Life gambling in riverbeds,

Panning the aurelian gold.

Washing the grime, Of hunger and thirst,

Smelting the stench of penury,

Euphoria dredges the

Miner's heart of insecurity.

Sometimes they found nuggets, digging them out with a butcher's knife. The ounces of ore were accruing, the days of drizzle whited out the sunlight, a sallow sun could sometimes be seen, behind grimy clouds. When the rain hailed down the canyons, like frigid glass filings, the diggers retreated to their canvas cocoons.

Across the Tasman, old scores travelled, even underground.

As he resoundingly hit Victorian earth, Mangus Munson heard his ribs crack on the buttress of rock that he had landed on. The broken lower leg he sustained, as he fell from the heights of his position, was situated on a nasty angle, with bone poking through the top of his shin. He managed to drag himself, and crawl into the crevice of a cave, before shock, pain and concussion enveloped his consciousness.

When he came too, an Aboriginal woman was putting a poultice on his smashed tibia, it appeared that the bone had been realigned.

"You been in fever for week", said the woman, "my people came to the caverns for water and shelter and find you."

Mangus knew, now he would survive to reap his revenge on his archenemies.

He scrawled his face into a pained smile at his redeemer, took out some tobacco and a pipe as an offering for continued service; the gears of his machinations, whirling into maelstroms of malevolence.

After much cerebration, Mangus had set his course to attain his final goals. He limped his way back to Ballarat, with the aid of a stout staff, and the Aboriginal woman who had salvaged him.

Meeting his uncle almost proved Mangus's undoing. Ann, dead at the hand of Satan's hand maiden. If Redmond had not stopped him, he would have plunged into the street shooting, and stabbing any and all who had been associated with his nemesis.

"Go", commanded Sir Redmond, "leave this place, I will advance you your share of the takings. The army are looking for you and will do an inquiry into the stockade disaster, there are some who accuse you of firing too early and killing too recklessly. Take this payday and leave the country. Our association is at an end, I cannot shield you more, my own affairs are under scrutiny at the highest level. See if you can contact your old cronies in Tasmania, Fred West is lurking about somewhere between here and Hobart town" Gunn concluded.

"Och, I hav my own personal vengeance to wreak, I'll nae be needing yer encouragement, there's plenty o men to be bought for little enough reward.

My old mate Fred West will return my favour, it's just the thirst for retribution that I need to sate now".

That late evening, Mangus took a fine bay stallion from the army stables, and headed out for bush ranger territory, to gather miscreants for his private payback.

Signing up as first mate on an army supply brigantine, made one of Mangus's goals just that much closer, he had also found a lover with a temperament that matched his own. A 'lady lifer', Kitty, had been transported at sixteen for stealing money from her employer, she was quite the beauty and very willing to please.

The captain of the vessel appeared extremely desperate for crew, even when he discovered Mangus, drunkenly entertaining Kitty and her friend Lotty, they were only given a warning and kept onboard, however the captain had an uneasy feeling in the pit of his stomach, that his forbearance was going to reap rotten fruit of the most bitter kind.

In New Zealand, alpine 'barrenness businesses', orchestrated temporary commercial premises, men looking for quick profit mushroomed on the craggiest outcrops, miner's lives depended on these shanty suppliers.

Gilbert walked to the back of the tents, to see six men round a gin packing case, deeply engaged in an unlimited card game of loo.

He recognised some of the participants. Fred Turner, an officer in the lancers, Lucan Windsor, a wealthy wine merchant's son, Charles Wilson, and friend, two old Harrovians and a police constable.

No one looked up as Gilly approached, he stood for several minutes watching the total absorption of play, Lucan Windsor was the dealer. Gilbert knew that at half a crown loo, anyone could win or lose a hundred pounds in a few hours, and that there was scarcely any person who could be sure of having fair play in this competition.

Lucan prepared to shuffle; he had a dexterous turn of hand, quick as thought, he made a flip with the deck, the shuffle was then made to his advantage. Putting the cards down to the right of his hand, also denoted he had an accomplice in the match. This was a signal he had a good hand; the stakes were high; some land claims and nuggets were being bartered for chips.

Some pack horses had just arrived, Gilbert decided to help disperse the chicanery. In his pocket he still carried some firecrackers, that he had acquired from Master Po. He took several out and surreptitiously slid behind the store canvas, lighting the small explosives, he hurled them under the hoofs of the ponies. The terrified animals reared up, braying in fright, then turned wildly in every direction, running in panic through all camp obstacles, to escape the blasting gunpowder.

Tane saw the rolling hills of Port Chalmers as he bent down and swung his swag up onto his shoulders, a small, snuffling nose caught his hand, followed by a scratching, scrapping, jumping on his thigh.

"Alright Cobber, we're almost there, land ahoy, you little mutt", said Tane, he sighed in relaxed accord with his homecoming spirits, his sense of identity, he could rest with his people, his 'turangawaewae'.

Ballarat, Victoria seemed a distant phantasm, just a page torn out of a crazy foreign dream. His mates had wished him well, Rangi and Rua, he knew he'd see them soon, Aotearoa shores called its son's home. One by one, ancestors blew horns of 'haere mai', welcome, to their people.

Shemus and Alice had married, Shemus belonged to Bunjil's clan now and they were finding territory to survive on, away from the gold mining industries.

Shemus and Alice had come into town one Sunday, some weeks back to visit the diggings at Bakery Hill. Haggis had trotted along in his mongrel glory, chest expanded and looking quite pleased with the world.

Tane laughed to see Haggis rollover, sit up, and jump for pieces of mutton.

"That Haggis, said Alice, "he off with the bloody dingos again, we cannot find him, they go walk about, come back, Haggis has his own pack!"

"Wha do you mean? asked Tane.

"She means", said Shemus wryly, "Haggis is a father of eight dingo cross pups, we've got puppies coming out our ears at the camp, they get into everything, they've chewed up the toes of me best boots, and ripped the arms of my coat, with their sharp little teeth. Not to mention, eating us out of house and home, I'm going hunting just to feed the blighters!"

Tane, Rangi, and Rua split their sides with laughter at the comical vision of a camp load of out of control, small canines.

"Haggis is no help; he just lays under a mulga tree and looks proudly on at the chaos his progeny lays waste to." complained Shemus further.

"We give puppy present for Gilly", said Alice to Tane, knowing he was heading back to New Zealand in a couple of weeks.

"You want me to take one of these tearaways to Te Waipounamu?" asked Tane.

"Of course," brightened Alice, "you just carry around neck" she explained.

In the end Tane could see no way of arguing the toss, a puppy was going to be expatriated to his homeland, they were supposed to be man's best friend he thought.

He only hoped Gilbert saw it that way and would still be his friend when the puppy parcel arrived on his doorstep.

Chasing rainbows ends, Gilly, Manaia and Rory moved on to the rumour of the next rush. Westward from the Mata-au, towards the Old Man Range.

They climbed precipitous rock faces and bluffs. As they looked down, they saw the mountains towering over the hills surrounding them, and at the very pinnacle they could see the dotted, ivory calico, of the miner's canvas.

Gilbert could just make out figures, clinging to the roulette wheels of hope, panning for fortunes, in the duplicitous tide of the serpentine river.

No timber could be seen, skyline to skyline, the snow encrusted slopes of the mountains, known as the Remarkables, scintillated in the far distance.

Once the hefty coverlet of snow crystals thawed, the sleek ascents of the Alps were adorned in a coarse, mustard coloured tussock grass.

Each swagger carried his tent poles in his hand, using it as a staff, looking like a pilgrim, who performs his penance, carrying a heavy load upon his back, as he drags his weary way towards the distant, hallowed altar.

It took Tane a full week to track Manaia and Gilbert down on Old Man Range. By the time his found them, Cobber had become a few inches taller, his fur coat had thickened up in the cold environment. He had also learnt to stay rolled up in Tane's swag, when the weather took a turn for the worse.

Soggy snow was something Cobber was still getting his nose and head around, he had a perchance to come into the tent, and shake his wet furry body all over the human, trying to stay warm and dry in there, much to Tane's disgust!

Gilbert was astounded at the 'replica Haggis' that bounded up to him on the steep slopes of the mountainside, he reached down and swept the dog up in a large bear hug, remembering Haggis, Shemus, Alice, Bunjil, Black Billy, Will and all their companionship, through the long duration of living in Ballarat.

Cobber seemed to sense Gilly was his intended soulmate, as soon as he had been enveloped in Gilly's embrace, Cobber was ready to dig anything for Gilbert.

The two had an accord; Gilly told Cobber about Haggis's heroism, Cobber dug every word and life on the barren steppes seem more bearable for Gilbert, with a warm bodied idoliser like Cobber to cuddle up to.

Chapter 16

Queensland; 'Wooloomooloo'

"Ah, just look at that satin smooth sea, Madam, 'one day a pearl, the rest to the oyster shell'", captain O'Malley declared.

Uileen stood at the ships railing, looking into the aquatic serenity before her. Just half an hour before, she had witnessed the perpetual progress of the humpback whales, and mid most of them all, one resplendent, cowled phantasm, breaching like a pewter hummock.

"Aye, the ocean is a wondrous cauldron of marvellous mysteries", Uileen sighed. William was absent from her side, as he had signed articles, to work for the voyage, to preserve the savings they had, and secure a better berth for the two of them than steerage, better provisions too.

They were Brisbane bound, out of Melbourne, via Sydney, it was the only vessel available to take them immediately, accommodating them both and providing passage without too many queries.

"I turn to the sea whenever I discover myself cultivating a grim visage, I am but a temporal man, fixed in briny reveries', captain O'Malley imparted further, looking intently at her for a response.

Uileen began to feel uncomfortably, the captain's bent of mind seemed slightly on the melancholic, even solipsistic, perhaps due to all the time he had spent in marine environs, alone.

She murmured her regrets about being 'too long in the sun and salt wind', and beat a hasty retreat to her minute cabin, where she dragged an ivory comb through her long golden locks.

William knocked their secret knock, and entered at Uileens behest.

"Will, you're as wet as a flounder", Uileen chastised.

William took his reason for being in his arms, and laughed.

"Och, I've been a lot wetter than this, believe me my love" he returned.

"It's a queer ship Will, the captain appears to be a seafarer with a despondent demeanour", Uileen confided.

"Aye, he's an odd fish, the mate and the carpenter seem at odds, the cook said he would not trust the bosun to sail the ship, even if his name were Noah!" William said. "Och, I hope we are nae sailing with an ill tide", worried Uileen.

"We hae better be prepared for every wind that blows" cautioned Will.

"Get those hatch covers off you scabs!" yelled the second mate.

"I hae better return to the deck, before we get our marching orders" said William as he quick embraced his wife and kissed her soft dewy lips.

Uileen sighed, she felt somewhat castaway, here at the frontiers of humanity. She picked up her cloth reticule, shook it and thought wryly, 'a purse is but a rag, unless you have something in it.'

Break of day saw the Wooloomooloo in the grips of a massive squall, the breeze from previous days had hardened into a violent gale. The crew were hard pressed to strike the topsails when they were rent from the bolt ropes, the chief officer Newsom, with a tremendous tenacity kept the ship on course.

Uileen was in her cabin being shaken and battered about like a cork in a bottle, William was hoisting sails for all he was worth.

"Help", screamed a distant voice. Will looked up to see cabin boy, Billy Bronson, swept overboard on a kraken-like wave, its watery tentacles dragging him into the tempest. Will threw a lifebuoy, but the gigantic wall of breakers bore the small, floating circle away from Billy's futile attempts to swim for it.

The Wooloomooloo was just maintaining her course, carrying foresail, fore topsail, mainsail, and foretomain stay sail. The wind was blasting a quintessential hurricane, a fearsome sea was running. Surrounded in thick, dirty weather, the vessel was thrown above each wave.

Will checked on Uileen a few hours after the rigging was secured.

"How are ye my darling? he asked.

"Black and blue - but clinging on to hope that ye are safe my love" Uileen whispered, the maw of terror holding her voice in its claws.

"We're riding it out best we can, looks like a cyclone has found us, I must be away lovely, I love ye and I will return for ye as soon as I can", Will smiled encouragement, as he left for his duty, in a heavy raincoat and south wester.

On deck, Captain O' Malley heard from the crow's nest "land ho off the starboard bow", "Bring her about", he roared to the able seaman at the helm, all that day the gale blew southeast to east southeast, flying about in sudden gusts, heavy rain and foam assailed the ship, then night closed in.

William called the watch; sighting the Cape St George lighthouse astern, but the 'peas porridge' weather was dense right down to the waterline, and naught else could be perceived.

At eight o'clock, a terrible shattering, graunching, splintering sounded. Wooloomooloo had struck a reef. Captain O'Malley, his face as long as his first mate's arm, directing his crew, rushed forward, the ocean broke onto the deck, driving him against the spars, he cried out in pain as his ribs were cracked in their chest cavity, several crew slipped and slid to his side, half carrying him through the watery blizzard, down the stairs to his cabin.

Enormous seas swept the decks fore and aft and in the dead of the night, all hands retreated to their cabins; Will went down to comfort Uileen, her face as white as the snow of the Shetland winters, his demeanour was grave as they lay entwined in each other's arms, in the narrow wooden bunk, bracing themselves from the banging, crashing demolition of the swells.

Morning appeared in a rain-soaked monotony. William and Uileen went on deck, they could see with horror that they were only one hundred and fifty metres from shore, cut off from all communications by a tremendous surf, drowning out their cries.

By noon the mizzen mast was cut, the rope caught Andrew Parnell around the ankle and whipped him over the side, nothing could be done in the gargantuan thrall of the ocean's temper.

Despairing, the crew watched as the cargo of tallow, wine, cotton, whale oil, coconut oil and all manner of boxes, continuously washed out of the hold.

Captain O'Malley forced his way against the blustery blows, but his rib cage was afire, his strength ebbing, and he gave way to the immense pain of nature's wrath, retreating to his berth.

Suddenly, Uileen saw the bulkhead of the cabin floating away from the rest of the ship, "Will, look!" she cried.

Grimly, the whole crew witnessed their captain's slow demise; he tried to swim back to his vessel, but the violence of the seas obstructing him, carried him, finally unconscious, far away out to sea.

The rupturing timbers of the fast-diminishing hull, and the ceaseless roar of rolling surges, drained the faith of the survivors, half drowned by the constant lashings of downpours.

William and Uileen sat buttressed together, on the fast-diminishing hull, along with the rest of the half-drowned crew and passengers.

During the interminable darkness of that endless night, the cook succumbed to his destitution. Uileen spoke a few quick words of farewell over his body, as he was committed to the depths of the inferno that raged around them.

'The Sailors Prayer

Journey out to the ocean again young mariner,

For where else should a seafarer be?

But bestride the white horses, savouring the brine,

Out there, on God's celestial Seas.'

Morning dawned, the nascent rays of the rising sun spread over the desolate, marooned company, the sea appeared marginally more clement.

Two sailors elect to attempt to swim to the shore. William and the first officer secure a line to Gerald Nash, an American tar. The survivors watched in horror as he was defeated by the behemoth breakers.

William resolved to try next, hugging and kissing a tearful Uileen, he executed an exemplary dive, conserving his energy riding with the waves, breast-stroking in between the sets. By all miracles he reached the beach; as she saw Will safe on the distant sand bank, Uileen garnered her remaining strength and determination, and dived down into the billowing surf herself.

Growing up by the ocean, and learning to swim in the cold Atlantic, stood her in some stead for the arduous attempt, but the beacon of love that shone from William, was her Eddystone, that is what she swum for ;her guiding galaxy.

Finally, as she was almost exhausted beyond all recompense, Uileen felt William's arms close around her beating heart, supporting her harsh breaths; the fatigue of her feat overwhelming her.

Will swam with his wife safely ensconced in his embrace, as they negotiated the final few feet of the swells, they stumbled onto the sand and lay panting in prostration, waiting for some energy to return.

The chief officer, Robert Carter, resolved to try his chances with the waves, but he was drawn into trough after sucking trough, the tide pulling him under time and time again. Eventually he lay face down in the foaming crest of a wave plummeting toward the shore, unable to fight anymore, William and Uileen ran into the riffle, dragging the bedraggled, half asphyxiated seaman onto the seashore. Will rolled him onto his side and he spluttered, choking, and coughing on the salt water lodged in his lungs.

Uileen found bits brush to place over the saturated sailor, just to keep some warmth in his veins, meanwhile William determined the best course of action, to gain succour. Aboard the fast decomposing vessel, three other sailors were swept away on the catastrophic currents, the remaining men having to endure without food or water, and they were becoming desperate.

For three interminable days and nights the captain's dog, Hero, howled with the wind's veracity and his master's loss, his mournful cries mounting as the dreadful, dismal moments ticked by; in his precarious predicament, each cry brought him closer to his sacrificial fate.

The carnivorous nature of the existing subsisters came to the fore, Hero's howls were ended, the remaining wretches descended into a primal subsistence gaining sustenance from the dog's raw flesh, staving off starvation through the poor beast's sacrifice. Hero's blood being caught in a Sou' wester, and shared around the thirsting group, like the lamb of God, an expiatory gesture from man's best friend.

Kaya, a young Aboriginal boy, was watching the waterside from the hills above the bay, his keen eyes gleaned the ships plight, as it lay wrecked on its side, plundered by the tsunami seas.

Fast, he ran, as swiftly as his fleet feet could carry him, to the sheep station five miles from the inlet. By the time he arrived, the lad was wheezing with the exercise; Andrew Parnell owned the station.

"Boss, Boss, white fella ship on the reef, sinking fast," cried Kaya.

"Right'o Kaya, you stay here," Andrew ordered "I'll saddle up and ride down to the beach, see if there are survivors, bring me some blankets!" Andrew called to his housekeeper.

By the time he arrived, five people were huddled on the sand.

"Here, take these blankets and provisions, I'll start a fire," Andrew said.

William went to help with gathering firewood.

"Thank ye for coming to our rescue sir", he said.

"Call me Andy, young man", said Andrew "I'm going to set you up with a fire, then ride for help, it's flooding all down the coast, this cyclone is a four day curse, so send up some prayers, we are going to need them, how many on the wreck?" he asked.

"Twelve, I think", replied William.

Parnell climbed on his roan stallion and rode away over the sand dunes and into the gloaming distance, Will went back to his companions and Uileen.

"We have a champion, let us be grateful for that mercy", said Will. The pyre caught with the aid of dry kindling, the meagre heat, and supplies were a manna from heaven, as the hungry few waited for deliverance.

The paddle steamer ,Soteria, received the SOS for the Wooloomooloo. It was past midnight when the chug of its engines sounded off the side of the wreckage and a great, clamorous cheer arose from the stranded mariners.

The Soteria's Captain tried to send down a lifeboat, but the ocean's fury had not abated enough, and the blackness of the atmosphere blinded their attempts.

It was the ipomoea of the dawn, that elucidated the emancipation of the final twelve compatriots, who were left just cleaving to life, whilst five others were washed ashore, and were lying lifeless on it's silica.

The ocean and elements had wreaked their havoc, devouring some, delivering others, the pitiful few who survived, were loaded onto carts bound for Terara, New South Wales.

What happens when the citizens of an obscure, rural township, hear of a treasure trove of bounty, being disgorged onto a local cove?

In a community of three thousand, mainly farmers, cut off from civilisation by remoteness, a cornucopia of exotic wares, with no obvious owners, was too much of a temptation to resist.

Hundreds of enterprising souls made their way to the beach, the small guard group had no recourse in protecting the bounty, the denizens came with drays loaded up, ironmongery, drapery goods, groceries, and clothing.

The creek cut the beach in half, and every time the police attended to one side of the divide, the marauders moved to the other side, and continued their plundering.

Of course, with the hundreds of gallons of spirits, the ambience on the beach became a bacchanalia of frolicking, fighting, and fooling about, as the population became saturated in alcohol.

Every member of the congregation was snickered, sizzled, and squiffy, the underwriters had no thought to give permission to sell the goods, so the officers could only watch helplessly, as the miscreants imbibed freely.

Two months later, Moon brothers, Jeb, and young Henry, were seen semi-naked, walking into town after being stripped of two crimson shirts, a pair of twill trousers, and a great coat that they found in the bark of a tree. Before the magistrate, they admitted that the clothing could have been loot of the Wooloomooloo, and were both fined five shillings, with seven days in the lockup.

Walking back to town was indeed chilly, as the stolen property was handed back to the underwriters, a lot worse for the wear.

Mirrie lights beckoned, Peter was taking home the nonpareil of his life, a talisman that had steadied his steps, guided his actions, and led him to family. Grace: what more could a man ask for in his endeavours? Peter felt blessed with good fortune, without finding a single fleck of gold dust he had hit the mother-load, his eureka moment, love struck, as he boarded the ship in Lerwick to reclaim his sister and stop the privateering of the Norwegian navy supply lines.

As they drew nearer land, Grace cheered with glee; the emergence of boundless pelagic birds, shrieking and pirouetting in curlicue tracks, they accompanied the vessel, and at times alight on the yards and stays.

The Orkney Islands loomed in the mist, off the starboard bow of the Aurora, the coastline came into view, deeply indented by the ravages of the seas, biting into the soft, old, red sandstone which resting uneasily on beds of metamorphic rocks, grey gneiss, and granite. Delineated ancient topography, written by seismic upheavals, layer upon layer, set down many millenia before the Vikings rowed their long boats into Scapa flow Firth, a thousand years before Uileen and Peter sailed in their bow-prints.

Scapa Flow, one of the great, natural anchorages of the world, bay of the long isthmus, sheltered waters, a boon to ships of sail and steam.

Mainland, the largest island of the Orkney archipelago, came into focus. The 'heart of Neolithic Orkney'; mariners from many ages found safe harbour in this fertile, low-lying isle, built of old red sandstone, the Pomona of the Scottish islands.

Uileen and Peter arrived in Kirkwall, Mainland's largest town late in the evening, twixt a crescent moon and low hanging clouds, chill wind wound its way through their woollen tunics, reminding them of its arctic presence.

An immense minster, stood before them, cut from rust coloured iron ore, tons of holystone, the same soft sandstone, used for scrubbing decks of navy ships, started in 1137, three hundred years in the making; a monument to the bishops of Orkney before the reformation. It dominated the Kirkwall skyline; Peter knew that it was the secret meeting place he had been told about.

Grace stood on the preface of stunned bewilderment and fear, as two cloaked figures emerged from the rubescent shadows, of St Mangus Cathedral, she fell back, torn between fight and flight.

All at once, two cheekily familiar countenances, were beaming at their sister's disarray, "Angus, George, what on earth are ye 'toe rags' doing here?" Grace asked.

It was difficult to see the twins, all grown and manly, in a strange environment.

"Och, hark at her, nae even a hug for her favourite brother", said Angus.

"Aye, sister dear, ye have lost yer good breeding in the wilds, and lest ye forget, I am the favourite!" announced George.

Grace flew at bothof them, unsure whether to box their ears, or hug them till the morrow, she chose the latter course of action.

"Och! will ye nae leave a mon some oxygen woman"? gasped Angus as he tried to wrench his sister's arm from his neck.

"I see ye had the good sense to bring Lars with ye", said George, when all the hugging and tears were swept away with relieved familial laughter.

"Aye, that I did, not only that, but say hello to yer new brother", said Grace.

"I was afraid that something like this would happen, putting the two of ye together," said Angus, "yer too good looking for anyone else".

"Aye", agreed George, "we should be matchmakers, a change of profession from spy, I think brother, what does our new brother think?"

"I think you would be dangerous in both professions actually! At present, the Norwegian Navy and the Shetland Police Force need you as agents for them."

"Och, just when it was getting interesting", said George.

Hugs were renewed all round as Peter Lars Tordenskjold was welcomed to the family, the twins were pleased as punch, that they had been the ones who made the introductions. When she had quite regained herself, and the gravity of the situation, curiosity overtook all else.

"What...agents...spys? asked Grace.

"Aye, that's us", admitted Angus, "so many Shetlanders and Orcadians have been cleared off their crofts by Sir Redmond Gunn's factor, Charles Munson".

"We could not just stand by and watch the pillaging of our people's and their homes." said George.

"How could Sir Redmond afford the land to do that?" asked Peter.

"That is what the navy and the police want to know: where is the finance coming from for the land clearances and the pirating", Angus continued.

"Och", answered George, "Sir Redmond has been heavily investing in African slaves, and a sugar plantation in the Caribbean, Jamaica, the profits he gains selling the sugar harvest, using free slave labour and land, then making rum and selling it to the British navy. Then he has gone into acquiring the island crofts for mutton farming.

He's worked out that mutton is worth a lot more than people, so the crofters are evicted, the Munson men are the burners, who work as a gang to torch the home's thatched wooden roofs, and smash the stone walls, so disenfranchised crofters cannot return to them."

Redmond Gunn poisons the well of all the poor people that he has anything to do with, he's financing the pirate raids as well" added Angus.

"We thought as much!" said Peter "now we have proof of the connections between Redmond Gunn, his dirty business deals, and the Munson's, finally we can deal some justice."

"Och, we are rearing to go, so are the small cadre of men we have put together to clean out those viper Munson's," said Angus.

Grace was still looking puzzled and unhappy, "what is going to happen now?" she asked, having a fair idea.

"Now my dear, we fight the enemy, face to face, and drive them out. Redmond Gunn is being investigated as we speak, he has been laundering monies from the Victorian commissioner's accounts for some time. A certain Chinese gentleman was able to give us the details about that." said Peter.

"What of the monster who started all this?" asked George.

"Mangus has been vanquished from the army, for kidnapping and unbecoming behaviours in battle, even Sir Redmond could not save his career, he may have died on the rocks of the caverns, we know not, but he will no longer serve as lapdog to the tyrant." said Peter.

The quartet then talked of family matters for some long time, after the first pressing business was concluded, eventually, after Grace could bear to part with her brothers, they receded to the lodgings that had been prepared, so a good nights slept could fit them for the conflictual days ahead.

Edward 'Bludger' Baines had slipped out of Picton harbour New Zealand, almost unheeded, except for the careen of gulls that collared his brigantine the Jabberwock, as the old ship lumbered out, into Cook Straits heading up the east coast of the north island and into the Tasman Sea, bound for buccaneering. The Jabberwock was an ex- opium runner, that leaked like a cray pot and steered like a dray.

Edward drew in a breath, spiced with the aroma of tarred hemp, canvas, and cordage, after leaving Queenstown under a cloud, he had been relieved to escape terra-firma for the oceanic freedom of sail.

They were headed for Brisbane River, to intercept a screw steamer carrying a cargo of gold for London, Baines could not wait to purloin the golden prize, then make a run for the Solomon Islands to start 'Blackbirding' for the lucrative contract he had just signed with Samuel Browns.

Browns wanted cheap labour for his cotton and sugar plantations and labour in Queensland was neither cheap nor plentiful. For Baines, this vacuum was a vast opportunity, for it was ungoverned by law, moral or civil; to entice pacific people into contracts they could not read, to work unlimited hours in agricultural industries, far away from the waters of their people.

His compass was his own and he often said, "I am a free prince, and I have as much authority to make war on the whole world, as he who has a hundred sail of ships at sea, and an army of ten thousand men in the field."

A first mate of his, had once said Baines was "the most successful man and treasure stealer in the pacific", and on this voyage, 'Bludger Baines' aimed to prove it true.

Eight thousand ounces of gold, thirty thousand pounds, was too much temptation for any marauder; Bludger had read about the horde, being taken by steamer out of Brisbane from the Gympie goldfields, in mid Queensland.

No one heard the silent, muffled oars of two rowboats stealthily sculling alongside the steamer Foam, there was only a skeleton crew on board as the captain, first officer, and mates had gone ashore for supper with the councilmen, who had travelled up with them from Sydney.

With no real jetty, the vessel had had to tie up to a tree, the men were rowed to the riverbank, then had to embark onto the mudbank mooring.

Uileen had taken to wearing Billy, the cabin boy's clothing, left behind when the typhoon overtook them, they were much more comfortable than a crinoline skirt on a ship. Upon her husband's advice, she had bandaged round her breasts, to make her female attributes, less noticeable to starved seaman, with much regret she took a pair of shears to her luxurious locks, cutting the beauteous tresses short, until they curled around her ears; pulled on the blousy, stripped breeches and leggings , the old ragged, linen shirt and an old baggy canvas coat, a woollen cap completed her transformation from married lady to cabin lad.

Will was much impressed at his new look wife, Uileen was soon giggling and laughing, rolling around their bunk with her cavorting husband.

At two am, the stillness of night rippled across the riverine waters, lapping lavishly at the steamers hull.

Sinister malignity stirred William's sleep, he tossed, turned, and tossed again in the confines of their wooden cot; Uileen stroked his restless forehead with worried frown. Will awoke with a start.

"Och, I feel something's amiss", he whispered, "its unnatural quiet, I'm going topside to check."

"Aye," agreed Uileen, "I feel an ill wind too."

Before William had emerged onto the midship, a hard cosh crashed down upon his head, he crumpled down the ladder, before burly buccaneers dragged him back up to the deck.

Uileen stood aghast for a few moments, in the affront of the force of this attack. As she crouched, hidden beneath the ladder, she could see at least a score of hooded pirates, climbing effortlessly about the steamer searching for booty. The thieves were fortified to their back teeth, carrying machetes in their mouths, and cutlasses and pistols in their belts, deadly spectres, taciturn in their larceny. Uileen drew back as a brigand made his way down the steps towards her, hideaway. Too late, he had seen her move, she was unceremoniously dragged from the cache, a hood was placed over her head, before she too, was knocked senseless.

Hours later, the new cribbed crew were about to get a rude awakening from the corsairs.

Captain Baines was in a merry mood, his coffer swelled with wealth, but avaricious never sleeps, and he had big plans for a fast fleet in the future.

"Sprag, throw a bucket of seawater over these swabs, let's see what the tide washed up", demanded Captain Bludger Baines.

William, Uileen and several other seamen from the Foam, were doused in cold bilge water. The small pile of captive humanity, came to awareness with the sun blazing into their squinting sight, with painful alacrity.

"You're on the Jabberwock now scabs, I want you to pay close attention to the law on this ship! said captain Baines. He them marched over to the helmsman, Snodgrass, took hold of him by the scruff of the neck and the strap around his waist and hoisted him up skyward as high he could stretch, then suddenly pitched him on to the deck.

Everyone watching, heard the snap of Snodgrass's arm and ribs, as he lifted his face from the unyielding floor.

Bludger Baines smashed his fist into his nose.

"There, now that'll teach you to steer the course I give you next time", he shouted; "and as for you new scum, I am judge, jury and executioner on my ship, understand?"

He did not wait for a reply, Baines turned to his first mate and carpenter.

"Get these lubbers to work" he barked, as he went below to check his charts.

Uileen tugged her cap down further over her ears, she had had the foresight to smear some tar on her cheeks and hands, whilst in her hiding place on the steamer, now she only prayed it would be enough of a disguise to fool their captors.

"You there squib, can ye cook?" Asked the first mate, Clegg.

"Aye Sir, he can. He was the kitchen hand on the Foam, but he's mute," answered William quickly.

"Mute eh; well as long as he kin savvy what he's told, no lips all the better" said Clegg. Uileen breathed a small sigh of relief, as she was shoved ahead of the carpenter down to the forecastle, cooking; the one chore on board she could accomplish without shame.

"Bandits like these used Brigantines, because they're quick, manoeuvrable, and nimble in a raid," said Will, when he finally had a chance to see Uileen safely.

"That is how they got in and out of Brisbane River so fast. There are also six cannons; three on each side, two harpoons and three cannonball barrels on board, I think they mean to blackbird around the pacific islands," Will added.

"What can we do?" whispered Uileen worriedly, knowing she was not to speak aloud. "We need to keep our heads and lie low," replied William, "this sea dog is a bully and a murdering brute, he will not hesitate to take anything he wants by deadly force", Will continued.

There were only enough hammocks for the captain, the gunner and the first mate, and some of the lesser pirates, all the recently 'acquired sailors' slept on woven mats with only a blanket for covering, and a salt toughened pillow, they found a space anywhere on the deck. Will and Uileen snatched forty winks fully clothed, essential for Uileens position, she always kept one shoe on and one shoe off, as they seldom got more than four hours sleep at any one time.

Uileen was grateful for the perpetual cooking, grubbing, mending, and scrubbing which kept her from many interactions with her jailers. The forecastle was lit with fatty tallow candles, that smoked relentlessly. She felt she lived her days in a small dark cave, without much light or warmth, it was always damp and mouldy, the space was malodorous, with a filthy floor in constant need of cleaning. The oven was a portable wooden box lined with clay, but only on calm days could it be lit, it was hard tack in inclement weather.

The chickens that had been brought as live meat, made Uileen truly appreciate the saying 'henpecked', as they were in her charge, it was difficult to say which bird felt more caged her, or the chooks.

"Articles of piracy are expected from all swabs aboard this ship", Spragg the quartermaster announced, his red face, bulbous in the tropical sun, a hideous 'P', emblazoned into his forehead, the mark of a branded pirate.

"Ye will line up and make yer mark or the devil take ye", he continued.

"Och! I'll Nae put ma name to any parchment that makes me a criminal!" stated William.

"So, we have a sea scum who thinks he's high and mighty do we?" challenged Spragg. "Right, bosun Clegg, bring up the tallow candles", ordered Spragg.

At gun point, William was escorted to the centre of the deck, his hands tied behind his back, as he was forced to sit on the deck, Clegg then proceeded to hold his nose and prise open his mouth, then Spragg thrust one candle after the other down Wills throat. Uileen cringed when she heard what was happening, she knew the composition of the candles, they were rendered mutton fat, a bilious brew if ever there was one. She was at her wits end as to what to do, until she thought of her charges, the chooks.

Surreptitiously, she slipped over to the avian nemesis's cages, and cut the bonds to release them upon the deck. A squawking flurry of feathers and claws flew around the perimeter of the pirate's position.

"How did they get loose?" roared the captain.

Uileen and cutlass Cleg, plus half a dozen others, chased the chickens from stem to stern, William was forgotten in the flying fury of the bird verses pirate melee.

Somehow the remaining candles went overboard, some of the fowls were corralled, and Spragg had hit anything that moved with his knotted bully rope, bruising and bashing. William was put on continuous watch for thirty-six hours to change his tune.

To be caught sleeping on watch was a death penalty, every time he nodded forward his helpmate was there with a bitter fowl brew called coffee, so when that seemed ineffective, a barrel of cockroaches was collected, and William was forced to endure twenty-four hours of the crawling creatures, creeping all over him in the meagre confines of that dark hole.

Uileens face shone in his mind along with the phrase: 'this too shall pass.' Stoically, he took his punishments, it meant they were not focusing on his loved one, and he held his line, knowing there would have to be an escape from this purgatory of piracy soon.

"Land ho on the starboard bow", called Will, he stood on the crosstrees of the fore and mainmast. The ship glided through the entrance in a kaleidoscopic coral barrier reef, the natural breakwater of an island. Will hardly noticed the rich, turquoise waters within the lagoon, as he gazed enchanted by the verdant, emerald hills which arose almost abruptly from the shore.

"Righto, look lively now lads, get that rowboat in the water, we've gots some negotiating to do, quartermaster and second mate, ye row me to shore, you five men take the other rowboat and follow me", said Captain Baines "takes yer pistols with ye, for safe keeping!" he added.

The islanders of the atoll arrived on the beach, brimming with curiosity.

Captain Baines, a bland smile plastered on his countenance, called for the chief to attend him. Upon his arrival, Bludger launched into his best pigeon Melanesian, English, "Yes, suppose you let him some boy go along Queensland.

We buy him altogether, my word good fellow. Very good, you let him boy come, good fellow place, he no work along sugar, you savey, he work along bully-me- cow" lied Baines.

The chief answered quickly.

"No. No boy, no like go ship, too much work Queensland, no good".

The captain countered.

"Suppose you come by and by. Island man plenty trade, muskets, powder, plenty sulu, waist cloths."

Etotosis, the chief's son said.

"Me go, very good, small fellow, ship-a-ship, no like Queensland."

Baines could see the villagers pulling back from his discourse, with distrust and suspicion in their bright russet eyes.

"Very well, you come ship-a-ship trade, we no trade on beach", he cajoled.

The chief, his conjurer tattooist, and the conjurer's assistant spoke to the villagers, none of whom spoke English. William, who had been one of the five sailors in the second boat, saw the ordinary islanders were naked, but their hair was dressed in extraordinary styles, men and women sported long black braids, hanging down their backs, the chief and his son, proudly displayed hawk feathers in their coiffeurs, the females with buns slicked up and mounted on top of their heads, supporting beauteous flowers of vivid orange, yellow and reds.

The islanders for their part, began to crowd around the seamen, looking with the utmost amazement at these aliens, some of them went about feeling the texture and fabric of the strangers clothing.

The freebooters rowed back to the Jabberwock, Bludger Baines organised his henchmen.

"Soon as those natives get below, ye knows what to do!" he said.

Spragg, Cutlass Cleg, Snodgrass and six other trusted bandits listened attentively.

Canoes were approaching the ship, laden with supplies, yams, coconuts, kava, and gourds of all descriptions, along with shells made into all kinds of ornamentations. Captain Baines bade the villagers to come aboard, rope ladders were slung over the side to allow easy access.

"There is a feast in the hold, you likee," enticed Bludger, as he motioned towards the open hatchway.

Etotosis and his people marvelled at the incredible vessel, so large and spacious against their canoes. Their amazement grew at the rigging, and fittings. Timidly, they climbed aboard and went down the open hatchway, natural curiosity claimed them as they espied on trestles that exotic foods had been placed, bread, roast chicken, and potatoes. Baines and Spragg made sure every islander, male and the few females, had entered the hold before yelling out:

"Throw the hatch covers on and bolt it!" shouted the captain.

"No!" yelled Will; but in the howling confusion of the captives coming from the prison of the hold, he was all but drowned out.

Back on the shore, the chief and his medicine man could see no sign of his son or villagers, the eyeglass he had been gifted showed him an empty deck.

A sudden dread fell upon him as he realised, they had been duped.

"Quickly, quickly," he called to his remaining warriors, get the canoes, we rescue Etotosis and the others!".

The island warriors sprinted to launch their war canoes, from the Jabberwock, Snodgrass the lookout saw the war party approaching.

"Enemy off the port bow captain" he cried.

"Damn their eyes, they're sharp as a marlin" cursed Baines. "Man the cannons, get that powder monkey loading", he called.

"Aye, aye captain" replied Spragg.

Gunner Sugden and his mate pulled the forward cannon into place, the heavy brass barrel was positioned in a firing mount. Uileen, being the most dispensable, was the human simian selected to hand the gun powder, packed into a canvas bag out of the storage barrel. She wore no shoes and a linen garment that would not generate sparks. Her hands shook as she passed the calico ball. The gunners mate shoved the ball down the muzzle of the gun, and used the rammer to ram it home, a wad of cloth was then stuffed down and rammed tight. The cannon was elevated slightly at an angle; then Sugden the gunner, now had to consider the pitch, roll and yaw of the vessel as well as the wind, wave, and enemy movements.

When all was ready, he called "fire in the hold!"

After applying a burning taper fuse to the touch hole, the cannon leapt back, recoiling with the blast; heavy ropes keep it from going wildly loose on the deck, the cannonball and wadding shot out at the oncoming canoes. The ball blew a hole through the front canoe carrying the chief, and several islanders were blown to pieces and the sea rushed into the fragile boat.

The men in the canoes behind rushed in to rescue the survivors. William strained to see if the chief was still alive, but the smoke and sea spray limited his vision, and he could not tell from the bloodied bodies floating in the sea; the triangular grey fins emerging making the carnage all the more calamitous.

Meanwhile in the cargo brig, Etotosis was aware of his predicament and the peril they were in, they had no weapons and in the darkness of the hold, it made any escape almost amaurotic. The four women were wailing, and the dozen men were clubbing the hatch cover and walls, but not a crack could they discover in their internment. After some hours passed, slowly one by one, they sank into the lethargy of thraldom.

Staring at the slop he had to eat, Josiah Jones felt he had endured enough indignities on this ship to last him his entire lifetime, but it seemed he was to be subjected to many more to come.

After being 'Shanghai'd' whilst enjoying shore leave in Auckland New Zealand, in an dingy alley, jiggered from a little too much rum, and too many enticements by sultry maidens, Josiah had been clobbered and kidnapped. He had been serving as sea surgeon on the British naval vessel, Amazon, now his chances of being in blighty again were slim to nil, as the bosun Clegg, had said when he had come to his senses

"There be a pox above board, a plague between decks, Hell in the forecastle and the devil at the helm." Life was cheap and quick on a pirate ship!

Unwilling as he was; the inducement of sitting immovably bound, with fingers splayed, and lit fuses burning between them with the resulting excruciating agony, Josiah eventually agreed to comply with Bludger Baines, and act as a Pirate surgeon.

So far Josiah had pulled teeth, set bones, injected mercury for syphilis, and staunched a lot of bleeding wounds, when he was not attended to the wounded or sick, he was confined to a small storage compartment, 'to keep him out of the way', the captain had decreed.

Fearsomely durable hard tack was all that Uileen was allowed to feed the slaves, most of the black oak, salted beef was gone. Snodgrass had carved some of it into buttons for his jacket.

The hold cover was removed for Uileen to carry down the rations, but Spragg stood over the hole double armed with pistols.

"If any of you hostages got ideas of escape, a bullet was all they'd receive" he declared. The conjurer's assistant and Etotosis led their people incantating menacing spells, eyes shining with hatred even as their limbs were shackled, their hearts were not, and their mind's thoughts were their own.

Bludger Baines brought his captives from their confinement one by one, the crew lined up in two lines. At pistol point William was told to 'run', between the lines, as he complied, the sea rats pulled out sail needles, stabbing viciously at his torso as he passed them by. After twenty continuous minutes, Baines said to the island men

'Let's see how you do, with blooding and sweating", the terror of the torture was vividly displayed in the shadows of their eyes. Lamenting in their own language, the men bore the torment, dripping in blood, scratched, and torn to shreds they crumpled to the deck writhing in anguish.

When the crew had finished their entertainment, and thrown saltwater buckets over the abused bodies, the captain brought out contract of indenture for his prisoners. Although none of the captives could read, Uileen could see the papers were as follows:

I, Etotosis, native of Tanna in the Pacific Ocean, have this day agreed with Captain Baines to serve the Jabberwock in the capacity of his ships, or as a whaler either on board or on shore, or as a shepherd or other labourer in any part of the colony of Queensland- to make myself generally useful for the term of 5 years.

"No, no" objected Etotosis, standing proudly defiant, magniloquent in his uniquely mesomorphic design.

All at once Captain Baines whipped out his razor-sharp machete, violently dissevering both Etotosis' ears, with a scream of rage and excruciation the young man fell to his knees his hands holding his head, blood spurting through his fingers, down his arms and pooling on the wooden planks like a crimson tide pool.

Uileen wrung her heart out at the sight of Will, and the island men's sufferings, they needed a plan and they needed it now, she thought, as she vomited behind a chicken coop, what little she had eaten.

'Isle de Erehwon' was a densely forested island with conical volcanic mountains, accompanied by freshwater cascades running down larval escarpments. Once the crew forced their way through the tropical undergrowth, they ran to dive into crystal clear, aqueous silver pools. Fresh water, the staff of life in the tropical heat, replenishing the stores on the Jabberwock was imperative or no one would survive the harsh environment of sun, sea, and salt, especially not the enslaved, chained in the hold.

Uileen was sitting, assisting Josiah Jones in gathering several herbal plants for his medicinal pharmaceutical collection. Josiah had learnt by talking to Pacific Islanders whilst sailing in New Zealand about the healing properties of the island plant remedies, such as banana leaves and piripiri.

Snodgrass was drying gunpowder on a silver plate some feet away, he was easily distracted by a stinging bug or the possibility of missing out on grub, Snodgrass had temporarily deserted his post. The sun's rays upon the metal drying disc were exacerbating the heating, a glowing furnace was being created, suddenly a loud explosion rent the atmosphere! A shrill, unholy, scream stabbed a hole in the fabric of the serene oasis, the acrid smell of burnt flesh and gunpowder filled the air.

Uileen lay writhing in the grey smog. Josiah rushed to the injured young woman, a secret he had only just discerned in the light of the explosion, one which he knew must remain hidden, along with the opiates he carried. It was fortunate indeed for Uileen, that the rest of the seamen were otherwise engaged, and were not immediately able to discern the gender of the injured party.

Josiah staunched the bleeding from the hideous gash in Uileen's thigh. He the grabbed the piripiri leaves he had harvested and crushed them in his mouth, placed them in a banana leaf and bandaged the wound. These leaves were said to stop infections and tetanus. He then cut a staff for the injured limb and braced the leg against it.

Uileen's conscious climbed towards the light, until a perforating pain struck her mid brain, a dizzying array of blue lights flashed in front of her awareness and she passed out again.

The next time she swam up to the surface of cognisance, Uileen felt Will's presence at her side. She was in the cot of the sea surgeon, and her leg was competing with her head for being the most painful. Perspiration was pouring off her blasted body, Josiah clamped a cloth of cool water to her brow, and slid it down her face, before repeating with her chest and arms, Uileen threshed in the jaws of agony, gritting her teeth to save crying out.

Josiah looked at Will and called him out to the corridor.

"Look," he whispered, "I know your secret and I know you were taken, just as I was, and those poor miserable sods in the cargo bay. You trust me to join forces, you are a sailor?"

"Och, aye, we must escape ship intact, we canna take anymore o this kind of punishment, yon lassie is ma dearly loved wife!" said William. He had already realised the surgeon was no part of Baines' gang.

What had happened to Uileen made their situation untenable, critical action was necessary, but it would need more than two to take the ship anywhere other than a reef.

The medicine apprentice of the Tanna men had used his dried herbs to heal Etotosis, and his magic stones to curse Baines and his minions. The oracle Narumin stones, told of an edible black magic that would be their salvation.

Baines had organised the men to haul one of the young pacific women away, Etotosis and his warriors fought and struggled to release themselves from the manacles that held them fast, the cowardly bonds of the oppressors.

As they disparately continued the futile attempts to free themselves, Bludger Baines defiled the poor young maiden; despair dredged it's way around the as hold, taking Hell to a new level, they could hear Tomeka's piteous wailing, it eviscerated their spirits, all the Tanna men's thoughts were on vengeance!

Josiah knew a small amount of pacific pidgin English from his naval experiences with the varying island peoples, he hoped he knew enough to savvy with the headman of this group.

Captain Baines had given permission for the captives to be examined, to ascertain health, and therefore value as a cargo, Josiah had been ordered to carry out the examinations in the hold.

In the diffuse light of lanterns, Josiah found himself encircled by a group of very muscular pacific individuals, who were extremely enraged at their imprisonment and treatment.

"I come no war, I no like captain ship, I prisoner, no good, same you , no good" said Josiah.

Etotosis looked at Josiah.

"No like go ship?" he asked suspiciously.

Josiah held up his hands "I medicine man, no pirate!" he said.

"What you want?" asked Etotsis.

"Escape!" answered Josiah.

Tepuna threw his stones to the floor and shouted something in his native tongue, was it a curse a blessing or an omen of the future, Josiah wondered.

The conversation was inordinately difficult; the traumatised Tannaese were distrustful and distant, Josiah had taken some bread and beef for them, and tried to be patient with the situation. He checked the physical condition of some, as best he could, they were suffering the bloody flux, amoebic dysentery, that often accompanied shipboard degradation.

Tepuna told Josiah of a 'howling rock' on Tanna, where the mothers of sons and husbands go to mourn their kidnapped kin, their cries of grief mingling with the winds and waves, forever haunting the archipelago.

Will tried to be as close to Uileen as possible in her sufferings, he poured his heart into her as she poured her heart into him, a mutual resuscitation of souls. Sometimes he would sit and tell her tales in the night, in other daytime dalliances he softly sang the keening lullabies of his childhood.

Sleep now, was just a distant memory for Will, as he, Josiah, the chief's son Etotosis and the conjurer's apprentice, and medicine man, Tepuna were busy weaving a net of their own.

After a skirmish with yet another set of islanders, in the hopes of more human plunder, Bludger Baines had finally caught a machete across the mouth, which had laid his teeth bare.

"Arh, yer stitching is array, ye 'cross eyed sawbones', can't ye do better than this?" Baines bleated.

Josiah had had more than enough berating by this sulking bully, in one stroke of his scalpel, he broke open the stitches.

"Sew up yer chops yerself and be dammed!" he exclaimed.

Bludger blustered, and bleated about this uncavalier turn of events, but Josiah held his ground, the captain knew he could not maim, or kill his sawbones, the most valuable man aboard except the gunner, the scar zigzagged across his face, giving him a grotesque grin to gift upon the company.

The sonorous sounds of a squealing pig were not to be ignored; Josiah for one had noted the acquisition of this porker with great interest. Spragg had bargained it off some islanders for some blankets and a musket and the crew were almost merry at the thought of fresh meat on the menu.

Uileen was back cooking with only a limp to show for her ordeal, her leg mending miraculously, with the herbal remedies Josiah had acquired from the pacific locals.

The 'cackle fruit', or eggs, from the chickens, had been on the wane and Captain Baines and the others had been exceptionally irritable about the short mundane rations, meagre as they were.

The fire box had been carried up to the deck to barbecue the pig, Uileen, and Josiah had discussed in detail a menu for the feast.

On a balmy evening, the porcine party was well underway, with grog being liberally distributed. A stew had been concocted from pork, yams, coconuts, taro and banana, inculcated with herbs and spices kept in the stores.

A sailor's jig was underway, accompanied by the discordant notes of an ancient violin, and a horn pipe, one of the pirates sang, then the rest joined in.

'A pirate's life is ever at sea
He follows the winds of his destiny
Sing high for Jack Tar, sing low for heave ho,
The devil has his seaman...
Dressed in blue and black
They ride the waves to hell they do,
And they never sail back.
Sing high for Davey Jones, sing low for dead men's Bones.
A pirate's life is ever at sea
He follows the winds of his destiny.'

Spragg gave out the pork stew, followed up with damper of flour and water bread, it was the first meat meal the raiders had enjoyed for some time.

Uileen and William were busy obtaining an escape for Etotosis, Tepuna, and the active villagers.

Captain Baines watched his men eating their fill, but his hackles were up, and his eyes narrowed, he felt unease in his waters.

"Where's that 'Scots rebel' and the boy who follows him?" he questioned.

No one had seen William for some time.

"I'll find him and his toe rag" roared Cleg, but as he got up from his meal he felt his head spin, he staggered on his feet, his breathing laboured.

"I, I need a drink" he said weakly. Other men around him began to experience headaches, some vomited onto the deck, or over the side, others had muscle tremors and cramps.

"I'm sick captain!" cried Sugden, as he keeled over breathing his last.

Baines looked aghast at his brigands, as one after the other they fell down in apparent death throws.

"Jones, where is surgeon Jones", he yelled.

Josiah made his way over the fallen bodies of sea thieves, towards the captain, who himself began to sway, woozily.

"What is happening, Jones? My mind is flapping like an undertaker's blind."

"Yes sir, that is to be expected, but it will cease in about ten minutes", Josiah explained. "What is this damned affliction Jones?" asked Bludger Baines after vomiting over himself.

Josiah stood his ground, watching as his nemesis folded in on himself with stomach pains, whilst loosing bowel control, to the power of the prussic acid that had been administered, colourless and odourless, it introduced itself with ease into the hot liquid cassoulet.

Down in the hold, the iron shackles had been removed, Etotosis, Tepuna, and companions roared with relief at the taste of freedom. They rushed up the ladder to face the sea dogs that had kept them enslaved. As they emerged from the abyss of the cargo hold, a 'pacific tide' of sinews and strength, the crew were in the final clutches of the poison's deprivations.

The islanders watched in astonishment, as their enemies dissolved into death in front of them, their ordeal at the hands of this madman was over.

William, Josiah, and Uileen stood with their newly acquired allies, trying to make sense of the sailing charts that Baines had kept in his chest.

"We must try to make for Cairns" said Will, "I think it is the closest land."

"No! We go home to Tanna, 'the land'", said Etotosis.

"I'm not sure I can navigate the distance", said Will, "it's the reefs in these waters, they are the devil's teeth for shipping."

"Aye, they are that" agreed Josiah.

"We go home now, I find the stars", Etotosis said, and he showed William the sun's trajectory from the orient to the occident.

Uileen looked meaningfully at William, they needed to find Vanuatu to return the stolen people.

"Yes", agreed Will, "you belong to your island not to white man's greed."

The Tanna people proved to be adept sailors on the brigantine, they were much more aware of the hidden dangers under their ocean currents. They knew of the swells and strong winds that could drive the ship on to coral canines.

As they voyaged into the crystal oceanic pacific, Tepuna undertook to teach Uileen herbal spells, and growing stone magic. The agricultural stones were placed amongst the crops of the Tanna gardens to help them grow, he also told her of the twin fortune to be germinated on her journey.

As they travelled, Etotosis told tales of Tanna; he regaled his audience in his pacific pigeon speech:

"Many die on Tanna from white man's disease coming" said Etotosis.

"It is much to be lamented that the voyages of Europeans could not be performed without being fatal to the nations whom they visited," said Josiah.

Finally, true to his word, Etotosis, the navigator and his people brought the Jabberwock, renamed the 'Kapiel' or magic stone, into the safe harbour of Tanna's Sulphur Bay.

Their welcome was a joyous one, the villagers ran into the bay as the returning survivors surfed the waves on the jollyboats. Everybody was grabbed and kissed in peaceful effusion, presents of bananas and other fruits were brought forward, and Uileen kissed all the small children, much to their delight.

That night, the beach was lit by many fires, and resonated to the boisterous sounds of chants horns, drums, and dancing. The coastal clan, had by sovereign rite, prepared a sea turtle, a Yao.

Only they, had the mystical stones to permit the capture of the turtles, in the caves where they sporadically laid their eggs, Tepuna explained:

"Our kastom has been here like the banyan tree, since the world broke open, it was here at the start."

By kastom, the oldest man was given the turtle's skull to eat in secret, to gain its supernatural abilities and perspicacity, absorbing the venerated totems sagacity.

The body of the turtle was divided five ways, which coincided with the paths of affiliation, Tepuna elucidated "that turtle blood was shared only with brothers who lived on the same enclave."

It was a supreme honour to be included in this sacrosanct ritual, William, Josiah, and Uileen knew, that the Europeans who had come before them had only given offence and spread afflictions.

Will was stunned on the universality of thaumaturgic stones; the Tanna islanders, talismanic stones were their foundation for kastom, Gilbert's lodestone from their island with its magnetic qualities, made its home in their hearts, the green stone, Pounamu, of New Zealand were the spiritual ancestors of the Maori, gold, the nuggets found in amongst rocks, produced the fire within prospectors, to search for the freedom to buy land. Cairns of rock were land marks, way posts, milestones and beacons for the weary and the lost, a monument for eternity to mark the passing of people in the past, the present and the future.

It had been several weeks, since they had at last accomplished the voyage back to Tanna, the villagers were overjoyed at the return of their loved ones, and their chief and apprentice medicine man, conjurer Tepuna.

Etotosis' father had been killed in the bloodshed of the kidnapping, as he valiantly tried to save his son and his people, the conjurer had also been wounded, but survived. Tepuna would be learning from his mentor for some time to come, until he took his place as medicine man, conjurer for the village, but somehow Uileen felt sure when the time came, Tepuna would be a great conjurer.

On the balmy pacific afternoon William, Uileen, and Josiah were taken by Etotosis in a canoe to the larger Vanuatuan island of Espiritu Santo, and were picked up by a merchant ship, the Mermaid, bound for Russell in the Bay of Islands, New Zealand.

In return for the ship, the Kapiel, Magic stone; the people of Tanna gave many gifts of mother of pearl and clay pots and carved wooden containers to the three who had returned with their loved ones and the bounty of sail.

"Land ho", came from the lookout.

"Where away?" called the captain lustily as he was brought his spy glass.

The moment the Mermaid arrived in harbour, at Kororareku Bay, large groups of Maori rushed to greet it, swimming out to gain access, climbing onto the ship.

Captain Johnson was not amused by being overrun by the local tribe.

"We are at the frontier of chaos!" he lamented, as pandemonium broke out, and in the ensuing melee, Uileen lost several items of clothing, some clay pots, a hair comb and a parasol.

"Every visitor, off my ship!" cried the captain, as he saw items disappearing with the invaders.

"First mate Hanley, will you remove these tourists" Captain Johnson requested.

Uileen felt the local's inquisitiveness was overwhelming, there was also a pervading hostile regard from the Maori men, and some whalers, of the ship, the captain, and the crew.

Josiah traded some of the Vanuatan carved wooden figures, with the Maori and old sea dogs who lived on the station. They told a sorry tale, which half explained the hypervigilance. Some weeks before their arrival, a brigantine called the Aphrodite, had called into the North Cape, some miles up the coast from Kororareka, the vessel had been commandeered by convicts out of Hobart, Tasmania.

It was a supply packet, carrying stores for the garrisons of Port Arthur and Hobart town, it had plenty of rum, wine, tea, flour, grain, and salt pork.

The filibusters were an ex -convict, first mate, an army deserter, Mangus Munson, a big truculent looking man, who knew how to use a Bowie knife.

Of that man, a whaler said, "charcoal would have left a white mark on his character."

The second bandit was Walter Levy, the pilot was an ex-convict, he had somehow steered the Tasman Sea to find Aotearoan shores.

They brought with them Dewi, an earless Taiwanese cook, and two female convicts, Kitty Lawson, a middle-sized woman with fresh complexion, much inclined to smile as her teeth were an attractive white. She spoke with a hoarse voice; her benefactor appeared to be Munson. He called her 'his queen of the cannibals.' She danced drunkenly around the men with a bucket on her head, lewdly lifting her skirts.

The other convict woman was Lotta Smeaton, a very corpulent figure of a female, with a full face, and thick lips, she was carrying her infant child Lizzy. Lotta was a pirate's bride they boasted, but no one knew which pirate, not even Lotta herself!

Dewi played the horn to accompany the musical exhibition Kitty provided. Armed with pistols, cutlasses, and a small brass cannon, fourteen brigands overthrew the Aphrodite's crew, putting them into the jolly boat or over the side, at last the ship put hard up, then headed out to open sea.

By the time they had made North Cape, the small convict crew were well under the yard arm, on rum and high spirits.

The Maori of the area had come down to barter with the Brigantine, but Munson and company had other plans, and abducted the chief's daughter, after killing three warriors and sailing away without paying for goods. The Maori were on the hunt for revenge, Utu, as they called it. Every ship was searched for the missing Maori maiden, Josiah had the answer to the mystery of being overhauled on the way in.

While Josiah was finding out about the vice, and general lawlessness of the port, one of the sailors, James Roper, lost his hat overboard. Will tried to stop him, but Jim immediately plunged over to retrieve it. Instantly he was seized by a shark, which Will could see had taken his head off, then it proceeded to take his left arm.

The Maori had already seen the shark and had left the waters, except for the few still talking to Josiah, all could see the fruitlessness of trying to rescue the unfortunate midshipman.

After witnessing the horrific incident, Uileen felt her introduction to Aotearoa was fraught with dangerous omens; the queasiness that she had been feeling for several months culminating once again, by losing her morning's porridge over the side.

The ship eventually docked and after everyone had been evacuated, the crew began unloading.

The wheaten, sandy beach girded the bay like a horseshoe, bush graced the hillsides down to the fringes of the sand. A small, white, sacrosanct building turned out to be Christ's church, delineating the missionary's stamp on the burgeoning society of Maori, whalers, convicts, adventurers, and sailors from every point of the compass.

The captain was due to marry a local lady, in the alabaster sanctuary of the Kirk in the morning, William and Uileen would have preferred to stay on board ship, however, being asked to act as witnesses at the wedding, they agreed to stay on shore for the night.

Chapter 17

To seek the calm beyond,
To know where we are going,
We need to know first-
What happened and why.

The New Zealand Company representative, Crispin Montague, was a tall, thin, round shouldered, twenty something toff, with dirty blond hair, and distant, ghostly grey eyes. He had become more and more desperate and aggressive, to keep up the supply of land for British investors and settlers in the region. He was one of the spoiled offspring, of wealthy English gentry who had scorned working for the family estate.

Before his ignominious ejection from British hearth and home, his father had stated: "Crispin, I would have done with you! You sir are a reckless reprobate, good for nothing, be gone, for you are no son of mine!"

Crispin felt a tad, miffed by his progenitor's lack of fortitude in the face of his failing fortunes, however he soon cheered himself up by borrowing a large sum of money using his father's name, drumming up credit in the city.

Catching the first steamer to the Antipodes was a gamble, but his luck could not be much worse and his connections to school chums in the New Zealand Company were about to be reconnected.

Stepping off the gangplank in windy, wet, Wellington harbour, a dishevelled Crispin made a beeline for the NZ land offices; time to cash in his chips and set up in a growing business.

The wooden facade of Wellington city plied the westerly wind, with a smoky haze that hung like a pall, over the houses planted about the high, hovering hills, forming an amphitheatre containing its citizens.

After hailing a Hanson cab to the offices of his new employers, Crispin went in search of the kind of villain he needed, to substantiate his investment in his new endeavours of land acquisitions. Especially the rich, reliable sort, that could be easily obtained by guile and deception.

"Can you do anything that looks official for the natives?", Crispin asked a shifty, small, weasel featured man in a peaked cap called Glum, who stood in front of plates used in printing.

"Have you official New Zealand Company paper?" Sherman Glum enquired crafty, in his conversation.

"Of course, of course man, I'm no amateur to this kind of toss!" affirmed Crispin.

"You'll have your documents for a price, it will cost you dear!" Glum stated wolfishly. "Pish! If we succeed, there will be plenty of pounds in your purse man, you needn't worry about that!" Crispin scoffed.

The two men greedily rubbed their smutty paws rapaciously, and got to work, Crispin drummed up interest in a valley, he had been told about on the boat near Nelson, it was a good grazing, and agricultural property, and a lot of colonials were looking for such real estate and land grabs had been on the rise in the northern areas of Te Waipounaumu.

In Queenstown, Manaia met with his cousins Tamatea, and Hinemoa, from the Nelson, the Golden Bay tribe, Ngati Toa.

"Our tipuna's lands, our great possession has been declining, more and more British settlers arrive, they invade, and our territory is stolen, our chiefs have no mana in the white man's eyes. This man, Montague, seeks to trick settlers and Maori alike, his greed is like a taniwha taking over our country! Come with us to defeat our enemy, the New Zealand Company, and the devil that does their dirty work." cried Hinemoa.

Manaia could not bear to see the wretched grief of these once proud warriors, saying

"I will accompany you to speak with the chiefs, Te Whakaiti and Manaakita, this theft of our land is bad, for when the feast is over, we will be but bones drying to dust, devoured by their acquisitiveness."

In the Wairau valley, the land was fertile and rich, fed by the Wairau River, the Ngati Toa tribe had been cultivating the area for many years, they had their Pa, fortified village, and their burial grounds in the verdant, abundant plains.

By the time Manaia arrived at Tuamarina, back in the north of Te Waipounamu, he was just in time for an important hui, meeting, of the tribal elders.

"This is a creeping European disease, this land creeping, when they buy take land, we no longer belong, we are aliens in our birth-right!" warned Te Atama.

"Would they sell their England to strangers from across the seas? Would they live under the yoke of estrangement from the lands of their forefathers?" demanded Te Rawiri. "See, the surveyors have put huts on our land, they say it has been sold to the New Zealand Company, we are to disperse from our homes like the driftwood on our shores."

"Never"! shouted the Ngāti Toa tribe, as one voice, determined to make a stand. A warrior ran forth with a flaming torch, setting fire to the survey pegs and surveyors' tents.

The smoke cloud of battle hung over the valley, as Manaia and his kin got ready for the trouble sure to follow their courageous stand.

The surveyors had been standing by, watching with growing concern, but Manaia and Hinemoa had removed their belongings.

Te Rawiri ordered a waka to take the surveyors and their gear down river, to a southern Pa at the river mouth, the warriors showed no anger at the government workers.

Retribution from the settler leadership was swift in coming. Crispin Montague was the leading protagonist, complaining bitterly in the Nelson Club, to the powers that be about the native rebellion. He had been conniving, to turn Pākehā fear of the Maori aggression into a full blown, military conflict.

Finally, gathered together, was a posse of forty-seven ordinary citizens, press ganged into soldiers and special constables, and along with Crispin and Sherman Glum, they crossed the Tuamarina stream, using a knotted titoki tree tied up their canoes.

The militia lined up in front of the Maori chiefs, Rangatira, with their rifles at their shoulders aimed at the speaker's heads, whilst Crispin, tried to order the handcuffs be placed on the lead chief.

"Have I stolen a single nail, that you should come and imprison me? Have I injured a single European, or touched anything in his tent, although pitched upon lands that you are plundering me of? You, and your own people, are the robbers and not me, go and manacle them, I will not go with you!" Te Rangihaeata cried.

Suddenly a shot rang out from the rank of unnerved militia, and a woman's scream filled the anger strewn air; Hinemoa clasped at her breast and sank to the ground dead. "Patua! Kia ngaro me to puehu pina aua e te liau!" cried Te Raupo as he watched his daughter breathe no more.

("Kill them, that they disappear as the dust that is known by the wind.")

Manaia, horrified by his countrywoman's demise, joined his countrymen in their reprisals, behind a flax bush he wielded his musket, shooting two soldiers as they stood. Gunpowder's grey smoke fell over Manaia's vision, the acrid smell invaded his nostrils, the valleys peace rang with gunfire, more men fell, until only six of the pakeha survived. Several Maori warriors had also succumbed to the lead balls of greed that the soldiers had lobbed, no man walked away unscathed that day.

The treacherous Crispin Montague, with his accomplice Sherman Gunn, left their lives on that field of battle, that they had orchestrated; Maori, the rightful owners, recording justice in their own way.

The forces of larceny on the West Coast also were gathering in tight, rapacious groups. When the New Year began, Velvet Ned and Tom Noon, his right-hand man, stood in the Hokitika Arms Hotel, a favourite waterhole of the erstwhile thieves.

At that moment, they were in full view, but unrecognised in this new country, and reminiscing.

"Munson was one smart gent for busting us out of that prison hulk, in Melbourne port", crowed Noon.

"That he was, right enough," agreed Ned. "It reminds me of the days, we had the coppers on the run, I reckon we gots the same chances ere, if we play our cards sharp! Let's nobble the silly buggers who gamble with digging, target thems that are loaded with loot, make a cert deposit in our own. pockets."

"Cor, its just info we need on the 'hatters' to holdup", said Noon.

"Lewy can provide us with that, he's bin buying bullion, up and down the coast, I've worked this bunco with him before, in Dunedin. They got me that time though, bang to rights, cause I be working on me own without im. Three and half years, hard labour, huh! Scurvy knaves! then thirty-six bloody lashes for trying to make an escape, well, not again, I means to avenge those stripes in coppers lives, see if I don't!" Ned vowed.

"Aye" agreed Noon grimly.

Ned had started to form an association, from old and trusted men, the 'Bounty-man' gang; they had co-opted three others. So far, they had just begun to terrorise the so called "lucky lads", lone prospectors, whose small fortunes had been made fossicking the newly found fields. They had already stolen two pistols, from the Hokitika police camp armoury, a bank hold up was on the horizon.

Tom knew one last associate was expected, he had been making his way south after his last caper; it was a personal mission and they would meet up soon enough, in the meantime, the law was scarce, and the pickings easy. Soon they would be on their way to Clyde, where, as Ned told it

"The banks were entirely at the mercy of any marauders who wanted to enter them." "I'm off to make sure we have a soft landing after we appropriate the loot", Ned mumbled; he wanted a few hours to reacquaint himself with his new lady love, Maude, a handy helper when an enterprising man needed a place to lie low, and a convenient hiding place for purloined possessions.

Maude Mendelevium knew women's work could be a shabby affair, housekeeping from dawn to dusk, with no light in the drudge-filled days. She had left one husband at the altar, somewhere in London Town, carefully remembering to pawn the ruby ring he had just brought her, choosing to attach her wagon to a wandering star, and gain passage to southern climbs without another 'husband' to start shifting her own affairs, that's what she was about, and where better to do that, than a world away, where no one knows who you really are, or what you are, unless you have a mind to say. But reinvention was the name of the game, time to 'borrow' from others for the betterment of self, Maude liked to think. She also thought a real lady had brains!

As the mother of five 'daughters', 'acquired' from the industrial school in Dunedin, it was with her newly found family that she set about garnering the wherewithal to run the 'Diggers Arms' Hotel.

The girls became very proficient at procuring pocketbooks, silk handkerchiefs, purses, and fob watches, one of them, Jenny had quite the fortune to find, was filled with gold dust from the carpets she was cleaning.

Maude worked alongside her recalcitrant brother Clarence, who had been wandering the waves, from the Barbary Coast to the Bay of Bengal, and at last feeling enough time had elapsed since his last misfortune; a mutinous sinking off the Melbourne coast, and thence to find a steamer to the latest fields of gold.

The siblings were setting up a clandestine receiving business, that they hoped would set them up for life. Clarence often spent evenings in the bar of the Diggers Arms, listening to the miner's tales, seeing the fortunes won and lost, his ear to the ground for another Aurelian rush. So, he was unsurprised when two villains came into the tavern, or to see Velvet Ned saunter upstairs after his sister. Here's a chance, he thought, we may be able to double our share out of this one and all! His motto was always 'It is better to do evil than do nothing at all!'

Maude was only too glad to entertain her swain; Ned was from the old country; he knew how to show a lady a good time and to pay for it too. He also had plans for enriching her coffers considerably.

"We just need a good hidey-hole Maudy" said Ned, "somewhere the coppers wouldn't think of."

"I have a place Neddy, but it will cost you, I have a lot at stake, if I'm nabbed."

"Don't worry my deary, I'll not leave you broke or under done, this is a big job, and we should all come out of it with 'new bib and tucker' to spare. We hav a couple of insiders on the case!"

Dunstan bank at midnight, on a Sunday, was really just two strong boxes kept in a gaol cell locked up. The gold escort had delivered two parcels of notes, and two bags of gold. Both crooks had donned disguises, a false moustache for Tom, and a long straggly beard for Ned, before the escapade, just in case some virtuous sleepwalker happened upon them.

Noon crept quietly up to the outer door of the building, he took out the key that he had attained for a tidy sum and opened the door silently. Ned examined the padlock bolt, then using some safe cracking keys, he drew the screws from the lock. Stealthily, they carried one, then the other box, out to the horses they had brought, the boxes were heavy, containing bullion and notes. A light went on in the shop across the street, someone seemed to be looking out the window.

"Quick! We may have been spotted!" whispered Ned.

Now Tom had bought with him, his horse 'Speargrass,' an old bay, who had been ridden over the Dunstan Range and back many times, and the poor horse had already staggered a bit at his load. Ned loaded his gelding and started off, however Speargrass was having some difficulty keeping up, Tom had to get off him to lighten the load.

"We can't stay here; it will be daylight soon" Ned said.

"This damn nag won't move any faster" complained Tom.

"Yer should hav brought a new one, on this kind of job, the troopers will be on yer, if yer don't get a move on." Ned admonished.

Tom pulled at his nag with all his might, but Speargrass had found a stubborn streak that rivalled his cousin mules, he would not budge.

The duo was on the crown terrace, overlooking the small town of Dunstan, sitting on the east bank of the Mata Au River gorge, embraced by rounded hills of schist, punctuated with large, craggy standing stones. The longer he waited, the more chance of being caught thought Ned.

"Look, see here, Tom, you hav to unload, bury a bit and catch up, I've got to be on my way, Maude's expecting me," said Ned.

"Alright" agreed Tom. As he took off half the pack, he took two heavy stones and covered a gold bag, hiding it under in a tussock mound. Then he lit a small fire, trying to burn his tweed coat and moleskin trousers, then he ripped off the false moustache made of horsehair and wax.

Velvet Ned made haste, to put as much countryside between his compatriot and himself as possible, all he knew, was disaster was very much on the cards, and it was time to lie low.

Maude was waiting for him several days later, as he slipped into the Diggers Arms. Unobtrusively, Maude was all business, ushering him into her private salon, as she directed Clarence to 'keep a look out.'

"They're on to us Maudy, that blithering idiot Noon took a dead horse, he gone over for sure!" complained Ned. "My horse went lame crossing the creek, I had to walk the last five miles carrying these saddle bags in pitch blackness", he continued to whine.

"Never you mind, Neddy love," crooned Maude, as she sharpened her focus on the contents of his bags.

Clarence was busy in the study, as Maude called to Ned,

"You stay here lovey, while I put this lot in my little nest."

Ned gratefully accepted the glass of rum she proffered, and propped himself up on the crimson chaise lounge, boots, and all; he missed the slight frown of disgust that ran across Maude's face at his uncouth behaviour, robbery or no robbery, his manners were appalling!

Clarence, eavesdropping outside the door, collided with her in the hallway.

"How's it looking brother mine?"

"All clear so far Maudy, me angel" replied Clarence with a smarmy smile.

"Right, let's get this booty away, before prying eyes and wagging tongues undo all our good works" ordered Maude.

"Right m'dear," said Clarence.

"I will attend to our brave solider in the salon" said Maude, with a significant look upon her face.

In the sharp delineation of a fine, autumn, alpine afternoon, the body of a man was found on Hokitika beach, weighed down by an anchor chain; the tide was washing over it, coming in, going out.

The coloured pebbles of the beach marbled about the figure, like a Roman mosaic. Velvet Ned was cemented in memory, by the native gravel stones of the West Coast.

Meanwhile, in Queenstown, the special constables had finally forced a confession out of Tom Noon. He had dobbed in the inside man, a policeman, who had provided a copy of the outer door key. He'd also mentioned a prisoner, that had been kept in the Dunstan gaol house some months earlier, Velvet Ned.

The police had worked out that Ned had used a screw wrench, to undo the padlock screws; a local blacksmith identified the wrench as one of his, that had gone missing a week before the robbery.

Time was ticking for the police to track down the rest of the guilty culprits, they had Tom Noon bang to rights, after finding the remains of his burnt clothing on the Crown Hills. Some of the gold dust was recovered under Toms directions, but the parcel of bank notes was conspicuous by its absence at the supposed cache.

The Sergeant at arms, Bill Grice, was a 'dyed in the wool' Scottish sceptic; he had been a policeman for most of his adult life and had become suspicious of shadows for most of that time. As he listened intently to the honeyed words, dripping of Maude Mendelevium's ruby lips, he detected the polished performance of a charlatan.

As she showed him to her study, she lamented that the police were not any closer to finding the murderer or the stolen bullion.

"I'm not safe in my bed, sergeant" she opined.

Bill caught himself losing good grace, and a lot of his patience, dealing with Maude's deceitful posturing and her brother's obsequiousness.

Apart from, 'yes madam' or 'no madam", Bill Grice kept his own counsel, checking alibis and any unusual occurrences. Of course, they alibied each other, neither could think of anything out of the ordinary happening recently. Clarence had never set eyes on Velvet Ned; Maude had a vague recollection of him in the bar months ago.

Whilst the question-and-answer session went on, Bill noted two unusual things about the room, one was the absence of a fire, even in the frosty evening air of May, and the other was the peculiar handle of Clarence Mendelevium's walking stick, with its curious diamond tip.

Uileen was quite certain she could hear a cricket chirping, or maybe her fecund imagination was just playing tricks with her hearing.

After a thorough search of the vessel, she at last found the perpetrator of her auditory hallucinations, secreted away in the bulkhead of the ship was an orphaned Chinese boy, who had spent most of his brief thirteen years upon the sea.

Physically slight, with a hang dog look, and not more than broom handle in height, Lee Shing as he was called, performed odd jobs, he was, he said 'number one boy'.

Uileen felt despair for this child of Asia, who, in the Antipodes was worth much less than cargo.

"I must get to the river of the arrow" pleaded Lee Shing, "I must find illustrious energy to return to family with honour" he continued.

As the ship made its way down the East Coast of the North Island, cabin boy Lee Shing hovered around Uileen, like a bright butterfly in the sunshine.

He could only just remember his mother; she was a nebulous figure in his imagination. Captain Welbourne had insisted he should wear European clothes, trousers, a shirt, and a battered hat, but sometimes he would dress in the saffron silk suit with a gilt embroiled cap, that a Chinese digger had given him before he expired from dysentery on his voyage to the gold fields.

On his sailing sojourn, Lee had made it his mission to learn many new things, and Uileen became his trove that he purposed to take possession of, his mother had been wise too, he was sure. Sometimes he would lay himself down, his ear against a crack in the heat-split, oaken door and listen to the adult intrigue that manipulated his life. He had taken to trailing his ideal lady, like a silhouette, as she was entirely new to his escapades.

When she cooked he kept vigil.

"Can Lee have a little rice and some dried fish atop... perhaps some vegetable?" he wheedled.

When Uileen frowned at his begging, Lee replied:

"Those who beg in silence, starve in silence." Uileen had to agree with that ancient wisdom.

Uileen had remembered Ah Sam, and their promise to help a 'celestial son', so when William's irritated countenance came into view at the sight of Lee Shing, she reminded her husband of their debt.

Will began to teach the boy to play the pipe and fish; Uileen sought to teach Lee better English, and to read and write. Josiah showed Lee anatomical drawings, taught him how to bandage a wound and what herbs worked for pain and fever, Lee revelled in his new teachings.

In the coastal beech forests, a kea parrot lay bitten and bleeding, at the base of a large tree, she had not seen the black rodent creeping up the tree, it had bitten onto her leg with its scissor-like teeth, just as she was about to fly away.

Clawing and flapping in fury, she tried to use her curved, grey-brown upper beak, to prise the creature from her body, but the rat had her, fast clamped. She fluttered furiously, fighting for her life should her leg be checked off, frantically shrieking with an alarm call 'keeeaa keeeaa.'

Joseph McCleary heard the kerfuffle of the parrot's panicked call through the silent stillness of the southern bush. As he pushed his way through flax fonds, ferns, and titree branches, he saw the epic battle for survival between the introduced, predator rat, and the native bird. An olive-green, plumed spiral, with an orange, red fire sparking underneath her wings, the kea was a magnificent sight, two feet long, with a bluish green tail with black tips fanned out in rage.

Joseph saw the grimy vermin gripping the kea's leg, he picked up a stick and struck the rat with deadly accuracy, the rat spouted blood from its nose and expired from the deadly blow. The parrot fell from its grip on the tree, with the rat still attached to its leg. Joseph leapt to catch the falling juvenile parrot, which was still crying as he came to her rescue and cut the deceased rats head off with his pocket-knife. He prised open its sharp dagger-like teeth from the kea's leg.

"That rat made a mess alright, bird, but ye are gonna be alright, with Joe tending ye" he said, "let's get ye cleaned up and bandaged at home, soon ye'll be as good as new!" Carefully, he picked up the large bird, swaddling it in his jacket. The bird felt contained, as she lay swathed in the boy's clothing and as they walked the bushland track, a trusting bond grew between bird and boy.

"I've got to giv ye a name, bird," said Joseph. "Perhaps 'Koru', for the colour of ye and the spiral of ye flight, it looks just like the new fern head, koru."

On the roaring West Coast, everyone wanted to be 'a homeward bounder', a man who made his pile and could return home, wherever that was. Gilbert knew that his life was just one 'stoush' after another, a bust up, then the pure excitement of the next wild gold rumour. He sighed, scratching Cobber's raggedy head, as he listened to his comrade on the steamer 'Land's End'.

Jock was relaying his prospecting experiences down the Hasst Gorge.

"I have seen the ice, inches deep along the banks of the river. Icicles in their thousands, hanging from every rock and tree beside the creek slopes. Diggers with their beards frozen, while using an iron crowbar so cold, it would stick to your hands, men lost skin that way".

They were on their way around the South Island, to join the hunt through deep, swift rivers, oppressive jungle-like rainforests, where it was always dripping wet. The miners were living on wood pigeons, 'Keruru', potatoes, fern, and konini berries.

One in every five men coming to the new 'bonanza' had made their way to the wilds of the West.

Everyone wanted the freedom and adventure that came, with just a dish and knife, no one else to set the day, except themselves.

However, some brave female souls, accompanied their prospecting men into the mountain's maws, finding light, in having families, when none was to be found in the monolith's eye.

Mrs Laura MacLennon was one such woman; matrimony was her mission, she was the proud progenitor of twelve children, with a wee bit of help from Mackenzie MacLennan, her husband, and her eldest, Joseph, it was she kept body and soul together.

The McLennan clan were living in a pit sawn, wooden house, with three rooms and an open fire, in a ravine, where the sun never reached the house.

It was there, that the eldest boy Joseph, watched his parents toil as influenza took his baby sister Katie, and his brother Jay. Two, snow white crosses lay in his memory when he thought of them, swaddled in grey blankets in the frozen earth.

When his Da did not come home for several stygian nights, Joseph went out into the blizzard conditions to find him. As he stumbled along the rocky, riverbeds, Joseph did not know what he would find, but he felt the responsibility of his parents welfare, and he knew they could not afford any more crosses to bear.

Meanwhile, several miles down the river, Gilbert, Cobber and Jock had found Mackenzie MacLennan underneath a boulder with a broken leg. Strapping Mackenzie's leg to a wooden staff, they made a temporary stretcher from clothing, and titree poles.

Joseph had caught up to the burdened duo, dog and Da, as they splashed and sloshed their way to humanity, and some medical intervention.

It was an arduous, agonising journey, the quintet made up the river, slashing their way through the dense foliage, walking in icy water with numb footfalls, when finally, Hokitika emerged, perched on the steppes where rivers met the sea.

"You go home and tell yer Ma; we'll keep an eye on yer Da" said Gilly to Joseph who seemed reluctant to leave their company.

"I guess Ma will be worrying", said Joseph.

He had enjoyed having the company of older men, who were more his age. He would miss them, and Cobber, his canine mate, Joseph thought as he threw on his jacket and his swag, for the long trek home.

Cobber watched his new friend depart, howling in dismay, he ran after Joseph, then turned, to look at Gilbert, with a question in his curious brown eyes.

"Och! Cobber, come back, ye daft, strange wee mutt. Joseph's off home, we'll see him again," called Gilly. Cobber whined, and returned on Gilbert's whistle, but Joseph's kindness was stored in his memory for future reference.

After exploring some of the West Coast's creeks and rivers with Jock, Gilbert was restless again, and ready to return to Otago claims.

Mackenzie MacLennan was back on his feet, fossicking again so Gilly made tracks to Potters Gully, one of the most remote diggings the country had to offer.

Chapter 18

Spring washed over the region, bringing balmy rains, melting the snows from their mountainous summits, for six days and nights this biblical deliquesce continually poured into the rivers. On the seventh night Gilbert, Manaia and Rory woke suddenly, it was after midnight and they could hear the thunderous whooshing of wild waters, above a wintery howling wind, other miners were running past, shouting at them as they peered out into the calamitous darkness.

"The river is overflowing, flood is coming", an old hatter shouted, as he ran past dragging his swag. The three men stared at the once quiet stream, to see a torrent of water and debris cascading toward them.

"Run!" cried Gilly, "Run for your lives; up hill, climb mon, hurry. Get up as high as ye can!"

The trio grabbed their boots, coats and valuables, Gilly grabbed Cobber, stowing him under his jacket, then they took a convoluted zig-zag route up the steep, bouldered banks of the raging waterway.

The inundation was complete, eight tents- including theirs, were swept away, as the pebbled ground that they had inhabited was completely engulfed.

Manaia stood looking into the chasm, watching the frothing, foaming waters wash away the wreckage of their lives.

"Come on!" called Gilly, "we have to find a shelter, from this storm tonight."

"I'm coming, but I'm looking at the gap, where Tom's hut was, do you think he got out"? Manaia asked.

"I don't know", replied Rory.

"Nor I", said Gilbert soberly, "it's going to be a while before we really know the toll that tidal wave has taken" he added.

The small, bedraggled party of survivors, clambered further still up, amongst the crags and crevices of the mountainside, until they found a small shelf of rock to take refuge under.

A pallid, leaden dawn opened its feeble curtains on the nocturnal destruction that was wrought upon the ravine. None of the four had slept, they had huddled together for warmth against the bitter, biting weather, the drizzling outlook filled them with gloom. Silently, they unfolded cramped limbs, and climbed into the sodden atmosphere, Rory walked off down the hillside to peer over a precipice.

"What are you looking for mon? called Gilly.

"Me boots", answered Rory.

"Ye hav nae forgot yer boots? Gilbert asked in disbelief.

"Aye, I think I dropped em, as we climbed up over the bluffs", answered Rory.

Manaia looked at Rory's badly swollen chilblained feet, cut, bleeding, and bruised.

"No good to anyone with no shoes!" I make paraerae, flaxen sandals." he said.

The trio of compatriots sat in the lee of the overhanging rocks, as Manaia gathered mountain grasses and began to weave them into string like ropes, for the soles of the moccasins. As Manaia wove, Gilly bought out his tinder, tobacco, and pipe, after a short contemplation, he found dry mosses and grasses to try to make a fire. Rory limped his way down the mountainside to gather rocks for a fireplace, as he looked out on the scene of majestic mayhem nature had unleashed upon the valley.

Their food supplies had dissolved into the onslaught's fluid depths, fortunately, or unfortunately as Rory was apt to think, Manaia had some dried leaves and roots that were edible, from the punta fern trees and koromiko bush.

Gilly and Cobber fetched some snow, they melted it in the only billycan that was saved, and boiling roots were soon perfuming the air with a pungent aroma.

"Ah, I've eaten this boggin scran before, it's a powerful brew.

"But no scurvy", replied Manaia, "no pakeha sicknesses".

When they finally managed to find their direction again, they came across a pitiful sight at a digging further over the 'Potter Gully.' As they looked into hut after hut, they found none but sick men, some bedridden, others just able to crawl, none in any way capable of the exertion of travelling to the nearest point, where fresh meat and vegetables, the only chance of life, could be obtained.

Manaia advised the still able-bodied, colonial miners, on which vitamin C rich plants, sow-thistle, koromiko, could sustain the wretches from the ravages of scurvy.

The roots of spear grass, called by the diggers 'wild Irishman,' was often all that could be found. Rory bellyached that "the flavour of a nauseous herb and more than all the toughness of boiled hemp!" They also dined upon sow thistle, puha, and cabbage tree hearts.

After traversing the gullies and gorges, of the mountainous arenas of the lower South Island, Gilly, Rory, and Manaia at last arrived in the Main Street in the middle of the settlement that had become the centre for the latest southern gold rush.

Queenstown grew like the magical seed from an Indian juggler. It's beginnings, from a remote pastoral holding, to a teaming town of tents was sorcerous.

Perched on the broad banks, of the languorous Lake Wakatipu, a fifty-mile-long lagoon, curvilinearly sensuous, and circumscribed by jagged mountains, aptly named the Remarkables.

Gilbert, Rory, and Manaia arrived to see a thriving hamlet, being run by an entrepreneurial landholder called Bill Threes. Bill had read the signs of a stampede, when two of his shearer's had snuck off to pan in the river, where they struck gold. Immediately, he gave his woodshed a new facade, painted a sign, and the diggers were soon sinking their grog and their money, into the Queens Arms hotel.

It also happened, that the Allingham clan had moved their theatre company into the embrace of the Queens Arms, as they were performing there, the very evening the trio walked down the Main Street.

Whilst Gilly, 'got the beer in,' the bartender told a bizarre tale.

"Captain Bludger Baines had fallen out with the Allingham's and was no longer their benefactor. He had syphoned away their songstress with promises of marriage, no ring had been forthcoming, only a child, born out of wedlock.

The stunned Allingham family had decided to challenge the bravest 'barbers' in the region, to find out if the captain's cheating at cards was true.

"They offered five pounds," huffed the bartender "fancy that!"

"Well," asked Gilly, "did they find anyone?"

"Oh yes," replied the barman, "the barber brought him in ere, after a few nobblers drinks, the clippers did their work most expertly."

"Well!" asked Gilly exasperatedly, "what happened?"

"Everyone saw that Captain Bludger Baines is minus an ear, a punishment from a worse pirate than he, if there is such a thing, he left town in high dudgeon. The Allingham's have written a farce about it, in one of their performances…serve the cheating beggar right I says!" the barman stated empathetically, as someone who had been swindled on many occasions playing cards.

The comrades paid for a claim, and assembled their tent outside of town, down the banks of the 'Shotover' River that drained out of Lake Whakatipu; the hunt was on. Several days later, Manaia met with some of his kinsmen.

"We have an amalgamated mining concession, some miles up the Shotover River, it is very valuable to our tribe." explained Hemi, the troupe's leader. "But we have been 'jumped' by professional claim jumpers, they use the same old lies about their land rights!" Hemi continued, "they say only white men should be entitled to claim, over men of any other colour!" Hemi snorted disgustedly. "The men have thrown their own tools onto the claim, they have thrown our implements away!"

Tama, a younger brother of Hemi added.

"We had an altercation with them, angry words were shouted, but we do not want another Wairau Valley affray, have you words of wisdom cousin?"

Manaia sat with his relatives for many hours into the night, when the crepuscular cape of nocturnal fog clothed the hillsides, and the men were encapsulated in their conspiracies.

In the predawn, the pure, silver chimes, of the tui and bell birds, like an angelus prayer, emulated through the ethers and continued, until the rising flames of first light.

The Maori men made the trek to their stake on the river, to find the 'jumpers' in high glee, thinking they had an easy victory over their competitors.

Some of them were looking at nuggets that they had found, trying to decide their weight and worth. In the climax of their euphoria and boisterous congratulations, several of the swindlers saw the Maori coming back in single file, each had a hatchet tugged in his belt.

Hemi, Manaia, Tama, and their kinsmen, proceeded to emphatically collect their tools, then resolutely replace them in their claim. After doing this, they deliberately took out their hatchets and prepared for prospecting.

The interlopers did not relish this kind of demonstration, and upon further consideration, with caution being the better part of valour, they decided to depart. However, they threw many a threat and taunt, about commissioners coming, with the wrath of the law.

Manaia and his whanau laughed, as they stood in the waters of generations of their people, cleansed in the knowledge that it was their life's essence. They heard no more than the stitchbird's song.

Across the Bay of Plenty's brilliantine surf-crossed sea, Mangus Munson watched through his telescope, Maori canoeists coming swiftly towards his safe harbour.

Little did he know that these warriors, ebullient in their belief, and assiduously set upon retribution, or willing to expire In the venture, made the ancient ocean fizz and boil, to the rhythmic stoke of their belligerent tuki, as their long, low, war canoes skimmed basilisk-like, over the oscillations of an open swell: it was noon as they approached Motiti island sighting the enemy ship anchored near the strand, at the isthmus.

The ignorant convicts rushed blindly forth in welcome, mistaking these Maori for the local tribe, with whom they were bartering, little did they suspect that this was a betrayed Northland tribe set on utu, avenging their stolen women.

Panic filled Munson, as it dawned upon him, that the minds and hearts of the oncoming warriors, were set for mayhem on the shipboard criminals.

In a split-second decision, he dived overboard, holding his breath, disappearing deep under the seas, silvery surface, he knew his only salvation was to swim unseen, as far beneath the eyes of justice as he could keep breath bated.

It seemed an age of anchor bobbing; the coming and going slowly down the East Coast. William and Uileen wondered if the vessel would ever make haste in its destinations.

As they met a melancholy, morning tide, coming upon Wellington harbour, they heard other passengers on deck, talking agitatedly about earthquakes, what the Maoris called 'ru whenua', the shaking of the ground.

Up on deck, they saw the tide surge forward in a strange tidal wave, the inhabitants of the ship looked helplessly aghast, as on shore people ran, in terrified confusion onto the streets, looking for open ground They could see, the ground itself appeared to be in a constant, tremulous motion with houses swinging to and fro.

They were unnerved; there were masses of brickwork from chimneys dislodged, the entire destruction of some tenements, the collapse of others, universal sacrifice of property, terror, and despair in the inhabitants.

When Will, and some other the other men from the ship disembarked, a slimy, mud liquefaction had overflown the main road, inundating everything in its path.

The subterranean convulsions went on for another twenty-four hours, accompanied by deep, hollow sounds and roaring. The front of the Union Bank was a perfect ruin, a rubble of bricks and chandeliers.

Had it been winter, Captain Welbourne was sure the fires from chimneys would have spread like the plague, consecrating the whole city to the ground. Lee had run for his sail-cover hatch when the quake first struck, he had never seen such a phenomenon having been more on water than land.

Uileen coaxed him out with some devilled eggs.

"We will be on our way to Nelson soon," she soothed, "ye must be brave now, we are safe on the ship."

But Lee saw the worried lines around his mentor's eyes.

Will went ashore to help citizens find shelter, out of harm's way, some were too upset to stay and gratefully accepted a berth on the ship. Just as Will was about to leave the quayside, he saw a small tabby cat, emerge crying from the rubble and bricks of a dockside building, quickly he snatched up the castoff kitten, 'this is all I need, a small tiger to take care of' he thought, as he took the small feline back onboard ship 'another mouth to feed,' the small cat purred contentedly, as Will absently scratched its head and ears, it was home.

Gilly slept the slumber of the exhausted soul, after delivering Mackenzie MacLennan to the doctor, Jock had taken up a collection for the MacLennan family, as it would be three months before Mackenzie was fit to fossick again.

A nymph stretched out her languid arms, as she floated through Gilly's orphic mind, holding out a familiar loadstone of aurulent hue. His senses were ensnared, by the tangling threads of feminine, fiery goldilocks, swirling around and around, in a sensual spiral, wrapping him, body and soul. Suddenly, a flash of glittering flecks burst the vision, sparks flew, and the sylph splashed back into the pool of fantasy from whence she emanated, taking Gilbert's dreams with her. He awoke, strangely refreshed and reflective, after his sojourn in the cradle of 'Morpheus' chimera', the dream always made him sad and happy at the same time.

It was late afternoon when Joseph MacLennan found Gilly's tent, near the beach, he called for Koru to come down to perch on his forearm.

"Och, that's one beautiful beastie, ye have there, son", said Gilbert, when he saw the magnificent mountain parrot. Joseph proudly paraded Koru past Gilly, the cocky bird clowned around, bouncing, and beaming on Joseph's forearm, flashing her yellow eye rings at Gilbert.

"What a jester" laughed Gilly, as he applauded the performing parrot.

"Yes, she's a rascal for sure" agreed Joseph, "just watch yer stuff, she likes ta collect shiny things!"

"I'll be certain to keep that in mind. To what do I owe this honour", asked Gilly.

"I just wanted ta thank ye for saving ma Pa."

"Och, twas the least we could do, how is yer family?"

"Ma's not too well, Pa's on the mend slowly, the rest are tearaways that don't listen to a word I tell them."

"Aye" agreed Gilbert sagely, "my brothers and sisters never listened to me either." "There is another thing if I could ask ye?"

"What's that son", inquired Gilly.

"Me Pa canna pan for weeks yet, I need to take his place panning, he taught me how, I'd be no trouble, I'll work hard," Joseph ran hurriedly on, hoping against hope Gilbert wouldn't deny his request, as the survival of his family relied on his fortitude to find fortune.

Gilbert's mien took on a stern expression, as he looked at the thirteen-year-old boy playing with his rescued bird, what could he do? He thought the large family dependent upon succour from gold and gold had to be dug.

Gilly thought of his own brothers and sisters, and how sad it was that childhood was so fleeting. The heavy mantle of manhood was descending on Joseph, without a lot of the lightness of being, a carefree child might have had. Worrying had worn away his chances of childish things. After this thoughtful soliloquy, Gilbert looked again at Joseph's determined, set face, he sighed, before saying:

"I must be mad, but if you can keep up with me, you're welcome to share my tent and company, as long as yer parents agree!"

Joseph was ecstatic.

"Ma and Pa already know I'm here", said Joseph, as he threw Koru up into the air, to watch the kea soar on the thermals and gully updraughts effortlessly.

The boy, the bird, and the mentor went surfacing, or beaching as it was sometimes called, looking amongst beach sands after stormy weather, for the gold that may have been thrown up.

Gilly began to teach his protege how to use simple equipment for surfacing, cradles, a portable sluice box with a hopper, a mercury coated copper plate, and a small tail sluice lined with carpet to catch very fine gold, shovels, and an old wooden wheelbarrow. "Beaching can only be done in storm season" counselled Gilbert, "rough seas, and wild winds combine to cut into the beaches, and produce large exposures of heavy black sand, we call those 'sniggers,' that's a claim of fifty feet square, and we can operate it between the two of us."

Joseph found his first twelve ounces, much to his glee, until Koru wanted to stick her beak into the shiny treasure.

"This bird is always looking for a sparkler!" said Joseph.

"She's got an eye for the main chance alright!" laughed Gilly, as Koru took to the air calling, 'Ke aa', as she ascended to the treetops and beyond.

"She'll be back when she wants some beetle larvae, and berries," said Joseph as he watched his companion soar, in clouds of glory.

"If you've still got some dysentery, Joe, Manaia told me, you should chew some Koromiko leaves, you will find the shrub all over this coast, here's one over here,"said Gilly, pointing to a drooping, willow leafed bush, six feet high, with light green, spear shaped leaves, in the spring summer, it has white and lilac flowers. Take some with you in case your family needs it as medicine, the Maori use it for ulcers as well".

"Thanks for all yer teachings, Gilly, soon I'll be headin back to check on the family, maybe now we will have enough to tide us over the winter" Joseph opined.

Gilly woke in an early morning panic, with a sudden, painful, clawing sensation about his chest and neck "what the blue blazes", he cried, as he came face to a curved beak with a beady pair of eyes with yellowed rings, all bedecked with green plumage.

"Koru, what are ye doing here?" demanded Gilbert. He got his answer soon enough, when he saw the renegade parrot with his sunstone, clasped in her scaly craw.

"Och, ye would rob a friend would ye, ye fly by nighter, ye foul feather-brained filcher!" Unperturbed, Koru stared back at Gilbert's wrath, and continued her efforts to acquire the gloriously glowing gem, for her agglomeration.

Joseph, swiftly appeared at the tent opening, with huhu grubs in hand; Koru's favourite snack, it was not easy to persuade the bird that 'one stone in the hand was worth two grubs in the bush', but finally the food won out, 'for now thought Koru, but there will be another time to take the advantage, she was sure!

After a quick breakfast, and a last chat about Joseph's future, Gilly said:

"Be well, young friend, don't forget to take yer clown with ye, she's a canny creature, for sure she is." said Gilly, as the two pioneers went their separate routes

Shetland Islands, Swinister.
'Home!' Grace could not quite believe Lerwick's harbour lights; they had seemed as remote as the stars in the far heavens. But there they were, drifting towards her, as they swanned into the bay. She felt buoyed up, upon remembering her inherent attachments to the people, place and time.

George and Angus stood strangely solemn on the deck, under the unfurled sails of the mizen mast, each had a lingering dread of the intelligence they had heard through their spy networks.

Whilst in Orkney, they had witnessed the passing of five or six men, forming a cadre; wrapped in long, loose capes, that disguised their lanky lean forms, with drooping hoods drawn over their brows, obscuring their fierce features, midnight eyes, and bronzed faces trailing them, tracked a caravan of burdened ponies and small wagons, on which were spread the feeble, the elderly, and the babes, all part of the exiles. The women wrapped in brown cloaks, with an 'earasaid' scarf wrapped round their heads. The bigger children, with bare heads and unclad feet, barely shrouded in thin clothes, tended the cortège.

Flora had spoken to the men; they had been burnt off their homes on the outer islands. "It was disgraceful said George, the children were sick with whooping cough, and they found themselves with no shelter in the weather, that was 'very cold, a nor easter'!" The brothers knew the grim mood of the Isles, as the lairds and landowners began to demand the land.

"Och, I hope the family are keeping safe from the predations", said Angus.

"Aye," agreed George, "we've been away a good six months, things have escalated a fair bit in that absence!"

They turned their eyes to shore, in time to view the stone citadel of Fort Charlotte, built for defence in the Anglo Dutch war of 1781, and still in use as the jail and courthouse. The tide was coming in as the quartet of Peter, Grace, Angus, and George walked the gangplank into the remains of the day and onto familiar soils.

A skeleton of charred, scorched stones greeted the riders, as they rode across the barren heath. The home they knew was abandoned, reduced to ashes in the wind.

The twins sat stock still on their ponies, as tears dropped down their ashen cheeks. Grace fainted at the sight, Peter caught her as she fell from her horse, her mind trying to turn in upon itself, to escape the desecration of her family home.

After hours of searching the countryside, the company final found their loved ones, camped beside the water's edge in a sod-turf hut, trying to resurrect whatever the flames had not completely devoured.

The tearful reunion became a wake for the loss of a living, hard held.

"Peter, we meet you at our lowest ebb" said Fiona, "can you see those burnt, charred, wooden remains? My husband made that crib the week before we married, I slept in that bed for thirty-five years, my eleven Baines were born in that bed and lay in the cradle beside it. My hearth is now a ruin, a pile of rubble, the fireplace where I fed my family, the place they grew straight and strong, nourished by their family and community, a heritage, a homeland," Fiona continued bleakly to describe a horror, beyond anything any of them could have ever imagined.

"The icy, winter winds, of an unrelenting avarice, clawed the countryside with a blizzard of destruction, blighting lives, leaving frozen wastelands in their wake. We have been blown to pieces. My is heart a congealed, leaden lump in my chest, my dreams are shattered like a broken winged bird. Where can we fly now? Banishments were orchestrated with abhorrent relentlessness and callousness, they were foreshadowed in February, by illicit burning of heath pastures, barns, kilns, and mills, so that stock and people were divested of substance and stores for the future."

"Grace, Peter, George, and Angus sat listening to the telling of the evil events that unfolded several weeks before their return.

"Och, the first I knew of the attack," said Thomas, "was Cathy screaming about burners, we had nae other real warning. Edith and Ma were inside making breakfast, break of morn, just a bit of porridge and tatties, it's all we could manage, with the shortages.

Da had gone off fishing with John and Agnes, to supplement the meagre supplies. I was in the piggery, feeding what I had foraged to the last remaining pig."

Old Gilbert came in from the hotel with a parchment.

"What do it say Da?" asked John.

"It's a proclamation, evicting tenants from the area." replied Gilbert.

"What can we do?" asked Ma.

"We can stand our ground with sticks and pitchforks" answered old Gilbert" but, they will have fire power and manpower to overpower us."

"Och, we hav ta fight, we canna give in to the likes of them thieves," said Thomas.

"We'll do our best, so will the neighbours I have been speaking to," said Da.

"Then they came," said Ma shuddering.

That very night, in autumn, when it was cold, twenty men, marched with fire-filled torches along with four sheriffs, in the pay of the Munson's, for sure," said Thomas.

"We crofters were ready with sticks and stones, but we were no match for brutes with burning eyes and blazing instruments of destruction." said Fiona.

"Aye, the money hungry lairds got rid of the highland sheep, that could live in the high hills, where some said, 'they could live on fresh air alone', then they want to replace 'em with black-faced English sheep, what can't climb hills and who can only graze the fields that we live on, to exist at all", said old Gilbert.

"Now, wearing the tartan, comes with the penalty of transportation across the seas to his Majesty's plantations, to remain there for a full period of seven years" stated Thomas.

"We were forced to build this felly hoose from pieces of turf", said Da. The younger children, Catherine and Agnes looked miserable, crying, and downcast, as the tale of woe was poured out in their misery.

John tried to be brave for his brothers and mother, but his eyes shone far too bright in the firelight, before he hung his head and walked away.

Little Fanny had begun to cough with paroxysmal force, Fiona rushed to nurse her, "She's flushed Da, I think we need to get a doctor, I canna help her with the whooping cough," her face drawn, lined and grey with care.

Peter looked inside the temporary shelter they had erected, the mud walls and floor were musty damp, the thatch roof leaky, as the wind moaned its way through the gaps in the sodden sides.

"Well, I know only one thing; you cannot stay here in a sod shack, the family must accompany Grace and myself home to Norway!" Peter declared with conviction. Everyone started clambering at once: Ma spoke to Da, Da spoke to Peter and Tom, Tom spoke to Ma, Da and Peter; Grace exclaimed to George and Angus, the twins spoke to their parents and Peter, the rest of the children shouted to each other and everyone else. Da motioned for Peter and Ma, to join him outside for a parley without the distractions of the distresses and delights of the rest of the company.

When they returned, another great raucous chorus ensued, until Da held up his hand, cleared his throat and called for silence.

"Well!" he said after a pause for quiet calm, "it is true we canna stay here, I dinna want to leave, but there's nothing here for us to live on, our livelihood has been expunged by the English lairds, and their Munson cronies. At least Peter, has a home to house our big clan without putting him out, he's one of us now, and we are part of his family. Uileen is his sister ye know, and she and Will are united in Australia.

Grace stood with Peter, her heart full of love for their salvation and his understanding heart, the younger children were afraid of leaving everything they had ever known, but she knew that a new start was the only road forward for the family.

Mangus had, by hook and by crook, hand over fist, found his way down to Nelson, and was embarking on a steamer for Hokitika. His contacts had been true to their word, and it was time to take up the offer of a new beginning, where no one knew his name, except for the one he was hunting.

A lantern burned brightly, in the upper story of the Diggers Arms, as Mangus was drawn to its light like a moth to its flame. He climbed up to the second-floor balcony, the muscles in his brawny arms, bulging and flexing in the shadow light with the effort.

The heavily draped French brocade curtains twitched, as a pair of darkly lined eyes and vermillion lips, bowed in delighted welcome, as Maude espied her long-term lover.

She rushed to her boudoir dresser, to apply rouge to her erect nipples, Maude pushed her already overflowing bosom up even further, from her lilac dressing gown, then she pushed up the sash window, as Mangus clambered over the windowsill and enveloped the perfumed vixen, in his huge bearlike hug.

As the bed springs heaved and strained to the lover's tempo, Maude panted

"I have news of the man ye seek my darling."

Mangus renewed his vigour in stoking Maude's desires ever higher, as he took in her good news.

Once the two lovers had taken stock of each other, Mangus made plans to join up with Clarence and his gangsters, they were headed to the Old Man Range, exactly where Gilbert was prospecting. A good, and desolate place for a reckoning.

Meeting Barbara Couper

In the hollow at the base of her throat, where her breath caught, lay nestled a glimmering, metallic grey heart, suspended on its fine filigree chain. Barbara circumspectly caressed this lodestone between her thumb and forefingers.

The threads of her life were unravelling faster than the holes in her shawl, there were so many loose threads, strings that tripped one up or snapped, when trying to hold on to them for support.

A beautifully carved wooden box had come into Barbara's possession, the wood was unlike any she had ever seen, certainly in Scotland. The designs were Celtic in nature, intricate knots woven one amongst the others, the receptacle was a puzzle, for its contents was naught but a cryptic note, secured into the underside of the lid and Barbara had almost missed it.

Her misty, grey eyes grew sadder than rain, as she thought of her dearest brother, lost to the rapaciousness of an avarice, which drew men in like a succubus, a black hole in the untamed wilderness of the Antipodes.

She shook her dark ringlets in dismay at fruitless endeavours, but at that present moment, there she was, launched off by a frostbitten old aunt, standing on the deck of a clipper. Outward bound, in search of a brother, absent for more than six years come July.

In the meantime, Scotland was being invaded by English landowners, famines plagued the crofters. To be a spinster, for the rest of her life, and an unpaid drudge, living on her aunt's parsimonious attitudes, was too much for any spirited young woman to bear. She was officially an emigre, an individual divided by loss and progress. At twenty-four, time was the servant of the devil, passing a young woman with no means by.

Marriage in Britain, even with the looks of a tempestuous, raven-haired beauty, was not on the cards for Barbara.

It had been her only brother, that had gifted her the heart necklace she treasured, he had found the stone adorning the top, of the Kirk church belltower, it had been struck with lightening and split asunder.

The metallic glint in the rock drew his fascination through geology, and he wrought it into pleasing shapes, sure that somehow the gemstone would someday become an asset.

Barbara loved it for her brother's artistry, his endeavours to shape a better life from a lowly stone, turning it into a valued possession full of charm and hope for the future.

Chapter 19

"You sir are a libertine!" Censured Barbara Couper impatiently, "I did not come here to be mauled or abused like a common harlot" she continued.

"Madam, I would not dream of compromising your honour", Sir Felix Wycombe protested.

"I would not have come to this place, these Elysian Gardens, if I had but known it would be a hedonistic retreat for lascivious pleasure seekers such as you, Sir Felix!" Barbara fumed.

Felix beat a hasty retreat, taking his arm from Barbara's waist as she turned her back upon the varlet, fuming in anger for allowing herself to be cajoled into his company, she knew it was a mistake, as a sick leaden ball had formed in her stomach while the journey to this place had proceeded on the small steamer, Diadem, taking her further and further away from her lodgings into an unknown boondocks.

"Calm yourself me dear, we will return to the orchestra rotunda if it's more to your liking", Felix placated.

"It would be more suitable for me to return to my lodgings, thank you Sir Wycombe", Barbara concluded.

The Elysian Pleasure gardens had been Sir Felix Wycombe's crowning achievement- twenty three acres of a very pretty concocted plantation, the whole thing laid out in walkways;

gardens spread out over the hillside with collections of ferns and stately trees, little bowers and summer houses for privacy, statues of goddesses adorned the shrubberies, tented tea gardens, and the rotunda with its voluminous stained glass windows, splaying dashes of violet, crimsons, purples and orange over the crowds as they danced and promenaded, delighting onlookers, to the enlivening strains of the band playing throughout the eve into the small hours.

They had been greeted on that February eve, with a resplendent illumination of pyrotechnics, rockets, sparklers, fire flowers and multitudes of 'golden rain' whiz banging, then flashing up into the velveteen skies above them.

Barbara had never seen the like of this enchantment before, she was spellbound in amazement, like a child with its first mechanical toy.

Not twenty-four hours off the steam packet, Southern Star, Barbara had encountered Sir Felix, who seemed to have business everywhere. They had nearly collided on the hotel's steps, as Barbara was setting off in search of employment as a lady's companion that had been mentioned by Sharach Jones.

She had the address and wanted to find a conveyance in which to travel into the unknown byways, of a bush laden bay. The wooden villas that were built on the peninsula were sparsely set about its hillsides, the verdant, native flora teemed with avian abundance, tuis, pigeons and wekas.

Echoing refrains of birdsong chimes greeted the morning break of day, Barbara had felt refreshed as she dressed carefully for her appointment. Abruptly, as she had commenced her descent into this brave new world, she walked into the 'moveable brick wall', that was Sir Felix.

"I do beg your pardon, ma'am have I injured you in anyway?" Sir Felix inquired.

Although her foot felt crushed, as if under the hoof of a bucking bronco, and the wind fairly flew out of her sails, she had managed to say only:

"No, no I'm perfectly fine thank you sir."

Sir Felix Wycombe stood back to behold a slightly dishevelled, slender auburn haired young beauty, with a small, straight pert nose, and flashing smaragdite green eyes.

She had every likelihood of being as tempestuous in nature as her fiery Gaelic forebears. Sir Felix was always heedful of woman of a certain quality, that could add distinction and desirability to his establishments. Here he beheld a diamond of the first water, obviously a fledgling just out of a strait-laced home in Scotland; her brogue was not strong, and she appeared elegant, in a slightly outmoded dress with a cultivated air about her.

To Barbara, this gentleman who had accosted her, was maintaining his observations of her for an inordinately inappropriate length of time. She drew herself up to her full height, of five foot five and one half, and commenced her departing speech.

"Sir, I have an appointment with an employer and must not be tardy on my arrival; goodbye day to you."

"My dear young lady, if it's employment you seek, look no further as I have the perfect solution to your dilemma. There is a position as a hostess in my pleasure gardens, you would be ideal for."

A prickling sensation crept down Barbara's spine, as she looked into the kasha-coloured orbs that had a spark of devilry secreted in their centres, the suave, aristocratic exterior, did not fully disguise the faint look of boredom, that hung around his sun bronzed and chiselled features.

Sir Felix was a classically handsome man in his prime, who had been getting his own way since he graced his family with his presence, although his latest escapades had led to his absconding to the Antipodes expeditiously, for a period of 'contemplation,' and a decompression from his creditors in Britain.

"I don't think that would be suitable Sir, I am seeking a more refined position as a lady's companion, nothing more and nothing less, please let me on my way," Barbara requested.

Deciding to give a little rope, Sir Felix stood aside, and with a short bow, bade his charming acquaintance adieu, whilst scheming upon how to ensnare one such as her, for his machinations.

Barbara was more than relieved to be free of Sir Felix's intent attentions, she felt somewhat spoiled by the encounter, although she could not put her finger on just why.

The Elysian Gardens was proving to be an experience that Barbara was caught fast in, the boat returning to the town side had already left the quayside, she had little money and not much room to maneuvere with a grouper like Wycombe. It certainly did not help that he was the owner of this farcical establishment, Barbara thought.

That evening was a Caledonian gathering, she walked over to the dancers of the Highland reels, the Strathspeys, and the flings, sighing longingly at the sight of home, the plaid leaping through her memories into a past, rich in heritage.

Alone in this foreign clime, choosing where, or to whom to turn, was as confusing as a kaleidoscope, especially lost in all these people.

Amongst the splendidly illuminated walkways, with glass lamps hung adroitly amongst the trees, she felt her feet taking a direction, any direction, to escape the bounder who held her in his persuasion. As she walked looking into unlit pathways, she could vaguely make out through the darkened passages, that this was oft times a scandalous meeting place for amorous adventures, 'private coteries' seemed to come alive with sensual shadows. The further she walked, the more illusionary and perplexing the pageant became, to her horror, there seemed to her to be a lot of rough trade, soldiers, and diggers loitering along the birdcage walks, waiting to capture their flights of fancy.

Felix was speaking in a low, ingratiating voice.

"Now you are abandoned and unaccompanied, you can work for me my dear, you will be kept in the lap of luxury, wanting for nothing, all I ask in return are a few favours, for select friends; a friendly, lovely, obliging hostess to host the wealthy visitor, decerning gentleman, if you take my meaning?"

Barbara felt like a bucket of iced water had been flung in her face, and the hairs on the nape of her neck stood up, fear crept through her veins, as her virtue stood at the abyss of abuse.

Gilbert did not know why he had bothered to come to the Elysian Gardens for Caledonian Eve, maybe it was the skirl of the Gael, the bagpipes 'never far from a tear,' or the promise of a purse from a boxing pursuit. But he had paid his shiny shilling, tossed the caber, drunk some good highland whiskey, and felt the stirring of Shetland blood pulse through his veins.

That may had been the extent of the outing, but his wayward walking led him to stop, as he beheld the image of his wildest dreams: her autumnal hair streaming behind as she ran towards him, her pursuer not far behind.

Suddenly, in a splintering crash, Aphrodite came to life, as over went, a virginal, white quartz, life sized statue. Gilbert stared befuddled, until he realised his beauty, was part Valkyrie, a shield maiden, if ever he had seen one.

As she had taken flight, like a frightened doe, Felix hastened to chase after her with his henchmen following close behind, they were perplexed to see their quarry duck off the path and were too late to leap completely out of the crashing marble statue's way.

Both collected a crack from stones as they flew randomly in their direction. Looking back, Barbara felt her heart fly into her mouth, as she evaded the debauchees chasing her in the 'notorious walk'.

Sara Beaumont-Connop

"You won't escape for long, my little dove", shouted Felix, as he lay dazed and bruised. "Get after her, you buffoons" he cried.

Suddenly, she felt as though she had hit solid granite, perhaps another statue hampered her progress, it was as solid, and did not move from its position. In the next instant, a long arm extended forth from the apparently alabaster sculpture and clamped about her waist in an intractable grip. Before her reason had time to clear, she was whisked up against a rock-hard structure, which now seemed far more flesh and blood, than any marble could have come close to replicating.

Whatever the nature of the one who presently detained her, one fact was certain, the form was assuredly not of feminine persuasion.

She was sustaining some asperity perceiving reality from illusion. The smoothly draped forest green skirt of her evening gown, and double-breasted Spencer jacket of cinnabar red, set off by a cream ruche, seemed inadequate protection against the unyielding frame.

The unidentified assailant looked hard at the feisty temptress who had flung herself up against him, slowly, reluctantly, he let his arms fall away and the lady reclaim her freedom.

She promptly flung herself back and stood on a stone, which quickly slid under her booted foot, throwing her completely off balance. Her arms lashed wildly about, in a frenetic effort to catch herself, as the man again reached for her.

In tribulation, she clutched the first thing that came within contiguity to her hand and her frantic pirouettes to recover her balance ended instantly, when her left thigh slammed into the manly groin.

Her casualty seemed to choke on her arbitrary assault, to her abashment, her skirts rode up to her knee, as her right leg slipped down the outer side of a hard, brawny limb, leaving her feeling rasped raw. Assiduously, she sought to redeem her decorum, as she strove to dismount the thigh.

But neither party could pull apart.

"My crystal necklace Sir, is caught on your medallion!"

The tall stranger appeared disconcerted in his attachment, all fingers and thumbs, trying to pull apart the two magnetised adornments.

"What warmth instils the reciprocal bonds in kindred minerals?" Gilly said.

Barbara put her hands to her throat and clasp the carved, crystal heart that hung from its chain, her pendant of protection. It was fused to a metal wire frame, that encased a yellow crystalline gem.

"These two ornaments would seem to have a life of their own", she muttered.

"Aye" said Gilly, "I've never encountered such an attraction before to the family sunstone."

"Nor I to my lodestone, given me by my brother." said Barbara, "'tis strange indeed" she murmured further.

"Hold on", she said, "I'm sorry, who are you sir?"

"Never mind who I am, who are you?" Gilbert strangled out.

"I'm someone in a hurry to exit, this den of iniquity post-haste Sir. Are you in league with the vulgar dandy who claims to own, this den of iniquity?"

"Nae lass! I'm just the poor, innocent sot ye hae just about gelded!"

"What do you mean Sir!" I don't have time to…"

As she stood facing him, hands on narrow sateen hips, about to enter a new affray, the previous one was just about to catch up with her.

Felix Wycombe and company, arrived at the grotto, in which Gilly and Barbara were standing.

"Stand away from that young lady, if you value your skin sir!" ordered Felix, his bully boys standing rubbing their heads and shoulders, after the solid stoning they had just received. Gilbert was not in the mood for small talk, with a trumped-up dandy and his minions, when the object of his most erotic dreams stood on the threshold of his evening. He carefully placed Barbara behind him before facing her attackers square on, and said:

"Och mon, I canna leave a lassie such as this, to the bilge-sucking hornswagglers such as ye."

"How dare you sir," cried Felix, and he directed his hired brutes to attack. Gilly had been in unfair fights before and jumped aside as the brawlers came at him swinging. He punched one in the jaw and pushed him into the other; the second villain pulled a knife, "Watch out!" cried Barbara "he's carrying a blade."

Gilly dodged the dagger as the varlet plunged it down into thin air. Meanwhile Felix reached for his revolver; Barbara picked up a large branch and launched it at her purveyor with all her might, the weapon fired, just managing to catch the ear of the second attacker, the man roared like a stung bull, as a lead-ball sliced his lower left earlobe from its attachment. Enraged, the man danced around the enclosure, looking for the matador, or at least a red cape, as blood streamed from the wound.

Felix decided that his pigeon was more eagle than fowl, he took the prudent course of departing through a convenient hedge row, Barbara struck his spine with her stout stick, as she saw him try to slide away.

Gilbert had his hands full, punching stomachs and making some head butts count, with all the muscle, heaving tailings, mud, sand, and rock had developed, not to mention bare knuckle boxing matches, his opponents finally lay where he had knocked them out. Barbara put down her war wand and glanced at her knight errant, from under her thick lashes. His handsome, open visage, with its darkly translucent, grey eyes, his well clipped sideburns, accentuated by the chiselled bones beneath sun-bronzed cheeks; she saw it all, in an instant, he surely was a handsome devil and from the auld country too, she thought.

"Help me." she asked impulsively, "I find myself in dire straits, I must flee this place, my safety is obviously in peril, and I have no one to turn too", she explained.

Gilly was instantly contrite, as he realised this was no simpering feminine game; these assailants had meant to enslave this vulnerable young beauty.

"Come with me," he urged, "we can take a small sailboat I have moored at the jetty, I had a feeling this was a place of debauchery when night blackened its environs."

Gilbert took Barbara's hand, she looked surprised, but upon hearing men, making their way through the park, being led no doubt by Felix, she took flight with Gilly, and ran down the terraced hillside as fast as feet could fly.

With no time to set the sail, Gilbert took the oars, after depositing his prize safely in the stern, and put his upper back muscles to good use, pulling away from the beach with all his might. The trip was arduous, as the small craft bobbled its way across the causeway bay, to finally reach the opposing shore.

But they were not out of the woods yet, Barbara could see a signal lamp flashing from the pontoon to the steamer; obviously Felix Wycombe had hired help stationed everywhere.

"Quick!" said Gilbert, "this way, hurry." He pulled Barbara with him, as they ran along the inlet, somewhere, amongst the rutted ground, Barbara had lost a shoe, which hampered her forward motion in no small amount, Gilbert, seeing this, swung her up into his arms, holding her sturdily against his broad chest, and continued to dash his way along the bush track, until he came to the boathouse, with his boat. Swiftly, he put Barbara in it, and went to check to see if they had been discovered and followed.

In the meantime, Barbara found herself being licked raw, by a canine of debatable heritage.

"Och, get down Digger!" ordered Gilly.

"I take it, that this overly affectionate mongrel is akin to you sir?" Barbara inquired wryly.

"Aye, Digger by name, digger by nature," said Gilbert, "he's a great ratter, something ye will be grateful for, sitting here by the water."

"Oh!" exclaimed Barbara. "Yes," she agreed as she scratched and rubbed Diggers already battered head and ears.

"Now young lady, who are ye, and where do ye hail from?"

"My name is Barbara Couper, and I come from Perth, Scotland. But I was educated by an aunt in Carlisle, on the border of England and Scotland."

"Ye wouldn't be any relation to Colin Couper, would ye?" asked Gilly, in a sudden rush of hope.

"Why yes! He's my long, lost brother," she cried.

"I canna believe it!" said Gilbert wonderingly, "my name is Gilbert Gilbertson, from the Shetland islands. Colin Couper was my best mate and firm friend, he never talked of his home or a sister through" Gilly added.

"No, I doubt if he would have talked of family, he had a falling out with our father, before he went away, then our parents died of influenza. He had already left Scotland and I had no way of knowing his whereabouts, except he was heading for the Antipodes."

"Och! No wonder he was such a lost soul, his heart was broken in on Scottish soil, he was working to redeem himself, to prove his worthiness for his Da and family", said Gilly sadly.

"Yes, I was but a girl of thirteen, and sent away to live with Aunt Ida, to furnish me with an education for marriage. But everything changed with my parents passing, my maiden aunt could no longer support us, so I was sent to be a lady's companion to an elderly Scots noblewoman in Edinburgh, but alas, she too died. Alone, and in need of funds, I decided to try to apply for a position in Dunedin, that was advertised in the London Times, but the position was already filled when I eventually reached the address, after a four-month journey."

"Do you have any kith or kin anywhere this side of the equator?" asked Gilbert.

"Only Colin- if he still be on this sphere," replied Barbara slowly.

"I am truly sorry to have to tell ye, that Colin died six months ago in Ballarat, Victoria. He gave his life to save mine." said Gilbert, his eyes silver with sadness, the grief of loss still raw.

The world swirled in front of Barbara's eyes, she sank to the dirt floor, as Gilly jumped to support her feint.

"Not Col as well!" she cried, tears coursing down her chalk white cheeks, "all this time I hoped and prayed that he would materialise back into my life, we could have had at least each other, for comfort from the bleak, coldness of forfeiture.

Gilbert beheld this fragile flower of womanhood, that he somehow had been fated to be caught up with, he could not believe his good fortune; all the prospecting, fossicking, digging, and caving, and here at last, in his arms he clasped a cornucopia of treasure, such that he would be mining for a lifetime.

Barbara's grief strewn eyes gazed into the depths of his grey lake-like stare, a shudder ran through her being, at the look they shared, the two necklaces had met once more, magnetised by their proximity.

"Yer heart seems to like my sunstone", said Gilly huskily.

"Yes", she agreed softly, "there is a definite attraction. Colin made this heart for me before he left, it's a lodestone, from the chapel bell tower of our town, it was struck by lightning; I believe that it is a magnetic stone that attracts iron.

"Aye, and my sunstone is wrapped in iron wire, so the two minerals are made for each other; just like compass needle is magnetised by a lodestone to find the bearings on a ship," said Gilbert.

They pulled the substances apart but smiled gently at the portentous experience. Digger sat watching the couple, he began to beg for attention, rolling about the floor, then jumping to catch imaginary flies, they laughed at his antics.

Gilbert knew Barbara would be going with him, wherever he ended up, she had not only captivated his sunstone, but she had also enchanted his senses, beguiled his mind with lustful fantasies, and brought out the protective worrier in his spirit. Such a charm could only add value to the vacant life his was, he could not wait to find out about the richness of his lady's existence.

Plans were made for Barbara to stay on a sheep station, with a Scottish family Gilbert knew, helping to look after the children. Gilly had to go for one final expedition, to Old Man Range. He knew Barbara would be safe, hidden in the hills, just one last good haul, and he would have enough gold for his own farm, it was the prospect he had always dreamed and worked for.

The Gods seemed to be lining it up and smiling, for it seemed to Gilbert, that in his sorrow, joy had been unmasked, Colin had given him more than just his life, and Gilbert intended to treat this gift with reverence, like the well-spring that it was!

The children who have left her,

Will re-echo from a distant shore-

The sounds with which they took their leave-

Ha til, ha til, ha til, mi tulidh! - we return- we return- we return - no more!

And when they ask-

Where are the highlanders?

They are answered

By the baaing, of innumerable sheep.

George, Angus, and Peter took turns looking through the telescope to spy the vessel, 'Vengeance', bearing twenty large guns

and six smaller. It was commanded by Gerald Munson, and anchored at Lerwick, Shetland Islands.

They had discovered that she was the main privateer committing various acts of audacious depravity by both crew and master.

Captain Munson had become so undaunted, by the inability of the locals to fight back, he not only came ashore, but gave dancing assemblies in the village of Scalloway. Before they had realised his true vocation, Gerald Munson had enthralled the affections and become betrothed, to Heather Scot, a young lady of some means.

Peter sent Grace to speak to Heather about Munson; it took a lot of persuading, including Grace taking Heather on a coach trip, to see the burnt-out villages, the broken shanties, and the lines of refugees, homeless, including her own mother.

Heather broke down on the way home.

"Och, how could I have been so blinded, the mons a monster, I canna believe I could have been fond of him" she cried and buried her head in her hands.

Peter, Angus, and George made sure the next masked ball that Gerald organised, at Heather's mansion, had plenty of local militias. Grace helped Heather spike the wine while Tom and Da volunteered, with other young men of the village stepping forward. The evening frivolity began with pipers, and a lively band with several singers.

As the evening wore on, the crew of the Vengeance seemed to be evaporating almost into thin air, as Gerald Munson tried to corner Heather alone, in the library.

Grace hid behind the curtains and Peter behind the door; with Gerald unsteady on his feet, they could see that the drugged wine had worked its opiate discombobulations. Peter made quick work of cracking Gerald's skull with his pistols, Grace sighed with relief, as finally, the ringleader of the burning gangs and murders, was in custody.

Standing in front of the Lerwick judge on the following Monday morning, Munson would offer nothing but his name. The judge, old justice MacAuley, took no nonsense from anyone, least of all a whipper snapper like Munson.

"Jumped up guttersnipe," he grumbled. "Bring in the guard!" he ordered, "put on the thumb screws."

Two guardsmen arrived with a whipcord, and squeezed Munson's thumbs until the cord broke, then they doubled it, and then they tripled the cord. The miscreant withstood the torture boldly.

"I hereby sentence you to death by hanging, Gerald Munson. Take him down!" pronounced Justice MacAuley acidly.

The scaffolding was prepared. Gerald scoffed that he 'no more feared death then a birthday party.' However, on the day of the hanging he had to be carried onto the platform and vomited before the rope was placed around his scrawny neck. As the floor fell away beneath his feet, he saw a great, dark shade come upon his vision, and cried out gagging, as his feet danced their final gallows jig, until they kicked no more.

Peter, Grace, Angus, George, Tom, and Gilbert watched the final minutes of the hangman's cotillion, satisfied justice had been served. One last jackal had been erased from the island's miseries.

It was time to turn their troubles into new opportunities; a clipper was waiting to take them to a new Norwegian home.

Meanwhile, Heather arrived too late to see Gerald alive, so she asked to see his body,and there, in the mortuary, she formally renewed her troth, for without a ceremony in auld Scottish superstition, Captain Gerald Munson's ghost would nae giv her rest.

It was Chinese New Year in Arrowtown, South Island, New Zealand, and even though it was an auspicious occasion on the

Chinese calendar, Li Shung knew he was marooned on this desolate, Antarctic Island, amongst the mountainous terrain.

His family had used a kinship responsibility, to raise the money and pay for him to travel to this 'golden prospect' opportunity. He was unable to return to his homeland, until he had sent enough money earned through prospecting for gold, back to his family to repay the familial debt, as well as some riches from his work after the debt had been paid.

So, he had left his beloved China, Guangdong, and joined with others of his land, as aliens in a barren tundra.

They had been outcast from the European diggings, so they built simple, sad, stone dwellings within the outskirts of the main camps.

These 'last-minute' miners were brought in by the Dunedin merchants, to keep the flow of gold alive, they lived small lives, on a bush bound creek, in the shaded Arrow River valley, which were often cloaked in frost and snow.

Pinned to their wooden doors, were red rice papers, festooned with Chinese characters wishing good fortune.

Li day-dreamed of his sister's family, and the little girl she bore, he had played for hours with his lovely, baby niece, before he 'castaway,' to stake his future. If only his meagre finds amounted to one hundred pounds, the equivalent of twenty years wages in China, he could return without loss of face, gaining his family's favour.

But so far, his market gardening only just helped to keep the wolf from his door, without needing to use the hard-earned gold dust, and few nuggets he had scraped together in the years he had been grafting.

Leaves, like fire flew, amber, orange, umber, vermillion, cerise and bronze- aflame, around the small Asian tenement; the bare trees cast their arms, into the autumnal afternoon, in silent surrender to nature's awesome confluence.

Lee arrived on a small, trekking pony, its brown mane plaited and beribboned, for the journey. It was the Chinese feast of lanterns, Yuan Xiao, honouring deceased ancestors, promoting reunifications, peace, and forgiveness.

Uileen had stayed behind in Queenstown, as her time for travel was ceased for now, bearing new life, was the only sojourn she could undertake.

Lee could just see the red lanterns bouncing in the stiff breeze, swinging in a lightness of being, it would be night before their true glory could be manifested.

With an intrepid heart, Lee asked for Li Sheng at the first small dwelling. The man looked at the scrawny individual in his doorway, and pointed to the last hut, before closing the door quickly shutting out the spectre of bad spirits coming to his home.

Lee pulled up the pants that were too big, and tucked in the oversized shirt, gathering up courage like the flapping, fiery foliage.

He approached the entry and knocked at the portal.

"Yes?" asked Li Sheng, "can I help you?"

"Are you, Sir, the Honourable Li Sheng?"

Li Sheng looked down, at the willowy waif that stood before him.

"Take off your cap young person," he said.

Lee gradually pulled the cap away from its customary perch, covering all the straight black hair, and waited for Li Sheng's response.

"Li, is that you, 'little flower', Li Mei, my sister's little girl? I have not seen you for thirteen years, it has been fifteen long years since your birth child." he gasped.

"Yes uncle" confessed 'Lee', "It is I, Li Mei, daughter of Mei Xing, named for you, my uncle, and the roses in his garden.

Li Sheng fell to his knees, in wonderment at the vision before him; Li Mei looked just as his favourite sister had looked, at the same age.

266

A New lunar year reunion was filled with reminiscing and adventures revealed, Li Sheng gave thanks for his niece's cunning in hiding her true identity, when she faced so many dangers on her long arduous journey.

Uncle and niece celebrated their New Year miracle with tangyuan, rice balls filled with fruits and nuts. Fireworks shot into the sky, but Li Sheng and Li Mei could only look at each other, for the sparks of joy bursting within them at their reconciliation, were much brighter than any seen in the ebony skies.

Joseph MacLennan had made his way to Arrowtown, he had heard a good stake could still be made on the riverside there, if one were patient, and besides, he knew Gilbert was only a ten hour walk away on the Old Man Range. It would be good to catch up with his mentor and learn more about prospecting in the mountainous country of Otago. Koru, in her infinite wisdom, had decided to follow her protege, whether that was real attachment or cupboard love, Joseph was not quite sure, probably a bit of both, he thought ruefully; still, it was comforting to see the flashes of bright orange wing feathers, and a cheeky beak waddling into his tent in the early morning light, then rooting around for trinkets and treats.

Joseph had been getting vegetables from Li Sheng, when he met Li Mei, she was like no one he had ever seen or encountered before, like an exotic perfume, every time he contemplated her, he thought of flowers, and lately, he kept having the feeling that he had been walking through a spring garden all the time.

The two teenagers took walks together, into the barren beauty of the countryside, looking at their surroundings and each other in a new light; it was the dawning of a new era for both.

Li Mei finally let her hair grow long and began to wear garments more feminine than masculine. Koru was not so enchanted by this new female rival for Joseph's affections, but when Li Mei rubbed her head, and fed her peanuts, she relented in her opposition, as Li Mei pampered her pride and prodigious love of food.

Will had left Uileen in Queenstown, in the hotel overlooking the lake. Uileen was feeling her condition now, and the constant weight of the baby, was making travel burdensome.

It was Will's mission to find his, 'lost in action' brother, and eventually reunite the family, such as it was, given it was in the ascendency with a newcomer on the way.

He was having one last drink in the bar, before heading off to Arrowtown and beyond, in his search for Gilly. Randomly, he glanced over at the bar, there, a man of familiar stature, stood learning his girth against the native timber structure, drinking, and seeking information about someone, William knew very well, Gilly!

"Ye know where Gilbert, the blackguard has gone then?" asked Mangus.

"Aye", said the barkeeper, "and for a sovereign, I'll tell ye!"

Mangus flicked out the coin, disgusted at the thievery, the barman caught the golden orb, bit down on it, and quickly pocketed it.

"He's fossicking up on Old Man Range", the man said.

Mangus finished his whiskey in one last gulp,

"I'm off", he announced, as he jammed on his hat, heading for the door. Will raised his head, staring after the enemy that had haunted them, ever since they were lads.

Gilbert's in trouble, deadly trouble, he thought, as he unfolded himself out of his seat, and followed Mangus outside; he had to find his brother before Munson did.

Will arrived at the Arrow River, hoping against hope that someone had heard of Gilbert's whereabouts, at the very least, he knew Lee was somewhere in the vicinity.

William's shocked face was priceless, when the door to Li Sheng's cottage opened and he saw the occupants. His jaw dropped, and he just gaped at the blossoming of 'Lee'! "What the-aren't you supposed to be a boy? Hang on! Och! Will someone tell me what's going on? I'm all turned about!" Will stuttered in confusion.

It took Li Mei sometime to explain the turn of events, to Wills satisfaction He was a bit hurt that she could not confide in them, but at last he could appreciate her dilemma, in the circumstances He remembered 'Uileen's stint on the Jabberwock, and realised she needed the disguise until she felt safe to discard it.

Joseph and Koru arrived some hours later, as William was sitting, sharing a tea ceremony with Li Sheng and Li Mei, discussing Gilbert's plight and the probability of where he had gone.

Li Mei, and Koru it seemed, insisted on accompanying any search party that was to be undertaken; reluctantly, William agreed, although he was not sure what a parrot with an eye for anything sparkling could contribute, as he wrestled his wedding ring from Koru's greedy grasp, for the fourth time.

Overall, William felt Joseph's arrival was a godsend, when through an effusive rush of introductions and explanations, they found mutual bonds in the form of concern for Gilbert. It was Joseph's knowledge of the area and mountainsides that William would rely on, as they packed to face the elements and enemy that stood between them, and Gilbert's safety.

Sargeant Bill Grice had been gathering steam, he discreetly followed Maude Mendelevium, as she surreptitiously slung around the few streets and outhouses of Hokitika. It was obvious, Maude was the brains of the operation, but try as he might with search warrants and extra men, Bill had still not been able to catch his canny quarry with any stolen loot. He was, however, more certain than ever, that Clarence had been involved in Velvet Ned's murder, the police surgeon had found an indentation wound of a diamond pattern, at the back of Ned's skull, which would have rendered him unconscious before he 'drowned' in the tidal beach pool.

At last, he had information that Maude was about to receive stolen goods, such as silverware, lace, silk, gold, pocketbooks, and pocket watches, as well plenty of cash.

Mangus Munson, Fred West, Jacob Dooley, Angus Clayborne, and Clarence Mendelevium, a collusion of ex-convicts turned gangsters, Britain's castoff subjects, a colonial nightmare in the making, had managed to get together and form a gang.

They had information from Maude, that four more of the 'foolish-fellows,' gold laden, were making their way to Dunedin, on the secluded tussock land track, where solitude, and distance from civilisation, boded ill for the undefended individuals, that were their prey.

Wearing a calico mask, with slits for eyeholes, Mangus jumped down from his horse, pistols drawn, and said to the rest of the gang:

"Ye keep where ye are, I'll put them up and ye give me your gun, while ye tie them up!" Three of their targets arrived within fifteen yards. Mangus stepped out onto the road, "Stand! Bail up!" he called out, and made the diggers fall back, on the bank of the track facing up the range.

Fred West and the others wore black bandeau's masking their faces, Fred tied the four detainee's hands behind their backs, and the whole gang marched the unfortunate captives, down the incline side of the path into a gully, six hundred yards away.

They all sat down on the crooked rocks, beside a dried-up old creek bed.

"Anyone waiting for you in Dunedin?" queried Fred.

"No, no one", said Franklin Hurst, the oldest of the miners.

Jacob set about searching the men.

"Is this all the gold you've got on ye? demanded Clarence Mendel.

"My gold is in my portmanteaus on the packhorse" said Albert Swain, the better dressed of the prospectors.

The other two hostages, Jeremy Smith, and Sydney Milton, submitted to the search, but looked sick at the incursion into their safety.

Angus Clayborne went back up to the road to recover the baggage from the horse on the trail, leaving the others.

"We'll relieve ye of yer valuables, and then ye can be on yer way!" said Mangus , to the fearful detainees. Fred leered at Mangus, as Clarence and Jacob began collecting wood for a fire.

Sydney Milton did not like the look of conspiracy, that flowed between the two, seeming leaders. Valiantly, he tried to struggle with the knots of the ropes around his wrists.

"Ye come with us, and ye can be on yer way", said Fred to Franklin.

Fred winked at Mangus and Angus, as he turned away and lit his pipe, puffing clouds into an empty sky.

Mangus, Angus, and Albert walked away from the impromptu camp, about one hundred and fifty yards into the scrub.

"We had best choke em, in case they report gunfire heard from the road", said Mangus. "But you said I could go free!", cried Franklin.

"I lied!" laughed Mangus, as he tied a handkerchief over Franklins eyes, and took off the sash around his waist.

"No, no!" cried Franklin, "I will give you more gold, no!" he pleaded again, "for God's sake have mercy", as Mangus put the sash around his sweating neck, and tightened the cloth to a strangling cord, which twisted Franklin, into a purple-faced, clawing frenzy.

It was a good ten minutes before the bedevilled victim, succumbed to death's sad surrender.

"That took you long enough," said Angus.

"Och, mon, I'm out of practice choking, a pistols more my opus, ye ken," said Mangus. "Ye do the next one then, if you've a mind", he continued.

"I will", agreed Angus.

Albert Swain's luggage contained two bags of gold, Fred relieved him of his riches, and escorted him up the hill, in the same direction as Franklin has previously taken.

"Ye turn round, and I'll cut yer ropes off yer wrists mate", directed Angus.

Albert was shaking, as he turned his back on his captor for his release. Angus had already taken out a garrotte he carried in his pocket.

As he went to put it round Alberts throat, Albert thrust his hands to his neck, and grasped the cord. The two men tussled to gain the upper hand, as they grappled each other, testing the strength of the opponent, Angus slipped on the angular ground, and slid away from his dupe. Albert knew it was his only chance, and he wrenched himself out of West's grasp, throwing his weight away he kept his balance, as the lighter, wirier of the two. Fred found himself, rolling on loose metal, downhill from his intended homicide as Albert headed up the hill, as fast as his legs could carry him, sheer terror adding wings to his feet.

Angus threw his Bowie knife, but it fell short of Albert's fleeing figure by several feet.

Down at the creek side, the final two men sat, sharing a pot of ti-tree leaf tea, waiting for their turns; Angus arrived back in a lather. He took Mangus aside and told him what happened. Mangus felt a cold rage pour through his veins, as he listened to Angus's feeble excuses, and he thought of the chump that had escaped, being able to raise the alarm.

By the time he could see past the red veil, that had fallen over his mind's eye, Mangus looked at his hands, and then looked behind him, at Angus Clayborne, who lay still with his limbs sprawled out in all directions, like a large rag doll, that had been thrown down the steep stairs of revenge.

When Mangus returned to the remaining detainees, blond haired, blue eyed, twenty-year-old Jeremy Smith, stared at him with petrified anxiety. Not a sound echoed in that rivulet's depression, the somnolent, dry, stony environs, seemed devoid of any other sights or sounds.

Suddenly a pistol shot rang out, a ruby slash of blood sprayed across a boulder, and Jeremy's pale white face with its anxious, indigo eyes, looked unseeingly up into the pale clear, 'for-get-me-not' sky. Jacob Dooley stood with a smoking gun, looking at his colleagues in crime with a questioning glance.

"Where's Angus?"

"Otherwise engaged" replied Mangus.

Sydney leapt up in horrified foreboding.

"Oh my lord! Don't you murder me", he cried, "help, please, help me someone" Sydney shouted, into a whisper of a wind.

"Hush, quiet now", warned Mangus.

"I'll be quiet, just don't kill me," begged Sydney.

Mangus walked slowly toward the fire and got himself a cup of tea.

"Clarence, ye walk this man up the hill", directed Mangus.

"Right, boss, here you, come with me."

Sydney Milton fought the desire to scream, tears streamed down his face, he could hardly see where he was going as Clarence pushed him up, along the rugged hillside.

A glinting shaft of metal thrust up and down, in the vapour strewn sunlight, a laceration appeared around Sydney's throat, it bled hot, scarlet fluid, onto his cheap, cotton shirt.

All that could be heard was a gurgling sound, as his last, gasping breaths were lost.

"Have ye lubbers finished digging those graves yet? Growled Mangus, "I have another engagement, I don't want to be late for."

"Almost", said Fred, chewing on tobacco, spitting red, brown juice onto a rock.

"This ground is mostly rocks", he complained.

"Just be thankful yer not under it too", muttered Jacob Dooley.

The gang arrived separately in Dunedin and divided up the takings. Each stayed alone, in a different hotel, under an assumed name.

Mangus took his leave as soon as possible, his final goal of revenge was set in his mind, as made his pilgrimage toward the inland mountain ranges, armed with his wrath, and the ammunition of avenging archangel, fighting for his family's honour.

On the pinnacles of Old Man Range, where the spectral glaciers shine, higher even than where eagles advance, up, where storm giants roam, and the air is as thin as a wafer; two, inter-generational male adversaries, faced each other. Each claiming the higher ground, one trying to divert the other, and the only weapons to hand were their bodies. Snow drifts made walking, like wading in cotton wool, the cold, clarity of the day, snatched the warm breath from their lungs, condensing it into fogged particles, the only visible signs of life in a still, silent, iced wonderland.

Gilbert had endeavoured to force his opponent off his trail, but in waist deep snow, the chances of extraditing himself from Munson's clutches were slim, an inevitable showdown was imminent.

Mangus had tracked Gilly for mountainous miles, fervent in his crusade to bring down his enemy, his family's nemesis, a rival for land and titles.

The swag, with Digger hanging out the side, and a sack of nuggets tucked deep in the bottom, weighed heavily upon his shoulder and back as he laboured up the steep side of the glacier. The cost of carrying all his eggs in his swag was adding to his misfortune. Mangus was rapidly gaining, hanging off his climbing rope and grappling with his pick to find hand holds in his ascent.

"Against ye I spin, to the last wrestle with ye, from hades heart I stab at ye, for enmity's sake, I spew my final breath at ye!" Mangus cried.

Gilly was waging another battle with his own conscience: did all his earthly possessions mean more to him, than the love that he was unearthing for Barbara, should he hang on to material gains, and loose the opportunity of discovering a greater treasure of loving embrace. He hefted burden of decision over and over, whilst kicking out at his protagonist, until finally, he just let go, and the ponderous load fell from his mind and his grasp simultaneously.

Suddenly, he heard a loud roar, high up the ice and snow crowned mountain, a huge avalanche was beginning. Gilly looked up to see bright orange sparks, flashing from the clash of falling rocks, he felt the air blast, then there was a boom as rock, ice and snow were pulverised as they fell.

"It's an avalanche!", Gilly yelled.

Mangus was a man possessed, he could no more stop his pursuit of Gilbert than tear out his own pumping heart. He had seen the final sacrifice that Gilbert had made, letting his gold fall where it may and in one foul swoop, he had scooped up the riches and clung to them, as he continued his mission for revenge. He could see Ann's sweet, heart shaped face, laughing into his own, he remembered the indignities that he had suffered at the hands of Grace and Uileen, he let the pure poison of hatred pour through his veins, strengthening his resolve like Circes' poisonous oracle predicting doom and destruction. Millions of tons of rocks, snow, and ice tore down the mountainside; the men were on the vampire rockface, Gilly clambered sideways and down as fast as his new freedom would allow him, he kept Barbara's embrace in his memory, as he hurried to find shelter and escape from the debris cascading, down spreading out in all directions.

Just as he was about to jump to a ledge below, he felt Mangus's fist smash into his right ankle with a bone shaking blow.

Gilbert hit out with his left foot at the madman's head but then a dust cloud erupted over the flooding landscape, grey fog descended, and Gilly felt himself falling into nothingness.

The South Island's alps grew in stature and magnificence as William, Grace, Josiah, and Lee sailed down the East Coast of Te Waipounamu towards their last destination, Dunedin.

Lee had never seen such majestic monoliths on land, he only knew the monster waves of the ocean's fury, he could not believe their altitudinous nature.

Dunedin bustled with businesses, farmers, prospectors, new settlers, and anyone interested in becoming prosperous, the steady stream of bullion coming into the town was being funnelled into buildings, sidewalks, and societies of all sorts. Such were the machinations of a town in its zenith, rising in stature like the ranges surrounding it.

The buildings were stone and brick, elaborated with carvings and ornate windows.

Of the sixty-five hotels and boarding establishments, the quartet chose Hopes Hotel, a medium-priced hostel, with bed and breakfast included in the price.

Josiah had prospects of work as a practitioner in the township and after seeing his room, went to make the acquaintance of the Doctor in residence at his Octagon, town square offices.

Lee prowled about the rooms like 'tiger' the kitten, anxious to explore his new situation, "Don't go too far," warned Uileen.

"Ok, I be back soon", promised Lee, as he leapt down the hotel hallway before she could change her mind.

William laughed as he saw Lee make a bid for freedom.

"He's nae used to the land life yet", he remarked.

"I only hope he's careful" worried Uileen.

"Och, he has to look after himself sometimes", said Will, "besides we have our hands full here with the load yer carrying", he observed wryly.

"Aye, I'll nae deny that this is becoming a wee bit of a burden now", agreed Uileen.

The pregnancy in its seventh month had made movement cumbersome, she said:

"I feel like a beached whale!

"But ye'd adorn the prow of any proud ship, my darling", cooed William.

"I look like a Spanish galleon", Uileen complained.

"Not to me, my love, ye are like the sun, wreathed in its stars, I find myself mooning around yer orbit, always drawn to your radiant beauty", said William.

"If I didn't know better Will, I'd think ye were up to something, with all these sweet words! Uileen remonstrated.

"Only angling for another kiss from yer sweet bonny lips, and a warm cuddle after dark, my lovely", promised Will.

"Oh, I'm starving said Uileen, "this sun needs a lot of energy to burn this brightly."

"Yer wish is my command my queen", bowed William, "a banquet for her majesty awaits."

"Ah ye are a tease, let's find Lee and eat now!" said Uileen, as she waved her bonnet at him laughingly, then fastened it on, with the hat pin he had made for her, complete with the head, an ornamental, carved pearlescent handle from Tanna, Vanuatu.

Along the corridor Fred West, mascaraing as Bentley Harcourt, was putting on a new suit and trying to decide which part of the globe he wanted to trot off to.

As he drew the door of his room open, he looked down the passageway, just in time to see a couple who sent him spinning into a sense of déjà vue. The man was very familiar, he was not so sure about the woman, he instantly stepped back into the closet of his room, coursing through his memory until he hit upon it: the Golden Spring, Will, the smart kid brother of that impudent swine, Gilbert, who thrashed him bare knuckled on the ship to win a bet.

'By God! he won't get away so lightly this time', thought Fred.

"I could not eat another bite, I'm quite stuffed", declared Uileen.

"Eating for two will make good fat?" asked Lee.

"Yes", agreed Uileen wryly, "I'm good fat, alright!" As she laughed with Will about the tact of a thirteen-year-old boy.

As they returned to their hotel room, William and Uileen stood opening their door, Lee came hurrying down the hall to request:

"Tiger sleep with me?"

"Yes of course, Tiger can bunk with you", said Will.

Lee pushed into the couple's room to scoop up the young feline before it escaped.

A menacing figure lunged out at Lee, from behind the curtains, Lee feinted left, then right, but a giant fist hit him in the side of the head, he crashed hard on to the floor. Will rushed in behind the boy, and saw the attacker, Uileen, following screamed as loudly as her lungs would allow.

A large knife sliced the air beside Will's head, he heard its ominous whistle past his ear, he balled his fist and hit his opponent's belly as hard as he could, West was winded, but he stood his ground; William tried an uppercut to his jaw with a punishing right hook, West shook his head groggily, then turned, and aimed his blade at William's heart, and plunged it home. William felt a cold sliver, pierce somewhere between his collarbone and shoulder, he shuddered at this barbed broadside.

Uileen looked aghast, as she saw William stabbed and disabled, she grabbed at her hat pin, pulling it from its perch and rushing forward, before West could turn on her and drove it right to the hilt, into his midback side with all her might.

Uileen's frenzied fight, turned to horror, as she realised West was still standing. Screaming again, with all the waning strength, she turned to the doorway. Just as it seemed all hope was lost, she glimpsed Josiah returning at the run, along with the hotel porter and manager.

"Hurry", she cried, "hurry, my husband and son are injured, and the assailant is still here!"

Fred West felt faint with the taste of blood in his mouth, his breathing seemed laboured, he was halfway out the window, when Josiah and the hotel staff rushed in upon the scene.

Lee had been knocked out cold, so William had Josiah pull out the dagger embedded in his upper chest, he reassured himself that his family was safe, answering his wife's anguished entreaties about his continued mortality, before neatly passing out, to Josiah's tender ministrations.

Fred West was captured by the hotel staff and the police constables, as he was trying to cross the roofs of the township. When they pulled him down in irons, his laboured breathing crackled in the starlit scene, and his monstrous shadow contorted in the jaws of justice.

Several days later, it took the prison doctor a good deal of finesse, to haul out the hat pin, a large amount of yellow, green pus accompanied its withdrawal. West was wheezing at its retraction.

"That bitch done for me, ain't she sawbones?"

"Well, if you weren't going to be hung next week, you would not last long with that infection", the surgeon replied.

West Coasting Hokitika

Coming in from the storm-lashed, heartless immensity of the Tasman Sea, every ship saw the implacable cliffs of the lee shore. The river, spewing its sediment load out into the sea, forever shifting its bar, treacherous, and magnetic to any vessels keel.

Gold diggers:

"A shaft is a chasm in the earth,

possessed by a deceiver."

-Seymour Silver

Rory had followed Manaia up the Grey River to Mawhera Pa, where the chief warmly welcomed them. Manaia's taste for gold was waning, his spirit was yearning for the discovery of pounamu, the nephrite jade gemstone of his people. He spent many hours in discussions with the Poutini Ngāi Tahu, at Mawhera.

Rory, in the meantime, spent a miserable month, as it rained interminably, he put on his coat to divert a flood from his tent, when he was done with the coat, and was becoming friendly with some Maori maidens, he suddenly found himself covered in maggots from head to toe, the Maori women hooted with laughter, and ran off giggling with glee, as Rory realised, the flies had blown the inside sleeves of his coat without his knowledge. It took him two days to be entirely free of the vermin and only by washing in the freezing waters of the river could he effect the expulsion process.

Manaia met up with his Northland Maori cousin, Hone, the two kinsmen decided to reconnoitre up the river, to a creek bed called Hohunu.

As a child in Northland, Manaia had been kidnapped by whalers, his tribe had been outraged by this, but the whaling captain had given a barrel of tobacco in exchange, so he was set in sail for many years, until he could escape whaling, the local tribe of Akaroa had helped hide him.

Rory sat petulantly stewing under his canvas awning, watching with narrowed vision, as the two young Maori men strode barefoot up the gelid rivulet.

Being an inveterate gambler and drinker, was beginning to wear on Rory, oh, he'd found his wages claims worth of gold, which would have made him comfortable, but the rash exhilarations of the dice, the cards, and the next race, were too tantalising to turn down. Rory had less than he had started out with, and Gilly had done the sums.

"For fifty-five thousand pounds they would break even, Rory had only found twenty thousand, in the year that he had worked every waking hour, of every day of every week, every month on.

He had not been marinated in the juices of gambling endorphins, racing through his brain, or imbibed the soothing, alcoholic narcotics to escape the indifference of the frigid, outside world; he missed being cocooned, where nothing could touch him.

Meanwhile, the search for pounamu went on apace, Waitaiki, Hone's sister, accompanied the men, they made good speed to the tributary Hohunu.

Rory followed behind, when he saw the trio stop, and Manaia dive down, into the turgid waters, he knew treasure lay beneath. Hiding behind a clump of punga ferns, Rory plotted the place Manaia dove into, he could hear cries of delight from Waitaiki and Hone, 'it must be greenstone' thought Rory.

Manaia, Hone, and Waitaiki, cut levers from the manuka bushes, on the edge of the river, and they set about cantilevering a boulder of the purest pounamu, from its bed. "Tangiwai," said Hone, "the tear water stone."

Waitaiki wept at its beauty, adding her tears to the streaming waters, as they rolled the gem downhill, onto the bank under the cover of the lush bushes, away from prying eyes and flash floods.

"Let us wait and look again when the waters clear", said Manaia.

Several hours later, they returned to see the muddied brook, running lucid once more. "Look!" shouted Waitaiki, as she pointed at the riverbed. Glistening through the glitter of the crystalline waters, was a pile of golden nuggets, sparkling in the sunlit copse.

Hokitika, West Coast, South Island.

Along this coastline, with its pestilence of black fly, the biting was beyond belief. Rancid bacon rub was the diggers only solution.

After waking up sober, with half his flesh red raw, bitten bloody, itching insanely, and the fumes emanating from his oiled, soiled skin, stinking like an old abattoir, Jacob Dooley was in no mood, to deal with the pleasantries of small town, West Coast living. Betrayed by his mates, as he saw it, unable to claim the greenstone-creek gold as his own, and with no stake to keep him from penury, Jacob Dooley was running low on options.

"Here's a new chum", called out an old digger, sitting outside the twentieth hotel situated on the main road of Hokitika. As a very tall, lean man, with extremely large bones, Jacob had a rather prepossessing countenance, but he tried to keep his head down all the same, pulling a slouch hat over his furrowed features, he was heading for the nearest hotel. After five hours of holding up the bar, Jacob, and his worldly issues receded into a blissful, black hole of drunken oblivion.

The next time he was compos mentis, he found himself chained up to a large log, lying opposite to, what was supposed to be, the police lock up. After a tempestuous time, of trying to gain his release in vain, Jacob could no longer ignore his violent thirst, and seeing that he could not release himself from his wooden anchor, he took a deep, strong breath, and hoisted the impediment up, onto his brawny shoulders, walking slowly, but resolutely to the closest pub, where the local policeman found him there, hours later, drinking his fill, complete with the lump of timber balanced still, upon his shoulder. Jacob figured he wouldn't be waiting long, for the real action to happen on this coast of crooks, he fancied his contact would not be long in coming.

After waiting overnight, for the Maori trio to depart and lodge their claim, Rory set upon his plan to expedite the removal of the bullion.

Dynamite! Rory was at pains to secret the sticks, in a safe dry cache, away from prying eyes, as he tenaciously made his way through the great treed canopy of totara, matai, kahikatea native timbers, all under-storied by tree-ferns, vines, epiphytes, flax, and mosses. The alarm calls of bellbirds, grey warblers, and tomtits, flew through the single- minded silence of his thoughts, his ship was finally coming in, he was going to make his 'pile' alone!

When he finally reached the Eldorado, that Manaia had discovered, Rory placed the dynamite around the pounamu boulder, lit the fuses, and with his hands covering his ears, took cover behind trunks of a stand of trees. The resulting explosion blasted the birds from the bush, scattering green, stone gems everywhere over the mossy carpet of the clearing.

Rory rushed to scoop up his ill-gotten gains in his two haversacks, he couldn't wait to claim the Canterbury provincial government, prize of a thousand pounds, for finding gold in the Hohunu, greenstone creek area.

He conveniently 'forgot' Manaia, and his Maori compatriots, greed had pulled the Midas mask over his mind, Rory's only thought, was of Rory.

When Manaia returned to the Hohunu creek side with Hone and Waitaiki, they found their precious artefact stolen, their ire knew no bounds for the pounamu was their birthright treasure, the stone of their ancestor's spirits, they were beholden to retrieve their heisted heritage.

The court case did not bode well, for the pillager of sacred stone, by the time he lost the ruling to Manaia, Rory Ramsey was not a popular character on the West Coast, and he was festering with resentment, for what he considered ill-treatment of a British subject, he vowed to get even with his compatriots. How dare he lose his prize to a native, he thought, saying:

"I will return yer 'Janus faced' dealings, whatever the cost!" Rory Ramsay was a man possessed; his greed was outweighed by his need for revenge, he planned a swift justice to his fellow diggers.

Rory registered his claim on 'a stringer', near Ōkārito, a West Coast area bounded by ocean, estuary, sea cliffs, and lush forests. From the banks, the viewer had an unsurpassed view of the southern alps.

On the roaring West Coast, the merest whisper, of a glint of a rumour, that a fortune could be made, in a convoluted, countryside creek mine, was enough to ensnare, and enraptured the imaginations of the bored masses of men, idling on exertion, extraction and alcohol, but finding only 'tucker ground around the area'.

Rory Ramsey was carefully observed and followed about his ablutions when he returned to Hokitika; men approached him to ask after his stake.

"Och, I'll be damned if I'm going to tell ye where I'm going, yer all a lazy, freebooting mob", he announced to all in sundry, supping at the hotel.

Soon as he could, he slunk off again, in the early hours, hoping his pursuers would still be sleeping it off, but by midday by his reckoning, fifty or more men were trailing him. Rory tried to use the densely crowded crofts of bush, to stay out of sight, to camouflage himself with the landscape, becoming incognito in the environs. But these tenacious prospectors, were the blood hounds of the territory, they stuck to their quarry like the snows on the glaciers they traversed.

Finally, Rory realised, he would have to give up his quest for singularity at his claim site, as dozens of diggers began to appear there, setting up their tents. At last, he threw in his lot, after working a frustrated week around the rock formations of the river.

"I'm heading back to civilisation, maybe I can make more sense out of the folk there, than this bunch of piratical pillagers." Rory declared.

The Okarito dig was worked for many weeks, after its discoverer disappeared into the distance of the mountainsides. Most of the miners found nothing, those that found anything, looked at the few flecks in their cradles.

They finally pronounced a 'Duffer's rush', saying:

It's a claim that has been salted with grains of gold dust, to fool people into coming there, distracting them from another site", said Aldous Brooks, one of the lead diggers. Many of the men ran out of provisions, on the way back to Goldsbough, the nearest town, Aldous found a poor digger consoling himself, by reading a cookery book, he was sitting down in the wilderness, to study the art of starvation, from the leaves of a culinary text!

Aldous thought this valiant individual a martyr, a true philosopher, but most just thought him a 'madman from Victoria.'

Meanwhile, Rory Ramsey was basking in the glory of a cornucopia of vengeance, as he struck it rich some miles downstream, and moved on to greener pastures.

Clarence beckoned to Jacob Dooley from behind the bar, Lowry, a small man, with dark piercing eyes sat far back in his head, and a mouth like a seam in a saddle bag, was yet another convict acquaintance of Fred West's and had joined the West gang.

"The banks are completely at the mercy of any marauders who want to enter em," said Fred West.

"Ahh, but lone diggers are easier pickings," interjected Jacob Dooley.

"Well now, we have plenty of em to pick from around 'ere don't we." West sneered.

Gilly's waking vision was a white nightmare, he came to, with Cobber licking his face, but the only sight he could discern, was white. He could feel the deep, powder scrunch of snow from Cobber's anxious jumping and hear his whining, as the dog was busy digging out the snowpack that surrounded them. With no other sensory information Gilbert thought, 'I have to get up, before hyperthermia sets in.'

In complete accord, Cobber danced around his master, barking, and pulling his moleskin pants to encourage his forward locomotion. With no idea if his adversary was out there somewhere waiting, Gilbert felt naked and vulnerable to the elements of evil, and nature both.

He again thought of what he had to live for, the love story that had just begun with Barbara, he knew from their first 'hello' that she brought a new meaning to his lonely, empty life. With her around, how could he be lonely? He'd reach for her hand, and she would always be there! It was about time he asked for her hand properly, and told her what was in his heart, suddenly, he could not wait to get back to her and tell her.

Gilbert felt his strength of resolve resume, all his efforts centred on returning to his true destination, a place that could only be secured with a single gold ring, no more or less, that's what he needed to offer with his heart, for life.

Still blighted by blindness, Gilly pushed his aching muscles to follow his canine companion's encouragements, he knew not where they were bound, but it could not be buried beneath tons of snow, on a cloud piecing mountain, lost from futures sight.

Lying prone, with Cobber trying to keep him warm, in the wilderness of whiteout, Gilbert again lost any bearing. 'If only my sunstone could help me now, if I could see, it would show me the way out, just by holding it up in the air for the solar direction.'

In that moment, as he lay blind, and helpless in the drifting snows, Gilly felt he heard Barbara's voice, urging him, to hold his talisman up anyway. Feeling foolish, he nevertheless pulled the crystal from its chain about his neck, and held it up, unseeingly. In the distance, he perceived the voice of the elevation blowing a mournful melody, as the final rumbles of rock, found resting places.

The escarpment appeared to go on forever in its infinite crags, ridges, and buttes, Cobber howled in frustration at their predicament.

Then, out of the white haze surrounding them, they heard a familiar cry, coming from the heavens far above them, 'kee aaa, kee aaa.'

"It couldn't be!" Gilbert thought, surely not, not Koru, Joseph's kea?"

'There are other snow parrots,' he thought, 'can't get hopes up' he said to his dog ruefully, Cobber barked anyway.

Koru loved the scintillating gleam of glass, the shimmering glint of golden crystal, it was all she craved, it's what she collected and crowed about. Down on the ridge line, she detected the glittering gem she had seen, and coveted before, there it was, sparkling in the sunlit snow.

Joseph, William, and Li Mei saw the parrot swirl round, in the frost blown sky, and began to lunge their way through the deep drifts of powder, to keep up with the feathered fiend.

Gilly was distractedly thinking of all this happening, the peculiar, overarching death of Mangus, the truanting of the sun from the heavens, the prodigious cold, and the oddness, and bizarreness of it all. He felt chilled and discomforted, but he tried not to ruminate upon his infirmity, as a creature of climate, and upon humanity's frailty in general, being able only to exist within the tight limits, of hot and cold. It surely was cold, he deduced, as he massaged his unfeeling nose and cheeks, with his gloved hand. Cobber whined, depressed by the freezing weather, he knew it was no time to be out in it, without a fire.

Gilbert's beard and moustache were iced, whitened by his crystallising breath, he noted numbness, creeping down into his fingers, he pondered about his toes, moving them about in his boots, he decided they were numb also. He felt a profound sense of exhaustion wave over his mind, down into his body, a draining of his senses, a great drowsiness, as he tried to remember what he was doing here.

Cobber saw his nemesis anew, that bloody parrot, his canine brain calculated, where she was, Joseph was sure to follow. Mongrel by nature, but purebred with courage, Cobber hauled himself over through the powdered snows, barking with an alarm, as he toiled his way to the rescuers.

William saw the black and tan mutt first, he felt weak with relief, they were on the right trail, there, in the distance, several hundred metres away, he could see a fallen figure, and he knew it was Gilly.

Will dragged the possum skin blanket from the sled, that they had brought from the Aboriginal people, what seemed so, very long ago, and ran to lay it over his brother, his kindred spirit.

Gilly opened his eyes, and looked into the laughing, azure twinkle of William's, and for the first time in a long time, he felt warm, they were going home.

With much joyful reuniting, mixed, with defending Gilbert's sunstone, from an obsessive parrot, Joseph, Li Mei, and Will headed to Queenstown with Gilbert, safely on a sled behind them.

Chapter 20

One last puzzle
Will it be? Do you hearken?
A fresh liberation melody,
Is resounding
Nae more shadow, nae more darken.
There is a new dawn
That is ushering,
Someone natural is the passkey
Only love gives us liberty.
It's so distant, it's so close
Nearly there, now disclosed.

The coffer had come from an oriental sailor, won in a game of chance, on Colin's long journey to the goldfields, it was a rose wood box, inlaid with a mother of pearl ornamentation of stylised leaves. Colin had kept it close to his breast for safekeeping, and when he reached Ballarat, he had buried it in a depression he dug into the ground of his hut, where he slept on his swag.

For he could not, in all good conscience, trust himself under the unsafe influence of the grog, for in all its elegance, it was an unassuming object, illusive in its value. It accommodated an arcane knowledge, hidden from the everyday curiosity of ordinary individuals, for even the tutored owner, a small metal implement was necessary to decipher the mystery.

It had taken Colin some days to find the keyhole to the cryptic core of the canister, it sprang apart, revealing an abstruse compartment. In this cavity, Colin stored his valuables, such as they were, he'd managed to hang on to some nuggets, coins, a few pounds, and a compass, handed down the generations from 1745, alas it was no longer magnetised north.

But that family compass had been Colin's cynosure, his aspiration to venture forth and seek his fortunes, fighting against the failures of injustice, strife, poverty, and mischance.

Sometimes, in the deathly hallows of lonely midnights, prolonged by winter's fierce bite, nostalgia for his roots would drive Colin to dig up his trove.

Looking at the familial direction finder, he remembered his intentions, to find salvation for his loved ones in their hardships, so no other man, could own their home and force them out. If only the compass could direct him now, he sighed, as he began to write a letter to his sister Barbara, explaining his predicament, his perdition, and his preferences if anything was to happen to him, in the barren harshness of this final frontier.

When Gilly, Cobber, William, Joseph, and Li Mei arrived back in Queenstown, Barbara opened the hotel door to them. She hardly recognised Gilly as he had a growth of whiskers, studded with snowflakes, covering his lower jaws, and beneath the deep hood of his coat, she could see that his brows and lashes had a hoary frosting of white. Gilbert felt as weak as a kitten, Barbara was overwhelmed by the number of newcomers that had suddenly descended into her life, but Gilly had insisted that his brother and friends met his intended bride, before he would consider any other action.

Cobber, of cause was known to one and all, as he jumped up on each, to get his fair share of attention and excitement, intermingled with treats.

Uileen was soon fetched by her doting husband, and proud father to be and Gilbert was awestruck by the miracle of life, beginning again anew, he was going to be an uncle! Uileen felt like a bowsprit on one of the sailing ships that she had arrived on, she only hoped that this child, would not be too big for her to bear. Doctors were fairly spartan in the area, and mid wifes were as well; she knew nature had a will of its own, hopefully they would weather the storm.

It was obvious to William and Gilbert, that Barbara and Uileen would be good friends and sisters-in-law. Joint trials and tribulations in loss, had seen to that.

As kindred spirits in wrangling the brothers, the two women conspired regularly, to keep their partners on safer paths of progression for the future.

Colin was mourned again by his friends and family, whilst Uileen came to grips with her cabin boy Lee, being Li Mei, and not male!

Joseph was also welcomed into the fold by the tight knit group, he basked in the warmth of their welcome.

There seemed an ethereal, antarctic gloom over the complexion of things, an elusive pall, that made the day dismal, a dreary blanket of clouds filled the sky.

Mangus's mind was vacant of thoughts, he could feel a brutal numbness afflicting his hands, as trapped by compacted snow, he tried to move and flex his fingers, to no avail. He was angry, and cursed his luck and Gilbert out loud, already, all the sensation had departed from his feet. He knew the frigidness of space, beset the unprotected spire, causing the snow to deluge down the mountainside under its own weight, and he had received the force of the full blow.

When he had been climbing and fighting, the blood had been pumping hot around him, his body aided and abetted, by rage and hatred for his enemy. But now he was trapped, it ebbed away, and sank down into the concavities of his body.

The extremities were the first to feel its loss. His damp feet froze the quickest, and his vulnerable hands numbed faster, though, they had not quite yet begun to be frozen. Sensations of his nose and cheeks, had abandoned him, while the skin of all his body chilled, as it lost its plasma, he felt his genealogy slipping away from him, all the glories he fought for, were receding.

He pictured being found on Culloden moor, lying in the snow-glanced heathers, the clan finding his body the next day, after the great battle. He pictured himself splayed out, claymore clasped in his hand, with Ann, weeping over him, wearing her best, crimson gown.

He knew he did not belong with himself anymore, for even then, he was out of body, standing with Annie, and staring down at himself, in the frozen field.

Mangus Munson's frozen body was found a month after his disappearance in the avalanche, his legs sticking out of a snow drift. His body was buried under a metre of snow, that had to be chiselled off with a pick. All signs of bullion had been excised by the raw power of nature's advance.

Gilbert sighed with relief, when he heard that the war from his past and present, would not follow him into the future. No one had gotten materially rich from such conflict, instead, it had stolen men's souls, planting them back into the atmosphere from whence they emanated. The old order of kings, crowns, and titles along with entitlement, was waning.

A new identity of opportunity was on the horizon, Gilbert was hopeful of change, in this, his new world.

Barbara was looking into the puzzle box Colin had left her again, and she again read his letter enclosed:

"I have not been all our father would have wanted of me, I have heard the beat of a different drum, and followed it. My gift to you, Barbara, is for you to find the freedom, of making the footsteps to your own fulfilment, no matter how distant, and far away from our ancestors that may be.

Sometimes, the old ways have lost their purpose, home is where you find yourself, with one who loves you best, think of me still, as I travel on this new plane of existence, use the compass needle I bore, to find and know, the riches of love, the fire within."

She, took out the compass from its case, pondering her brothers meaning; picking up the container, she searched for a clue to the mystery of his words, and as she turned the vessel over and around, she saw a microscopic hole in the side of the lid, just big enough for the compass needle point.

Taking a chance, she slid the needle tip into the aperture, and was rewarded with a soft click. A secret compartment, from the side of the box sprang open, and there, flickering under the candlelight, were rubys, emeralds, topaz, diamonds and opals, a myriad of precious gemstones, scintillating, as the heavens brightest stars.

Overwhelmed, she summoned Gilbert, and the two castaways cried in each other's arms, at Fate's fickle fortunes.

Colin's loss, their gain, and the chance to begin a life for the first time, on their own terms.

Gilbert found Blueskin Bay, while climbing through the bushland, to Mihiwaka with Manaia. They stood together on the bluff dominating the bay, the region encircling Dunedin, unfolded about them.

"This bay named by pakeha, 'Blueskin', nickname for local Maori man, with ta moko over his body, but Maori call it Waiputi, on clouded days, the bay becomes a blue-grey mirrored colour." explained Manaia, "it is a good food gathering site for Maori, especially for shellfish, cockles, pipis and toheroa", he went on to say.

"Would we be welcome here, on this land, your land? asked Gilly anxiously.

Manaia looked out over the vaulted mountains in the distance.

The auction, for the Blueskin Bay farmland, was being held in the offices of the land sales co-operative. Manaia knew that Barbara and Gilbert were keen to purchase land of their very own, freedom for the future, he knew to the pakeha, progress and civilisation was attributed not, with uninhabited bush, but a well grassed paddock.

Life was changing, he understood his people would have to adapt with it, the land would have to be shared, with the gold rush, the new world had caught up to the old one. "Your bones will be buried here with mine, we will be of this place, our children's children will walk upon our paths, it is from our seeds that this country will grow" Manaia said.

The two men stood together on the edge of a tomorrow; new beginnings, each trusting the other's friendship, to share whatever they needed to do, to live together.

Around the wilds, on the outskirts of Dunedin district, pigeons, and pigs were in abundance and some said, that it was more providential to have a cow, than a child, in that, bush-covered backwoods.

It was back breaking work, grubbing the hillside land of scrub and debris, but for a young couple, Home Farm, looked like a paradise for the making, a place of their own. Gilly had seen the flyer in the newspaper, 'Home Farm - Blue Skin Bay': To be sold by public auction by Messars Landress, Hepburn & Co, at the Dunedin Club, 2pm Saturday, March the 15th.

When they went to see him, the estate agent was most effusive, in his description of the property and the financial situation.

"Yes sir!", Harold Landress expounded, "The terms are of the most liberal character, 5 pounds cash deposit, and the balance extending over four years, at 8 % per annum."

After a trip out to the plot, and a look at the bay, Barbara was keen, to live near the sea, Gilbert liked the idea of seeing gulls flying over their farmland, winging away north, south, east, and west.

Acreage was not easy to be had, most of the South Island hill country had already been taken, and converted into large sheep stations, of thousands of acres in size, vast farms for provisioning the 'mother country' Britain, and commonwealth countries besides.

When the crowd of buyers and onlookers, congregated in the main auction room of the Dunedin club, a mix of old and new identities stood, sizing up the opportunities.

Barbara was horrified to see Felix Wycombe, smirking in their direction, whilst speaking to the auctioneers.

"I cannot abide that blackguard, he's up to no good, for sure", she said furiously to Gilbert.

"Och! never mind my love, pay him no heed, we are more than a match for him and his lackeys, as he has already found to his detriment".

"Aye, that we are my champion", she sighed, holding his arm, thinking of his lips on her own.

Seymour Silver attended, to transmit the property situation to the community, although, the way news travelled in this part of the world, he often wondered if he needed to print it.

Shadrach Jones started the flame to the wick, the bidding blazed with the burn, making quick work of the first half of the candle. Barbara could almost not bear the suspense, of the competition in the room, it was like a red-hot cinder, burning her insides and sometimes, she closed her eyes, to try to gain relief from its tortuous sting.

Gilly watched the candle inexorably burn down, as the bidding continued to climb, he tried to keep his bids quick, with fast paced responses to others in the room.

As the candlewick started to smoke and splutter, it was obvious, that Felix Wycombe had converted his land, and was using vast sums of capital, to try and push the price beyond Gilbert's reach.

Just as the final bidding was in progress, the door of the venue was opened, and a sudden gust of wind blew in, and the flickering wick fell into the drowning wax, extinguishing it.

"Who had the final bid? Someone yelled.

The room was silent with anticipation.

He knew the day was coming, but he over-hoped that there would be several months leeway, to put affairs in order; to grease palms, commandeer a ship, and put to sea -before the wheels of justice squealed up to his doors.

Like the foolhardy Icarus, Sir Redmond Gunn had flown too close to the sun, in his fool's paradise, thinking himself above the reach of British law.

The gold commissioner's position had given him access to wealth, other men could only dream of, and he had mined his way through Antipodean resources, and plowed it into his estates in Scotland, the Shetland, and Orkney Isles, and into funding slave procurement from Africa, for his plantations in the Caribbean.

Gold had paved his way onto landed wealth, beyond even his early dreams of avarice. If only he could escape the noose that had begun to tighten around his neck, as the English and Australian authorities started to check his figures and books.

Agatha had been slinking in and out of the house now for some weeks, he did not have time to watch her every move, however, one of his agents had tracked her spending a great deal of time at the Chinese camp.

Perhaps she'd taken up 'opium eating' he thought distractingly, I'll have to sort her out, he decided, putting it on his list of loose ends.

But it was too late for all his plans and schemes he realised, as he saw, out the net curtains of the office window, troopers marching down the street towards his front door, he recognised the chief magistrate, and the chief of police, at the head of the military detachment.

Turning away from the on-coming foe, he faced the room.

"Nothing for it now." he said out loud, to the ticking clock on the mantlepiece...

Sir Redmond sat upright, cloistered behind his ostentatious, Tasmanian oak desk, in a plush, upholstered dark green, velvet chair.

The door inched open, and Agatha's thin, pinched visage, poked around it.

"I thought I'd find you locked away in here," she said bitterly, "where else would you be, if not counting your money or your mistresses!"

Redmond stared through her, into the Gates of Hell; he had already mounted a vessel and was being carried over the river Styx.

The pistol smoke glissered, around her fingertip. Agatha felt the numbness of nothingness, she turned, and saw men in red uniforms battering down the front door. "Time to pay the piper", she thought. All this dreary life, come to naught, but a cold dungeon of desperation, but it had to be done, a final sacrifice to all those other tormented souls, that Redmond had reduced to ruin, and damnation.

Soldiers surrounded her now, questioning everything, including her sanity. That, she felt, was all she had left now that was sacred. The rest had been systematically shredded, by deception, and a destructive desolation of an uncaring despot.

One of the lieutenants was speaking, and through the veil of disassociation, Agatha looked up, to see Redmond's flaccid features hang forward, as the investigator pulled his body from the chair.

Although his chest bore the open wound of Agatha's vengeance, it was obvious, to the room of observers, that the gaping hole at the back of his head, where a bullet had exploded, was the cause of Sir Redmond's demise.

Another revolver was retrieved, from the dead man's clenched hand, it appeared the devil had finally claimed his own, Redmond, had taken the only way out.

"Well madam! We cannot prosecute you, for shooting someone who was already dead, however homicidal you may have behaved", pronounced the Ballarat magistrate.

"You are free to go".

Leaving the courthouse, Agatha felt her life could finally begin, she was stunned and exhilarated at the same time, she walked in a euphoric haze to the Chinese quarter of town. Ah Sam greeted her, at the door of his humble abode, and the two disparate outsiders embraced, in the knowledge that they could at last be together, in a new era.

Birthing tomorrow today, Uileen felt like a jumble of contradictions, as she negotiated the twin hurdles of getting around the small house, whilst containing an extra load over her feet. She was excited to begin their new family, but she sorely missed Grace and Peter; it was lonelier without them, even though Will tried his best to console her. Especially now, when the time had come that her shoes could only be wielded by Will, for she could no longer bend in the middle, to reach even her big toe.

Their child was going to be a bouncing one, they already kicked like a mule trying to get out of the barn, gladly, she would give release to their protestations; as soon as possible.

"Oh no, not now!" she thought, as she was alone, and waiting for William to return from visiting Gilbert and Barbara, "I'm not ready now!" But her water had broken, and she was having labour pains that were so close together, she knew instinctively, that the baby was coming, ready or not!

Since leaving the pirated ship, Josiah Jones had been weighing up whether to start a small hospital or stay in private practice. Partially, he wanted to investigate his best options, but mostly he wanted to move to within a horse ride of friends. So, he had pulled up in Queenstown, looking for medical opportunities and his 'friends in adversity' William and Uileen, not to mention Lee.

As he stood outside the door of the hotel, he could hear Uileen's cries, and immediately knew that she was in labour, so he kicked the door in.

Uileen was never so glad to see anyone, other than family, as she was to see Josiah come flying to the rescue. The pains gripped her, until it seemed every muscle in her body, ached with the strain.

"Hold on Uileen, it's going to be a bumpy ride, but we can take the waves together" he said, as he carried her to the large bed, and helped the process of birth begin.

William arrived an hour later.

"My God, it's the baby!" he said, stunned and mortified he had not been there sooner, but he stood, holding Uileen's hand, as she held on to it for dear life.

"Can ye not do something for the pain Josiah?" Will enquired, feverishly mopping his own brow.

"No old fellow, I'm sorry to say, there's nothing I can do, it's nature's way of preparing us for life's difficulties", Josiah said.

With each contraction, William became more distraught, but he could not leave his Uileen, he wiped her face with a damp cool cloth. Finally, after what seemed to everyone like a lifetime, the head of an infant, made its way into the world with a last scream from its mother.

Will came out of a daze to see the red, wrinkled face of his son, bawling his eyes out, the child was wrapped carefully in a swaddling blanket, and placed in its father's arms. Suddenly, Uileen, who had been exhaustively looking at her new child, and his father smiling, felt a new pain seize her lower body.

She breathed deeply as the pain eased, but her relief was short lived, and she was tortured again.

"What's happening?" cried William, as he watched his wife's agony begin again. Josiah checked his patient again.

"Well, I never!", he exclaimed, "William, you are about to become a father again!" "What? said Will weakly, as he sat nursing his son. But Josiah was again focused on Uileen, who clung to his hand and gritted her teeth, and bore down for a second time.

At last, the small girl, entered the world, ten minutes after her big brother, whilst her cries were more delicate, she left the room in no doubt, that she could make a noise that would be heard!

'How could two people, be so happy to see, two more people', Josiah thought tiredly, as he finished up. 'Ah well, new life was always a mystery, until it was consigned to the world alive and intact', he decided, secretly pleased, that he had been about to be present at this double miracle.

Lerwick Harbour, Shetland Islands.

On the other side of Earth's circle, hardships and circumstance had prevailed, Grace had pulled her family from the fires of foment. Once again, they were flowers on the wind, the seeds of today, blown onto the shores of tomorrow.

As a patriarch of a clan disposed, Gilbert spoke to his bereft family:

"Shetland's paths are sundered for us, severed in this commotion, time to look at Polaris our Northern star, as our ancestors did, and find the forbearance of the phoenix to start anew. Like the selkie, seal folk, who change from seal to human by shedding skin, therianthropy, our myth of old, we must be brave, shed our auld skins to make this reincarnation, and we may find our new nature. Our family sailed from Scotland over one hundred years ago, in the midst of misery, destitution, and despair, we changed our names, our clothing, our cultivation, but our hearts have never wavered, we kept our strength, in winds of change we bend, but do not break, our love endures, traditions are held in hand, our clan remains, we have survived!"

Selkie

We are a people from an island
Trying to be free,
When we are cut from every strand,
Shapeshifting is our way to be.

The West Norwegian pearl, Bergen, is the gateway to the fjords, in the peninsula of Bergenshalvøyen, a city encircled by seven mountains, meaning, Peter announced, 'the meadow among the mountains', rich in events and spiritual tremors, and Vagen, was the city's harbour and heart, where foreign sailing ships brought fresh breezes from the wide world, full of a melting pot of sailors, speaking dialects that only they know, a Babel of voices, with one vision - the sea.

Peter introduced his new family to his cousins, the Griegs, their grandfather, a Scottish emigre fleeing from the Jacobite rebellion.

In the 1770s he set up as a shipping merchant in Bergen, marrying Peter's aunt and making Peter, a cousin to Evard Grieg the composer.

Gilbert, Thomas, Fiona, Edith, John, Catherine, Agnes, and Fanny were invited to stay at the Grieg's summer estate, 'Elsesro,' where they were treated like royalty or so they felt. Thomas and his parents looked for farms outside of the city, while at Elsesro the children were surrounded with music, and opportunities to learn all kinds of new skills and languages.

Grace stood in the famous Bergen fish market, shopping, smelling the odours she felt sure would stay on her clothing for the next week, trying to absorb the impulses of the city. Excitement ran through her veins, at all the possibilities open to her family, now they were reconstituted at Peter's cousins, the world's oyster opened to them, here in Bergen, she could feel the cosmopolitan beat.

Tied up to history at Bryggan, the Hanseatic wharf, was the steamer Odyssey, where Peter was becoming reacquainted with an old naval friend.

"Peter Lars Thundershield! For me, you will always represent something of the best and noblest I have encountered along my way. Our paths have been severed for too long, in life's commotions," said Evard. "I want you to Captain the pride of the fleet, to begin a new era in steamship passenger voyages, you will never be happy away from the sea for long, my friend."

Peter looked around the American steamer, it was a wooden hulled, side wheeled steamer, built in 1850, one of the largest, fastest, and most luxurious transatlantic vessels of its ilk.

"Liverpool to New York, how about it my friend?" Asked Evard again, "we could set the transatlantic record, give the English a run for their money!"

"My new wife will be the deciding factor", said Peter, for he knew no ship, could lure him away from her.

"Bring her aboard, man, get her used to the luxury life of modern steamship travel, she's welcome to join you onboard, if the sea is in her soul". Evard pressed.

Peter reflected on what the Odyssey would bring them, more adventure, and more travelling. Would Grace want to put her feet upon the deck of another floating caravan? Did she need dry land at her heels to be happy? Where was she anyway, she was supposed to be meeting him at the wharf, he had a violent need to see her, talk to her and hold her.

Meanwhile Grace had been threading her way through Bryggans. The wharf was a collection of compact medieval storehouses, long slender buildings with gabled facades facing the harbour, left behind by Germanic traders of the fourteen hundreds. Constricting, wooden passages hemmed her thoughts in, all she wanted to do was find Peter, the maze of structures leaned down over her, out of the shadows, rats scuttled past, making her jump back in fright. On the side of the alleyway, Grace had turned down, a looming silhouette ran up the wall, she dropped her bundle of fish and turned to flee.

The Odyssey steamship was designed to accommodate two hundred first class passengers, in one hundred and fifty separate berths, including several large 'honeymoon' cabins. All the rooms were commodious, including two washbasins and a chaise, in addition to the four posted bed, the berths were finished in lustrous amber satinwood and draped with an elegant damask green curtaining.

All this opulence he thought, Peter wanted to take his wife on a honeymoon voyage, if he could locate her in the shambles of buildings, with their disguised nooks and crannies, would she agree? How would being in dry dock, suit a sailor with salt in his blood, he questioned himself, where was she?

As Grace stood riveted to the spot, a tall, wavering phantasm took shape, as it stepped towards her –

"Peter! "Grace! Where have you been? They both asked at once.

Sighing, in exhausted relief, Grace threw herself into Peter's welcoming arms.

"Don't do that again", Grace admonished.

"Do what?" asked Peter perplexed.

"Lose me!" replied Grace emphatically.

"I solemnly promise to not mislay you, my precious cargo, again, especially if we are going to New York!" Peter intimated mischievously.

"What do you mean, New York, what is this about America? Not gold again, is it? asked Grace in quick succession.

"Never that my love", Peter avowed, "this is pure adventure, on an opulent scale, come look for yourself", I can hardly wait to show you."

Grace could not believe the sumptuous saloons of the steamer, the rich carpeting, multihued Italian marble, opalescent tables, the furniture of the highest plushness, comfort and quality, interiors finished with a combination of woods, rose, satin and olive, so the captain informed her.

She walked with Peter and Edvard into the first of two saloons, and saw that each salon, the smaller dining and the larger main, were illuminated by several large well-ventilated columns of variegated glass, which stretched from the floor to a skylight in the spar deck above, while splayed out around the entirety, ethereal colours flickered like flames from splendorous stained-glass windows in the stern.

Grace was speechless as she toured the magnificent ship, she felt the tang of salt air in her nostrils, a frisson of fire in her blood, and she felt the arms of Oceanus reaching out to the selkie in her spirit.

"Will this truly be our abode?" she asked wonderingly. Peter who had been watching his love with anxious eyes, waiting for a sign of approval, laughed at her acceptance.

"All this, and much more can be our journey, if you, my darling wife, can join in it with me", he said.

Grace threw her arms around her husband's neck.

"I will take that as a yes", said Edvard, beating a hasty retreat for privacy's sake, but the two venturers had already lost themselves, entwined in each other, body, and psyche.

Auction outcome

After the auctioneers had called it, it taken a few moments before the outcome sank in, slowly, Gilbert's face lit with glee, he turned to Barbara, kissing her deeply, then swung her about in pure joy.

"By all that's holy we have it! We finally have our own home", he could hardly believe it was theirs.

While waiting for the official paperwork to be done, Barbara stood outside the Dunedin Club, still finding herself in shock at becoming a landowner, trying to stay calm, by stroking and feeding Koru perched upon her forearm. They had become fast friends via small food favours, it had been a day of extremes, and she was doing her best to take a break from the auction's tensions.

Felix Wycombe had saddled up his stallion, after losing out to his competition, and not being satisfied with menacing the maids, children and infirm, he felt Barbara's unruffled composure squelch what was left of his good humour. Felix reigned in the horse and then, kicked him forward in her direction.

Barbara was appalled when she realised, she was being charged at, but her moment of fright only seemed to embolden Felix, his mirth rose to a booming roar, igniting her resentment. In obstinate defiance she stood her ground, refusing to capitulate to the abuser any further gratification, as the monstrous charger clattered toward her.

The sight of that horrendous brute, racing toward her, very nearly peeled away Barbara's fine facade of bravado, but contra to an almost overwhelming urge to bolt, she kept her place, gripping the terrified, clawing parrot, until the vulgar fiend, hauled back on the reins, and brought the horse to a swerving stop, right in front of her.

Then she pitched the hissing, biting bird at the steed.

When the Kea landed, it raked its claws right down the stallion's muzzle, as it grappled for a hold with its sharpened, curved beak, eliciting forth a horrified scream from the horse.

Like some feral, deranged beast, the creature leapt and flayed about, trying to displace its persecutor, while the similarly petrified bird shrieked, flapped, and clawed with all it's tenacity onto the mount.

Unlike the rider! Caught off guard by this abrupt turn of events, Felix sailed through the air with extremities flailing impotently, until he thudded back to earth, landing flat on his back, with a discernible 'whoof' as his breath left him, and he endured an anxiety filled moment, as he struggled to regain it. Incensed, he cursed and recoiled to his feet, like a geyser belching in violent fury.

As he scanned around, on the branch of a nearby tree, he saw the preening parrot, having relinquished its hold on the horse. Koru arrogantly eyed him, the clear victor of the fray, and like an evil lunatic, she danced up and down.

Felix's apoplectic anger turned to Barbara, who realised her predicament at once, and beat a hasty retreat into the auction rooms to her husband's side. Gilly knew immediately something was wrong, when he saw Barbara's face, it did not take much guess work, to realise Wycombe would be the cause her distress.

She spoke quickly to him, in low undertones, he excused himself from the clerk he was dealing with, and stood like a stone wall between his wife, and the brute in pursuit. Felix's ire cooled slightly, as he realised the flames of his wrath had masked a greater threat to his wellbeing.

Gilbert walked, quietly, deliberately, toward the 'dandified gentleman,' his face a mask of contempt.

"So, ye pick on people half your size and defenceless animals, ye gobbershite ruffian!"

"Hardly defenceless!" Felix derisively spat.

"Och well, step outside laddie, and we shall even the fight, and we will settle this, for good and all!", taunted Gilbert.

Felix hesitated, as he began to think a bit more clearly, but Gilbert had already reached the spot he was riveted to, Wycombe looked about, the hall was full of acquaintances, businesspeople, and a few friends, satisfaction was demanded, and his reputation was at stake.

Outside, Gilbert took off his jacket and rolled up the sleeves of his blue serge shirt, he drew out a ring in the grey dust of the street with a dead tree branch.

"Let's be having ye then", he goaded.

The two men advanced to meet each other. A crowd of onlookers gathered, Manaia, and Jock stood with a worried Barbara, several surreptitious bets were placed. Felix held his fists up in true public-school form, moving back and forth toward his opponent. Gilbert was in and out, and in again, like a finely balanced device of steel and springs, he dealt a left to the eye, and a right to the ribs, Felix folded a little, like the beginning of an origami swan. As Felix was swaying and staggering, Gilly threw his first real punch - a hook, with the arm rigid, and all the weight of his half-pivoted, muscular body behind it, a perfectly timed fist of retribution. Felix caught it on the side of his nose and jaw, he was felled like an ox, face first, eating the dusty sidewalk. After being rolled over, and several cold buckets of water in the face, Felix came too, his nose oddly misshapen and oozing blood, gingerly he inspected his face.

"You bloody broke my nose", he shrieked in a high-pitched nasal whine, no one was listening much, as a disgusted bookie was paying out ten to one to his punters, the magistrate, and the chief constable amongst them, looking decided pleased with the turn of events.

Gilbert rolled down his sleeves, hugged his wife, picked up his jacket, shook Manaia and Jock's hands, and hired a buggy to ride out to Blue Skin Bay, it was time to claim Home Farm for their own.

Hokitika, South Island, New Zealand.

Finding the loot had not been easy, Sergeant Bill Grice had many a sleepless night, putting all the pieces of that jigsaw together, it had all come down to the mysterious gaffer they called the 'toy man'. He had been the purloiner of many a fine bit of frippery, tortoise shell snuff boxes, silver tankards, pocketbooks, gold rings, silver watches and a bracelet set with garnets. It was the bracelet that had tipped Bill off, when he saw Maude wearing it, after a visit from Rory Ramsey.

The toy man was a well-known thief, who employed youngsters to help pass on the stolen items once they had been uplifted, often from drunken diggers, or their tents and huts when unguarded.

A lot of houses had been burgled in Nelson or Dunedin, and the proceeds ending up mysteriously, down Hokitika way. Still, Bill and his men had to find the hiding place, he had heard Clarence was away down in Dunedin, so a visit to Maude was perfectly timed.

Maude was dolled up to the nines, in a screaming rose pink gown, embellished with feathers, and trimmed with furs, she reigned supreme over her establishment, and Bill was not surprised at her cool calm expression.

They proceeded to her parlour, Bill feeling more like fly, and less spider, in the company of such a courtesan, and accomplished actress. There were no flies on Maude, she could shift with the best of em, Bill figgered.

Still, when he saw a mouse run into the fireplace, he knew he had her, bang to rights. Calling in his two constables, to guard the duplicitous diva, he proceeded to investigate the fire, grate, and chimney, remembering that there were never any fires set in it.

Low and behold, he found a thin wire at the back of the flue, that pulled a dumb waiter down into the fireplace, and there upon it, were a myriad of stolen items, plus bags of gold dust, and notes from the bank robberies.

Maude, realising the jig was up, tried to make a dash for it, by stabbing a letter opener into the arm of one of her guards, but she was no match for Bill, and the other constable, who was unafraid to use force on a woman. She was soon handcuffed and taken to the lockup, where Bill began the interrogation; who were her accomplices, who killed Velvet Ned?

'They still hang women', she was reminded by Bill, it was at this point that she sang like a canary pointing the finger in all directions.

Down on the docks, a few near-do-wells loitered, looking for the next goldrush, fight or another drink, they lounged on the quayside as a ketch pulled in, Rory Ramsey was dropping off one last load before hopping the South Island scene.

As he departed the vessel with his swag, Sergeant Bill Grice, and his disguised loitering men, leapt out to collar him.

"So, Toy man, thought you could get away with another swipe and swindle?" asked Bill. Rory hung his head in retracted silence.

"Nothing to say?" said Bill, "well don't worry Toy man, I'm sure this loot will speak for itself", assured Bill, "take him down constable", he added.

An invitation arrived in the mail, that Sergeant Bill Grice could not refuse, his investigations into the robberies and stolen good receivership, as well as Velvet Ned's murder had all born fruit, he was on his way to Dunedin, where they had all the culprits of the crimes in custody.

Night bore no benevolent silence to the prison dwellers of the Empire's fourth largest gaol, as clinking chains, cries, and moans of the condemned rent the air.

Fred West and Clarence Mendel along with Jacob Dooley stood manacled to the wall, each in a private Hades of his own. They each had an appointment on the morrow with Jack Ketch, the hangman's noose, a singular affair, and one there would be no return from.

The clamour of hammers and splitting wood was an ominous noise upon the inertia of eventide, it foretold dismal deeds were going on within the confines of the prison. It grated with dreadful consequence, on the ears of those, whose destruction it was so concisely to be fundamental.

A sturdy scaffold had been erected, seventeen feet high, thirteen feet long, by nine feet wide. The 'drop' was in the centre of the construction, measuring three feet wide by nine feet long. Inhabitants of that fair city, had rushed to various eminences adjoining the gaol, from which it was anticipated, some vista might be procured in the final ghastly locus, of this appalling apocalypse.

Fred arrived, attempting to speak of heaven and angels, but his speech fell on deaf ears, clanging to the ground, as the few prison visitors watched him with disgust. He kneeled before a black, hooded hangman, whilst his hands were tied behind his back, and a white hood was placed over his contorting face.

Crying out: "The devil take ye," at the last, he danced the hangman's jig, until the asphyxiation finally did its work, he crowed no more.

Clarence expostulated in the most woeful tones of his innocence, but all protestations were smothered at the end of the rope. As Jacob Dooley came to the author of his demise, he railed at life's inequities, despising all men, for their inability to find mercy for his poor beginnings. His shrill, discordant voice could still be heard shrieking in throttled overtones, as the executioner hung on his legs, to weight the noose down, to at last strangle his words into oblivion.

A black flag flew from the jail mast, and a cannon sounded from the Dunedin hills, on that funereal Friday.

It was a morning destined to inspire the sagging spirits with hope, prognosticating future bliss. The ambrosial day, in all the freshness of a precocious summer, was gladdened by the beams of sunshine. The day a wedding should happen, Gilbert thought, with a buoyant heart.

Just a week ago, a hen party arrived at Barbara's dwelling, small crowds of neighbours, acquaintances, friends, and family. They carried hens, salted mutton, dried fish, oatmeal, butter, and whisky for the wedding, but what really brought tears to Gilly's eyes, was William, bringing up the rear of this provision procession, in full kilt, playing the bagpipes.

They had an afternoon, evening, and night of festivities, celebrating the joy of the joining of two perfect people, at the beginning of their dreams together.

Barbara and Uileen, had taken the special feathers from the hen party, and used them to stuff a wedding quilt, for the long, arctic winters, they had fashioned together.

"Come on, grab them quick, before they catch on," a voice whispered loudly.

"What are ye doing", cried Gilly.

"Ye'll find out in good time lad, a Scottish voice replied.

Before he knew it, Gilbert had been trussed up like a turkey, smothered in soot, treacle, flour, and feathers, and was sharing a cart, with his beloved bride to be. With much mayhem and merriment, they were carried through the streets by their captors, better known as friends and family.

"Och, its tae ward off the evil spirits, ye know", called out an auld Scots woman, Clara Macdougall.

Barbara and Gilbert were helpless in the hands of older and wiser than they, so they stood, resigned to their fate for the sake of good fortune in the future.

"It's not every day, an ice princess becomes a fairy queen", Barbara ruminated as the dress makers maid and Uileen, helped her into a creamy, Ecru lace and satin gown. "You look divine" said Uileen, tearing up at the happiness she saw in Barbara's eyes, and she knew that Gilbert had discovered such exhilaration, finding his other half.

In a still moment, Barbara stared into the looking glass and saw her all fantasies come true, she remembered the night Gilbert stood outside her bedroom window, in the moonlight, to ask her to marry him, playing on his pipes, a song about the eternity of their love.

True love.

Trust me, if all those enchanting young charms

Which I gaze on so lovingly today,

Were to change by tomorrow, and fly from my arms,

Like fairy trinkets waning away -

You would yet be cherished, as this second, thou art,

Let thy comeliness wane as it will.

And round the dear relic, each desire of my heart

Will entwine itself luxuriantly still!

A wedding, against the background of the mighty Remarkable mountain's vivid splendour, brought into focus nature's awesome mysteries and how they fit together. William could see undulating stratocumulus clouds, languishing against the alps as he stood beside his brother, and Gilbert recited his marriage vows.

"With this ring I thee wed, with my body I thee worship, and with all my worldly goods, I thee endow......"

As Will listened to Barbara's answer, he thought about how far they had all come, a whole world away from their beginnings to these new ones, he looked across the happy couple to his own wife, his best friend, the bearer of not one, but two bairns, and he winked a promise wrapped in the words they were hearing.

Uileen stood at the bride's side, her arms overflowing with flowers, her face wet with joy, she did not know if she had room for more, her babies were cuddled in Li Mei's and Joseph's embrace, as they too watched the weddings progress.

With the final pronunciation, of "Man and Wife", by the beaming minister, Gilbert reached out, and took his bride's fingers within his clasp, and then, with his free hand, he drew her head slowly forward for a long, lingering kiss.

Dawn's new awakening saw the festivities still being celebrated, as a welcome break from all life vicissitudes.

At the end of it all, Gilbert took up his pipes and played the melody, that haunted his ancestry and carried him across the oceans. Then William took over the piping, and Gilly sang for his wife, what was in his soul.

Sprint Bonnie ship,

Like a warbler on wing-

Forward the mariner's cry

Ferry the lass that's born
For my ring,
Here our hearts we'll tie.